I0571507

KAIJU SEEDS OF DESTRUCTION

KAIJU DEADFALL BOOK 3

JE GURLEY

SEVERED PRESS

HOBART TASMANIA

KAIJU SEEDS OF DESTRUCTION

Copyright © 2017 JE Gurley
Copyright © 2017 Severed Press

WWW.SEVEREDPRESS.COM

All rights reserved. No part of this book may be
reproduced or transmitted in any form or by any
electronic or mechanical means, including
photocopying, recording or by any information and
retrieval system, without the written permission of
the publisher and author, except where permitted by law.
This novel is a work of fiction. Names,
characters, places and incidents are the product of
the author's imagination, or are used fictitiously.
Any resemblance to actual events, locales or persons,
living or dead, is purely coincidental.

ISBN: 978-1-925711-42-4

All rights reserved.

1

August 11, 2019
Paris, France –

The weight of centuries of history rested upon Gunnery Sergeant Lowden Francis LaBonner's broad shoulders, and the pressure bowed him like an old man. Although only 32 years old, he felt as decrepit as the oldest edifice in ancient Paris, as if the timeworn cobblestones of the streets had replaced his bones and crumbling mortar his blood. His heart and sinew were strong, but his head reeled with the hopelessness of the situation in which fate had placed him, fate, and his determination to get the job done. Surrounded by iconic architectural wonders and priceless works of art facing imminent destruction, he could do nothing to protect them. The Arc de Triomphe, the Arenes de Lutcee, the Louvre, the Eiffel Tower, the Basilique St. Denise, La Conciergerie – all the pretty postcard wonders to which tourists from around the world flocked to see – would soon be obliterated by a nightmarish creature that a year ago, Parisians could not have imagined. Not even the dark, fertile minds of Giger, Goya, Dali, or Bosch could have birthed such a monster that now faced Paris.

Yet, for all their cultural and architectural significance, buildings were mere mortar, brick, plaster, and stone; paintings only canvas, oil, and acrylics. Engineers could reconstruct buildings; artists could copy paintings. LaBonner realized his first priority was to the citizens of Paris, those who had not fled already ahead of the deadly Kaiju's rampage.

The reek of blood, sweat, and grime assaulted his nostrils. The sweat and the grime was his, now a part of him after days wearing the same uniform. Dried splotches of blood staining his tunic belonged to one of his dead men. He racked his memory but failed to remember which one. All their agonizing deaths blended into one grim scene that replayed repeatedly in his mind like a looped trailer for a horror movie. Watching men die in battle was nothing new to him. Whether quick and merciful, or slow and suffering, the deaths had been a natural consequence of bullets, explosives, or cold steel. Nothing about his men's deaths had been natural. They had become victims of alien monstrosities.

He needed time to think, to clear his head. They had pursued the Kaiju for two days, waiting for the opportunity to destroy it. So far, they had failed. He needed another plan of action, but his whirling mind refused to cooperate. Exhaustion plagued him and sapped his will; rendered him indecisive. He had not slept for over forty-eight hours. To lie back and close his eyes for a while would have been a godsend, just a few minutes alone to purge the dreadful things he had witnessed from his mind.

Blaming the heat for his vacillation, he wiped the beads of perspiration from his forehead with his sleeve. Immediately, more replaced them, as if squeezed from his pores by the pressure of the situation. Rivulets of sweat streamed down his face, burning the fresh scars on his square chin through the three-day-old stubble. The afternoon temperature hovered around 94 degrees, and the humidity made the rank, cloying air difficult to breathe. Paris in late summer reminded him of his home state of Louisiana, minus the ubiquitous alligators and mosquitoes. Right now, he would gladly take them both, plus a few cottonmouths, over the horrors around him.

In Plaquemine Parish at the mouth of the Mississippi, when the heat grew too intense to bear, he would sit beneath the shade of a willow tree with a glass of iced tea or a cold beer and watch the sun slip behind the Mississippi River levee. The ground would tremble with the passage of large freighters up the river to the Port of New Orleans to disgorge their cargo, their huge propellers churning water the color of his coffee-and-cream eyes. The gentle vibration would often lull him to sleep on hot, humid nights. He would gladly trade the remainder of his life for just half an hour inhaling the sweet fragrances of gardenias and magnolia blossoms, or the heady aroma of crawfish and heads of garlic boiling in a black kettle over an open flame.

He ran his finger under his opened collar. *God, I'm suffocating!* He longed to shed his TEP armor and BPP. Combined, the Torso and Extremities Protection plates and Blast Pelvic Protector weighed over thirty pounds and tended to shift at awkward times, throwing him off balance. The body armor trapped perspiration against his body, roasting him like a rump roast, but at least it offered a small measure of protection against Fleas and Wasps, two of the deadly creatures hosted by the Kaiju, its foraging battle units.

Around him, protected by the burned-out hulk of a double-decker *Transilien* railcar, the four remaining members of Kaiju Killer Team

Charlie sprawled in varying degrees of fatigue. Corporal Sid Thayer lapsed in and out of near delirium from toxins injected by the bite of an alien Flea. The modified IFAK each soldier carried offered little remedy – a bandage for the deep laceration of the bite, Quik Clot to staunch the bleeding, and a Povidone-Iodine solution to cleanse the wound. Field first-aid kits were for bullet wounds or trauma, not infectious bites from alien creatures.

LaBonner had given Thayer two aspirin for his fever from a bottle he carried in his shirt pocket for one of his migraines, which seemed to come on more frequently lately. It was all he had to offer the stricken soldier for the pain. Proper medical help was beyond reach for the moment. They could expect no medical evacuation by chopper. The sky above the Champs de Mars was under the control of the Wasps, and the ground was the domain of the Fleas. LaBonner hadn't seen a *Mirage* 2000N jet, or a *Tiger* EC665 or *Gazelle* SA341 helicopter in hours. Most of the French ground troops either were dead or had fled east to form a new defensive perimeter around the Parisian suburbs. *Maybe they've just given up, as I want to.*

Kaiju Paris had landed a few miles south of Rouen, France, three days earlier and blasted its way through Mantes-La-Jolie, Poissy, and the French countryside on its way to the heart of Paris. It had made short work of the 1st and 8th Artillery Regiments, stomping through the double line of 155mm AUF-1 self-propelled and 155mm TR-F1 towed cannon placed outside Poissy.

They had come across dozens of French *Leclerc* Main Battle Tanks from the 1st *Spahis* Armored Cavalry Regiment abandoned along the streets. Their 120mm cannon and 80mm grenade launch tubes were no match for a giant Kaiju, and their remotely controlled 7.62mm machine guns weren't fast enough for the hopping Fleas or darting Wasps. One tank lay on its side, the heavy steel armor gouged deeply by Wasp claws, attesting to the combined strength of the creatures. The only trace of its three-man crew was the dried blood staining the turret hatch, a mini-scenario representing similar scenes taking place all over Europe.

Crossing the Seine at Boulogne-Billancourt from the *Rive Gauche*, the Left Bank, the Kaiju, as much manufactured weapon as biological entity, now sauntered down the Avenue de New York on the *Rive Droit*, the Right Bank, as casually as a Mademoiselle out for a Sunday stroll along the riverbank. The Paris Kaiju was a condensed version of its 900-foot predecessors, smaller, but just as deadly and just as gruesome. The hulking ebony monster measured over 600 feet in length. Its multiple, overlapping body segments acted as impenetrable armor ending in razor-sharp spikes. The ebony armor also served as an energy collector, absorbing solar energy or any kinetic energy directed at it, and converting it for power. The creature used the very weapons aimed at it to fuel its rampage.

It scuttled across the landscape on twelve, 60-foot-long needlepoint legs – three pair in front and three pair at the rear – that stabbed like massive pikes into the soil and asphalt, shattering buildings, ripping up chunks of concrete and asphalt, and shaking the ground with each powerful earthquake step. Eight bulbous protrusions surrounded the gaping vertical maw in its head. LaBonner had seen the protrusions in action, a sickening sight. Uncurled, they became 80-foot tentacles capable of snatching people from inside buildings or from the street and transporting them to its hideous mouth. He had witnessed the horror of Sanders drawn into the dark chasm screaming at him for help. He could do nothing but watch.

Of all the deaths LaBonner had witnessed, those were the most gruesome. Inside the mouth, multiple rows of razor-edged teeth macerated anything the Kaiju ate into a paste and delivered it to a pool of digestive acids from which Wasps, Fleas, Ticks, and other assorted denizens of the Kaiju fed. The stench of death surrounded the creature like a miasma rising from a fetid swamp. LaBonner wished he could channel his hatred of the creature into one massive bolt of energy to penetrate its dark heart. He had watched his men die one-by-one, helpless to do anything about it, taking their deaths onto his conscience, as he could not take their dog tags home. So far, the mission had cost the lives of four of his team, and it seemed more would pay the ultimate price for victory before they stopped the creature.

As he curled his hands into fists to stop them from trembling, he noticed the dirt and blood beneath his fingernails. His mother would say, "*La proprete est proche de la saintete.* Cleanliness is next to Godliness, mon cher." *If she could only see me now.*

Corporal Ellis Chalmers interrupted his reverie. "Sarge," he said, "we'll never get a shot from here."

LaBonner drew himself back into the present and stared at Chalmers, trying to bring the corporal's face into focus. Everything seemed a blur, as if his eyes, like his mind, refused to accept the reality of the situation. Chalmers, barely out of his teens, a tall, lanky Ohioan from Dayton, was the team's weapons specialist. His constant contumaciousness bordered on insubordination, but his expertise with heavy weapons made him a vital member of the team. Finally, Chalmers' thin haggard face with its hawkish nose and jutting chin cut through the mental fog enveloping LaBonner's mind. Chalmers no longer looked like a boy. His grim mien spoke of the days of stress and fatigue that plagued the entire team. His nasally, whiny voice had become more strident and irritating over the past few days. LaBonner resisted the urge to smash Chalmers' face with his fist for stating the obvious. *Keep your shit together, Francis.*

The broken windows of the railcar's upper observation level provided an excellent view of the Kaiju, but the firing angle was wrong. They needed a higher vantage point. He had considered the Eiffel Tower, within view and the most obvious feature around. At eighty stories high, it was tall enough, but it offered little protection, and crossing the open ground around it opened them up for attack from above by Wasps.

Chalmers continued to stare at him waiting for an answer. LaBonner clenched his jaw to keep from yelling at him. "No shit, Chalmers," he responded with a sharp edge to his voice. "We'll keep falling back ahead of the Kaiju."

Chalmers mumbled something unintelligible. LaBonner was certain it was not supportive, probably derisive, but he let it slide. He didn't have the energy to argue. He understood Chalmers' frustration. They had fallen back ahead of the creature for three days, and it had gotten them nowhere. More of the same seemed futile. He studied the wrinkled map in his hand. The lines of streets and avenues danced across the page, twisting like worms in a bait bucket. A bloody fingerprint stained the upper right-hand corner of the map. His gaze focused on it for a moment, unsure how it got there. *Is it mine? No, I'm not injured. Whose?* He shook his head. *It doesn't matter.*

"There's a church nearby, the *Eglise Saint Sulpice*. It has two towers perfect for the job."

LaBonner was certain the creature would re-cross the Seine to destroy the Eiffel Tower. The 1,063-foot tower was too conspicuous an artifact to ignore. Then, it would continue its path of destruction through the Latin Quarter and on to the *Ile de la Cite,* home of Notre Dame Cathedral. After that, the heart of the city was just a few monstrous strides away, unless he and his team could stop it.

Chalmers glanced down at Thayer. "He'll never make it that far."

In spite of his agony, Thayer roused long enough to pull the Fentanyl lollipop from his mouth and smile. LaBonner had brought a handful of the painkiller treats for just such an emergency. Sanders had carried most of their medical supplies with him into the Kaiju's mouth. With his curly blond hair, teal eyes, and smooth cheeks, Thayer looked like a kid with a sucker, a reward for a trip to the dentist.

"Don't worry about me, Chalmers," he replied in a low growl. The effort of speaking drained him.

LaBonner had removed Thayer's heavy armor to ease his labored breathing and made a pallet of charred bench cushions to make him more comfortable. Thayer pushed himself into a sitting position using his Mk17 SCAR-H rifle for support. He looked up at LaBonner with his face drained of color, and slapped the rifle.

"Just leave me some extra ammo, Sarge. I have a great view of the Eiffel Tower." He coughed twice, wincing in pain. "I always wanted to visit Paris, and there aren't many tourists this time of year. Wish I had my camera."

Thayer's casual acceptance of the situation infuriated LaBonner. He had lost enough men. He could not bear to lose another. "We're not leaving anyone, Thayer. You can make it. I'll help you. Dig down and suck it up."

"Don't be stupid, Sarge." Thayer reached down to pat his hideously swollen right leg. The rip in his pants exposed flesh bruised and discolored from the toxins in the Flea's bite. The grave expression that crossed his sweat-beaded, pallid face revealed the pain the gesture caused. The pain-suppressant lollipops were no longer working. His chest heaved with each labored breath, as his lungs slowly filled with fluid. "I'll slow you down. Besides, I don't think I can hold out much longer. It's getting hard to breathe."

"Shut up, Thayer," LaBonner snapped at him. "Let me think."

Thayer was right, but he had already lost four men and had yet to get close enough for a shot at the creature. His greatest fear was that he had spent their lives uselessly. Each time he replayed a decision in his mind that had cost lives, it only made making new decisions more difficult. His questioning his leadership ability was one thing. Having his men question it, was something altogether different.

The Wasps overhead were as thick as a murmuration of starlings. He had watched such flocks as a child, fascinated by the sheer poetry of motion exhibited by the birds, swooping and swirling but never colliding. He sensed none of that joy watching Wasps. The swarms of black and yellow Kaiju spawn and the dark clouds of smoke from the inferno sweeping through parts of the city effectively blocked the sun. Daylight had become little more than dreary twilight. The gloom seemed to sap his strength and his ability to make decisions. *So damned tired.* He checked his map again, searching for a safe alternative. His mind spun. *So damn hard to think straight.* He bit down on his lip. The pain helped him focus. Still, only one option came to mind.

"We'll use the sewers," he announced. "Underground is safer. Yeah." He nodded, trying to convince himself his decision was a wise one.

Chalmers scowled and rolled his eyes. "Wading through French shit ain't my idea of fighting."

"The army issued you big boy boots for a reason, Chalmers." He looked at Privates Jack Spence and Kris Mayer, the two remaining members of his team. Spence, a thin-as-a-rail twenty-year-old from Dry Fork, West Virginia, and Mayer, a burly, twenty-four-year-old redheaded former roughneck from Odessa, Texas, kept an eye on the terrain. Both looked as if they could use a long nap. *Don't we all.* "Gather our packs and the launchers. Chalmers and I will carry Thayer."

"No way, Sarge," Thayer said. He released his grip on his weapon and fell back onto his pallet, moaning. "It's over a hundred yards to the sewer entrance. You'll never make it carrying me." He waved his hand. "Look out there."

On the neatly clipped grass of the Champs de Mars, mottled brown from the intense summer heat, hundreds of Fleas hopped and leaped about in search of prey. Each of the dun-colored, German Shepherd-sized creatures could cover ten feet with one bound. Their legs ended in sharp killing tools, and their vicious bites spread disease. They were the Kaiju ground shock troops, providing prey for the Wasps to ferry back to the Kaiju. The Wasps were the air support. Together, they were an invading alien army. His team was five men, one of them injured.

"We'll —"

Thayer shook his head. The effort made him dizzy. He rolled onto one side and groaned. "Forget it. I'm not going anywhere." His chest heaved as he gasped for breath to continue. "We both know I don't have a chance. I won't cost other lives. You need every man you've got, even assholes like Chalmers." He glared at Chalmers. "I'm staying right here."

LaBonner stared at Thayer, torn between pulling rank and facing reality. The hell of it was that Thayer was right. The mission came first. Too many innocent lives were at stake. He nodded. "Okay. Good luck. When this is over, we'll come back for you."

He meant it, but he didn't think Thayer believed him. A fit of coughing racked his body. When it ended, his face was ghostly pale and his lips thin and drawn. In a weak voice barely above a whisper, he said, "You do that. Bring a bottle of good French Bordeaux wine and some brie."

"Roger." He turned to the others. "Check your weapons."

Each of them except Chalmers carried a 7.62mm MK17 SCAR-H rifle loaded with rounds tipped with bits of ebony Kaiju material, the only material hard enough to pierce the Wasps' armor. Chalmers carried a 7.62mm M134D-H minigun. He handled the 41-pound weapon with the ease of a traveling salesman carrying his samples case. The minigun's six rotating barrels could spew death at 6,000 rounds per minute. In addition, each soldier carried a Beretta 9mm pistol and two fragmentary grenades.

They were running low on ammunition. Chalmers had started with six bandoliers. Now, he was down to two 2,500-round belts draped across his chest. Each man carried two extra magazines for the SCARs. The bag LaBonner carried held eight extra magazines of 7.62 rounds, four 9mm magazines for the pistols, and a handful of MREs. They could expect no more supply drops. The Wasps saw to that.

The small arms were for protection against Wasps and Fleas. They were no threat to the Kaiju. As part of the U.N. Early Response Force, better known as Kaiju Killers, LaBonner's Army Ranger team carried two Mk-54B boosted fission, nuclear-tipped, shoulder-launched rockets, each capable of delivering an equivalent of 20 tons of explosive power to a chosen target. His job was to get his team close enough to fire a rocket into an open blister of the Kaiju. The mouth would not do. The same energy-absorbing ebony crystalline material that formed the creature's exoskeleton lined the creature's mouth. An explosion there caused little serious damage. The ebony exoskeleton would only absorb the energy of the blast and use it to power the creature.

It had been an arduous task. The oblong, nine-foot by six-foot blisters along the Kaiju's flank opened only when disgorging swarms of Wasps and then remained open for only minutes. Guiding a rocket through the flying mass of Wasps and into the open portal required split-second timing and a lot of luck. A near miss did nothing but cause more destruction. Only an enclosed explosion could produce significant damage to cripple or kill a Kaiju.

Major Walker had been the first to prove that with the monster Nusku in Nevada. Six months later, when Kaiju Kiribati, an aquatic Kaiju, struck the South Pacific, nuclear weapons were not an option. Instead, Walker and his team delivered K-2 nerve toxin to the heart of the creature. Though successful, K-2 was much too dangerous to use near populations. LaBonner didn't know if a mini-nuke posed less threat than toxic nanites, but he followed orders. Due to the very nature of the threat, few people survived long in close proximity to a Kaiju or its subordinate creatures. Radiation was the least of their problems.

Making as little noise as possible to avoid alerting the patrolling Wasps, LaBonner piled benches from the train around Thayer's position to form a barricade, hoping that if the Fleas did not see him, they would not attack. He hoped to send help back in time to save Thayer, but the odds were against him. Thayer knew it as well. As he placed the last bench, Thayer said, "Don't worry, Sarge. I knew the risks coming in. It's a tough job, but someone always gets the short straw."

LaBonner nodded. The brass had handed them the short straw on this mission. He unwrapped the last Fentanyl lollipop and placed it in Thayer's trembling hand. "Try to stay quiet."

A spasm of pain washed across Thayer's face. When it had passed, he nodded.

LaBonner's men were ready. He hoped he was. He surveyed each one for a moment, assessing how much they had left to give. They were on the edge of physical collapse and emotionally drained, but they were not beaten. They all understood what was at stake, if not the fate of the world, at least this little piece of it.

"We'll make a dash for the storm drain using the flower beds and hedgerows along the sidewalks for cover." He glanced at Chalmers. "Chalmers and I will go first. We'll open the drain and provide covering fire for you two." He fixed Spence and Mayer with his gaze. "I'll signal you when to start out. Not before," he warned.

He watched until a large group of Fleas hopped by and disappeared behind a grove of trees. The nearest Wasps were five hundred yards away over the Seine. He tapped Chalmers on the shoulder and started across the open parkland at a sprint. Chalmers followed close on his heels. Three days earlier, the Champs de Mars had been a place of joy, a rendezvous for lovers, and a favorite spot for tourists viewing the Eiffel Tower. Now, he tried to ignore the dried bloodstains on the concrete sidewalks and the scattering of personal items – purses, parasols, books, blankets, sunshades, telephones, and cameras – detritus left behind by fleeing or dead sunbathers. That was the eerie thing about the aftermath of an attack by Kaiju: unlike a conventional battle, no bodies remained, neither human nor alien. Even dead Wasps and Fleas became fodder for the Kaiju.

Feeling as if every alien eye in the city was staring at him, he raced across the open ground. He kept his gaze focused on his goal with one thought only in his mind – killing the Kaiju. Making it to the small gazebo-like structure housing the entrance to the sewer unscathed came as a surprise. However, their luck did not hold. Within minutes, the first Wasps arrived, drawn by the slightest movement. A hexagonal-shaped metal door comprised of eight triangular sections covered the entrance to the sewer. While he worked feverishly to lift the heavy lids, Chalmers cut loose with the minigun, spraying the Wasps with a lethal dose of ebony crystal-crusted lead. The creatures' ebony armor made them difficult to kill, but the furious rate of fire from the minigun chipped away at the crystalline armor. A few bullets found the vulnerable spaces between armored plates, killing two Wasps, but too few rounds struck home to make a dent in the gathering horde.

As he feared, the noise drew more unwanted attention to them. Fleas by the hundreds began converging on the area. They were running out of time. He clicked on his throat mic, hoping it still worked. They had no more batteries, and they had lost their solar charger.

"Spence, Mayer. Go now!"

Lugging the heavy launchers and their weapons, the pair moved slowly. LaBonner mentally urged them to hurry. 22-year-old, 5'8" Kris Mayer was as strong as any man on the team; her muscles toned by lifting heavy drill rig pipes in the Texas oil fields, but the days of stress and the heavy armor had taken their toll on her. She struggled to keep pace with Spence. When the shadow of a Wasp fell across them, she turned and fired her SCAR from the hip without slowing, hitting the Wasp in its thorax. It flapped away, licking its wounds.

Spence tripped while leaping a flowerbed wall, tumbled headfirst, and disappeared from view. Mayer reached down, dragged him to his feet, and slapped him on his helmet. They continued their crossing, but they had lost precious seconds.

Both LaBonner and Chalmers poured intense fire into the Wasps, keeping them at bay, but it would be a tossup as to who arrived first – his team or the pursuing Fleas. LaBonner stood aside as Spence and Mayer rushed up, almost out of breath, and dropped through the drain opening. Mayer urged Spence to hurry down the steps by shoving him in the back. Chalmers fired one more burst from his minigun and joined them.

The sound of another SCAR drew LaBonner's attention to the railcar. Thayer stood outside the car, leaning against it and firing his rifle in short bursts at the Fleas, providing cover fire for the rest of the team.

"Go back, Thayer!" LaBonner shouted into his mic, but Thayer did not have his helmet on and couldn't hear. He focused his attention on the thick mob of Fleas pouring across the Champ de Mars. LaBonner watched in horror as a Wasp dropped down from directly above Thayer, enfolded him in its four pairs of legs, and jabbed him through the back with its three-foot-long stinger. Without his TEP body armor, the slender stinger easily pierced his chest. Venom spurted from the tip, dripping down the front of Thayer's shirt. He stopped firing and dropped his weapon, hanging limp and transfixed upon the deadly stinger as if upon some macabre crucifix. LaBonner hoped he was already dead, as the Wasp jerked Thayer's body into the air for the short trip back to the Kaiju.

LaBonner dropped down the opening just as a Wasp made a lunge at him, ripping through the gazebo roof. Pieces of splintered 2x4s and plywood fell on him. He reached up and pulled the metal covers back in place. A ripped piece of a poster announcing a Paris air show dropped in front of him. He stared at it as if a tarot card a reader had lain before him on a dark table. Paris had gotten its air show all right, but not the kind they had anticipated.

A length of plywood prevented the last section of grate from closing. As he struggled to dislodge it, the Wasp shrugged aside the remains of the flimsy gazebo, and landed beside the cover. It poked two legs inside the narrow gap and threw the triangular section aside. LaBonner stared up into the Wasp's face. As the two stared at one another, he detected no intelligence in its alien countenance. The creature was simply a cold-blooded, organic killing machine. This was no meeting of two intelligent alien species. It was a case of predator and prey. It cocked its head to one side to get a better view of him, while emitting a high-pitched droning sound. LaBonner didn't know if it was a sign of the creature's irritation or a call to its brethren.

The opening proved too small for the Wasp to force its way inside, but he was certain it would eventually open enough grates for the Fleas to pour into the sewer. He poked his SCAR through the opening and fired into the Wasp's triangular head, aiming for the green band across its face that served as its visual sensor. Viscous yellow ichor splashed over his arm and face. Injured, the Wasp backed away but refused to abandon its position. It stamped at the opening with four of its legs, rattling the metal grates until the sound thundered down the sewer tunnel, drowning out the echoes of his team's fleeing footsteps.

He abandoned the opening to join them. The power remained on, and the lights strung along the walls of the drains illuminated their way. Behind him, the injured Wasp or one of its companions had returned, scratching frantically at the steel cover. Glancing back, a patch of sunlight illuminated the opening. Moments later, more light appeared, as the creature lifted a second panel. They were learning fast.

"Hurry," he yelled. "We have company."

2

August 11, Homeland Security, Washington, DC –

Major Aiden Walker sat unmoving and uncomplaining in the straight-backed wooden chair he believed was designed to increase the discomfort and vulnerability of anyone visiting the office of Homeland Security. Nervous tension gave him cottonmouth, but he didn't want to disturb the busy receptionist for a glass of water. He didn't see a water cooler or door marked bathroom. He wondered if she made the long walk down the outside corridor whenever a call of nature occurred. He swallowed hard to wet his parched throat.

The Secretary's receptionist, a young woman so absorbed in her work that she had not glanced in his direction in twenty minutes, looked up, frowned at his barely audible interruption, and then resumed her duties. Walker glanced at his watch. His appointment had been for 10:30. It was now 11:15. He was military. He was used to waiting, but the time seemed to drag by on leaden legs. Each minute blurred seamlessly into the preceding minutes, marking no distinction between one moment and the next.

That the office was so quiet astonished Walker. Equally surprising was the fact the Secretary of Homeland Security had a single receptionist and not a full staff. He had expected a bustling operation. In 2016, before the first Kaiju had arrived, the annual budget for Homeland Security had been just 41 billion dollars. This year's budget was three times larger – 120 billion. Protecting the country from terrorists had been child's play compared to protecting it from alien Kaiju.

The Secretary, former Air Force General John C. Robinson, had summoned Walker from London where he had been coordinating fighting techniques with U.N. Kaiju Killer teams. He was not happy with the summons and unsure of the reason for the meeting, but one did not refuse or dally when Washington called. Even after the seven-hour plane ride from RAF Lakenheath, his blood still boiled from the images of the

12

devastation and carnage of flattened cities. The east side of London lay in smoking ruins from Edmonton to Dartford, and north to Bishop's Stortford. They had lost two insertion teams before bringing down the Kaiju on the banks of the Thames. So far, they had managed to destroy only the London monster and the one threatening Tiran, Albania. Large swaths of Europe still lay in the path of the remaining creatures.

After the defeat of the last alien Kaiju monster in December, the world had breathed freely for eight months before the arrival of the next batch of Kaiju. Now, the alien Nazir had gone gangbusters, sending ten of the creatures to devastate Europe in their bid to annihilate humanity. These monsters were smaller and more mobile, but just as deadly as the originals. Swarms of Wasps and Fleas released by the creatures wreaked havoc on the human population, reducing humans to food to fuel the creatures. The Kaiju – giant, unstoppable, ebony bulldozers – pushed across the landscape, destroying everything in their path.

The first alien Kaiju invasion exactly twelve months to the day as this third-wave attack had caught the Earth unawares. Crawling from their impact craters, the three giant creatures, code-named Ishum, Girra, and Nusku after Mesopotamian fire gods, had destroyed San Francisco and parts of the West Coast, as well as Chicago and a deadly swath through America's heartland. Walker had led Fire Team Bravo, which had infiltrated the insides of Nusku north of Las Vegas and delivered a baby nuclear bomb. It had been the first taste of victory in the war with the aliens, but it had not been enough. The sacrifice of astronaut Commander Erwin Langston when he crashed his *Lunar One* Orion spacecraft into the alien communications pod on the moon had finally stopped the creatures, but not before tens of thousands of people had perished and millions displaced.

Six months later, a single Kaiju landing in the island nation of Kiribati in the South Pacific had almost succeeded in detonating a gravity bomb that would have activated most of the tectonic plates of the Pacific Ocean, causing global destruction. Walker and a special team, including Sergeant Costas, had entered the Kaiju while submerged and had delivered a container of deadly K-2 nerve toxin derived from Wasp venom and Novichok A-230, a Russian acetylcholinesterase inhibitor. Microscopic nanites flooded the creature's blood, producing prodigious quantities of the deadly neurotoxin.

The two incidents made him an expert Kaiju killer. He now wondered why the politicians in Washington had interfered with his job. He slumped slightly in his chair and stretched out his long legs to soothe the cramps in his calf muscles. The secretary glanced over at him. He thought he glimpsed a flicker of sympathy in her avocado green eyes as he smiled at her. Maybe he did, for two minutes later, with no intercom buzzer, phone call, or signal he could detect, she dropped the sheaf of papers she had been perusing on her desk, turned to face him, and said, "Secretary Robinson will see you now, Major Walker." He wondered if all visitors received the mandatory forty-five minute waiting period.

He stood, grateful to stretch his back. His rigorous training schedule had pushed his body to its limits. He needed a long rest, but it was unlikely that was the reason for his recall. *No rest for the weary.*

"Thank you," he replied.

She brushed against him as she ushered him into a surprisingly small office. The contact was fleeting, but Walker detected a spark pass between them. Some people had called him handsome, so he attributed her subtle body contact as a sexual advance, one he would have gladly reciprocated, but her smile as she looked up at him was not coy but one of pity, an emollient to his bruised ego. She turned and closed the door behind her.

The Secretary's office was Spartan in detail. A dark mahogany desk sat before the single window, its polished surface marred only by a telephone, a desk pad, and a gold-framed photo. A single leather chair faced the desk. Two more of the uncomfortable wooden chairs he had endured in the outer office lined a wall in case of multiple visitors. A picture of the capitol building, the Washington Monument, a portrait of the President, and a photo of the general in his uniform standing beside a B2 bomber graced two of the walls. General Robinson sat behind the desk in a worn leather chair, a black man of about 56 years old with thinning cottony hair and a frown on his haggard, deeply lined face. His hazel eyes looked tired but still hinted at the force of character that had propelled him to his high position. As an African American, Walker was proud that someone of his own race had reached such a powerful position, a position that, due to the war with the aliens, was considered by some more powerful than that of President of the United States.

"General," Walker said as he entered.

"Mr. Secretary, now," Robinson replied. "My generaling days are behind me. Have a seat, Major."

Before Walker had settled in the chair, infinitely more comfortable than his previous seat, the Secretary began. "I guess you're wondering why I pulled you from your job."

"Yes, sir. There's still a lot of work to do."

Secretary Robinson's eyes smoldered like embers. He made a fist with one hand and rested it on the desk. "Well, it's urgent, or you wouldn't be here."

"So I assumed, sir."

Walker noted the tension in the Secretary's haunted face and decided Robinson did not direct his ire at him personally. The reason for the visit was direr than he had expected. A sense of despair wafted from the Secretary like cheap aftershave.

Robinson took a deep breath, held it for a moment, and then released it. His tone softened but the tension remained. Walker noticed a slight tic in his right jaw. "The gravity detectors on the LISA have picked up multiple pods inbound for Earth."

Walker frowned at the unexpected dismal news. Because the current ten Kaiju were smaller than the originals, 600 feet long instead of 900 feet, many of the experts had decried the aliens were running out of raw material. More Kaiju meant big trouble. It also meant the experts were wrong. What else were they wrong about?

He cleared his throat before asking, "How many?"

"Thirty."

An icy hand gripped Walker's heart and squeezed hard. His hands dug into the padded leather chair arms for support as he half rose from his chair in shock. The room closed in on him, as the air became too thick to breathe in. His mind numbed, refusing to grasp the number the Secretary had just announced. It seemed impossible, inconceivable.

"Thirty?" he repeated. His voice cracked with the question, hoping the Secretary would correct him; say a much smaller, saner number.

The Secretary glanced down at his hands folded on the desk. One hand gripped the other tightly, as if trying to keep it from trembling. His voice lost some of its assertiveness, as he said, "This could mean the end for us."

Walker could not picture thirty more Kaiju set loose upon the Earth. The destruction and loss of life would be catastrophic. He knew instinctively the thirty Kaiju would land across the globe, leaving Earth's already stretched defenders unable to bring their full potential to bear. He feared the Secretary could be right.

"How long do we have?"

The DRS detectors had given them only hours advance warning for the first Kaiju. The Laser Interferometer Space Antenna hurriedly launched and placed in Earth-Sol L1 orbit after Kaiju Kiribati arrived, had increased the detection of gravity waves tenfold, improving the warning time to eight days for the ten creatures now rampaging in Europe.

"The first ten will arrive in four days; the others, a week later."

Walker's chest tightened. It was barely enough time to determine landing sites and move teams into position, even if he had enough trained teams to do the job. "Why such a short a lead time for the first swarm?"

The Secretary waved his hands in the air to display his agitation. "They mentioned something about planetary alignment and the grouping of the pods. I don't know, Major. It doesn't matter. Bottom line is we're about to be hit hard."

Walker shifted in his seat. "Up until now, the Nazir tactics stymied me. They are obviously superior technologically, but seemed haphazard in their attacks. Three Kaiju, and then only one – it didn't make sense." He sighed. "Ten Kaiju in Europe and thirty more inbound. I guess they got some new generals."

"Maybe they underestimated us before. We sure as hell underestimated them. They mean business this time."

"I'll retrieve Costas from London, and we'll start building more Kaiju Killer teams."

"By all means bring Sergeant Costas here, but we have a different task in mind for you."

Walker's senses tingled with dread premonition. He wasn't going to like what the Secretary had to say. "Different?" he asked.

"What do you know about *Project Javelin*?"

Walker squirmed in his seat. He was certain that he was supposed to know nothing about it, but his friend Gate Rutherford had let slip the name during a conversation a few weeks earlier. "I've heard the name mentioned," he replied.

Robinson raised his eyebrows. "I imagine you know quite a bit more, but we'll let that slide for now. Are you familiar with the SR-80 *Lance*?"

"A little," he hedged. He didn't know how much of his previous missions the Secretary was aware. "The Kaiju in Nevada, Nusku, intended to destroy the base at Groom Lake where the new orbital aircraft were being tested."

Robinson smiled. "And you stopped it. Equipped with a smaller version of the Kaiju gravity drive, the *Lance* is now capable of interplanetary flight." He paused and gazed at Walker as if offering a challenge. "We are equipping twenty of the *Lances* with nuclear missiles, attaching them and a couple of habitat modules to a framework with a much larger gravity drive engine, and sending it to confront the aliens. *Project Javelin*, a weapon aimed at the heart of the aliens."

Walker didn't know what to say. He was delighted they were going to at long last take the fight to the Nazir, but it seemed a pitiful response and much too late to save the planet in view of the impending invasion. "An apt name, I guess."

"You will lead the assault team."

The Secretary's words caught him by surprise. "Me, sir? I'm no pilot."

"You won't have to fly. In addition to the *Lance* pilots, we're sending a select strike team of ten specialists. You'll be in command of an assault team consisting of members of your Kaiju Killer teams. The *Lance* group will be at your disposal, but commanded by an Air Force colonel. Your task is to assess the situation as you find it and decide on an effective plan of attack. It requires on-the-spot analysis and quick thinking. You've proven yourself capable of both."

The idea of hurtling through over 5 billion miles of space did not appeal to him, but striking a decisive blow against the aliens did. "I'm honored, sir, but what about the inbound Kaiju? Wouldn't current K-Team members be better utilized training new recruits?"

Robinson frowned. "Not your problem, I'm afraid. The U.N. Security Council is considering more drastic measure for the newly arriving Kaiju."

Walker was incredulous. The Secretary was talking about nukes, and the aliens purposefully aimed the Kaiju at heavily populated cities. "That could kill millions."

Robinson clenched his jaw so tightly it quivered. His quick response indicated he had faced the same accusation before and did not like repeating himself. "We're trying to save a world here, Major. Tens of thousands or even millions against billions – what would you do?"

Walker sank back into the seat. The Secretary was right. They could never train and field enough teams to handle so many Kaiju is such a short time. It had taken six months to train a dozen teams, and two of those were now gone.

"Yes, sir. I understand."

"Believe me, I fought the decision. The President threatened to fire me if I opposed him. He's in a difficult position. People are running scared and rightly so. The environmental groups raised holy hell over the release of toxic K-2 nanites into the ecosystem." He chuckled, but it was not a humorous laugh. "As if the Kaiju aren't doing enough damage, they're worried about Mother Nature getting her panties in a wad. The U.N. speaks of evacuation as if it were an easy task. Millions are already on the move. Where do the city populations go? How do we get them there? How do we house and feed them?" He waved his hands again. "Ah, enough bitching. It's going to happen no matter what you and I do or think. God help us if any of these new Kaiju hit here. We're still reeling from the last attack."

"When, sir?"

"You will leave in three days."

"What about Costas? He's capable of taking over my job training Kaiju Killer Teams."

"Yes, he is, but Costas will accompany you."

Walker smiled. "He'll love that."

A faint trace of a grin curved the Secretary's lips. "Better you deliver the news than me. Go get some rest. The next few days will be hectic."

In spite of the fact the general was not in uniform, Walker stood at attention and saluted. He left the Secretary's office wondering if he could find a quiet corner to perform his *Dhuhr* midday prayers. His need for solace had just grown exponentially.

* * * *

"Haumea," Costas asked, wrinkling his brow. "Is that in Jersey, 'cause you know I don't like Jersey?"

Sergeant William Costas filled the tiny wrought iron ice cream parlor chair with his huge frame, which contained not an ounce of fat. In his bright red tee shirt and Bermuda shorts, he looked more like a tourist than a master sergeant in the United States Army. The flowing Fu Manchu moustache he now sported wafted in the breeze. His face and arms bore faint scars from previous Kaiju encounters. Walker had chosen the outdoor café both for privacy and because he needed the fresh night air to clear his head. After leaving the Secretary of Homeland Security's office, he had spent the intervening nine hours since summoning Costas in meetings with the Joint Chiefs of Staff, the President's chief of staff, and a video conference with the commandant at Groom Lake.

"It's a chunk of rock in the Kuiper Belt, you big doofus," he said, knowing that Costas knew where Haumea was. He just liked to play dense sometimes. "We're attacking the Nazir on their home ground."

Costas tried his best to look offended. "*Moi*, in a spaceship? You've got to be kidding. All that distance with no broads and no booze. Why, it ain't human."

Walker made a show of searching for someone. "Who called you human? Point them out to me. They should be ostracized."

"Hey now. I'm potty trained and everything." Though they were the only customers at the café, he leaned in closer to Walker. "You really mean we're going out to meet the aliens, maybe kick some Nazir ass." Costas smiled and rubbed his hands together with unashamed glee. "I could handle that."

Walker smiled at Costas's comment. Mark Talent, a Tohono O'odham Native American from Arizona whom they had rescued from a stricken cruise ship, had joined his team inside Kaiju Kiribati in the South Pacific. The aptly named Talent had discovered a talent for killing the monstrous creatures attacking the cruise ship and inhabiting the innards of the Kaiju. He had also uncovered a series of markings unlike the indecipherable cursive alien script. The lines resembled the Latin alphabet letters N, A, Z, I, and R. Their true pronunciation and meaning were anyone's guess, but Nazir had stuck as the name of the aliens.

He wished Talent was going with them to Haumea, but Talent was a civilian content to remain in Arizona and train people to combat the Kaiju.

Costas reached for his beer and finished it off in one gulp. Walker, as a devout Muslim, drank only coffee and tea. That lapse might offend the mullahs, but he was American. Not drinking coffee was un-American. He had skipped dinner. His lunch still sat heavy on his stomach, roiling in the digestive acid ensuing from his troubling meeting with the Secretary. At sunset, he had dutifully performed *salat* for his *Maghrib* prayers, but neither they nor his noonday *Dhuhr* prayers had helped settle his queasy stomach. He suspected he could not pray away his problems. Sometimes, direct action was required.

"It won't be fun or easy. We have no intel as to what we'll face once we get there, but we have no choice."

Costas stared at Walker's face and frowned. He jabbed a finger at Walker. "I know that expression. You're holding something back. Spit it out."

"Thirty Kaiju are on their way here."

Costas paled; then swore. "Holy shit! Ain't we got grief enough?"

Walker agreed with Costas' sentiments. "We can't beat them. The U.N. has decided to nuke the landing sites."

Costas slammed his beefy fist onto the table. Walker grabbed his glass before it bounced off the table. "They're fools! Hell, they'll do as much damage as those ebony bastards."

A waiter standing by the door started toward them. Walker waved him back. "They're running scared. We've managed to stop only two Kaiju. Eight more are still loose in Europe. The European Union is breaking down as countries hoard vital resources. Thirty more?" He shook his head. "We can't win."

"Still seems like we ought to stay here and fight."

"We could never defeat them conventionally. If we destroy the alien manufacturing facility on Haumea, it might give them pause to reconsider invading our planet."

"How long will this little jaunt take?" Costas leaned back in his seat. "I only ask because I've got a date lined up with the Demarcos twins. I promised them a visit to the Lincoln bedroom in the White House."

"According to the commandant at Groom Lake, the ship they've constructed can make the outbound leg in ten days. The return trip … who knows?"

Costas' face turned grim. "We might not have to worry about that."

Costas, as always, was direct and to the point. Walker liked that about Costas. Consider yourself dead already and you didn't have to worry about dying. "There's always that possibility.

"Just you and me and some fly boys, huh?"

"We'll have a ground assault team of ten drawn from the ranks of the K Teams, all volunteers. If the aliens are dug into that rock, and I'm assuming they are, we'll have to go in and root them out."

Costas performed an exaggerated shudder that made his jowls flap. He rubbed the shoulder injured by a Wasp inside Nusku, the scar a vivid reminder of the dangers they faced. "I suppose they'll have Fleas, Ticks, Wasps, and Squid for defense."

Walker shared his sergeant's disgust. Each creature born inside the Kaiju crèches was designed for a specific purpose and deadly. He had a special hatred for the Squid introduced by Kaiju Kiribati, as dangerous aboard a ship as they were in the water.

"All the classic critters you've come to love, Sergeant. Maybe a few more surprises as well."

"Not too many I hope. I'm a fragile individual. My doctor told me to avoid excess excitement."

Walker smiled. "What about the Demarcos twins?"

"Them? That falls under relaxation." Costas' face clouded. "What if one of the new batches of Kaiju is headed for Groom Lake? They tried to take it out once before."

Walker had considered that possibility. "In that case, my friend, we're royally screwed."

As he sat there, allowing Costas time to digest all he had revealed to him, a young man walked by carrying a sign reading 'End Days are here. Kaiju are God's angels.' Costas growled and rose from his seat. Walker nudged him in the knee with his foot.

"Sit down, Sergeant. I don't need you in a jail cell for roughing up a Judgment Day acolyte."

Costas sat back down, but he did not appear happy with Walker's admonition. "Ignorant bastard needs his ass kicked. You know where I'd like to shove that sign he's carrying."

"Maybe," Walker agreed, frowning as he watched the young man trudging down the sidewalk as if the weight of the world pressed him into the concrete, "but let someone else do it. He has the right to protest, even if he is an ignorant bastard."

"It's un-American."

Walker sighed. "People are afraid. It looks like we're losing the war, and people turn to God. Some just go overboard. There have always been End-of-the-World cults."

"But these guys start fires and try to hamper evacuations. They want people to die."

"I've heard that too. I don't know if it's true, but no one on their side is denying it."

"Well, if one gets in my face, it'll be the end of his fucked up world." He shook his head. "The wrong people get eaten."

Walker let Costas have the last word. The Judgment Day cult disgusted him as well. It was giving up, and he wasn't about to give up, not while he still breathed.

3

August 11, Paris, France –

The stench inside the sewer was not as bad as LaBonner had expected. The cesspool odor was strong enough to singe the hair in his nostrils, but he had grown up in the Louisiana bayous with an outhouse instead of an inside bathroom. A similar pong permeated the Paris sewers, the familiar ammonia smell on a hot summer day. He rushed along the narrow, raised walkway beside the flowing stream of effluent, trying not to notice the water's red taint from blood seeping into the sewers. Dozens of water pipes, pneumatic tubes, and electrical conduits ran along the ceiling and walls, servicing the city through the 1300 miles of sewer tunnels. The Paris sewers channeled 1.2 million cubic meters of waste to the treatment plants each day, a veritable river of sludge produced by the city's two million inhabitants and eight million people living in the suburbs.

He paused for a moment at a junction to get his bearings. Plaques on the walls bore the names of the streets above them, eliminating wandering aimlessly through the maze of tunnels. He was glad his Cajun parents had drummed French into his head as a child. The northern branch of the junction led to the Sewer Museum situated along the banks of the Seine. He pointed down a tunnel running southeast.

"This way. The Rue de Grenelle runs to the Rue de Sulpice."

"Where are the rats?"

LaBonner threw Spence a questioning look. "Why?"

"I heard the Paris sewers swarmed with rats big as a West Virginia coon dog. Where are they?"

"They're smart," Chalmers answered. "They hauled ass out of here."

LaBonner hoped Chalmers was right, but the answer seemed too simple. He didn't have time to dwell the reason for the lack of rats, but he kept it in the back of his mind, one more nagging thought to vex him.

The tunnel was narrower than the previous tunnel and the ceiling lower. They ran in single file. 18-inch diameter cast iron pipes crossed the tunnel, forcing them to duck beneath them, slowing their progress. The section of sewer was old. Chips in the plaster revealed areas of the original stone casing from the 1800s. The walls bore the names of past sewer workers and intrepid visitors scratched into the plaster with pocketknives and tools, forever frozen in time. LaBonner wondered if the names would remain long after the city had fallen.

When they reached Rue de Sulpice, lack of sleep and fatigue during the days of keeping just ahead of the Kaiju began to catch up with him. LaBonner leaned against the sewer wall and closed his eyes. The ghosts of his dead men's faces haunted him, pleading him to make their sacrifices worthwhile.

"Take five," he said, fighting to catch his breath.

He repositioned the heavy bag of extra ammo magazines on his shoulder. The strap had rubbed a raw groove into his flesh. He suspected Spence and Mayer, lugging the heavy rocket launchers, and Chalmers with his heavy minigun, were in worse shape than he was. They all badly needed sleep and a hot meal, but it seemed unlikely they would have the opportunity in the foreseeable future. The air was thick and damp, difficult to pull into his lungs, and smelled like the aftermath of a battle, a sickly stench with which he was intimately familiar.

"That ain't *merde*," Chalmers noted aloud. He had recognized the fetid odor as well – rotting flesh.

Sniffing the air, LaBonner traced the foul odor to a small oval opening in the wall, a cobblestoned side tunnel. A trickle of water ran from the tunnel into the main sewer at their feet. Blood stained the water red. The warm air pouring from the tunnel smelled of an abattoir.

No rest for the weary. "Lock and load," he said. He had delivered the same short homily so many times it had almost become a prayer or an incantation to guard against death.

He froze at a faint scratching sound from inside the tunnel. It could have been the missing rats, but he doubted it. They couldn't be that lucky. He shined his flashlight into the tunnel and quickly drew back, as his light fell upon the angular outlines of dozens of Fleas placing dead rats onto a pile of carcasses reaching almost to the ceiling. From beneath the rats, two pairs of human legs protruded, two unlucky innocents who had sought shelter in the underground sewers as had his team. It was a grisly sight, a vivid reminder of events continually taking place above them. The creatures assimilated anything, living or dead, into the Kaiju food chain.

He motioned for his men to back away from the tunnel. So far, they remained undetected, but that would not last long. The creatures had a keen sense of hearing and an even stronger sense of smell. They would have to pass the opening to reach the church. He pulled an M67 fragmentary grenade from one of his pockets and pulled the pin. As he tossed the 2.5-inch diameter grenade into the tunnel, the spoon popped off with a distinctive *ping*. The Fleas stopped what they were doing to take note of the small object bouncing toward them. Five seconds later, the grenade detonated. The 6.5-ounces of high explosives packed into the device sent shards of metal casing flying outward in all directions. The deafening noise echoed down the tunnels for several agonizing seconds. LaBonner worked his jaw trying to pop his ears. Dust and chunks of loose rock from the ceiling sifted down on them.

Glancing inside the tunnel through the haze of dust and smoke, a few of the Fleas had survived, shielded by their comrades and the now smoking corpses of dead rats and human remains. Their dark, glistening eyes focused on him. He motioned to Chalmers, who stepped forward with the minigun. They disintegrated under the onslaught of a stream of alien crystal-coated 7.62mm rounds. Chalmers grinned maniacally as he held down the trigger. His fusillade of bullets struck several of the pipes in the tunnel. A stream of water sprayed Chalmers in the face from a ruptured water main.

"Ew!" he moaned, wiping his face frantically with his hand, as the six-rotating barrels spun down to silence.

"It's tap water, Chalmers," LaBonner snapped. He reached out into the stream of spraying water, collected some in the palm of his hand, and used it to wash the Wasp ichor from his face. The water was warm, but it refreshed him. "Get a grip."

"That took care of them," Chalmers said, inspecting his handiwork.

"But not their buddies," Spence announced, as he stared back down in the direction they had come. The skittering of the knife-like points of Flea legs and their high-pitched chattering filled the tunnel. Making a stand against so many Fleas would have been suicidal.

"Move it!" LaBonner cried.

They raced down the tunnel as fast as their exhausted bodies would carry them, but the Fleas were faster and tireless. As they neared the exit to the street above, they maintained barely a fifty yard lead over the pursuing Fleas.

"Up the steps," he urged.

LaBonner positioned himself beside the steps as his men climbed to safety. He leveled his MK17 but held his fire until the Fleas were less than fifteen yards away. The bullets tore through the creatures' bodies.

Ocher-colored blood sprayed the walls of the tunnel. Their chatter became frenzied, as they clambered over the bodies of their dead brethren. LaBonner continued firing as he backed up the steps.

Near the top, Chalmers leaned past him and cut loose with the M134D-H, cutting a wide swath of destruction through the massed creatures. Once outside, both men tossed grenades down the steps. Body parts from the Fleas and a geyser of blood erupted from the opening. They slammed the cover back over the entrance and held it in place, while Spence and Mayer pushed an abandoned, canary yellow postal service Renault Kangaroo from the street to help block the opening. It was a finger in the dike. The Paris sewers had entrances every fifty yards. The Fleas would eventually find a way out.

For the moment, the sky above them was free of Wasps. That would not last long. The latest batch of Kaiju, though smaller than the first to attack Earth, reproduced Wasps and Fleas at a prodigious rate, much faster than the previous Kaiju. The Wasps patrolled the air like fighter squadrons, drawn by any sight or sound of human presence. Soaring on two pairs of leathery wings, the Wasps were both fast and silent. Their venomous stinger was not their only weapon. Each of the sharp-edged legs could sever a limb, and their mouths could rip off a human head in one bite.

LaBonner's team emerged on the Rue de Bonaparte on the west side of the church. They hunkered down in the entrance of *Herve Chapelier*, a Parisian handbag manufacturer. The mobs fleeing the city had smashed the windows and looted the store, as if purses and handbags were a priority during an end-of-the-world scenario. The off-white façade of the *Eglise de Sulpice* peeked above a line of horse chestnut trees a block away, its mismatched twin towers rising into the smoke-filled sky. *Almost there.*

He tried to stand, but his legs would not cooperate. A fear washed over him, deeper than any he had experienced while under fire from the Taliban in Afghanistan. His new enemy was deadlier and alien. It harbored none of the human characteristics, however misguided, that he could understand or relate to. This misanthropic enemy wanted to devour him, much as he would eat a crawfish or a bowl of gumbo.

He pushed his fear down as far as he could and steeled himself. He stood. "Let's move it," he ordered.

They reached the open square without incident, but as they passed the Font de Sulpice dominating the square, the first Wasps appeared overhead, only a few at first, but more would soon arrive following the alien pheromone trail the creatures left, like foraging army ants. He pointed to the west façade of the church, whose open-colonnaded terraces reminded him too much of the Roman Coliseum and the deadly gladiatorial events that took place within it.

"Spence! Mayer! Make for the towers. Wait for the Kaiju to get close enough before taking your shot. We'll cover you."

Spence glanced up at the approaching Wasps as if unhappy with LaBonner's order to abandon him. Nevertheless, he nodded and started across the square at a fast trot. Mayer followed. As they raced across the courtyard carrying their nuclear-tipped rockets, LaBonner and Chalmers climbed onto the top tier of the French Renaissance fountain and took positions on each side of the tall pinnacle bearing seated statues of Bossuet, Fenelon, Flechier, and Massillon, four mid-Seventeenth Century bishops marking the cardinal points of the compass. LaBonner knelt waist deep in the water spilling over the top of the basin. Chalmers pushed up against Massillon's marble feet.

The barking of his SCAR and the whir of the M134 drew the Wasps to them, as LaBonner expected, allowing Spence and Mayer to reach the church in safety. He conserved ammo, waiting until Wasps got within a few feet before firing. This tactic was also more effective, as he pinpointed the more vulnerable areas between armor plates. However, Chalmers used his minigun like a broom, sweeping it back and forth, and firing without letup into the mass of gathering Wasps, wasting precious ammunition.

Chalmers' expression of disgust as he fired worried LaBonner. Hating one's enemy was understandable, especially one as inhuman as the alien creatures, but Chalmers seemed to take each attack as a personal affront. Killing Fleas and Wasps was incidental to the mission. Destroying the Kaiju was of foremost importance, their true mission. Chalmers' delight in killing Wasps and Fleas had seized control of him, become a priority, leading him to take too many chances. As he took a step away from the cover of the pinnacle to the edge of the fountain, LaBonner warned him back.

"Chalmers!" he shouted. "Take cover!"

Chalmers ignored him, caught up in a mad killing frenzy. Two Wasps attacked in tandem. Forced to swing the minigun from one to the other, he left an opening for the Wasps. One Wasp took the brunt of the gunfire, its body disintegrating in a spray of blood as the flurry of bullets tore into it. The first creature's sacrifice allowed the second Wasp to close in. It leaped over the body of its companion and landed on Chalmers' back, dragging him backward. Off balance and unable to bring the minigun to bear, he dropped it as he fell at the feet of Bishop Massillon. He pulled his knife and began stabbing at the creature's head. He inflicted serious wounds to the creature's eyes, but it continued to hack at Chalmers' body with two of its forelegs. He rolled into the basin with the creature on top of him.

LaBonner splashed across the basin to aid Chalmers. He jammed his rifle against the Wasp's head and held down the trigger. The creature's head exploded into a gory mess of flesh, yellow blood, and ebony crystal. One of the wings thrashed through the water and struck his ankle, knocking him down. He came up spluttering, spitting out a mouthful of water. The decapitated Wasp didn't move. He pushed it from Chalmers' body and lifted Chalmers' head from the bloodstained water. His eyes were open and his lips moved, but blood spilled out instead of words. He bled from a dozen wounds. He glanced up at LaBonner and coughed up a mouthful of blood and water.

"Damn you, Chalmers!" LaBonner yelled. "Don't you die on me!"

It was too late. Chalmers couldn't hear him. His eyes closed and his head rolled limply to one side. He lifted Chalmers' body and laid it on the ledge of the fountain. LaBonner could do nothing for Chalmers, not even save his body from the fate of so many others, that of feeding the Kaiju. He picked up the M134 minigun, dropped down from the fountain, and ran for the church.

Mayer leaned from the second-level terrace, firing her weapon at the Wasps pursuing him. LaBonner waved her back under cover. She carried one of the rocket launchers. She was too important to expose herself to save him. He reached the entrance just ahead of a Wasp. Inside, he fell to one side, turned, and fired a five-second burst from the minigun into the creature, as it scrambled through the door. It continued to lunge at him in its death throes, stabbing one of its knife-edged legs into the plaster beside his head and raking a large chunk of masonry from the wall. He fired one more burst to be certain it was dead; then, closed and barred the door. The heavy wooden door would not resist a determined onslaught by the Wasps, but it would slow them down.

His head pounded as bounded up the stairs. *Bad time for a migraine.* He bit down on his lip to ignore the throbbing. The Kaiju waded across the Seine in three enormous strides, crushing the Pont D'Iena Bridge beneath its ponderous tread. It halted in front of the Eiffel Tower as if posing for a photograph; then, reared and pressed its bulk against the tower. The massive creature rose over halfway up the open girder structure. The screams of the stressed metal sounded like the city dying. A cloud of paint flakes and rust chips exploded from the warped girders, falling around the tower like dirty snow. The bizarre scene mesmerized LaBonner. Despite the danger, he stopped to watch.

The iconic tower swayed drunkenly as the Kaiju pressed into the network of girders. Its front legs became battering rams, pounding the

130-year-old wrought iron. Finally, pushed beyond its structural limits, the tortured metal gave way. The northwest pillar supporting the tower twisted and buckled under the strain. Concrete exploded at the tower's feet. The tower canted far to one side for several moments, seemingly in defiance of the laws of gravity, but the Kaiju pounded it until the 1,000-foot-tall edifice toppled.

As if curtseying, the tower bent forward at the waist, folding at the second observation level. A 300-foot length of steel girders peeled away from the structure and collapsed into the Seine. Waves splashed over the banks and across the garden, washing away many Fleas in its wake. Its integrity compromised the rest of the structure split apart as rivets popped and welds cracked. Steel girders plummeted onto the Champ de Mars, embedding in the concrete like toothpicks in a tray of canapés.

Satisfied with the Eiffel Tower's destruction, the Kaiju dropped back onto its twelve legs and resumed its leisurely trek into the heart of the City of Lights.

4

August 11, Johnson Space Center, Houston, TX –

Doctor Robert Wingate 'Gate' Rutherford stared out his office window at the Memorial Grove near the facility's main entrance. A slight breeze rustled the leaves. His mind was on Commander Erwin Langston and the freshly planted tree dedicated in his honor. His heroic sacrifice in stopping the alien communications pod on the moon, thereby stopping the Kaiju, deserved higher honor than a tree and a posthumous increase in rank, but the world had bigger problems to deal with, and as usual, heroes were shunted aside.

Gate had attended the ceremony ten days earlier. The three surviving members of the *Lunar One* crew attended as well, adding their praise to that of the gathered dignitaries. That such an observance had taken place in spite of the current turmoil around the world spoke highly of the world's high esteem for Commander Langston. His was not the only sacrifice, but it was the most widely known. So many had died in the U.S., the South Pacific, and in Europe, it was difficult to keep track of the unsung heroes. That news of yet another swarm of Kaiju pods marred the solemn occasion only emphasized the sacrifice Commander Langston had made.

Gate rued the fact that some newspapers called him a hero as well. He reserved such accolades for better men and women than him. He had joined then Captain Walker's team, entering Kaiju Nusku hoping to learn more about the creatures. The possibility of dying had not seemed important. His anger at seeing Chicago trampled and witnessing tens of thousands of people dying had supplanted his natural sense of self-preservation. Crawling around inside the guts of a monster Kaiju had changed that. If the terror he experienced then, and the fear the memories evoked when he thought about it did anything, it proved to him that he was no hero – Foolish, maybe, but no hero.

He tore his gaze away from the window and focused on the report lying on his desk. He had read the words numerous times, but the full impact had yet to set in. It was a case of emotional overload. Ten more Kaiju would arrive on the Earth within four days. Twenty more would follow seven days later. It seemed an impossibly high number. He had warned that the Nazir would escalate their attempts to eradicate mankind for possession of the planet, but even he had not fathomed the resources at the aliens' disposal. As a former catastrophist for NASA, he feared for the end of humanity. Humans had proven resourceful and to some extent cooperative, but as the Kaiju destroyed precious infrastructure, feeding and relocating tens of millions of humans became an increasingly impossible task. Earth was near her breaking point. More Kaiju could tip the balance.

Earth's primary defense had been her early warning systems – LISA, the DRS satellite, and the gravity wave detectors scattered around the planet. Now, even those had failed them. They had only days to prepare for the new onslaught of giant Kaiju.

When the *New Horizon* probe had flown past Pluto in 2015 after a 10-year journey and snapped photos of Haumea and her twin moons, Hi'iaka and Namaka, the icy outer worlds had looked benign, offering no hint of the diabolical plot unfolding even then. No one suspected that when *New Horizon* went off-line just hours just before its rendezvous with Pluto, it had been the first shot in an interstellar war. Gate was convinced the brief loss of contact that had required a complete computer reboot had been an alien attempt to hack into the system to retrieve information about Earth. Later, when the probe had proved an annoyance to the aliens, they had destroyed it. NASA had planned new probes using the gravity drive, but none was presently past the drawing board stage.

Working alone and without NASA's sanction, he had discovered the alien base on Haumea, a stony, planetary fragment beyond the orbit of Pluto in the Kuiper Belt. Until the military had reverse-engineered one of the alien gravity drives, the enemy had been impossibly far away, too far to strike. Now, a slim hope grew in his chest that *Project Javelin* would work. It was mankind's last chance.

The Air Force had developed the SR-80 *Lance* as a Near-Earth Orbit tactical fighter, capable of both atmospheric and space flight as a defense against China or Russia, the main threats at that time. With the advent of the alien Kaiju invasion, the Air Force had retrofitted it with the new gravity drive. Even so, it could not travel 5 billion miles to the Kuiper Belt among the Trans-Neptunian Objects. For that, it needed a lift. The *Javelin* was a stripped down spacecraft, an open framework fitted with a large gravity drive engine and habitat modules. The SR-80s would dock with the *Javelin* and ride piggyback to Haumea. There, they would confront the enemy in its front yard.

Gate could not go. His heart was not in it. His hatred no longer burned hot in his chest. Having seared away all his passion and anger, it now smoldered like a banked fire. He had seen Kaiju and witnessed the aftermath of their path of destruction close-up and intimately, and he had no desire to confront them again. He had satisfied his morbid curiosity concerning the giant alien creatures. His and Walker's observations had aided the Kaiju Killer teams in Europe. For that, he was delighted, but he had learned something about himself during the encounter of which he was not proud. He was afraid.

His fear was not as much fear for his life as a fear that he would change even more than he had. He was not the person he had been a year ago before the Kaiju. What would he become if the alien onslaught continued? He did not want to find out.

As a NASA catastrophist, people, cities, and countries had merely been numbers on a chart, which he could manipulate. He had no emotional investment in the outcomes of his projections. Their futures were purely the results of cause and effect, a consequence of math, and a throw of the cosmic dice. After following Kaiju Girra and witnessing its path of destruction through Indiana and Chicago, his interest had become personal. The numbers now became people and the buildings someone's home. Each death diminished him. He wanted to stop the aliens as quickly as possible to save as many lives as he could.

Sometimes, his desire to stop the Nazir drove him to push himself beyond his physical limitations. After Nusku, he had thrown himself headlong into his work, ignoring friends and his own body. He had lost considerable weight, becoming a scarecrow of his former self. His health had deteriorated, and the nightmares intensified. Sleep became secondary to his pursuits. When Kaiju Kiribati had arrived, followed by the gravity bomb meant to disrupt the Pacific tectonic plates, his personal fear had grown to encompass the entire planet. Even after the threats had passed, his hatred had not abated. He had managed to temper it somewhat by focusing on astronomy rather than catastrophic predictions. He sublimated his hatred of the aliens beneath the same blanket of ennui that separated him from friends and colleague. His weight and overall appearance had improved, but he was still a shadow of his former self, moody, withdrawn, and prone to sudden outbursts. Walker, seeing him after months of isolation, had told him he did not play well with others. He struggled to change that aspect of his life.

He had learned from his sources that Major Aiden Walker would go on the mission, as would his faithful companion Sergeant Costas. He applauded the decision. He only hoped Walker did not learn he had suggested his name to the Joint Chiefs of Staff as mission leader. In spite of any ill will the military had for Gate, they recognized Walker's abilities. Gate hated to see his friend face danger again, but Walker had a knack for getting the job done, and that was what the Earth needed if it was to survive the war.

His desk phone rang, startling him from his reverie. He fumbled the receiver as he picked it up. "Rutherford here."

"Dr. Rutherford, this is Director Stevens. Can you meet me at Mission Control in thirty minutes?"

He tensed, certain the director had bad news or else she would not have called. Unlike former Director Caruthers, he and the new director were not friends. In fact, she resented his unique position at NASA, deeming him an outsider. "Sure. What's up?"

"We may have to launch early."

He sat up abruptly. She had touched on one of his worst nightmare scenarios. "Damn. Be right there."

An early launch of the *Javelin* meant a complete computation of new course parameters. Even a few hours could make a large difference on a 5-billion-mile flight. He suspected the director had not summoned him for that reason. The flight control crew could handle the computations. His role in the actual mission was minimal, that of a paid consultant. He had made enemies at NASA and in the military by stepping on toes and bypassing the normal chain of command during his search for the Nazir. Former Director Caruthers had shielded him whenever possible, but as Caruthers had warned him, the military had a long memory.

Heads had rolled after Kaiju Kiribati, and many who had barely escaped the ax held him responsible. He had learned to live with it, but Caruthers had grown tired of the constant infighting and had taken an early retirement. He now lived in a condo on the beach in Galveston. Gate envied him his freedom.

Gate, as a consulting astronomer, was included in the mission more as a nod to his past contributions than for any new input he could provide. The mission team had all the data he had accumulated concerning Haumea. Once the gravity drive fired up, Fire Team Alpha would be beyond interference by well-meaning NASA technicians. *Fire Team Alpha.* He had wondered why Walker's previous team in which he had been included had been designated Fire Team Bravo. Now he knew. Fire Team Alpha was the *Lance* pilots.

The walk to the *Christopher C. Kraft, Jr. Mission Control Center* was the first time Gate had left his office in two days. Sleeping on the short sofa had put a kink in his back. He contorted his body to stretch his muscles as he strode purposefully down the sidewalk. The south Texas day was hot, muggy, and dusty. His long-legged stride ate up the distance between his office in Building 20 and Mission Control in Building 30 M. He listened to Herbie Hancock's *Nightwalker* on his iPhone, in his opinion one of the legendary jazz master's best works. He reluctantly turned it off and removed his earbuds as he entered the building, replacing the sounds of calm serenity with those of frenzied activity.

The room, with which he had become so familiar during the approach of the first three Kaiju, was unusually chaotic. In addition to the preparations for the launch of the *Javelin* and her sister ship, *Assegai*, NASA's Mission Control handled all activities aboard the International Space Station and the Orion mission to place a new optical observatory in trans-lunar orbit. The noise level in the control center pulsed, as reports from technicians caused a stir, and knots of conversation spread around the room like ripples. He nodded at a few familiar faces, noted the increased security, but aimed his steps toward Samantha Stevens, NASA's new director. As usual, a sea of frazzled, white-shirted technicians bearing clipboards surrounded her, assiduous to her every word. At a mere 5'5'' tall, she was barely visible in the crowd. The crown of her easily recognizable bun stuck up like a Spanish comb. To an outsider, the short, frumpy, matronly looking director might not seem an imposing character, but those who had worked with her or under her knew better.

Samantha Stevens had fought her way up from an astrophysics department when women in NASA were a rarity. Lacking many of the social graces of her male counterparts, she bulldogged her way to the top using her expertise and her unshakable belief in herself and in NASA. She was neither colorful nor very likable, but she was efficient and dedicated to her job. Also to her credit, she did not step on toes. The military liked that; one of the reasons she presently held her position, not that she did not deserve it. Even Gate believed NASA to be in capable hands.

Today, as usual, she wore a simple two-piece gray tweed dress suit with a white blouse. An American flag pin adorned her jacket lapel. She glanced up at Gate's approach, her expression grave. "Ah, Doctor Rutherford. I'm glad you wasted no time."

"Moving up the launch is worth a quicker step."

"Quite so. It will require a few schedule changes and many hours of overtime, but it is necessary."

"Why has the launch date been changed?"

Stevens frowned. "We noticed a small adjustment in one of the incoming pod's path, in fact, several course corrections. It is possible it will intersect *Javelin's* orbit. We cannot take a chance."

Gate nodded. He had suggested a slowly changing geo-stationary lunar orbit that kept the moon's bulk between the *Javelin* and her sister ship and any incoming pods. The military had disagreed with him, deeming rapid access to the ships a military necessity. "I see."

"You need not say, 'I told you so,' Dr. Rutherford. I concede you were right yet again."

His cheeks reddened. He had wanted badly to tell her just that. "My job is to predict catastrophic events. The math was in my favor."

"Be that as it may, the mission clock has started."

That startled him. It also explained the increased activity in the control room. "So early. When are you launching?"

"In eight hours."

Gate was so astounded, he sputtered as he replied, "But-but that's not enough time to calibrate a new flight path." An early launch jeopardized the entire mission. His anger at the aliens rose in his chest, threatening to consume him. The veins in his temples throbbed. He clenched and unclenched his fists, as he struggled to control his temper. Lashing out at the director solved nothing.

"We either launch now or risk losing our only offensive weapon."

As daunting as recalibrating a course change was would be, he could tell she was reluctant to broach the real reason she had summoned him. He closed his eyes against the spinning room and took several deep breaths to calm himself. "I still don't see why you require my help. Your people are quite capable of doing the math, even under such a rushed timeline."

She stared at him with intense green eyes that sparkled like fire-lit emeralds when she focused her attention on someone. "You predicted the Nazir would do anything to stop the *Javelin*."

"I don't know if they are aware of the *Javelin* in particular, but they surely expected us to retaliate in some manner. They know we have interplanetary capabilities, and now we have their gravity drive technology. It would seem obvious that we would combine the two to strike at them."

She nodded. "That's what the Joint Chiefs believe as well."

"I still don't see why —"

"Doctor Rutherford, I want you to accompany the mission to Haumea."

Her words were like a pronouncement of doom, as if his doctor had dropped the Big C-word during a physical examination. He had worked hard to make his role in the fight against the Kaiju one of numbers and astronomical data. The pain, death, and suffering he had witnessed still lay too heavy on his heart, a constant threat to his sanity. Now, she wanted him to jump into the flames carrying a can of gasoline. His anger faded as quickly as it had arisen, as if quenched by the new emotion seeking a home in his mind – Fear. His palms perspired. He wiped them on his shirt.

"Me?" he spluttered. "I-I-I can't go to Haumea. You've got a dozen –"

She cut him off with a stern look. "Doctor Rutherford, NASA and JPL are currently controlling five missions simultaneously." Her voice was even and composed, but nevertheless strong and forceful, reinforcing why those she had intimidated called her a bulldog. She was a woman used to getting her way. "Our resources are limited. Any changes to *Javelin's* course will take far too long to enact in the event of an emergency. We need someone there to navigate the Kuiper Belt safely. You are one of the few scientists capable of doing so. You've spent a year studying it." A quick grin flashed on her lips. "I'm betting you have some of the orbital data memorized."

She was right. He had always been good with numbers. "I ..." His voice trailed off, as he realized her encomium was a tool to sway him. He took a deep breath to reign in his emotions and think more clearly. He had no ready reason not to go other than fear for his sanity and the more prosaic fear of death. Was mere fear reason enough to refuse when so many other people faced death? Should he value his life more than they valued theirs?

The director noticed his hesitation and pounced. "I would not ask this if it were not vital to the success of the mission, Dr. Rutherford. The Joint Chiefs want me to make it very clear that they will not order you to go. I'm not sure they could in any event. It is a request from a country very much in need of heroes."

Heroes. The curse still followed him. His shoulders sagged in defeat. He knew when he was beaten, and she had smacked him down good by calling upon his patriotism and his ego in equal proportions. The problem with being a hero was that heroes tended to die. In a roundabout way, he was responsible for Walker's inclusion on the mission. He wondered how Walker would feel when he learned the director had hoisted Gate on his own petard.

"I guess I don't have much choice, do I? I mean, given the circumstances …" He sighed. "I'll go." He scratched his neck where the imaginary noose tightened around his throat.

"Thank you, Dr. Rutherford." Some of the darkness left her face. *Had she expected him to refuse?* She motioned to an Air Force sergeant standing by the door. He walked over and stood behind her, his arms clasped behind his back. "Sergeant Brockton will accompany you to Building 32. Good luck."

As Gate followed the guard to the Space Environment Lab for an all-too-brief session in a space suit in the thermal vacuum chamber, his mind scrambled for a way out, a means to avoid his fate. He wondered if he would ever see Mission Control again. Given what he faced, it did not seem likely.

5

August 11, Paris, France –

The blood of the Wasps LaBonner's team had killed released alien pheromones that reminded him of the smell of rotten magnolia blossoms. Swirling through the air, the potent scent attracted hordes of the deadly flying creatures. The high-pitched susurration of their calls and the flapping of their leathery wings drowned out the groans of the approaching Kaiju. Each stride of the massive creature sent tremors racing through the Church of Saint Sulpice. Plaster cracked and sloughed from the centuries-old walls. Heavy candelabras danced across the tiled floor and fell. Inside the church, the stained glass window depicting the crucifixion shattered and fell. Wide cracks despoiled Delacroix's famous frescoes on each side of the main entrance. The church had stood since 1646, but every step of the giant Kaiju wrote its doom.

The army of Wasps kept LaBonner's team penned down in the north tower of the church, determined to wipe them out at any cost. It was almost as if they sensed the danger to the Kaiju LaBonner and his team posed. He and his two remaining teammates fought them off with a flurry of gunfire from their SCAR-H rifles, the M-134D minigun, and a handful of grenades.

He had no time to mourn Chalmers, Thayer, or his other dead men – Sanders, Anderson, Mackey, and Westlake. His fight now was to keep the list of the dead from becoming any longer. He pulled the pin on a grenade and rolled it down the steps into the midst of several Wasps climbing from the second-level terrace. The explosion shattered their bodies, but did little to impede the advance of the massed creatures behind them.

Private Spence's position in the top turret of the tower allowed him to fire at Wasps attacking him and those attacking LaBonner and Mayer in the lower tower level. Louvers covering the windows partially protected them from the Wasps' full fury, but the resolute Wasps ripped away boards at a pace faster than the three could kill them.

LaBonner had chosen the north tower both because its windows were covered and because it looked as if the Kaiju would pass closest to it, if it did not simply destroy the church, as it had so many other of Paris' ancient buildings. LaBonner hoped they could hold out long enough to take a shot. He peeked around the corner and fired three quick bursts into the advancing Wasps. There seemed no stopping them. Each time he created a barricade of dead Wasp bodies, the other Wasps simply hacked and chewed them to pieces, as if they were an obstacle to remove and not dead crèche mates.

The incessant attack prevented Mayer or Spencer from breaking away to prepare for their shot at the Kaiju. It looked as if they would have to choose one or the other – defend themselves against the Wasps or fire their nuclear-tipped rockets at the Kaiju.

"Mayer!" he yelled. "Join Spence up top. Load your rockets and get ready. I'll keep them off your backs while you take your shot."

He didn't know how long he could hold off the Wasps, but the Kaiju loomed closer with each enormous stride. The stench of putrefaction mounted as it neared. He estimated the pair had two minutes to line up accurate shots before it passed out of range or crushed them beneath it. He fired the minigun until he emptied the last ammo belt. He released the trigger and the six barrels spun down to silence. He dropped the minigun and slipped his SCAR from his shoulder.

Mayer passed him her two grenades. "Good luck, Sergeant."

"Yeah, I'll see you on the other side. Now, get moving."

He watched her disappear up the steps, and then moved to the center of the room with the stairs behind him where he could cover all the windows and the door. When one Wasp ripped away enough louvers to poke its head through, he fired a long burst into its head. As it died and fell away, it enlarged the hole. A second Wasp took its place, clawing its way inside. More Wasps pushed through the door. They bunched together, impeding their progress. He continued firing, as he edged backward toward the steps leading to the top level.

He tossed two grenades across the room behind the leading line of Wasps. The twin explosions reverberated in the enclosed space almost deafening him. His ears rang. As he took a step backward, a sharp, burning pain in his side drew his attention. He glanced down to see blood. Shrapnel from the blast had peppered his uniform, exposing the TEP armor beneath. Blood seeped through his uniform from a wound in his side the armor had not covered.

"Son of a bitch," he muttered.

A rage surged through him. He emptied the last magazine of his SCAR, spraying the Wasps in the door and at the windows. He tossed the empty weapon to the floor and drew his 9mm Beretta. As he hobbled up the steps to join Spence and Mayer, he suspected they would not be coming down from the tower. This would be their last stand against the Wasps. He didn't want to die for nothing.

The pain of his wound and the knowledge of certain death brought clarity to his mind that had been missing. The fear subsided like an ebbing tide. As he entered the top tier of the tower, Mayer aimed her rocket launcher at the Kaiju, while Spence fended off Wasps with the butt of his rifle. She had a difficult time lining up a shot because of the Wasps bunched around the window. LaBonner picked up her discarded SCAR and joined them. The Kaiju was still 200 yards away, but looked like a fleet of ebony C-17s landing on top of them. Its broad belly blotted out the sky. Each stride brought the 600-foot monster fifty yards closer. To their credit, they had drawn the Wasps away from the Kaiju to attend to them. A fresh batch of Wasps spilled from the Kaiju to attack the tower, leaving the blisters open, the chance they had been waiting for.

Mayer let out a loud curse. "I can't lock on from here," she said. "I'm going to the roof."

They both realized it was a suicide move. On the exposed roof, she would have seconds to fire before Wasps descended on her and ripped her to shreds.

He nodded. "Take the shot, Mayer," he said. "Do me proud. Spence, cover her. I'll hold the fort down here." He tossed Spence the SCAR.

Using his 9mm, LaBonner fired single shots at Wasps trying to enter the tower. He wasn't trying to kill them, only to keep them occupied. Mayer opened the trap door to the roof and crawled out. Spence stood on the top step firing up at Wasps buzzing the tower. A plume of fire shot from the rear of the launcher as the rocket left the tube. Mayer kept the laser pointed at an open blister along the creature's side. LaBonner prayed the blisters remained open; hoping his presence in a church would wing his prayers along to the proper recipient.

The rocket soared toward the Kaiju. Mayer disappeared over the side of the tower, as a Wasp swooped down and snatched her up. She didn't have time to scream. Spence picked up her launcher and realigned the targeting laser, ignoring the danger. LaBonner held his breath as the rocket, programmed to travel as deep into the Kaiju as possible before detonating, entered the blister. He hoped it reached the main corridor running the length of the creature where it would do the most damage.

He perceived the detonation in his chest before any visible sign of the explosion. A heartbeat later, the Kaiju's ebony armor, designed to absorb and utilize energy, flashed a bright azure, as it tried to absorb the energy of the nuclear blast. It could not. The blast spread throughout the creature's honeycomb structure, vaporizing flesh and killing the thousands of host creatures inside it, including the immature Wasps in the crèche nursery. Light erupted from each blister, from the spaces between armored plates, and from its open maw, as the blast disintegrated the internal organic components of the alien cyborg creature. The Kaiju stumbled when its legs folded; then, it fell prostrate on the ground, crushing houses and businesses beneath its bulk. The ground shuddered from the impact, collapsing buildings in an expanding concentric circle. The blast incinerated all the Wasps within a thousand yards. The Wasps confronting him stopped attacking as confusion set in.

A wall of superheated air swept across the square and struck the church. LaBonner ducked into the corner beside the window to shield himself, but the blast sucked him from the corner and rolled him across the floor beneath the feet of the milling Wasps. He slammed into a wall, stunned, his flesh scorched by the intense heat. The heat felt as if it was sinking through his flesh to the very core of his being, cooking him from the inside. *Now, I know how a microwaved burrito feels.* The wall behind him cracked and fell away. He slid down the suddenly tilted floor; then, the floor disappeared beneath him, and he plunged into space. He remembered screaming, but little else, as oblivion struck.

The tower cracked at the base and fell into the square, but the church itself, though seared and shaken, endured. An uneasy quiet settled over Paris. Ten minutes later, the peal of hundreds of church bells rang out across the city. Paris would live, scorched but unbowed. However, the fate of the rest of Europe remained in question.

6

August 12, Area 51, Groom Lake, Utah –

Four hours after leaving Washington, Walker and Costas stood inside a cavernous hangar at Groom Lake, called Dreamland, Paradise Ranch, Homebase, and Watertown, but better known as Area 51. A hot wind blew in from the desert through the open hangar door, parching Walker's skin. The moon perched just above the peaks of the Reveille Range casting his and Costas's long shadows through the door and into the darkened hangar. The SR-80 *Lances* stood in neat rows, each in its own pool of light, as workers readied them for flight. He recognized the 45-foot-long fuselage as that of an F-35B *Lightning*, but the Groom Lake engineering team had transformed the former high-orbital fighter aircraft into a hybrid spacecraft. With the wingspan reduced, the *Lance* looked every bit as sleek and fast as it was capable of flying. A compact version of the alien gravity drive engine developed from the recovered communications pod on the moon allowed the *Lance* to reach speeds of 40,000 mph, placing the moon within six hours travel time. The alien base was a lot farther than the moon.

The enlarged cockpit allowed for a crew of two – a pilot and a copilot/weapons specialist. A Gau-22/A 25mm cannon mounted in the nose and four weapons pods slung beneath the fuselage made the modified aircraft a formidable weapons platform. The SR-80 carried eight AIM-120B missiles armed with conventional warheads in the wingtip weapons pods. The six European *Meteor* missiles in the outer weapons pods were fifth-generation laser-guided weapons capable of evading the Wasps and delivering modified B61-11 low-yield, ground-penetrating nuclear warheads. Unfortunately, there were too few *Lances* to be effective against the Kaiju. As Earth's only offensive weapons, they were far too important to risk as Kaiju Killers.

Costas shook his head. "Man, I wouldn't want to fly one of those things."

Walker glanced over at Costas. In spite of the darkness, the sergeant wore his shades. He wore his cap pulled so low Walker could barely see his face. "Why not?"

"Could you imagine wearing a spacesuit for days on end?" He made a face of discomfort and rubbed his crotch. "I'd get diaper rash."

"The crews will ride with us in the habitat modules for the outbound trip. They'll board their *Lances* when we approach the alien base."

He knew how Costas felt. The pilots would be entirely dependent on their aircraft for nutrition, water, and oxygen while wearing the necessary spacesuits. The cockpits were too small to allow freedom of movement. The pilots would remain confined in their seats the entire time they were aboard their aircraft.

"Can they make it back to Earth if something happens to our ride?"

Walker smiled. Costas was asking if his team could make it back to Earth. He had asked the commandant the same question. The answer had dismayed him. "They have oxygen for twenty-four hours plus another six from their suit tanks. The trip back in a *Lance* would take about 14 years."

"That sucks."

"A second ship will launch two days after us with a two-man crew with additional supplies. If anything happens to our ship, we'll rendezvous with it for the return trip."

"A taxi, huh? I hope the driver speaks good English."

"What does it matter? You barely speak it right."

Costas scowled at Walker. "Women understand me well enough."

Costas might have said something more, but Walker didn't hear him. A Sikorsky MH-60G *Pave* helicopter flew by low to the ground on one of its periodical security grounds sweeps. Walker clamped his hands over his ears to muffle the noise. The *Pave* was capable of whisper-mode flight if necessary, but Area 51 did not openly flaunt its technology, adding to its air of mystery.

They had seen a group of protestors gathered around a bonfire a few miles outside the base's fences, a mixture of Judgment Dayers, alien enthusiasts, curious tourists, and people hoping for a sighting of one of the rumored new advanced aircraft. The soldier standing in the open door of the chopper manning an M134 GAU-17 Gatling gun indicated just how sacrosanct Area 51 considered its secrecy. He was certain any observers got the message.

"So we're Fire Team Alpha now, huh?" Costas said when the chopper had passed.

"Yeah, I guess we got a promotion from Fire Team Bravo."

Costas scratched his chin. "I always wondered who Alpha was. I was kind of jealous being the B-team."

Walker, too, had been envious, but to Costas, he said, "We're all on the same team."

"Yeah, but the first-string players get all the cute chicks." Costas plucked a fat, stubby Cameroon *Nub Olivia* cigar from his shirt pocket and jammed it in his mouth. As he reached for his lighter, Walker stopped him.

"You might want to reconsider lighting that," he said, pointing to an ordinance crew securing a weapons pod to the underside of a *Lance's* wing. "They're arming the *Lances*."

Costas replaced his lighter, but left the cigar in his mouth. "Maybe I'll just suck on it for a while like a pacifier."

"Good idea."

"I won't be able to smoke them on the *Javelin* anyway. One more thing I'll have to give up for this mission. Hell, I could apply for sainthood when I get back."

"I'll see you get a Purple Heart for your sacrifice."

Costas scowled. "Yeah, I'll add it to my collection of baubles and trinkets in my keepsake drawer. Say, I just thought of something. How can you tell which direction Mecca is for your prayers?"

"I'll face the rear of the ship and imagine Ka'aba, the holy mosque in Mecca. I'm sure Allah will understand."

Costas smiled broadly. "You'll be the first Muslim in space."

Walker shook his head. "No, there have been quite a few. In fact, a National Fatwa Council in Malaysia determined rules for Muslim prayers in space, based on local time at the launch site. Because of the lack of water, a damp cloth will replace ritual bathing before prayers. See, Muslims aren't so backward after all."

"After so many years in the bombed-out ruins of Iraq and Syria, you couldn't prove it by me."

Walker ignored Costas' crack, as he watched a man with Asian features stride across the hangar floor toward them, his back as straight as the crease of his pants. He wore a major's insignia on his immaculate uniform. He stopped as if coming to parade rest when he reached them. He looked them both over before extending his hand.

"Colonel Hideo Sakiri, U.S. Air Force. You must be Major Aiden Walker."

Walker extended his hand. "I am. This is Sergeant Costas."

Sakiri's grip was firm but not forced, as he were a man sure of himself and had no need to assert his authority. He turned his head slightly toward Costas. "Sergeant." His gaze did not waver, as he looked Walker in the eye. "Major, although I outrank you, your team falls entirely under your authority." A brief flicker of annoyance crossed his face. "As a matter of fact, I am to, I quote, 'Utilize your expertise while making my decisions on deployment and mission targets.' I am not pleased, but I will comply."

Walker decided he needed to smooth Sakiri's ruffled feathers. Space was no place to carry grudges. "I understand your frustration, Colonel. Just get me and my team down on Haumea or whatever other ice ball the Nazir have occupied and I'll stay out of your hair. I think this will be a steep learning curve for both of us."

"I appreciate that, Major." He glanced at Costas. "Perhaps you two would like to join me in my quarters for a nightcap before you turn in. Your sergeant looks thirsty."

Costas smiled and smacked his lips. "It would be a pleasure, Colonel, sir; a bit of scotch to wash this damn sand out of my mouth."

"The *Lance's* are beautiful aircraft, Colonel," Walker said, as he admired the sleek lines.

Sakiri beamed but did not smile. "Yes, they are exceptional *ships*," he said, emphasizing the word ship to remind Walker they were not normal jets. "I feel they will do us proud on this mission. I understand you've been here before?"

Walker smiled. "Not here, exactly, but in the neighborhood."

"Ah, yes. I have you to thank for saving my ships from Kaiju Nusku."

"I wasn't alone."

"Nevertheless."

The pair followed Sakiri from the hangar through a side door. The hangar blocked the worst of the wind, but dust swirled around them. Costas made a show of coughing to prove he needed a drink to clear his mouth of dust. "Did you volunteer for this little space adventure?" he asked.

Sakiri raised an eyebrow at Costas. "Of course. Didn't you?"

"I don't volunteer for nothing that don't involve women or booze. I go where they send me and bitch the whole time. It's the army way."

"What about you, Major?"

Sakiri was feeling him out, but Walker didn't feel like playing the 'whose balls are bigger' game. "I go where they send me, Colonel." He stared at Sakiri. "I don't question orders, not when the world is at stake. As long as I'm fighting the Nazir, I'm satisfied."

"True enough." Sakiri paused. A slightly upturned corner of his lips could have been an attempt at a smile or a sneer. "Perhaps more than one drink is called for."

"Amen to that," Costas replied, tapping his chest. "A man after my own heart."

As they crossed to the officer barracks, an airman raced up out of breath. He held out a note for Colonel Sakiri. Walker tensed, sensing ill tidings, as Sakiri read the note.

"Bad news, I'm afraid. They found no survivors of your Paris team."

Walker shook his head. "Damn, that's three teams down. Sergeant LaBonner was a good man. At least they completed their mission." LaBonner had been one of the first men he had trained. He had shown great potential. As soon as he learned not to take every death personally, he would have made a good group leader. At the rate at which they were losing Kaiju Killer teams, none would remain to deal with the newly arriving creatures, and seven Kaiju yet remained in Europe. He glanced at Sakiri and noted the look of concern on his face. His gut tightened for the other boot to drop. "What else?"

"The mission launch has been moved up. We go in eight hours. They want us at a briefing ASAP."

"What?" Costas growled. "Before a drink?"

"I'm afraid so, Sergeant."

"Why the rush?" Walker asked.

"One of the incoming Kaiju pods has moved to intercept *Javelin* in orbit. If we don't launch quickly, we might lose her."

"Fucking Kaiju bastards," Costas spat out. Walker didn't know if he referred to moving up the launch date or missing his cocktail.

"I agree," Sakiri said.

* * * *

August 11, Ellington Air Force Base, Houston, TX –

Between cursing the director and his own stupidity for allowing her to maneuver him into such a situation, Gate paid little attention to the scenery on the drive to Ellington AFB where four SR-80 *Lances* waited to transport him and three equally distraught NASA technicians joining him on the mission to the *Javelin*. The crew for the *Assegai* would launch from Russia on one of their new STK rockets two days later.

His fellow passengers looked as pleased as he was. He wondered what method the director had used on his companions to cajole them into cooperating. Any of them, including him, would be thrilled to venture into space, but in this particular case, the odds of returning were abysmally small. He did not want to calculate them for fear of forcing him to jump out of the car at the next traffic light and run like a frightened jackrabbit for the nearest church to seek sanctuary.

They had allowed him only his laptop as personal luggage. On it, he had downloaded his entire jazz collection, hoping it would keep him sane on the journey. The guard at the gate waved them through. The driver crossed the field and pulled up in front of a large hangar. His first view of an SR-80 *Lance* awed him; then, he remembered he would be riding it into space. A fast attack craft, yes, but as a spaceship, it looked too small and fragile for such a journey. A sergeant directed them to a room where technicians waited to fit them with excursion suits. He had expected to wear the bulky EMU Extravehicular Mobility Unit spacesuit he had worn into the vacuum chamber at Johnson. Instead, the modified Z-suit they offered him closely resembled the type worn by early Mercury astronauts. The cloth suits were lightweight and compact, less than half the weight and bulk of the ones worn by the ISS crew on spacewalks. Its thinness also meant less protection from the hazards of space – cosmic rays, UV, micrometeorites, extremes of heat and cold. One of the technicians stepped forward.

"Gentlemen, these are your second skin. When not wearing them, you will keep them close by at all times. In the event of a severe hull breach, you will have less than one minute to crawl inside, seal it, and secure yourself to something to avoid being blown into space." He paused to let that sink in. "Now, first, you will don jumpsuits. Then we will teach you how to safely insert yourself into your suits."

"They look flimsy," Worthen, one of the NASA technicians, remarked.

"They are durable and lightweight, not flimsy. Instead of the old LCVG – Liquid Cooling and Ventilation Garment – this model utilizes micro-pore tubing built into the suit material to maintain an optimum temperature zone. If you need to venture outside for any length of time, lightweight ceramic plates attach to the chest, legs and arms like armor for more protection. Believe me, if you wear one of these for long, you will appreciate the flexibility."

Thirty minutes later, on his third attempt, by lying on the floor as instructed, forcing his feet and legs into the lower half of the suit, and then contorting his body into the upper half, Gate managed to wriggle into his suit without help in less than five minutes, a far cry from the one-minute threshold. The effort exhausted him. Few of the others did any better.

"Now," he said, "let's try adding the PLSS."

Gate picked up his Primary Life Support Subsystem, a white, rectangular box that contained his oxygen supply, a carbon dioxide removal system, and air conditioning and heating system. It weighed forty pounds.

"Don't worry," the technician said, noting their worried expressions. "In space, it will weigh nothing."

Gate attached his to his suit, almost falling over in the process. One of the NASA techs tripped over his feet and landed face down on the floor, grunting in pain.

"Don't feel too badly," the training technician said with a grin, as he helped the man to his feet. "Astronauts and our *Lance* crews undergo hours of rigorous training for this. You will be in the hands of a professional. Trust them. Under any circumstances, do not panic. Aboard the *Lance*, your suit will hook into the plane's internal systems. The short hop to the airlock will take a minute at most. In the event of a complete oxygen failure, your suit contains sufficient air for that length of time."

The same NASA technician who had complained about the flimsiness tugged at the loose sleeve of his suit. "What if the suit rips?"

"Slap on a patch from the repair kit on your belt."

"What if I can't reach it?"

In a deadpan voice, the technician replied, "In that case, you'll die."

Four more airmen entered. The Ellington technician nodded to them.

"These men will escort you to your assigned ships. Good luck and good hunting."

Gate waddled across the hangar to the waiting *Lance*. It took two men to help him up the ladder and seat him in the copilot's seat. He was out of breath by the time they strapped him in.

"My name is Peters, Dr. Rutherford," the pilot announced over his com link. "Sit back and enjoy the ride."

The *Lance* rolled out of the hangar to the middle of the runway. Gate waited for it to taxi down the runway for takeoff. Instead, it lifted straight up. The only sense of motion he experienced was a brief bout of vertigo watching the hangar disappear below them, as if he was falling, but it passed quickly. The take-off was much smoother than any airline flight he had ever taken. He regretted he had forgotten his camera. The *Lance* climbed over Texas. By the time they reached the West Coast, they were at 120,000 feet. When the first stars appeared outside the canopy, Gate realized he had not looked at the sky except on computer screens for over a year. Knowing that aliens were out there determined to wipe out humans took away some of the novelty.

As they approached the *Javelin*, two other *Lances* were in the process of docking. Peters waited his turn. Gate watched one of the pilots glide gracefully from his *Lance* to the airlock, while his passenger tumbled like an out of control boomerang. He vowed to do better when his turn came. A Russian *Soyuz-MS* orbiter floated a few meters away off the starboard side of the *Javelin*. A silver umbilical ran from a tank attached to it one of the *Javelin's* two oxygen tanks just aft of the habitat modules. A third contained water. Peters docked his craft gently. The two clamps thudding against the side startled Gate. Peters exited first, lifted the canopy, unhooked Gate from the plane's umbilical, and gently pushed him across the open space toward the airlock. Gate focused on the airlock door, forgetting to breathe until his gloved hand gripped the metal rail.

They cycled through the airlock together. He was glad to have walls around him again. Space was so vast and empty that the eye became lost trying to find some point on which to focus. His limited perspective on a computer screen had not prepared him for the reality of the vastness of space. His mind still reeled from the experience. Zero gravity made removing his suit more difficult than putting it on. Even while bracing his feet beneath the low rail as directed by Peters, he swayed like a drunken sailor in a typhoon, or an advertising air puppet outside a used car dealership.

Through the hatch, he entered a melee of bodies floating at all angles, re-instigating his vertigo. The cacophony of voices made speech almost impossible. Gate noticed the size and closeness of the bunks. There would be no privacy on this trip.

Peters floated in close and yelled in Gate's ear. "Your quarters are on the bridge forward."

"Thanks."

He pushed through the double hatch into the next compartment containing a small galley with a row of stools along a narrow bar that looked like a street diner. Two storage compartments graced either end of the room. A few more bunks lined the walls of the narrow corridor leading to the portside airlock and bridge. From the size of the galley, it looked as if they would eat in shifts to accommodate them all. He also noted the lack of stoves. Their food would be military MREs and NASA frozen meals heated in microwaves. He passed a door upon which someone with a sense of humor had posted a crude drawing of a man floating upside down while urinating over his head, the Zero-G bathroom.

The ship's designers had situated the forward emergency airlock opposite the bathroom for a reason Gate could not fathom. He hoped it had more to do with engineering than the possible need to visit the bathroom to clean the inside of one's spacesuit after a spacewalk. A touch of queasiness visited him when he passed through the double hatch into the bridge and noted the explosive bolts securing the bridge module to the habitat module. In an emergency, they could jettison any section of the ship. Since the bridge had no airlock, he now understood the imperative to keep his spacesuit handy at all times.

Unlike the bridge of imaginary movie starships, the bridge of the *Javelin* was a small compartment with three consoles along the port side and a bank of video screens on the forward wall. Two small viewports on either side of the screens and a single port on the starboard side of the cabin provided the only direct visual access outside the ship. The bridge looked nothing as he imagined the control center of a starship would. It more resembled non-partitioned cubicles in an office.

His three companions were already at their stations. They glanced up at him as he entered. He recognized two of them from Mission Control, Steven Goodman, an environmental systems technician, and Brad Worthen, communications specialist and assistant gravity drive engineer. Both were highly competent technicians. The third, a haggard-looking young man of about 22 or 23 years, seemed in distress.

"This is Jess Blivens, Dr. Rutherford, our gravity drive technician," Goodman said. "I'm afraid he's a bit under the weather. I don't think he enjoys Zero-G as much as he thought he would."

Blivens scowled at Goodman and grumbled, "Fuck you, Steve."

Goodman chuckled. "Now, Jess. Play nice. Take another Tums."

The dismally small bridge compartment would be his new home for the next three weeks. In Zero-G, he could sleep anywhere, but under gravity, he would prefer a bed. Three bunks inset in the portside wall were for the bridge crew. They all looked too short for his long legs. As a last-minute add-on, he wondered where he would sleep.

Goodman glanced around the bridge, and then back at Gate. As if reading Gate's mind, he said, "It's smaller than my dorm room at Cal Tech. I don't think they designed the bunks for a man your size. There are some hammocks in the storage area. You can hang one from the ceiling in the corner. It should be more accommodating than the bunks."

Gate nodded and slipped his laptop inside a small wall niche, and then strapped his space suit beneath a net attached to the wall beside the others.

After a loud belch from Blivens, Goodman said, "We'll have gravity soon, Jess. Hold on until then. If you spew chunks, you clean it up." To Gate, Goodman added, "I'm afraid Jess isn't very pleasant under the best circumstances, but he is one of the best gravity drive technicians in the country."

Blivens shot Goodman a withering look but remained silent.

The bridge crew's attitudes reminded Gate too much of a frat house. No one seemed in charge. As much as he disliked assuming authority, his age and experience compelled him to lay a few ground rules.

"Gentlemen, it's going to be a long voyage in very close quarters. I suggest we make an extra effort to get along. To be safe, I would also suggest as little mingling with the *Lance* crews and the Rangers as possible. The military has their own way of doing things, and it often clashes with the civilian method. They don't mind placing their lives in our hands, but they would rather we didn't remind them of that fact. We'll take our meals here. It might reduce the chance of conflict."

"Fine with me," Worthen replied. He acted relieved that Gate had stepped up. "Some of those grunts looked like they would just as soon shoot you as talk to you."

"Military types tend to get jittery before a battle. Err on the side of caution with them."

Goodman grinned. "That's right. You've had some experience with the military when you helped tale down Nusku. Maybe you can tell us about it."

Inwardly, Gate shuddered. He shook his head. "No, I don't think I will." He pulled himself to the wall and strapped in. "Where are we in the pre-flight?"

"Gravity drive is green and ready to engage," Goodman answered. "Environmental control is ramping back up after the sudden influx of bodies. The *Soyuz* will be moving off soon. Course is set for the initial leg of the flight. We're ready to go."

Once they were beyond the orbit of Mars, Gate would compute the first course corrections. Since no one had tested the gravity drive under real-life conditions, he would have to see how the *Javelin* reacted before that. "Colonel Sakiri will give us the word as soon as he arrives," Gate replied.

"Please hurry," Blivens moaned. His face was pale and beads of perspiration dotted his forehead in spite of the cool cabin temperature. "I can't take much more of this."

Gate sympathized with the young man. Space sickness was a serious condition, but it was too late to replace him. "Just a little while, Blivens. Grit your teeth and hold on."

Blivens nodded but said nothing. Gate's stomach did flip-flops of its own, but not from the Zero-G. The journey did not bother him. It was an adventure. He tried not to dwell on what awaited them on the other end of the voyage. He had faced Kaiju twice in his lifetime, but, unlike the adage, he suspected the third time would not be a charm.

7

August 12, Rome, Italy –

Fifty-six-year-old Johan ten Boom stared down at the smoking billowing from Vatican City and Saint Peter's Basilica. He was too numb to cry and too frightened to be angry. Pope Francis was dead. In spite of the danger, the Pontiff had refused to leave his Vatican office. Now, Johan was the new Pope, appointed and elected by the Church of Cardinals in a hastily convened conclave before evacuating. There was no white smoke, no waiting crowd on St. Peter's Square. The mantle of office was only hours old and already the weight of the world, one that he thought himself unworthy to bear, rested on his shoulders.

He rubbed the knuckles of his right hand with his left thumb, massaging away the ache of arthritis, one of many afflictions God had bestowed on him to keep him humble.

"What shall we call you, Your Holiness?" his aide, Bishop Peter O'Bannon, asked.

Johan had given his choice of papal name little thought in the rush to escape Rome. Now, he had no choice but choose one. "I shall be Clement XVI," he said in a moment of inspiration. "Clement V was Dutch, as am I."

O'Bannon raised one bushy eyebrow, as he stared at Johan. A slight sardonic grin creased the corners of his mouth, as he asked, "The Pope in office during the plundering of Rome in 1527 by Charles V's mutinous troops?"

O'Bannon's statement struck him as odd. He had forgotten about Clement V's reign over the sacking of Rome. He regretted the irony of the name, but he would keep it nevertheless. God had inspired his decision. Perhaps the Church needed a fresh start in a new world. "I prefer to remember him as the Pope who commissioned Michelangelo's *The Last Judgment*."

The two men stood in the courtyard of the Church of San Pietro in Montorio on Janiculum, a hill south of the Vatican. From his vantage point, he could witness the destruction of Rome by the Kaiju, a great ebony demon sent from hell to punish the wicked and the saintly alike. The lengthening shadows of early evening highlighted the carnage. Modern Rome closely resembled the ruins of Ancient Rome dotted throughout the city. Raging infernos swept up the sides of Rome's fabled seven hills, leaving in their paths only devastation and desolation. The Tiber flowed sluggishly with debris beneath its fallen bridges and Roman aqueducts. The Ponte Principe Amedeo and the Ponte Palatino were broken stubs protruding from the river. Johan tried not to look at the dark waters too closely, knowing that some of the small dots floating by were human bodies.

He stood absorbed by the annihilation around him, as the aliens tried to obliterate mankind from the face of the planet. He wondered if the aliens understood the significance of Rome, its place in history as center of a far-flung empire or home of the Holy Catholic Church, or if it was just another city, a hub of destruction designed to inflict the most damage.

O'Bannon grabbed his elbow. "We must leave soon, Your Holiness. The ship will leave Marina de San Nicola at dawn. They dare not wait longer. The roads will soon clog with refugees. It will be a slow journey."

A patron of the Church residing in Ladispoli on the coast had offered his yacht to transport Johan and his retinue to Malta. "Yes, yes," he answered, irritated by O'Bannon's urgency, but his aide was correct. Italy had not seen such a movement of displaced people since WWII. The need to observe the destruction of Rome and to record it for posterity overwhelmed him, but matters pressed too hard. The faithful needed a pope. *A pope and hope*, he mused, but did not feel the humor of his poor rhyme. "We must begin our journey, a dark, painful trek whose end only God can foresee. I suppose I must place my faith in his will."

"His will and the skill of our driver and that of the Swiss Guards," O'Bannon added.

Johan glanced at the men who had accompanied them, *Oberstlieutenant* Rene Bossard and a contingent of eight *Guardia Svizzera Pontificia*, or Pontifical Swiss Guards, dressed in blue uniforms instead of the ceremonial Medici blue, red, and yellow banded outfits. They carried Heckler and Koch MP7A1 semiautomatic rifles firing 4.6x30mm rounds, each tipped with Kaiju-piercing coating, and Sig P220 10mm pistols instead of ceremonial swords and halberds. How the Guard had obtained the specialized Kaiju rounds usually restricted to various militaries, he did not venture a guess. The *Oberstlieutenant* was an unusually resourceful man.

The stoic gaze of the Swiss Guards never wavered, as they watched the swarms of Wasps darting across the skies of Rome. Standing in their midst, Johan did not fear for his immediate safety. The Swiss Guard was among the finest military units in the world. They had been guarding popes since Pope Julius in 1506.

Watching the cloud of dark smoke gather over the city, a mood of melancholy fell over him, darkening his heart and quelling his spirit, as if the ominous cloud separated him from God's grace. A deep guilt troubled him at abandoning the Holy See. As Bishop of Rome, he should be there among the people, offering what solace and comfort he could in their darkest hour.

He sighed. "Do you believe we will ever see Rome again, Father O'Bannon?"

O'Bannon hesitated. "I'm a pragmatist, Your Holiness. I know that is odd for a man of the cloth, but I'm also Irish. One can always hope for a brighter morning, but one must plan for the darkest night. Candles are often more effective than prayers."

"Indeed. Why not a candle and a prayer?"

"Aye, both together, but the candle first. Prayers in the dark seem so bleak."

"Light your candle then, for I fear prayers are much needed."

Malta, their destination, was 90-percent Roman Catholic, its official religion. At 316-square kilometers in area and with a population of 450,000, it was one of the most densely populated countries. Johan suspected the population would balloon with the influx of refugees.

"Our quarters will be at St. Paul's Cathedral in Mdina. The *Zghazagh Azzjoni Kattolika*, the Catholic youth group, will provide security," he glanced at the Swiss Guards, "along with our Swiss shadows."

Johan shook his head. "Children with guns." The idea appalled him. "Children should play games, not war."

"There are few children now, Your Holiness. The aliens have seen to that. The *ZAK* is receiving military training in case of invasion."

"You speak Maltese?"

"As a lad in the British army, I was stationed at Pembroke before they turned it over to the Maltese in '79. I picked up a smattering of the language, some perhaps a bit too delicate for a Bishop to repeat, but that was before my conversion. I've been brushing up the last few days."

"Perhaps you can instruct me. I will need to say mass soon. Saying it in Maltese might ease some tension."

"Most people speak English, but using the local language might make a few friends."

"We will need friends, I think, Father O'Bannon."

O'Bannon smiled. "Please call me Peter, Your Holiness. Father or Bishop sounds too formal."

"Okay, Peter, upon you I will build my rock."

O'Bannon chuckled at the Biblical reference. "Good luck with that, Your Holiness."

From the corner of his eyes, Johan saw the *Oberstlieutenant* drop to one knee and raise his rifle. O'Bannon noticed too and shoved him toward the waiting armored Cadillac Escalade Limousine. Johan observed the bishop held a Sig P220 pistol in his hand, produced from a shoulder holster beneath his jacket.

"We must go now," O'Bannon urged.

The Swiss Guards opened up on a pair of Wasps patrolling the hillside that grew nosy and flew too close for comfort. Their fire was deadly accurate. One of the creatures fell from the sky on bullet-riddled wings and struck the cobbled courtyard. Now flightless, it remained nevertheless dangerous. It rose to its eight legs and scampered across the courtyard toward them. Three of the men concentrated their fire on the grounded Wasp, shooting until it fell to the ground, bleeding thick ocher blood from a dozen wounds. It kicked its legs for a few moments before growing still.

The second Wasp, enraged by the pheromone of its dead brethren, dove toward them. No man moved or sought cover. They fired round after round into the creature's thorax and head. However, the driver, a civilian, panicked. He left the safety of the limo and ran for the church. The Wasp veered from the contingent of Swiss Guards and attacked him. He turned just as the creature stabbed at him with its harpoon-like stinger. The stinger struck him in the left side of his chest and exited near his right shoulder. He screamed in agony as the creature lifted him into the air, ripping flesh and snapping bone. The venom quickly did its job, rendering him helpless and silent.

Bossard and another Guard raced toward the Wasp before it could carry him away. From only a few feet away, both men fired into the back of its neck until it, too, struck the ground. *Oberstlieutenant* Bossard climbed atop the creature's back and emptied his weapon into the side of its head. It stopped struggling. Satisfied that it was dead, they calmly reloaded their weapons.

Johan made the sign of the cross with his fingers and hurried toward the wounded driver. O'Bannon grabbed his arm and dragged him back.

"More will come soon, Your Holiness," he said. "We cannot linger."

Johan struggled but could not break O'Bannon's firm grip. "I must offer the Viaticum."

"He cannot hear you. He is beyond the last rites."

O'Bannon pushed Johan into the back seat, opened the front driver's side door, and slid behind the wheel. As he cranked the Limousine, Bossard walked up. "He is right. It serves no purpose for you to die here. You are needed in Malta."

Johan relented and moved over to let the lieutenant colonel sit beside him. He did not know if it was from fear or acceptance that many in the city, and across the globe, would die without last rites. He nodded and began to pray silently.

With Johan, O'Bannon, Colonel Bossard, and one other man in one limo and the remainder of the Swiss Guard in the second vehicle, they left the mountain. O'Bannon drove fast, heedless of posted limits or the sinuous curves of the narrow roads. Johan held tightly to the door handle, as the vehicle slewed left and right. The 420-horsepower engine roared like an angry beast, as O'Bannon pressed the accelerator as if trying to push it through the floor.

"We'll follow the Via Aurelia to the SS1," he said. He stared at Bossard through the rearview mirror. Johan wished he would keep his eyes on the road. "The A90 will be impassable. We'll go through the mountains, through Malagrotto and Castel di Guido."

Bossard agreed. "The creature came up the Tiber Valley to Rome from the coast. There have been reports of Fleas and Wasps both ahead of it and in its wake. We should avoid the area. The hills will be safer. These limos have BR6 armor, rated against hand grenades and 7.62 rounds. We shouldn't encounter anything bigger than that."

"Do you fear our fellow man?" Johan asked. "These vehicles bear the Papal crest."

"Not everyone is Catholic, Your Holiness, and they are desperate. To many, these limos offer a means of escape."

"Perhaps I have more faith in my fellow man."

"If there were no need for us, Your Holiness, the Swiss Guard would be in Switzerland, not Vatican City."

Johan had no retort for that. The *Oberstlieutenant* took his job seriously. Colonel Bossard had accepted his role as papal bodyguard, agreeing to accompany the new pope to Malta, while the remainder of his men joined in the battle against the Kaiju and its deadly minions. He would not fault the *Oberstlieutenant's* judgment.

The streets filled with people fleeing in all directions in their panic. No authority directed them from the city or to shelters. With O'Bannon leading the way, the two black vehicles weaved a dance in and around the throng, ignoring people pounding on the side of the vehicle. Many of them made the sign of the cross and burst into tears when they recognized the papal crest of two keys wrapped in red cord. They could not distinguish the vehicles' occupants through the dark glass, but Johan had an excellent view of them. He tried to meet each pair of eyes, allowing their desperate gaze to sear his memory so that he would not forget their anguish.

They reached the SS1 without mishap, but crossing the horde of refugees along the A90 corridor proved difficult. If not for the ingenuity of Colonel Bossard and the Swiss Guard, it would have been impossible. They blocked traffic and moved stalled vehicles from the roadway. Against Bossard's wishes, Johan stood beside the road blessing the travelers as they passed. The regalia of his office, his Triregnum, his red pallium, and mantle were locked away safely in the trunk, but in his long, flowing, white cassock, white zucchetto skullcap, and white pellegrina draped around his shoulders, newly elected Pope Clement XVI was easily discernible among the flow of people. They did not yet know his name, but they recognized his authority. He held his hands out to the knot of people gathered around him. The Ring of the Fisherman, so recently gracing the finger of Pope Francis, was clearly visible on his finger.

To those headed south, he said, "Go north. South lies only death and devastation. Seek the hills." To those headed north, he said, "Help your brothers and sisters. We must face this trial together."

Johan's heart broke at the shared look of misery and hopelessness on the faces of the refugees – men and women so weary they stumbled with each step, children dull-eyed and weeping clinging to parents' hands, and the elderly and infirm pausing often to rest. None looked back. Most did not look forward. They simply moved, a slow tide of humanity flowing around stalled automobiles and highway guardrails like rocks in a stream.

"The way is open, Your Holiness," Bossard said a short time later. "We must leave."

With great reluctance, Johan entered the limo. O'Bannon noted his disheartened expression. "You turned them north, Your Holiness. You probably saved lives here today."

Johan took no solace from the priest's words. He shook his head. "Not enough. They need more than my pitiful prayers and a few words of caution."

"It looks as if your prayers have been answered, Your Holiness," Bossard said.

Johan looked of the window. A flight of eight Eurofighter *Typhoons* from Grosseto flew overhead in formation, and then fired the afterburners on the jet's twin Eurojet EJ200 engines and veered east toward Rome at Mach 1.5. Slung beneath each delta wing were three RBS-15 air-to-ground missiles, two KEPD-350 *Taurus* missiles, and a GBU-10 *Paveway II* bomb.

"Yes!" O'Bannon shouted. "That should do some damage to that big behemoth."

"Sorry, Father," Bossard replied. "Normal tactical weapons are useless against a Kaiju. They're on their way to blast the hell out of the Fleas and Wasps." His face reddened and he glanced at Johan. "Sorry for my language, Your Holiness."

Johan flashed a quick grin. "It is not a problem, my son. I share your enthusiasm."

The small caravan passed through the edge of Massimina and climbed into the hills surrounding Malagrotto where they encountered the first Fleas Johan had seen other than on television. Like airborne troops, Wasps cradled the smaller Fleas to their thoraxes and dropped them onto the ground, where they massed and attacked people and animals. Signs of their passage lined the roads, dead bodies and the carcasses of slaughtered animals in piles awaiting conveyance to the Kaiju. A line of the yellow-and-black creatures marked the path between Malagrotto and the Kaiju.

The stench was powerful even inside the air-conditioned vehicles. O'Bannon drove slowly, hoping to avoid the creature's interest, but their luck did not hold long. The tan creatures surrounded the vehicles, blocking their way and stabbing at the armored metal with their sharp legs. None of the appendages pierced through the thick door.

"We can't plow through them," O'Bannon warned. "There are too many."

"Stop the vehicle," Bossard told him. He exited the limo firing his HK MP7 in short bursts. The Guard in the rear vehicle followed suit. Unlike armored Wasps, Fleas were vulnerable to small weapons fire. The 30mm armor-piercing bullets easily punctured their brittle exoskeleton, shattering limbs and organs. Soon, Flea bodies littered the ground around the two limos. When Wasps detected the carnage with their sensitive olfactory organs, two of the Guard produced an RPG launcher from the rear of the vehicle. With one loading and the other firing, they brought down half a dozen of the creatures.

O'Bannon noticed the new swarm of Wasps rising from the buildings of Malagrotto before anyone else, but they were upon the group before he could shout a warning. He honked the horn, getting Bossard's attention. Bossard waved the others to their vehicle, but the two men firing the RPG, caught up in their killing frenzy, did not see him. Wasps descended on the second limo. The Guard with the RPG launcher fired it at point-blank range at a Wasp. The rocket bounced off its armored exoskeleton and exploded. Shrapnel killed both men. Two others died as Wasps riddled their bodies with stingers. Bossard covered two men as they ran for the first limo. They dove into the back seat just as Bossard slammed shut the door.

The driver of the rear vehicle, now alone, gunned the engine to ram the Wasps on the ground. The creatures surrounded the vehicle. Its armor, able to stop small arms fire and hand grenades, was no match for the hardened stingers that pierced the doors, roof, and windows. They clung to the limo, as the driver, unable to see, careened out of control. The vehicle struck a building and exploded. The Wasps continued their rampage against the engulfed vehicle heedless of the flames from the burning gasoline.

Bossard took one last look at his dead men and waved O'Bannon forward. Johan looked out the side-view mirror at the men sworn to protect him. They had lost over half the Swiss Guard and had only driven a few miles. He feared more would die before they reached Malta.

8

August 12, *USS Javelin* –

"It's even more beautiful than I had imagined," Walker said. He could not keep the awe from his voice, sounding like a pre-teen boy getting his first glimpse of a girl's breasts. The Earth spun slowly below him with only a few wispy, cottony clouds shrouding his view of the Nevada desert and the West Coast. It was a breathtaking view; one everyone should have the opportunity to experience during his or her lifetime.

"It never gets old," Sakiri replied. Walker noted the colonel seemed more at ease in his ship, now a pilot and not a commander.

"It looks so different from the NASA videos or the movies."

"It's too large for a television or movie screen to capture properly. That would be like seeing the Grand Canyon through a keyhole."

Walker sat enfolded by the SR-80 *Lance's* copilot seat behind Sakiri. The seat swiveled 360-degrees to provide access to the array of weapons panels, communications equipment, radar screens, and video screens surrounding the seat. Fifteen of the *Lances* had already ferried personnel to the *Javelin*, including Costas and Walker's team. Four more of the craft had departed from Ellison with the team of NASA technicians. He and Sakiri were among the last to make the journey to the *Javelin*. Sakiri's last-minute meeting with the base commander troubled him. They had not invited him, and he didn't like secrets.

Walker looked down at the vivid scar across the land that had been San Francisco and the path of destruction leading southward along the coast, a dark line amid a sea of lights. The Golden Gate Bridge was still under construction, as were many of the city's toppled skyscrapers. It would be years before many of the surviving population returned to their former homes. Tens of thousands had died in the attack. Unlike Chicago, San Francisco had no warning before the Kaiju struck. There had been no time to prepare for the tsunami it caused or to flee the creature's rampage. Tent cities dotted the outskirts of the ruins and clustered in former parklands. It reminded him of photos of the aftermath of the great San Francisco earthquake of 1906. As then, the city would rebuild, unless the Kaiju struck the West Coast again.

"We'll reach the *Javelin* in fifteen minutes. We'll launch right after we dock."

"They're not wasting any time."

"If we wait any longer, we'll have to take a longer elliptical orbit around Mars to avoid the Kaiju."

"What would that matter?" Walker asked. "We won't burn fuel."

"With a gravity drive, it's not a matter of fuel; it's a matter of consumables. Every extra liter of oxygen or water or pound of food takes up additional space. It's going to be close quarters for the next few weeks as it is. An extra day or two of travel time would make it real cozy."

"We wouldn't want that. Costas doesn't do crowds well."

"Your sergeant seems a bit, uh ..."

"Unorthodox?" Walker suggested. He had heard it all before. "He has his own way of doing things, but in a fight, you couldn't have a better man at your side."

Around them, stars blossomed in the darkness, a thousand colored pinpoints of light. The closest was farther than they were going, but they were on no short hike. They would be going farther than man or woman had ever ventured with all the inherent risks of such a long flight, and at the end, they would face an enemy they knew little about.

Walker's first sight of the *Javelin* did not inspire confidence. Rather than a sleek, pointed weapon aimed at the enemy as the name implied, it resembled the open-girder skeleton of a skyscraper under construction. Two cylindrical modules graced the front of the craft, while a third containing the gravity drive nestled in a framework at the craft's stern. A smaller module in the bow was the bridge. Between the habitat modules and the gravity drive compartment nestled three smaller spherical tanks containing the ship's oxygen and water supply. An array of antennae and dishes protruding from the bottom of the craft provided communications links, radar, and gravity wave detectors.

Nineteen *Lances* attached to the framework like limpet mines. Walker gripped his seat tightly, as Sakiri maneuvered his *Lance* into an open slot between two craft. Only a slight bump rattled the craft as it settled into its niche; then, another jolt as two clamps extended to secure it in place. There was no walkway, safety cables, or nets. To reach the airlock, he would have to exit the *Lance* and float across open space. That was the part Walker had been dreading. Operating in zero gravity had not been a factor in his all too brief training with a space suit. He was glad they were on the night side of the planet. He was afraid vertigo might overwhelm him staring down at the Earth below him in full daylight.

Colonel Sakiri went first. His graceful movements showed he was no rookie in space. He pushed off evenly with both legs, did a somersault midway, and landed feet first on the narrow ledge in front of the airlock's outer hatch. He grabbed the bar beside the door with one hand and waved Walker over with the other. Walker took a deep breath and pushed off, trying to emulate the colonel. He focused on the airlock, ignoring the splendor around him to avoid dizziness. He would have time to appreciate the view later. In spite of his efforts and his intense hour-long training course, he twisted and began to tumble, grabbing frantically for the holding bar beside the airlock door. As he sailed past it, Sakiri caught his outstretched hand and reeled him in like a garden hose.

"Not bad for your first spacewalk," Sakiri said, as Walker grasped the bar with his other hand and planted his feet against the module.

He felt foolish, like a green recruit. "I'll have to do better than that to fight the Nazir," he replied, fighting to keep his excited breathing off the open com line.

"We'll have time for spacesuit training along the way. By the time we reach Haumea, you'll be an expert."

In spite of Sakiri's reassurance, he doubted it. "I'm a Ranger. Spacewalking is like parachuting – necessary to get us to the fight. Unlike you flyboys, a Ranger fights best with both feet planted firmly on the ground."

Sakiri's voice became serious. "That will be difficult on Haumea with its low gravity. We're all going to have to learn a few new tricks for this war."

"True enough."

The airlock door was almost as wide as the module. When Sakiri punched in the code, the door popped outward two inches, and then soundlessly slid to one side. The airlock was large enough to accommodate a dozen people wearing excursion suits. For this, Walker was grateful. He did not wish to remain outside alone while Sakiri cycled through in case he couldn't remember the cycle procedure from the briefing.

They exited into a ready room the size of two shipping containers positioned side-by-side, less than 650 square feet. Spacesuits stowed on racks lined the wall. Weapons racks hung suspended from the ceiling. Removable panels in the floor were marked Weapons, Ammunition, MREs, First Aid, and FSRs. The First Strike Rations were high-caloric paste or liquid rations that plugged into recesses in the space suits. A feeding tube inside the helmet allowed its occupant to eat on the go. Walker had witnessed the process demonstrated with limited success during their briefing and did not look forward to the necessity.

The habitats were cylindrical, but the rooms inside were rectangular, the intervening space filled with the wiring and ductwork necessary to keep them alive in the harsh environs of space. The space also contained the shielding material to help block deadly cosmic rays, although in theory, the operating gravity drive's magnetic bubble would perform that task. The normal-looking rooms camouflaged the fact that they would live inside a rocket, more specifically, a section of NASA's now-defunct Space Launch System. The SLS, larger than the Saturn V that propelled man to the moon, needed only a few paintings, a comfortable chair, and a window with curtains for a touch of home. To Walker, who had spent so many years in various military barracks buildings, the room looked reassuringly familiar.

He counted the spacesuits – eleven, with space for one more. "Where are the rest of the suits?"

"Pilots, copilots, and technicians will keep their suits near their stations in case of a leak. This module is for your assault team. You'll sleep in hammocks slung from the ceiling. Your weapons and gear are stored here. The module detaches from the ship for a soft drop on Haumea. The enlarged airlock allows your entire team to cycle through together. There is a smaller emergency airlock forward near the bow of the ship. Four Zero-G toilets are located forward as well, not many for fifty-six people, as you will probably soon learn."

He had noticed the size of the two habitat modules as they had approached the ship. The airlock and his team's quarters took up fully a quarter of the habitat space. They would be packed in like clowns in a clown car.

"Clip your feet under one of the raised rails along the edge of the wall to brace yourself while you remove your suit."

Walker glided across the room, pulled himself down to the floor, and slipped his boots under the bar. Sakiri was almost out of his suit before Walker could get more than his helmet off.

"Yeah, I know," he said. "I'll get better at this too, I suppose, with practice."

After stowing his suit in the space provided, Sakiri opened the double hatch into the adjoining compartment. The pungent smell of human bodies was already strong after only a few hours. With fifty-six men and women cooped up in a space the size of a large Manhattan apartment and only an occasional sponge bath available, he hoped he acclimated to the pervasive odor quickly. The perspiration odor overlay a more subtle tang of disinfectant and ozone.

"About time you showed up."

He recognized Costas' loud, gruff voice before the crowd parted like the Red Sea and he appeared. Men and a few women sat strapped to benches along the wall or floated in the air. A few sat at the two tables playing cards using magnetic cards and poker chips. The bunks reminded him of submarine crewmen berths, stacked four-high with no headroom. They were for lying down, not sitting in. Curtains provided only limited privacy. Everything in the module, including the bunks, folded away for more space. The accommodations were strictly military with no luxuries.

He watched Costas clumsily thread his way through the crowd using their bodies as handy handholds for pushing off, mumbling, "'Scuse me," and "Outta the way." It was not a good way to make friends for the long voyage. Like the others, he wore a one-piece Air Force flight suit. "Man, this place is as packed as an *Al-Khaleej* brothel on Saturday night after payday."

His reference to the seedy entertainment district in Bagdad brought a smile to Walker's lips. It had been one of Costas' favorite downtime haunts during their Iraq missions. "Maybe you had better be a little more polite to the clientele."

Costas turned and looked at several men glaring at him. He scowled back. "That's okay. What this place needs is a good brawl to get everyone better acquainted."

"We need every man in good health when we arrive." He wagged a finger at Costas. "No fighting. That's an order. Now, have our team assemble in the aft ready room immediately so we can see who they sent us."

Costas shook his head. "No can do. We're to strap in until after launch in," he glanced at his watch, "five minutes. Come on. I saved us a nice secluded spot on a bench." As Walker crossed the crowded space, Costas said, "Would you believe there are exits signs above the doors. Like, where the hell are we gonna go in an emergency?"

A soft chimed signaled the two-minute warning. Everyone searched for a place to sit and strapped in.

"Okay, everyone," Costas called out loudly, "make sure your trays are secured and your seats are in the upright position."

A single chime announced the engagement of the gravity drive. Walker expected some kind of inertia, as he had seen on Cape Canaveral liftoffs. Instead, only a gentle pressure pushed at him as the artificial gravity engaged. It stopped at .8 Gs, leaving him feeling a little light.

"Not bad," Costas said, grinning. "I could get used to this." He glanced at the four female pilots and copilots. "I wonder if any of them would like to join my Hundred-Mile High Club."

"Keep your flight suit zippered, Costas. We're not here for fun."

"Too bad. That redhead looks inviting."

An overhead view screen flared to life displaying the Earth rapidly receding behind them.

"Hell, we must be at the moon already," Costas remarked.

Sakiri walked over to them. "Not quite, Sergeant. Twenty more minutes, but we're just cruising so we won't disturb any satellite orbits on the way outbound."

"Maybe they'll play Pink Floyd's *Dark Side of the Moon* as we go by."

Walker stood, staggering slightly as his body tried to shift his 168-pound frame that now weighed 34 pounds less at .8 G. "Fire Team Alpha to the aft briefing room. Bring your gear. It'll be your new home for the next few weeks."

Costas rose, an unlit cigar jammed in his mouth. "You heard the man, you space grunts, move it! Pack your gear and move your rears. Your luxury accommodations are waiting. Room service is available until I say it ain't. Don't worry. If NASA can train a chimp to go into space, I'm sure you mangy curs can manage." He turned to Walker. "Don't worry, Major. I'll make men of them before we reach a hot LZ. Except Cantrell, of course," he added. "She's already a better man than most of them."

* * * *

The *Javelin* launch was flawless, for which Gate was grateful. Sitting in a ship constructed of steel girders and new technology consisting of a bastardized hybrid of alien and human hardware. The ship boosted away from Earth orbit with hardly a shudder. They were already moving faster than any human had ever traveled, and they were barely pushing the drive. Blivens had recovered from his bout of space sickness with the return of gravity and seemed a more pleasant individual. He watched the minute fluctuations in the drive pulses on his screen with the eyes of a wary hawk, eager to maximize the drive's efficiency.

Gate studied the gravity gradients of the outer planets, hoping to use their gravity wells to boost the ship's speed. They would need to place as much distance as possible between them and the oncoming Kaiju pods, while leaving maneuvering room in case the aliens decided to sacrifice one of the Kaiju to stop the ship. Gate hoped it didn't come to that. Space battles were a new thing and the *Javelin* would be at a great disadvantage. She carried no on-board weapons system. They would have to stop to launch the *Lances*. Two operating gravity drives in close proximity presented a unique set of problems. In time, they would be able to compensate for such occurrences, but for now, it was too dangerous.

By chance or fate, Mars, Venus, Saturn, Jupiter, and Pluto were in rough alignment with Earth. They would pass near all five planets on their journey. This allowed Gate some leeway in his computations. It did not help that the fate of the ship, the crew, and perhaps the entire planet rested in his nervous hands. He continued working until a chime reminded him that his meal slot had arrived. He was too anxious to eat, but he needed to keep up his strength.

The galley was full, but he would eat at his station. He chose a beef stew MRE from the bin, and waited his turn to microwave it. Many ate it cold from the bag, but he preferred a hot meal. He chose a piece of flatbread to go with it, and a fudge brownie for dessert. The coffee was lukewarm but strong enough to keep him awake. He was halfway down the corridor when a familiar voice called out.

"I thought you were through risking your life."

He turned and grinned at Walker. "I thought you might need someone to keep an eye on Costas."

"Yeah, he's a handful alright. So, you're our navigator."

He hugged the wall, as someone pushed by. "I'm afraid so. It seems NASA thinks I'm indispensable." He shrugged. "The way things are looking one place is as safe as another. Come join me on the bridge. It's less crowded. Somewhat," he added.

On the bridge, Goodman and Blivens were busy at their stations; Goodman checking ship's systems and Blivens playing a video game. Worthen was asleep in his bunk with the curtain drawn. This allowed Gate and Walker a modicum of privacy. Walker leaned against the wall, while Gate sat in a padded folding chair beneath his hammock that had become his workstation. They spoke softly to not disturb the others.

"I'm afraid I'm the reason you're here," Gate confessed, hoping his forthrightness would soothe any of Walker's misgivings. "When word of the mission to Haumea came up, I knew you would be the man for the job."

Walker rolled his eyes. "Thanks. Nothing like a shitload of responsibility dropped on you to make your day. By the way, I wouldn't tell Costas. He might take it the wrong way."

"I know how he feels. I found out I was going eight hours before I left Ellis."

Walker's eyes bored into him. "You could have refused."

Gate stared back at Walker. He knew he could not lie to him. "No more than you could. We've been inside one of the damn things. That changes a man." He tapped his head. "In here." He could confess to Walker. Walker understood what he meant. He had been through it too.

"You got that right."

"Can we do it?" He hated to ask the question. It seemed defeatist, but he trusted Walker's judgment. He knew Walker would not lie to him.

"Defeat the Nazir? We can try. It's certain we can't continue to fight them on the home front. They're winning that battle." He paused. "With this new invasion of Kaiju, they could win the war before we reach Haumea."

A sharp pain sprang to life in Gate's temple. That was also his worry. If the countries began using nukes on the Kaiju, how long before someone accidentally dropped one on a neighbor and started WWIII. With tensions already running high, it would not take much to provoke a global confrontation. The aliens would win by default. In his estimation, the aliens had only one flaw.

He gently massaged his temple. "The Nazir are methodical to a fault. They seem intent on defeating us before taking our world. The logical course would be to attach a few gravity drives to a large asteroid and send it hurtling toward Earth. They could wipe us out in days or weeks."

Blivens overheard, looked up from his console, and hissed his disagreement. "You have something to add?" Gate demanded.

"Don't jinx us by naming our death," Blivens snapped. "Besides, it would be tricky to synchronize so many drives to operate simultaneously."

"The Nazir invented the gravity drive. Do you doubt their ability to do it? They crossed between star systems, tens of thousands of Astronomical Units. We're trying to travel reach Haumea just 53 AUs away."

Blivens glared at him. "No, I don't doubt their ability. That's why I chose to come. Eventually, they will stop fighting us in a conventional manner and decide to eliminate us in one massive attack. I came to try to stop them. I didn't realize we might be too late. "

"You're referring to the inbound Kaiju armada, aren't you?" Walker asked.

"You've seen how they operate, always adapting, tinkering. What makes you think these incoming pods are the same as the last batch, just more Kaiju? They could contain bombs or biological weapons. Maybe they've decided to forget about terrorizing us or destroying cities and simply wipe us out en masse."

Gate's face paled. "My God, you mean Armageddon." He had written about end-of-the-world scenarios, but reality was too terrible to contemplate.

Blivens nodded. His looked as if he had swallowed a lemon. "Yes, something like that."

"You could be wrong."

"I hope to hell I am. It's just ... well, I can see them creating large numbers of Kaiju. They're essentially cyborgs – some organic material, some ebony crystalline material, and a bit of technology. Gravity drives, on the other hand, are highly complex technological devices. Wasting them to send Kaiju to Earth seems counterproductive, even if they intend to recover them afterward."

"They tried a gravity bomb, if you recall," Gate reminded him.

"Yeah, but why just one?"

Gate set his food on the deck beside him, his appetite gone. He had asked himself the same question after Kiribati. "They want Earth as intact as possible for colonization."

"We're assuming that because the Kaiju and their parasitical creatures can breathe our atmosphere, the aliens do too. Suppose they don't. What if they designed the Kaiju specifically for our atmosphere? If they want our mineral wealth, it seems plausible they could mine with cyborg creatures of their design no matter what the atmosphere." He shook head. "No, I don't think we can assume that. They had their choice of mineral-rich outer planets. Why Earth? Until they provided us with the technology, we couldn't reach them to stop them."

"They want the one thing Earth has in abundance," Walker suggested, "water."

Blivens turned to face Walker and shrugged. "Maybe, but the solar system is rife with ice comets and frozen seas on various planetary moons. Major, what does the military do in a protracted war?"

Walker caught onto Blivens' train of thought before Gate did. It surprised him when Walker answered, "Test new weapons systems under battlefield conditions."

Blivens nodded. "I think that's what the Nazir are doing. They could have ended the war earlier, but they're preparing for the next world they encounter, the next war."

Blivens' suppositions left Gate reeling. His temple throbbed even harder. Blivens' statement explained the slight modifications of each wave of Kaiju. The aliens were tinkering with their new weapons system, tailoring them for Earth. Why hadn't he arrived at that conclusion? *Because I'm no soldier. I'm a catastrophist. I think in terms of cause and effect. Blivens has probably played video games his entire life with scenarios very much like the one taking place in real life.* He glanced at Walker and spotted the concern etched on his face. Blivens' conjectures had struck a nerve with him. Anything that worried the imperturbable Walker concerned him.

Blivens continued, "We could be too late. Win or lose, we might not have a planet to return to."

Despite Blivens' certainty, Gate's gut told him not to despair. "I refuse to believe that," he countered. "Things might look bad for humankind, but we're adapting. This mission proves it. For the first time, we're taking the fight to the Nazir. We can stop them or slow them down."

"Yeah, if we don't blow ourselves up in the meantime."

Walker cleared his throat. His eyes smoldered. Gate wasn't sure if his ire was for Blivens or the Nazir. "Small, well-executed raids have often turned the tide of a war. The Doolittle raid on Tokyo and the Dambuster raid on the Ruhr Valley dams in Germany are two good examples."

"We knew who we were fighting then," Blivens said. "We know nothing about the Nazir."

Walker's face tightened as he clenched his Jaw. "We know they want to kill us. We have to kill them first."

Gate hoped it was as simple as that, but somehow, he doubted it.

9

August 13, Marina de San Nicola, Italy –

Johan ten Boom, now Pope Clement XVI, stood at the harbor at Marina da San Nicola. His heart lay heavy in his chest, not so much for his own suffering, but for the trials and tribulations he had witnessed the people of Italy suffering on his flight from the Vatican. Throughout the long night, the images had played in his head like a newsreel loop, driving home the blight that had come to Italy and the entire world. He had found no sleep and little rest. They had undertaken the journey to take ship to Malta. They had arrived too late. A few miles offshore, a white yacht with blue trim sailed south along the coast. The rising sun glinted from the windows.

Bishop Peter O'Bannon stood beside him swearing softly to himself. "Careful, Peter," Johan warned. "Do not blaspheme."

"Forgive me, Your Holiness. My anger consumes me." He pointed to the yacht. "That is Simon Ponte's yacht. He said he would wait until dawn. He sailed early."

Johan did not allow his disappointment to show. O'Bannon had tactfully not pointed out that it was his fault they had missed their boat. If he had not insisted on helping the people along the highway in Rome, they would have arrived hours earlier.

"Perhaps our benefactor waited as long as he could. The crowds grow larger each hour. He might have feared to lose his boat."

"But, we are stranded here."

"God will provide."

Lieutenant Colonel Rene Bossard and his few remaining Swiss Guard formed a protective semi-circle around Pope Clement and O'Bannon to keep the pressing crowd at a distance. His wary eyes scanned the throng for any sign of danger. For now, they were merely curious. Most had recognized the Papal insignia on the vehicles, though they did not recognize the new Pope. Johan closed his eyes and prayed.

He should have prayed more on the journey, but his mind had been embroiled with other matters he considered important. Now, they seemed less so. Even in their peril, or, more importantly because of it, they could not forget God's grace.

"We should continue north along the coast," Bossard suggested. "We might find another ship. At least we can avoid the crowds."

"Not yet, Colonel," Johan replied. "I feel I should remain here for a time."

"Has the Lord spoken to you?" O'Bannon asked.

Johan observed the disapproval in his aide's eyes and caught the flippancy in his question. "Do you not think God might speak to me?"

"I wish he would tell you to listen to Bossard." He glanced at the crowd. "It is not safe here, even for a Pope."

"In perilous times, it is not safe anywhere. This place will do as well as any other."

O'Bannon shook his head. "You vex me, Your Holiness. How can these few men – I number myself among them – protect you? Crowds draw the alien creatures. The military is busy elsewhere."

Johan understood his friend's concern, but he was tired of running. Malta was his destination, and no other place would do. He stared out over the sea. The water was as still as a golden mirror slicing the cloudless sky in half. "God will watch over us."

O'Bannon sighed and turned away. A soft murmur rippled through the crowd. Johan checked the skies, but they were empty of any threat. Then, he spotted a motor launch approaching the dock. People pushed and shoved to reach the dock, but Bossard stopped them. The boat drew alongside them. A man in a white uniform hopped out and went to his knees in front of Johan.

"Your Holiness, I am First Mate Antonio Aldo of the *Doria*. Captain Marcello apologizes for leaving early, but the Navy was impounding ships and felt it unwise to remain. He sent me to fetch you and your entourage." He glanced at the four Swiss Guard. "I thought there would be more of you."

"There were more of us when we began our journey. Please rise, Antonio." He glanced at the crowd. "Is there any way to take some of these people?"

Aldo looked uncertain if he should interpret a suggestion from the Pope as an order. He hesitated, and then said, "It is but a small ship, Your Holiness, only 46-meters. If the situation demanded it, we could squeeze maybe a dozen people onto the deck, no more. If the seas became rough, it would be dangerous for them."

"More dangerous than here? Colonel Bossard, please inform the people that we can take only a few. I suggest women and children."

Bossard glanced at the crowd, and then back at Johan. "They will riot, Your Holiness."

Johan smiled. "I think not. Tell them the children are our future. Remind them Jesus said, 'Let the little children come to Me, and do not hinder them. For the kingdom of heaven belongs to such as these.'"

"I will have to make two trips to the *Doria*, Your Holiness," Aldo said.

"Then take the children first. If the others see that I remain, they will not panic."

"What if … what if …?"

"What if I am wrong? In that case, my son, there is no hope left for mankind and dying here will serve God's will."

He was not certain he was doing the intelligent thing, but he was doing the right thing. Abandoning his flock here to minister to another flock on Malta seemed too easy a way out. Any he could save, he would.

Aldo crossed himself. "I pray you are right, Your Holiness."

Johan smiled. "As do I, my son."

10

August 13, Budapest, Hungary –

Aleksandr Belovol had not wanted his mission, nor had his weapons specialist Sergei Andropov. Since the arrival of the Kaiju, Russia had reasserted its dominance over Ukraine. The newly installed politburo was now in charge. The conflict had been brief, a matter of three days, as five thousand Russian troops and one hundred T-99 tanks with 125mm cannons surged over the border, and the Ukraine government collapsed. So far, Russian territories had remained free of Kaiju, and they would go to great lengths to keep it that way. His Sukhoi SU-24m *Fencer* attack jet carried four R-60 *Aphid* air-to-air missiles for defense and a single Kh-102 cruise missile as its payload. The nuclear-tipped weapon delivered a blast of 350 kilotons, sufficient to destroy a Kaiju, or a city.

The Kaiju was in the heart of Budapest. Moscow did not want it to move eastward into any newly acquired Soviet territories. Toward this goal, they were willing to go to great lengths, even risk an international incident while NATO had its hands full in Western Europe. The once independent former satellite states once again became cozy with Russia when the aliens attacked. Russia intended that newfound love for Mother Russia did not fade once the alien menace ended.

Belovol wasn't sure it would end. Each alien attack drained resources and further divided Earth's defenders. Using nuclear weapons on the cyborg creatures was doing the aliens' bidding.

"Forty kilometers to Budapest," Andropov whispered in his headphones. "Time to arm our payload."

His weapons specialist's voice was calm and even. Belovol envied him his serenity, but then, Andropov was not the one firing a missile that might kill 1.7 million people. He was. Though Andropov was in charge of weapons systems, Belovol had insisted that, as pilot, he be the one to accept the responsibility. He would spare his friend that heartache. He clenched and unclenched his right hand to shake off the cramps from squeezing the throttle too tightly.

"Green light on my readiness panel," he replied. He reached over with a shaky hand to flip the arming switch. "Arming light green," he reported.

He could see the city of Budapest ahead of him. Budapest, really two cities – Buda on the west bank of the Danube, and Pest on the eastern bank – looked like a war zone. Smoke curled from countless buildings, while a line of flattened buildings, the Kaiju's path, cut through the heart of the city. The creature lay across the Danube just north of the *Erzsebet Hid*, the Elizabeth Bridge, creating an ebony dam. Rising water flooded the low-lying Pest portion of the double city, inundating the Inner City's many shops, museums, and historic homes. The creature had decided to destroy Budapest by drowning it. In the early evening light, the water looked like dark blood spreading throughout the city.

"Do you think the United Nation's special unit managed to kill the creature?" Andropov asked. "It is not moving."

Belovol wondered the same thing. If the Kaiju were dead, it would be the height of infamy to fire his missile.

"I'll approach from the north over Margaret Island," he announced to Andropov.

"But ..." his copilot began.

"Say nothing more," Belovol warned. His superiors might be listening to their radio conversation. It would serve no purpose to radio base for verification or new orders. His orders had been clear and left no room for argument. He was to fire the missile. If he did not, command would dispatch another *Fencer* to complete the mission and shoot him and Andropov from the sky as traitors.

He banked the SU-24 sharply to starboard, crossing north over the city until he reached Margaret Island north of the city. He did not look down, afraid he would see the movement of people below him. He had no wish to look upon the faces of his victims. He turned due south, aligning the SU-24 with the river into the city's drowning heart.

"It does not matter," he said, in an effort to convince himself rather than his copilot. He shook his head and repeated, "It does not matter."

He almost smiled with glee when a swarm of Wasps rose from the city and flew toward his aircraft. "Prepare yourself, Andropov. We have visitors."

"Firing missiles."

Four lances of fire shot ahead of the *Fencer,* the Aphis missiles. They exploded in the middle of the swarm, knocking dozens of the creatures from the sky. Dozens more remained. The rattle of the Gsh-6 23mm cannon on the belly of the jet shook the craft, as Andropov targeted Wasps closing with them. In spite of the savage cannon fire, the Wasps intent on colliding with them to bring down the *Fencer,* did not disperse.

"Hold tight," he said, as he pushed the throttle forward, urging power from the twin Saturn/Lyulka AL-21-3A turbojet engines. He shot skyward at a 70-degree angle, leaving the slower moving Wasps below. Andropov raked them from above with cannon fire. The Su-24 M could reach speeds of 1600kph, but if he tried to outrun them, he would burn all his fuel. They would not make it back home. Instead, he hopped over them and resumed a level course at two thousand feet.

Five kilometers from target, he fired the Kh-102. The jet jerked as the heavy weight of the cruise missile fell away toward Budapest.

"Missile fired," he said, his throat dry from tension.

He pushed the throttle forward and veered east back toward Ukraine. The glow of the missile's solid-fuel engine in the dying daylight dwindled as it sped away toward target. His Sukhoi was twenty kilometers away when the missile detonated. The bright flash was behind him, but it illuminated the clouds ahead of him. *Almost two million people – literally gone in a flash.* He forced the image from his mind. He reversed course to verify target obliterated.

The fireball radius of a 350-kiloton yield is over a kilometer. The air blast extends for 2 kilometers in all directions. Radiation affects anyone within 5 kilometers, causing third-degree burns and a 50%–90% casualty rate. The blast over Budapest was typical. The blast flattened the city. Ironically, the blast extinguished the raging fires spreading through the city. The waters of the Danube steamed and hissed. The bridges lay submerged in the river.

The Kaiju remained where it was. It looked as pristine as it had looked a few minutes earlier on his first pass, black, shiny, and almost invisible in the dusk. Nothing moved around it. There were no Wasps or Fleas, as the Americans had named them. There were no people, only ruin and destruction delivered by his hand.

"*Panchart!*" he yelled into his mic.

"True. We are all bastards," his copilot agreed. "Let's go home."

Belovol shot the throttle forward, eager to reach his base at Lutsk and drink himself stupid to forget what he had done.

11

August 14, *USS Javelin* –

Two days into the voyage, Gate sent word he needed to see Walker. Walker wondered why he called for him instead of simply coming to see him. After all, it was only a matter of a few steps. He got his answer when he spotted Gate sitting cross-legged on the deck with his computer on his lap. He recognized the look haunting the scientist's face as one he had seen before inside Nusku, a look of determination. Gate glanced up as Walker entered the bridge. His hollow-eyed countenance betrayed no emotion, but as his fingers danced over the keyboard, a graph displaying intersecting elliptical lines moved on the big view screen.

"I think I know how we can help Earth," he said.

"We can help Earth by defeating the Nazir."

Gate pointed to the graph on the screen. "Each time we changed course, one of the pods moved to intercept us. The aliens know our location, have probably guessed our destination, and intend to take us out."

"We expected that." Walker studied the graph for a moment. A large gap remained between the two craft. "Can't we shake them, zig when they zag or something?"

"It's not a car chase, Aiden, but I have an idea."

"I'm listening." He didn't know anything about gravity drives or celestial mechanics, but he trusted Gate. He noticed the heated look that passed between Gate and Blivens, indicating some dissention between them. Clearly, the two had discussed the subject at great lengths and did not agree.

"If we continue moving farther out of our original flight path, we add days to our journey. The advantage goes to the aliens. Because of the distance involved, they need make only small corrections to intercept us. I can't guarantee the aliens aren't willing to sacrifice a Kaiju pod to stop us. If so, we can't avoid them."

The news was a swift kick to Walker's midsection. He struggled to inhale a lungful of the stale cabin air already rank with the odor of too many bodies. "Then we've lost."

"No, not yet. We can use the aliens' determination to destroy us to our advantage."

His interest now piqued by Gate's comment, Walker asked, "How?"

"We can change course to intercept the pod swarm. Then, when we're close enough, we blow the ship's gravity drive."

Walker choked, as he replied, "Destroy the ship? That's suicide." He couldn't believe Gate would suggest such a thing.

Gate shook his head. "No, no. We first stop and release the habitat modules and *Lances*. The *Assegai* can rendezvous later and pick us up. We can preset a course, remote control the *Javelin* to the swarm, and destroy it."

The idea of destroying the pods appealed to him, but the risks were great. "Our bosses aren't going to like sacrificing a multi-billion dollar ship. Will it work?"

Gate hesitated. Walker read much into the astrophysicist's reluctance to answer the question. "Theoretically, it should, if I did the math correctly. Blivens here helped me with that."

Blivens raised an eyebrow but said nothing. Walker wasn't afraid of taking risks, but risking the entire mission was another matter. "Using the *Javelin* as a super bomb might give Earth a fighting chance, but I don't like dropping off the *Lances* and the assault team to wait for the *Assegai*. If the rendezvous fails, we're dead. The mission to Haumea will be a scrub."

"I admit it's a risk, but I believe a slight one." Gate stood and paced. His long legs made short work of the small confines of the bridge – Six paces, turn, then six paces back. "The rear module is detachable. If we disconnect oxygen #1 as well, the module should maintain a breathable atmosphere for forty-eight hours; the suits will extend that by another six hours. I'll make certain a timely rendezvous with the *Assegai* is possible before we commit to the endeavor."

"Even so …"

Gate's arms and hands danced in front of him as he explained. "Yes, yes, I know. Both oxygen tanks would be best, but the liquid oxygen from tank #2 also serves as a coolant for the gravity drive. We can't use it." He sighed. "It would be great if we could pump oxygen from #1 to #2, but no one anticipated the need. We'll have to settle with one tank. If we guide the *Javelin* into the flight path of the incoming Kaiju pods, they won't pass up the opportunity to destroy it, as they are already attempting. We've calculated," he indicated Blivens, "that the yield from an uncontrolled gravity anomaly explosion should destroy all the pods, the first ten anyway. The others are too far away."

Blivens added, "Provided they don't suspect a trap."

That mirrored Walker's thoughts. "What if it's only the one pod that has already changed course to intercept us? What if the others ignore us and continue on their present course?"

Gate scratched his head. He ducked under his hammock and came up on the other side, leaning on it and swinging slightly. "Then I've killed a lot of people on Earth and here and wasted a lot of taxpayer dollars, Aiden." He threw his arms in the air. "Look, I can't guarantee anything. It's a risk, but doing nothing ... That seems far more dangerous. Ten more Kaiju is an armada. Thirty is a death knell for planet Earth." He paused. "I've calculated the first ten will land in North America. If they separate too far or change their speed to intercept us, they will miss their destinations. The Nazir are too methodical to take that risk. I'm certain they will use only the one pod."

Walker wanted to believe Gate's plan would work. He wanted to believe it with a passion. The U.S. couldn't stand another attack. It was barely beginning to recover from the first attack. In spite of the inherent risks involved, Gate's plan offered a chance to even the odds. However, it was a decision he could not make alone.

"It's up to Colonel Sakiri," Walker said. "I'm only in charge of the ground operation."

"I know, but if I can convince you, maybe he will agree as well." Gate stared at Walker. "Have I?"

Walker took a deep breath to marshal his thoughts. "If we can give Earth some breathing space and still complete the mission on Haumea, I'm in. You do realize that sacrificing the *Javelin* means that if anything happens to the *Assegai*, we're not coming home."

"If thirty more Kaiju hit Earth, we might not have a home to come back to."

Gate's point struck home. The entire mission was a risk. One more shouldn't matter. "Let's speak to Sakiri."

* * * *

Just as Walker figured, Sakiri thought it was a bad idea. Sakiri's mission was to deliver his fleet of *Lances* to Haumea. Betting all their lives on Gate's plan, a man he did not know, struck him as an unacceptable risk.

"If you're wrong, Dr. Rutherford, we could lose this battle and thereby Earth."

Gate didn't accept Sakiri's rejection gracefully. Walker had argued with him before. He could be persuasive. "I don't know if we can make course corrections fast enough to evade whatever the Nazir throw at us. It depends on how determined they are. If we can eliminate part of the first swarm, Earth might have a chance."

Walker watched Sakiri's reactions, as the colonel mulled over Gate's idea, gauging the depth of his concern by the set of his jaw and the way his gaze shifted around the room. Like him, Sakiri understood the odds of success of their mission were low. Any relief they could offer Earth's beleaguered defenses seemed a no-brainer to Walker, but Sakiri had been working on the *Javelin* project for months. Suddenly abandoning his mission ran counter to his training and his mindset. Walker might feel the same way under similar circumstances, but he had the advantage of having witnessed the devastating destructive power of a Kaiju close hand. In his opinion, saving Earth from a single additional Kaiju would be worth the risk.

"You were added to the crew for just such a reason," Sakiri said. "Your job is to avoid the incoming Kaiju pods. It is the reason we launched early." He narrowed his eyes and stared at Gate, as if blaming him for the early launch. "Are you now telling me you're not up to the task?"

Gate didn't rise to the attack by trying to defend himself. He shrugged off Sakiri's insult. "I think I can avoid the Kaiju, but it might lengthen the voyage by days. However, if they decide to chase us down … I don't know. It depends on how badly they want to stop us. The aliens know more about the capability of gravity drives than we do. We're just learning."

"I see." Sakiri's gaze moved to Walker. He felt like he was a specimen slide under a microscope as Sakiri watched his face. "You're in favor of this?"

Walker had expected Sakiri to seek his opinion, not that it mattered. His authority didn't begin until they reached Haumea. In the end, it would be Sakiri's decision. He sighed. "Yeah. I trust Gate. Killing Kaiju is my job. I've seen what they can do. Killing ten in one fell swoop seems like an acceptable risk to me."

Sakiri didn't like his answer. His disappointment showed in his eyes. "It doesn't to me."

Sakiri's outright dismissal of the plan before carefully considering it surprised Walker. The inherent risks were inescapable, as they were in any mission. If it failed, it left the crew and the *Lances* vulnerable. The destruction or even the delay of the *Assegai* would sign their death sentence. Many variables had to mesh perfectly to succeed. The plan was bold and uncertain, but perhaps it would catch the Nazir by surprise.

"Thirty Kaiju could wipe out half the planet before we even reach Haumea," Walker countered. "Millions will die. I agree it's damn risky, but it could work."

"If we make this attempt and fail," Sakiri explained, "Earth will certainly be doomed. This is not a warship. It is a transport vehicle delivering the only offensive weapons we have, twenty armed *Lances* and a team trained to penetrate Kaiju defenses. The only viable weapon the *Javelin* possesses is its gravity drive. You're proposing that we intentionally destroy the drive and the ship to eliminate a third of the incoming Kaiju armada, and then stake all our lives on a rendezvous with the *Assegai* to continue our mission." Having succinctly stated his case, he paused. "No one has ever tried this before; yet, you are willing to risk everything on this slim chance of success. I cannot in good conscience agree."

"I understand, Colonel. I really do. As you said, no one has ever tried it before. Maybe we need to make things up as we go along."

"I'm against it; however, you are technically my co-commander, so I feel I cannot decide the fate of this mission over your head. I'll forward your proposal to Groom Lake. They'll have to inform the President, and he'll take it to the U.N. I'll let them make the final decision." He glanced at Walker with sympathy in his eyes. "I'm not blind to what stopping the Kaiju would mean to Earth, Major, but that would be a single battle. I'm concerned about winning the war."

"It will work," Gate said. He sounded certain. Walker wanted to believe him.

Sakiri tore his gaze from Walker and focused on Gate. "If they agree, it had better work," he replied.

12

August 14, Nantes, France –

The first thing LaBonner realized when he awoke was that he was still alive. He hurt too badly to be dead, from his toes to the crown of his head. The only parts of his body that didn't ache were numb. A Dextrose intravenous line ran to his blistered left arm strapped to a board. A white burn salve coated it from wrist to elbow. The same pungent ointment coated his right arm to his shoulder. He gently probed his head with his right hand and touched a bandage wrapped tightly around his forehead. Bits of singed hair protruded from the bandage.

Above him, the white fabric of a tent snapped in the wind. Large fans stirred the air by pulling in hot air from outside. The smell of alcohol and disinfectant fought with the sickening stench of death. He lifted his upper body to look around, and a shooting pain raced up his side burning like a hot poker. He glanced down. Bandages wrapped his middle torso. He remembered the shrapnel and the church collapsing, but nothing after that.

Spence and Mayer. Where were they?

People moved around him. He wet his lips and tried to speak but only a weak croaking sound emerged from his parched throat. His stirring attracted a nurse. She rushed over and offered him water from a glass with a flexible straw. He took a few sips of the lukewarm water and forced it down his throat. He nodded, and she removed the glass.

"Where am I?" he asked in English.

She shook her head. *"Je ne parle pas anglais. Parlez-vous Français?"*

He remembered where he was – France. *"Oui."* He repeated his question in French.

"A first-aid center in Nantes," she answered.

Nantes was near the coast on the Loire River over two hundred miles from Paris. "Nantes? How did I get here?"

"Some children found you in the Eglise St. Sulpice in Paris after the Kaiju stopped. Many of the injured from the city came here by truck, by train, by helicopter. So many."

"What about my team, Spence and Mayer?"

She shook her head and frowned. "There was only you, monsieur. No others."

He remembered Mayer in the clutches of a Wasp after she fired her rocket. He had lost his entire team, eight good soldiers, to bring down the Kaiju. It was a steep price to pay. Sometime during his sleep, his subconscious mind had sorted through his fears and hit the reset button on his hatred of the aliens. He focused on that hatred. He could not just lay there while other Kaiju threatened the rest of Europe.

"When can I leave?" He tried to sit up again. This time, he ignored the pain until his feet dangled over the side of the bed. Then, he stopped to catch his breath.

"No, you will tear your stitches," the nurse reprimanded him. She laid her hand against her side to indicate his injury. "The doctor removed shrapnel from your side, here. Your burns are very bad. You are very lucky to be alive."

He didn't feel lucky. He had killed his team. "Get my clothes. I have to report in."

"Your clothes were too badly damaged to salvage." She touched his arm gently, but he still winced at the pain. "I will bring the doctor to explain why you must stay."

He didn't have time for explanations. "Yeah, you do that," he told her.

He struggled to slide off the edge of the bed. It took all the strength he could muster. He ached all over, as if a building had fallen on him, and realized it had. His head spun. His muscles cried out in pain. He focused on his surroundings and noticed scores of people, mostly civilians, in serious condition lying on cots around him. Nurses and volunteers raced around the tent helping where they could, but they were obviously understaffed and overwhelmed. People moaned, prayed aloud, or cried depending on the severity of their wounds. Some of them suffered in silence, dazed and in shock by what they had endured.

He noted a Geiger counter on a stainless steel rolling tray near the section of the tent in which his cot sat. Around him were several patients with severe burns, possibly from the nuclear rocket his team used to kill the Kaiju. They would have received a large dose of radiation, as he probably had. The number could have been higher. Most of the populace of Paris had evacuated the area prior to the blast. The nuke was small to limit fallout, but radiation would contaminate the area for years. Those few affected by the radiation, including him, were unfortunate collateral damage.

He spotted two dozen bundles wrapped in sheets lying on the ground near the rear wall. A cold, hard knot formed in his chest when he realized that they were bodies. Not everyone had made it to the hospital alive. In no mood for arguing, he did not wait on the nurse to return with a doctor. He stood, wobbly at first, and forced his feet to move. His legs worked. He yanked out the IV and left it dripping on the cot. He winced as he loosened the Velcro strap securing his arm to the board, as it also removed hair and blistered skin. He walked barefooted across the canvas floor, avoiding still wet spots of blood. Near the exit, he passed a rack with stacks of folded hospital scrubs. He stopped long enough to shed his hospital gown and don a pair of green scrubs, noting the livid bruises and numerous burns covering his torso. From a box of polypropylene booties on another shelf, he grabbed a pair of the disposable shoe covers and slipped them over his bare feet.

Outside, the night sky was ablaze with stars. Because of the smoke and dust from the Kaiju landing and Paris burning, it was the first time he had seen stars in days. The tent was one of a dozen erected in the parking lot of a hospital. The sign read *Hospital Bellier*. Nearby in a railroad marshalling yard, ambulances and trucks unloaded rail cars filled with more injured from Paris and the surrounding cities. The hospital normally dealt with hundreds of patients. The thousands descending upon them overwhelmed their resources. They didn't need one more reluctant patient. He had to get back to his base in England to report on his mission, and, if possible, cadge an assignment to another Kaiju Killer team. He just wasn't sure how to accomplish it.

The fear and indecision that had gripped him for days had vanished, almost as if the nuclear explosion had expunged it from his body, leaving behind a throbbing ache for revenge. The others had all died, and yet, he had survived. He had to make that count for something. For all he knew, the radiation might have saturated his body. He might only have months to live or weeks. Cowering behind his wounds wouldn't accomplish anything. He wanted to go out fighting like a soldier.

A U.S. Army *Blackhawk* helicopter passing overhead gave him an idea. He watched it land in an open area a short distance away and headed that direction. He was still unsteady on his feet and stumbled over the multiple railroad tracks, barely making it out of the way of an oncoming train. The rocky ballast was sharp-edged and cut into his feet through the thin booties. He tiptoed across it until he reached bare dirt. A couple of tents, portable buildings, and a handful of military vehicles sat at the edge of the lighted open space in which the *Blackhawk* had landed.

He pushed through some bushes and startled a sentry. The young private raised his rifle and eyed LaBonner suspiciously, taking in his hospital garb and bandages.

"Who are you?" the private demanded.

"Sergeant L. Francis LaBonner, service number 1325468991 with Kaiju Killer Team Charlie. I was in Paris."

The sentry scratched his head and lowered his rifle. "No shit. You helped take down that monster."

"My team did. They're all dead."

"Pardon my saying so, Sergeant, but you look half dead yourself." He glanced toward a collection of portable shelters, trailers, and trucks. "Do you need a medic?"

"I need a lift back to England."

"Maybe you had better talk to Colonel Mitchell. He's in the second shack. Ask for Lieutenant Muldoon. He's the duty officer."

"Thanks, Private." He took a step and wobbled.

"You sure you don't need a medic?"

LaBonner shook his head. "No. No medic." A medic would take one look at him and send him back to the hospital.

The first truck was a mobile communications unit. A satellite dish on an extendable mast protruded from the roof of the vehicle. A portable generator hummed away between two DRASH tents. The first Deployable Rapid Assembly Shelter was a barracks. The second was an office. He walked up to the open door. A fan sat on the canvas floor in an attempt to fight back the heat.

Muldoon was a young second lieutenant sitting in front of a laptop scanning maps. He glanced up at LaBonner when he entered; then, did a double take. He noted the scrubs and the bandages. "How can I help you?"

LaBonner snapped a crisp salute. The sudden movement sent another spasm of pain shooting up his arm. "Sergeant L.F. LaBonner, K-T Charlie reporting in, sir."

"Kaiju Team Charlie?" Muldoon pulled up a chart on his screen, quickly scanned it, and then looked at LaBonner. "K-T Charlie was assigned to Paris. How did you get here?"

"No idea, sir. We took out the Kaiju, and a church fell in on me. I woke up here in a civilian field hospital."

"Well, good job, Sergeant. We thought Team Charlie was KIA. Glad you survived. What can I do for you?"

"I need a lift to England, sir."

"Hmm. I'll inform the colonel. Wait here."

He rose and passed through a door into the colonel's office. He returned less than a minute later with his superior, Colonel Mitchell, a tall, older man with a sunburned shaven head, who looked LaBonner over for a few seconds, and then shook his head.

"You look like shit, son, but I commend your desire to get back in the game. Under normal circumstances, I would send you straight to a hospital for some R&R and TLC, but we need you if you think you can cope."

The colonel's statement puzzled LaBonner. "What circumstances, sir?"

"You haven't heard?"

"I just woke up a few minutes ago." LaBonner noted the expression on the colonel's face – fear. "What's going on?"

"Then you've been out the better part of three days. Word is thirty more pods are inbound for Earth. ETA for the first ten is 1400 hours GMT tomorrow. Twenty more follow a week later."

LaBonner's legs folded as if someone had punched him in the gut. He collapsed into a metal folding chair beside the lieutenant's desk, suddenly dizzy and weak. He glanced at the lieutenant. The lieutenant had heard the news before, but his face still blanched as the colonel pronounced Earth's doom. "My God," LaBonner gasped. The vein in his temple throbbed to the beat of his heart. He resisted the urge to reach up and massage his temple.

The colonel nodded. "Exactly."

"Where?"

"We don't know yet, but it looks like the States, Eastern seaboard. The others," he shrugged, "who knows."

LaBonner swallowed hard and tried to shake off the panic burrowing like a mole to get inside his head. What had it all been for – the deaths, the devastation, the mass exodus of cities? Were they just trying to prolong everyone's misery? They couldn't deal with the eight remaining Kaiju. Now, the aliens were sending thirty more. It was hopeless. The urge to curl up on the floor and cry threatened to overwhelm him, but he didn't. Now was no time to lose it. He reached down deep inside, as he had advised Thayer to do, found one small spark of courage, and tried to fan it into flame.

"What's the plan?" he asked.

The colonel clenched his jaw and narrowed his eyes. "Plan? Why, we fight the bastards to the last man. There is no alternative. They mean to wipe us out."

He could handle that. He was probably dying from radiation poisoning. Dying at the hands of a Wasp or a Flea would be quicker than a slow, lingering death, if any of them got the chance to linger.

"Can you get me to RAF Lakenheath? That's Kaiju Killer Team command."

"Can do, son. You got lucky. I'm sending my reports to London HQ by chopper. I'll have Lieutenant Muldoon here inform the chopper pilot that you'll be joining him. He's refueling now. You'll be there within an hour."

LaBonner saluted. His finger trembled slightly as he held the salute. "Thank you, sir."

Colonel Mitchell returned his salute. "My pleasure, Sergeant. You get back in the game as soon as you're able. We need your experience."

The colonel returned to his office. Muldoon looked at LaBonner and grinned. "Let's get you home, soldier."

LaBonner relaxed and rubbed his temple. "Do you have any aspirin?"

Muldoon stared at him a moment. "I think I do. Maybe you need a shot of Jim Beam to wash them down."

"I could use a jolt, sir."

* * * *

LaBonner learned from the chopper pilot that K-Teams in Hamburg, Germany; Tiran, Albania; and Sophia, Bulgaria, had eliminated their Kaiju targets. Two of the teams had suffered heavy casualties but had made it back to Lakenheath. K-Team Foxtrot in Hamburg had failed to report in. That left five Kaiju: Malaga, Spain; Zagreb, Croatia; Rome, Italy; Brussels, Belgium; and Budapest, Hungary. They were batting .500 – Not high enough to win the pennant in this league.

Colonel Mitchell had insisted he allow a combat medic check him out before he left France. The 'Doc' had tsked LaBonner's leaving the hospital as unwise, but relented and rewrapped his head wound, bandaged his left hand, and reapplied burn salve to both arms. He had stood by, eyeing LaBonner like a mother hen until he swallowed two pain pills. The pills had knocked the edges off the aches but left him groggy. He wanted to curl up for a long nap, but already he had wasted away over fifty hours while unconscious. He couldn't afford to sleep.

Over the English Channel, they flew over a fleet of U.S., British, and French warships sailing north toward the North Sea. It was an impressive sight, two carriers and sixteen escort ships, but not all the ships in all of the world's fleets would be enough to deal with thirty more Kaiju. For the first time since the aliens had sent the Kaiju monsters, LaBonner wondered if Earth's best was good enough. The aliens were grinding humanity down to the point that rising again would be impossible.

At Lakenheath, he learned just how much had happened while he was unconscious. Command had ordered surviving members of hard-hit Kaiju teams and key personnel from existing teams to Groom Lake. He was the only unassigned Kaiju Killer remaining. Whatever mission lay in store for them, he would not be in on it. He cursed his luck. *A day late and a dollar short*. He expressed his disappointment to Kaiju Killer Team commander Colonel Leonard Eckhart.

"I wish to follow the others on the next available flight, sir," he said.

Eckhart looked him up and down carefully. His close-set sea moss green eyes squinted beneath bushy brown eyebrows showing the first hints of gray. "Sergeant, you look like you were on the receiving end of a gangbanger ass kicking. I'm surprised you can stand."

"Mostly bruises and a little flash burn," LaBonner lied, fighting to stand straight and not wobble. "I can fight." He put as much force in his words as he could muster.

The colonel expressed his doubt just as emphatically. "Sergeant, you couldn't fight my eighty-year-old arthritic mother, but I admire your spunk. Look, I know you want to join your unit, but emergency flights only have clearance to fly until the pods land. Fact is your fellow unit members are no longer on Earth."

LaBonner's jaw dropped. He wasn't sure he had heard correctly. "No longer ... Where the hell are they," he demanded; then, remembering he spoke to his superior, added a respectful, "sir."

"They're on their way to fight the aliens on their home turf."

The colonel's answer punched him like a hard left jab to the kidneys and left him gasping for breath. "You mean ... The Kuiper Belt?"

"That's right." Eckhart shook his head. "I don't know all the details. That's above my pay grade, but rumor is we're using the aliens' gravity drive technology now."

"Is Major Walker with them?"

"He's leading the assault team."

LaBonner was crestfallen. Walker needed him. He needed to be with Walker's team. "Damn it to hell!" The words slipped out before LaBonner could catch it. It didn't faze Eckhart.

"I know how you feel, Sergeant. I'm sitting here fiddling while Rome burns. My Kaiju Killer Teams are giving everything they've got and coming up short." He shuffled a few papers on his desk as he considered something. LaBonner hoped it was good news for him. It wasn't. "We're losing this war." He hung his head and shook it. "We don't have the resources to stop the aliens. Individual nations are taking matters into their own hands."

A cold knot formed in the pit of LaBonner's stomach, sending icy tendrils into his arms and chest. He had heard rumors. "You mean nukes?"

"I do."

"Aren't the Kaiju causing enough destruction without us adding to the carnage?"

"People are scared. Nations are scared. Frightened people aren't rational. Sometimes they do stupid shit."

LaBonner's shoulders sagged. Every hurt and pain he had endured to stop Kaiju Paris fought for dominance. "The Nazir must be laughing their asses off."

"No doubt. Captain Caulder will be arriving shortly."

"Finally, some good news." LaBonner knew Caulder. He was a good man, dedicated and obstinate. He saw the grim look on Eckhart's face. "Any casualties?"

"Most of them. Only Caulder and one other member of his team survived."

"I know how he feels. He has my sympathies."

"Washington wants me to withdraw all American personnel and bring them home to meet any new threats on U.S. soil." He made a fist. "I'm ignoring the order. They can damn well court martial and hang me. Hell, they can draw and quarter me if it will make them feel better, but I won't abandon Europe to those … those things, not yet. I've giving the teams in the field time to do their jobs. They've spent too much blood to quit now. Instead, I'm putting together as many teams as I can from survivors, new recruits, and volunteers. You will be leaving for the States tomorrow morning. Get some rest, son. You look like you need it."

LaBonner could not give up so easily. "Sir, I …"

Colonel Eckhart's face turned stone cold. "Sergeant, I can just as easily send you back to a hospital for a few weeks."

LaBonner looked into Eckhart's eyes and realized he had lost the argument. Eckhart was bucking command and might pay a high price for his treason in the name of commitment. He saluted. "Yes, sir."

The colonel reached into a drawer. "Before they court-martial me, I'd like to do one final thing." He pushed a small box across the desk to LaBonner. The box held a pair of silver captain's bars. "This is your reward for a job well done, more headaches. You've earned them, Captain."

LaBonner saw the glint of the silver bars and cringed. The last thing he wanted was more responsibility, having the power of life and death over more men and women. The colonel defied procedure by jumping him from sergeant to captain instead of to a second lieutenant. "I don't want –"

"Captain, you don't get the luxury of refusing. We need your experience if we're going to win this war. You can do more good as a captain than a second looie."

LaBonner was not happy. He didn't want more responsibility. The loss of his team was too poignant a reminder that he didn't deserve a promotion. His first impulse was to shove the bars into a certain part of the colonel's anatomy. Instead, he reached for them.

"Yes, sir. Thank you, sir." He hoped the colonel couldn't read his thoughts.

13

August 14, Hamburg, Germany –

Captain Beman "Buzz" Caulder stared at the broken Hamburg skyline. A tear rolled down his cheek. The salty drop created a clean furrow down his soot-smudged face. Once, Hamburg had looked old and inviting, like a comfortable chair or grandmother's house. Weathered brick, towering church steeples, dock cranes, placid canals, and bridges; it had been the greenest city in Europe, an industrial hub, a busy river port, and home to 1.7 million people. Now, it lay in ruins, a mound of smoldering debris, blackened corpses, and broken dreams.

Caulder's Kaiju Killer Team Foxtrot had achieved their mission goal stopping Kaiju Hamburg, but it had cost him seven men. They had saved tens of thousands of innocent lives, but he hadn't known any of their names, as he had his team. He would not see the faces of the citizens of Hamburg haunting him in his nightmares. He would see the faces of his dead team.

Kaiju Hamburg had crashed into the heart of Gluckstadt on the banks of the Elbe River sixty hours earlier and marched relentlessly through the German countryside and into the heart of Hamburg, Germany's second largest city. His team's nuke had stopped the creature, but not before it had smashed the city flat.

Sergeant Ron Warski, the only other survivor of K-Team Foxtrot, walked up behind him. "Our ride's here."

Caulder watched the Blackhawk helicopter circle the area searching for them; then, land in a clearing near a canal, raising a cloud of dust and ash that swirled above the chopper. Caulder noticed the dark waters of the canal bore detritus from the dead city – bodies, charred wood, half-sunken boats, broken and splintered trees, and dead animals – rolling northwards toward the North Sea. Eventually, the Elbe would cleanse itself. His soul could not. He had witnessed too much death and destruction. The single tear smearing his cheek was all he could shed for the dead. It was just too much to comprehend, too vast to wrap his mind around. He reached up a dirty finger and wiped away the tear.

"Yeah, grab your gear."

London, Paris, Tiran, and now Hamburg – four Kaiju down out of eight. How many more people would die over the next few days? He shook his head.

"We've got work to do."

The copilot greeted them as they boarded. He leaned out the door and yelled so that Caulder could hear him over the roar of the rotors. "I expected you guys to call in yesterday."

"It took all day and night to worm our way through the rubble." He didn't add that he and Warski had spent half the day digging through the rubble of a collapsed building searching for Private Hayden Lollar. They had finally found him pinned beneath a steel I-beam. They had sat with him for two hours, as he died, a deathwatch. Caulder had Lollar's dog tag in his pocket with the others of his team.

"Yeah, the city's a real mess, isn't it?" the copilot said. "Too bad."

"Yeah, too bad." *Too bad, I lost seven men. Too bad, it took three days to stop the Kaiju. Too bad, there are more of them.*

The pilot nodded to them as he and Warski boarded. A private stood behind a mounted M134 7.62mm minigun eyeing the landscape, wary of stray Wasps. Killing the Kaiju had slowed their rampage and befuddled them. With no way to feed, they would soon die, but they retained enough of their drive to kill to continue to be a menace. An unmanned GECAL50, a .50 caliber Gau-19/A, stood at the opposite open hatch. Without saying a word, Warski strode to the Gatling gun, clicked off the safety, and strapped himself into the harness, helping the other gunner keep watch over the dead city.

Outside, located above each door, a wing-like assembly held two removable pylons. Attached to one pylon on each side, AGM-114 *Hellfire* air-to-ground rocket launchers stood ready to take down any target on the ground. Having seen the Fleas and Wasps at work, the heavy armament did not offer Caulder any peace of mind. He sat back against the rear bulkhead as the chopper lifted off.

Just before leaving the German coast, a small swarm of Wasps attacked. Warski behind the GECAL50 and the private manning the M-134 killed six before they could get close enough to damage the Blackhawk by diving into the rotors, a common tactic they employed. Still confused by the death of their Kaiju host, the remainder broke off the attack and flew away.

Once over the North Sea, the chopper kept low to the water. A squall had blown in from the north, driving six-foot white caps before it.

Between the heavy rain and the choppy seas, Caulder thought he might get his feet wet. Some of the waves looked as if they would roll right into the chopper. He donned the earphones and queried the pilot.

"What's with the wave hopping?"

"Sorry, sir. Just got the word to keep the air corridors clear for emergency flights. They're moving a lot of equipment and personnel around."

"Why?"

The pilot smiled. "I just fly back and forth. I don't ask questions."

After killing the Wasps, Warski had taken the opportunity to catch forty winks. Caulder couldn't sleep. Every rattle of the chopper jingled the wad of dog tags in his shirt pocket, seven of them – Benson, Edelman, Hodges, Hollister, Lollar, Maget, and Richter. Richter had been born in Bremerhaven less than sixty kilometers from Hamburg. He had been familiar with every street, had a story about every bridge, and knew the owners of many of the quiet *rathskeller* that now lay in ruin. Now, Richter's body lay entombed with them, his dog tag all that remained. Caulder didn't sleep because he worried that his decisions had killed his team.

Warski would never admit his concerns if he had them. He was a perfect soldier with no opinion on anything. He went where they sent him and killed what his superiors told him to kill. He slept the slumber of the innocent. He was a killing machine and did his job with a clean conscience. Caulder didn't have that luxury. Command would assign him more men over whose lives he had complete control. Colonel Eckhart had assured him of his complete confidence. Caulder wondered if his confidence was misplaced.

He stared at the blackened scar of East London through the rain; a mirror image of Hamburg's blackened rubble. Even in the downpour, smoke rose from a hundred heaps of smoldering debris. If they didn't stop the Kaiju, all of Europe would look similar. He didn't have the luxury of second thoughts. For every man he had lost, tens of thousands had died in Hamburg and the surrounding countryside. Every effort he made to spare his team cost more lives. As soldiers, they were expendable. As long as the mission succeeded, their lives didn't matter. That was what he told himself, but his heavy heart would not let him believe it.

He nudged Warski. "We're home."

Warski blinked, glanced out the window, and growled, "Fucking rain. Does it ever stop raining in London?"

"It'll keep the stink down."

The Blackhawk passed low over a building with the word 'Eagles' written on the roof, a reminder that the 48th Tactical Fighter Wing with its F-15 *Eagles,* called RAF Lakenheath home. A few German *Tornados* were visible in front of the hangars. The chopper set down at the northeast edge of Runway 24 beside a rundown Quonset hut, HQ for the Kaiju Killer Teams. It wasn't much to look at, but the teams didn't spend much time there. For all its lack of comfort, it was home.

Corporal Chance Vance, wearing shorts, a faded Van Halen tee shirt, and an Atlanta Braves cap stood in the doorway of the hut holding a beer and watching the chopper land. He held onto his cap with one hand to prevent the wash of the rotors blowing it away. As Caulder approached, Vance took a long swig from the bottle and nodded.

"Caulder. Glad you made it." He glanced at the chopper, noting that only Warski emerged. "Rough one, huh?"

Caulder said nothing about Vance's lack of respect for his rank. The Kaiju Killers were a relaxed outfit. "They all are."

"I just got here from Albania a few hours ago. Alone. Sergeant Stoddard died on the way here. We gave him a beautiful burial at sea. His mama would be proud." He took another swig. "Better than the rest of my team got." He jerked his head toward the hut. "I'm it. Everyone else has gone already."

Caulder stopped. "Gone where?"

"The States. Some hush-hush project. Looks like we rode the slow horse here."

"What did the colonel say?"

Vance shook his head. "He didn't say anything. I haven't seen him. I did hear some scuttlebutt though."

"What?"

"Wilson's team is dead. The Ruskies nuked Budapest while they were there."

Caulder's chest tightened. "What was our response?"

Vance shrugged, but Caulder noticed a slight tic in his clenched jaw. "Not a damn thing as far as I can see. NATO hasn't said anything, but a lot of hardware and personnel have been moving north over the last twenty-four hours. It doesn't look good."

"Stupid Russians. What did they think would happen?"

"They're gamblers. They think NATO and Europe has enough to deal with already. They may be right."

"What do you mean?"

Vance took another sip of beer, savoring it before swallowing. "Rumor is more Kaiju are on the way."

Caulder stared at him in disbelief. "You're shitting me."

Vance held up three fingers in a Boy Scout salute. "I swear. I got it from a girl in communications. Lots of Kaiju."

"Can you say, 'We're fucked'?"

Warski walked up. "Good. More for each of us." He pushed past them into the hut.

Vance jerked his thumb at Warski's back. With a questioning look, he said, "Is he all right?"

"Just being sarcastic. He watched a lot of buddies die."

Vance lowered his gaze. "Yeah, been there, done that. Want a beer?"

Before Caulder could answer, a jeep pulled up in front of the hut. It stopped just long enough to disgorge its single passenger, and drove away. As the man approached, limping heavily, Caulder recognized him. He took in the bandages and the burn ointment on his arms and forehead and read a lot of pain and agony into the reasons. "LaBonner. You look like shit."

"I get that a lot." LaBonner glanced at the two men. "Is this it?"

"Warski's inside, but, yeah, the others are gone."

"Yeah, I know, to Haumea."

Caulder stared at LaBonner wondering if the injuries had addled his mind. "Haumea?"

"They're going to fight the Nazir in their backyard."

Caulder recognized the disappointment in LaBonner's voice. As much as he hated aliens, Caulder didn't think he would have volunteered for a space voyage. Clearly, LaBonner did not feel the same way. "I wish them luck." He noticed LaBonner's new bars. "A promotion. Good for you."

"Yeah, if you say so. The colonel insisted."

Caulder noted LaBonner's lack of enthusiasm. "Sounds like we'll have plenty to do here."

"Yeah, ten Kaiju hit in less than twenty-four hours and twenty more a week from now."

Caulder's face turned ashen. He sucked in his breath and exhaled. "You're sure?"

"Just got it from the colonel. Maybe you had better report to him. You still have the rank. We're hopping a transport for Dobbins first thing in the a.m. In the meantime, I'm getting some sack time."

"Dobbins?" Vance asked, watching LaBonner's back. "What's up with that? We've got Kaiju here."

Caulder shook his head, but he suspected it wasn't good news. A knot grew tighter in the pit of his stomach. The Russians nuking Budapest, the additional movement of personnel and matériel, and transferring K-teams to the States all spoke of big plans afoot. If more countries decided nuking the Kaiju was the only solution, all hell would break loose. With Russia flexing its muscles and China shutting down all outside communications, the aliens might be the least of their problems.

"Stupid fucking humans," he growled.

Vance turned up his beer and finished it; then said, "You got that shit right."

14

August 14, *USS Javelin* –

Walker filled the hours waiting for word from Washington about Gate's idea by pressing his team harder. Training made them forget about home and their destination. Only by focusing on the immediate threat would they have any chance of succeeding. The mission's success concerned him more than survival. Failure was not an option. If they failed, there would be no home to return to. The time passed agonizingly slow. The information had to precede through the proper channels – first the Joint Chiefs, then the United Nations, and possibly even NATO, before the President made a final decision. The *Javelin* was a U.S. ship, but the U.N. had invested a lot of money in its construction and demanded a place at the table. He only hoped they didn't debate it to death.

Walker firmly believed the President would turn them down. The U.N. had already agreed to nuke the incoming Kaiju. Risking the mission to stop a third of the Kaiju would not be an easy sell to politicians who clung to the hope of future elections, as if such a thing were inevitable in such apocalyptic times. Sakiri had forwarded the proposal with little enthusiasm. Walker was sure he had added his own objections to the message as a way of asserting his overall command of the mission. Walker did not begrudge him his opinion. If they failed, the majority of the culpability would fall on him.

Costas did not suffer the anxiety of the wait alone. Deprived of his booze, cigars, and women, he growled at every Alpha Team member like a bulldog guarding its bone. No slip-up or failure escaped his wrath. Walker considered speaking with his sergeant to get him to ease up, but decided that allowing his team to focus their hostility toward Costas was better than their resentment of him. Some might have construed his inaction as cowardly, but Costas could handle the pressure. Walker had sufficient worries to occupy his time.

Each of Fire Team Alpha's ten members had endured rigorous training for a spot on a Kaiju Killer team. Most were former Rangers, Seals, or British SAS, and were among the best-trained and disciplined soldiers in the world. Now, necessity demanded they fight and possibly die in an entirely alien environment – deep space. Most of them had stared death in the face. Each had been a member of a team that had faced a Kaiju. No team escaped unscathed. Some did not escape at all. Many teams had fallen to take down their monsters. Millions owed their lives to the few brave men and women in the room who had volunteered to venture to the ends of the solar system to face an even deadlier foe – the Nazir.

Sakiri pushed through the hatch. Walker studied the colonel's face, but the *Lance* pilot revealed nothing in either his mannerisms or his expression. He had a perfect poker face. Walker would have hated playing cards against him. "That's enough for now, Alpha Team," Walker told the group. "Grab some chow and leisure time."

Costas narrowed his eyes at Walker but said nothing. The others filed through the hatch, eager to place some distance between them and the claustrophobic sergeant. After a few moments, Costas swung up into his hammock and closed his eyes muttering to himself.

"Any word?" Walker asked Sakiri.

"They agreed under certain conditions."

The answer both pleased and surprised Walker, but the added codicil annoyed him. "What conditions?"

"They won't risk any more *Lances* or risk the *Assegai* remaining in orbit any longer than necessary. She left Earth a day ahead of schedule with her original two-man crew."

Walker sighed. "Well, that's that. I expected as much. I guess we're lucky they agreed at all."

"They almost didn't. Homeland Secretary Robinson lent his support to you. It looks like you have a friend in high places." Sakiri's tone implied that he resented Walker's high-level support. "We'll shut down the drive in six hours and strip the *Javelin*. The *Assegai* will increase speed and rendezvous with us in fifty-six hours."

Walker made a rapid mental calculation and didn't like the answer. "Whew! That's cutting it close."

"They are afraid to push the gravity drive and risk the ship. If the *Javelin* does the job, it will have been worth it. If not, we can expect the aliens to retaliate. If they do, we'll give them a fight."

You will. I'll just be sitting here in a windowless box waiting. Something in Sakiri's manner bothered him. He held something back. "Why did they agree? I was sure they would turn us down."

"Things have changed. Ukraine nuked the Budapest Kaiju. It obliterated the entire city. Now, the U.N. plan to nuke the Kaiju is falling apart. World leaders are afraid the use of nuclear missiles might mask a covert attack by China or Russia. Some heated discussion erupted on the floor of the U.N. when Germany suggested that changing the mission benefitted the U.S. at the expense of the rest of the world. The President pointed out that whittling down the incoming Kaiju might give the U.N. a few extra days to bring some muscle to bear against the second wave. We could prevent a global war. I guess they feel the risk is acceptable."

"What about you?"

Walker scanned Sakiri's face for some hint of his true feelings. The U.N. had approved the plan, and he harbored no doubt that the colonel would do everything in his power to comply, but he needed to know Sakiri's true mind. It could raise a shadow over any future suggestions Walker might make. He needed Sakiri's full support, but did not want to step on his toes. He wouldn't like it done to him, and Sakiri would undoubtedly feel the same way.

Sakiri's face remained neutral. Walker thought he might have detected the slightest quiver in the corner of his cheek, but it could have been his imagination. Sakiri cleared his throat before answering.

"I will follow my orders," he said.

Walker didn't want to press, but the answer did not suffice. "And then?"

"If the *Javelin* fails to stop any of the Kaiju, I am to assume complete authority of the mission."

The announcement was a hammer blow to his ego. "I see."

"I did not ask for it," Sakiri added. "The Joint Chiefs added it as part of their agreement. I do not wish to dictate terms to you or your team."

"Unless you feel it is necessary."

"Yes."

Walker let the tension flow from his body. He could not afford a confrontation under any circumstances. He had to trust that Sakiri would keep his word. The news about Budapest hit him hard. The team leader, Wilson, was a family man from Leeds. Another entire team was gone, this time killed by the Russians, their supposed allies in the war against the Nazir. He considered the bombing of Budapest a betrayal of humankind, even if they wished to place the blame on Ukraine. The world knew who pulled the strings.

"When this is all over, we'll have to do something about the Russians. If they refuse to play nice, we need to kick them off the playground."

"One enemy at a time," Sakiri said.

Walker appreciated Sakiri's attempt to defuse the situation. He was right. "One enemy at a time."

"Then let's do it." Sakiri turned to Costas. "What about you, Sergeant?"

From his hammock, Costas growled, "Yeah. Anything beats sitting in this damn coffin."

Sakiri reached into his jumpsuit and pulled out a small silver flask. When he sloshed its contents, Costas opened one eye and stared at him.

"How about a drop of *Ballantine's*?" He handed Costas the flask.

"Ain't this against regulations?" Costas asked, holding up the flask and caressing it with his gaze.

"I always keep a bit of Scotch handy to celebrate a victory."

"Isn't this celebrating a bit early?" Costas opened the flask, took a deep swig, and smacked his lips. "Not that I'm complaining, mind you."

"I thought perhaps we might celebrate before our victory, just in case."

Costas' face darkened. "Yeah, good idea. What about you, Major? Does the Koran make allowances for victory drinks?"

Walker smiled and shook his head. "None for me, but my spirit is with you."

Costas lifted the flask. "Here's to good Scotch spirits."

Walker decided to let Sakiri and Costas celebrate alone. "I think I'll inform Gate that his wish has been granted. He should be pleased."

"I'll bet he's already figured out a worst-case scenario," Costas said.

"Sergeant," Walker said, "this *is* the worst-case scenario."

* * * *

After three days in flight, the pilots and copilots had settled into a routine closely akin to normalcy. Except for the fact they were in an enclosed environment in space 450 million miles from Earth, the compartment very much resembled an aircraft carrier's ready room. However, there was no board showing flight movements, the ubiquitous Ouija Board. When the time came, they would all be in their *Lances* reporting directly to Sakiri. Men and women reclined in bunks, sat on benches or chairs, played cards, read magazines or Kindles, had bullshit sessions, joked, argued, and complained. A poster taped to the wall written in black marker declared the compartment "Ready Room KA" for Kick Ass. Walker admired their enthusiasm and hoped it was as high on Day 10 as it was on Day 3.

Threading his way through the crowded galley, the aroma of baked chicken greeted him. Four crewmembers had decided to avoid the miasma of so many different foods heating in the microwaves by choosing the same meal. It reminded Walker of the chow line at Fort Irwin in California on chicken potpie day, one of his favorite meals. The pre-packaged meals provided by NASA supplied the proper balance of nutrients and caloric intake. The taste was acceptable, nothing fancy, but palatable. However, the cacophony of aromas from so many different meals mixing in the air muddied the individual flavors. Each bite absorbed a minute trace of someone else's meal. Most of the crew did not notice or else ignored the slight discrepancy between smell and taste. He could not. In spite of his love of chicken, for some indefinable reason, the smell repulsed him. He blamed the tension of the mission, that ever-present viper hissing constantly in his ear, "Failure."

He walked onto the bridge in the middle of an argument. Gate and Blivens faced off inches apart, the tall astronomer towering over Blivens, whose face was a bright shade of coral. Gate stood with his right hand balled into a massive fist at his side. Walker had never seen the astronomer strike anyone, but he presented an intimidating figure. Goodman and Worthen sat silent at their consoles, looking as if they had rather be anywhere else, glancing up only occasionally. When the pair noticed Walker enter, both their faces flooded with relief. Gate and Blivens stopped yelling and turned to stare at him. Feeling the heavy tension in the room, he almost turned around and left, but he figured the disagreement had something to do with the proposed course change. He needed to step in to prevent further escalation. He looked at Gate and raised one eyebrow.

"Blivens here has changed his mind," Gate blurted.

"I didn't change my mind. I formulated better data, that's all."

"You're saying it is impossible," Gate countered.

Walker stepped between the two men and led Gate to the wall a safe distance from Blivens. Blivens relaxed his stance, but the angry expression on his face did not waver. "Start at the beginning," Walker said.

Blivens spoke up first. "I reran some numbers on the drive. It has been a learning curve. There are still things we –"

Walker stopped him. "Just the pertinent facts, please."

Blivens sighed. "I can't overload the drive with sufficient accuracy to assure an explosion within the vicinity of the Kaiju pods." He shook his head and shrugged. "It's impossible."

Gate glared at Blivens. "His original estimate from build up to explosion was .08 seconds. Now, it's almost double that."

"New factors, new data."

Walker cut short Gate's retort to Blivens with a shake of his head. "Does a tenth of a second make that much difference?" Their concern puzzled him.

They both stared at him as if he had spoken gibberish. Gate answered. "It's a matter of celestial mechanics. You're a sniper. It's somewhat the same principle. With two objects approaching one another at the speeds we're talking about, tenths of a second could mean a hundred thousand miles."

"I see. The Kaiju could pass the *Javelin* before the explosion. They approved your plan, by the way, so we have to come up with a workable solution soon. Earth depends on it."

He expected a look of triumph on Gate's face. Instead, the lanky astronomer looked appalled. "They agreed?"

"Look, why can't we disembark everyone to await the *Assegai*, and then move the Javelin a few million miles toward the Kaiju and stop it? Make it a sitting target for the aliens."

"Same problem – timing," Gate replied. "The aliens might continue to divert a single pod. They might change speeds or ignore it entirely. We need to meet the entire group to do as much damage as possible. Otherwise, we're wasting a ship for very little gain."

As much as he hated it, Walker could think of only one option. "Someone will have to remain with the *Javelin* to initiate the overload."

"Are you crazy?" Blivens shouted. "That's suicide."

Gate stared in stunned silence at Walker's suggestion of a suicide run. Walker ignored Gate and turned to Blivens. "Can you teach me the process? Not everything; I just need to know enough to trigger the explosion. The rest is automatic, right?"

"Yes, but –"

"No buts. We have to stop the Kaiju. This is the only way. It's my job." He glanced at Gate and smiled. "I've been killing Kaiju since Day 1."

Blivens threw his hands in the air and shook his head. "It's impossible. You can't pilot the ship."

"Okay. Then you and I go. Two lives to save Earth. It's a bargain."

Blivens stretched to his full height and thrust out his chin in defiance. "No! I won't do it. I'm not stupid!"

Walker was at his wit's end. He had tired of Blivens blustering, but he couldn't order him to go. "Then show me what to do."

"It's useless. You have no idea –"

"I'll go," Gate said. He spoke quietly, and his voice cracked on the last word. His Adam's apple fluttered up and down in his throat as he swallowed several times. "I can do it, I think." He shook his head. "I mean, I can do it. I'll go."

Blivens raised his hand and pointed at Gate with a smirk distorting his features. "He's not qualified."

Beads of sweat dotted Gate's forehead, eliciting a pang of sympathy from Walker. Clearly, his friend was afraid, but he had volunteered anyway. Walker gave him credit for courage. He flicked a smile at Gate. "He's more qualified than I am."

Blivens put his hands on each side of his head and moaned. "This is insane. You're both crazy."

"Someone has to do this. Unless you wish to volunteer ..."

Blivens glared at him and stalked away facing the bulkhead.

"There's the magnetic bottle," Worthen said; then, looked stricken, as if he had spoken aloud what he had been thinking.

Blivens whirled on him. "We discussed that earlier. It would never work. The field is too weak. It will cause a cascade effect in the drive."

"It might, but we can't be certain."

"I'm certain," Blivens stated with defiance, daring Worthen to challenge him.

"What?" Walker demanded.

Worthen stared at Walker and licked his lips. He had the look of a deer startled by headlights. He did not like the attention focused on him. "It might be possible to allow the drive to go near-critical but contain it within the magnetic bottle surrounding the unit. Collapsing the bottle will initiate an immediate explosion."

Walker looked at Blivens. "Is this true?"

"Theoretically, but there will be seepage – gravity distortions, magnetic anomalies." He shook his head. "We don't know how much seepage. It could affect the ship and cause a cascading systems failure. I doubt anyone could survive long enough to initiate the collapse at a given time."

"Someone will need to do the math," Gate said. "The physics of two moving objects is complicated. Neither Worthen nor Blivens is qualified." He grinned at Walker. "For sure you can't."

Walker understood where Gate was heading. "No way are you coming. You're too vital to the mission. They might need you on the *Assegai* in case of an emergency. You plot an intercept course and program the ship. I'll do the rest."

"It's not that simple." Gate shifted his weight on one foot. "Besides, it was my idea. I can't allow someone to take my place."

Walker understood Gate's dilemma. He attempted to soften the blow to Gate's conscience. "I've sent men on missions knowing full well they might not survive. It's all part of assuming responsibility. You've done your bit. It was your plan, but that's as far as it goes."

"No, I must be the one to do this, Aiden. My reason for coming was the necessity of making course corrections en route to avoid the Kaiju. By destroying them, we're eliminating that problem, thereby negating my original purpose. Your job is to fight the Kaiju on Haumea. I can't do that. We each have our specialties. Yours is being a hero. At heart, I've always been a numbers nerd. I'm not looking forward to dying, but I fully understand the risks involved."

A glimmer of an idea began to form in Walker's mind, a way to save Gate. They were essentially turning the *Javelin* into an Improvised Explosive Device. Walker understood IEDs. Terrorists triggered them by cell phone. "Can we do it remotely?"

Blivens hesitated, but Worthen spoke up. "Yes, but only within a limited range. The spatial distortions will increase exponentially with distance instead of the inverse. The waves gather momentum as they expand."

In spite of the jargon he did not understand, Walker perceived a slight glimmer of hope. "How limited?"

"It would depend on the local gravity fields of nearby planets. Mars is closest and will have the most influence. I'd say a few thousand miles. Any farther, and you risk stray gravity waves initiating the sequence."

"Good. A *Lance* can do that distance in minutes."

Gate looked puzzled. "I don't understand."

"We send a *Lance* with the *Javelin*. You initiate the gravity drive overload, bottle it up, and detonate it by remote control from the *Lance*, running like hell. You can rendezvous with the *Assegai*."

Gate shook his head. "I appreciate what you're attempting to do, but there are far too many variables to your plan. We risk a *Lance* and a pilot."

"It's a chance. There are more Kaiju coming after these," Walker reminded him. "We'll still need you to avoid them."

"No, by then, the *Assegai* will have moved too far from their course to matter. We can't do anything about them, and they can't stop the *Assegai*. This first group is the problem we must deal with, for Earth's sake."

He hated to admit it, but Gate was right. In spite of Gate's persistence, he did not feel right allowing him to assume full responsibility, but he could think of no alternative.

Gate was silent for a minute, as he paced the room. Finally, he faced Walker. "I can do this, Aiden. I don't need you to hold my hand."

Walker wouldn't give up. "We still have a few hours, right? Maybe you four geniuses can come up with a better plan before then."

Gate collapsed on his bunk. "It's doubtful. Now, all I need is a *Lance* pilot as stupid as I am."

It was unlikely they could stumble upon a better solution in the limited time remaining. To save Earth from the first onslaught of Kaiju, someone might have to place himself or herself in harm's way. He just didn't like the idea that it might be Gate.

15

August 14, *USS Javelin* –

Gate could not believe what he had done. He had backed himself into a corner from which he could not escape. When he had volunteered to make the journey to Haumea, the director had placed him in just such a corner. He hadn't fought then; he could not fight now. Considering all the factors involved, he was the best man for the job. If anything, Walker had taught him that the right tool or weapon sometimes made all the difference. In this instance, he was both. When the idea had formed in his head, he had not expected that he might have to sacrifice himself. He hadn't expected anyone to die. Now, he regretted having conceived the plan, but it was too late to back out.

No, that's wrong. Saving countless lives on Earth is worth the risk, even with the certainty of my death. He found ironic humor in the fact that he had thought himself finished with facing death after his ordeal with Nusku. He wasn't a natural-born hero like Walker, or a cynical, but dedicated soldier like Costas. Both men had trained to face danger and kick ass. Courage flowed through their veins as mathematics and probability flowed through his.

He could use a little of their courage. He had faced death and discovered a spot deep within himself he had hoped never to again revisit; a dark place like a cancer that needed little encouragement to grow and devour him – fear. It did not help that it was his idea. Sacrificing the *Javelin* had been a bold gamble he thought worth taking to spare Earth a portion of her coming misery. Now, the full horror of his proposal had come to rest on him. It was his onus, his albatross.

Maybe I should create a catastrophe probability flow chart with all the permutations that lead to a disastrous outcome. No, why tempt the devil?

He, Blivens, Worthen, and Goodman spent the next few hours brainstorming and arguing over trivial points until he thought physical violence would erupt, but they found no alternative to Worthen's original plan. They agreed that Walker's remote detonation scenario offered at least a slim chance of his surviving. Gate would guide the *Javelin* on an intercept course with the inbound Kaiju, adjusting his trajectory to keep them bunched together for a viable target. When the Kaiju pods were within range, he would abandon ship aboard a *Lance*, remotely release the spatial fury magnetically bound within the gravity drive, and hope he and the pilot could outrun the resulting blast.

It seemed simple on paper, but numbers never lied. They might mislead, but they never lied. A thousand things could go wrong – *okay, fifteen really*, he admitted – any one of which doomed the plan to failure and him to death. One slight miscalculation created a cascade of failures that ended in catastrophe. He understood because that had been his field – catastrophe analysis.

The moment he dreaded finally arrived. The planning stage was over. It was time to implement his plan. Taking the gravity drive off-line brought the *Javelin* to a standstill in space within minutes, something that would have taken days with a normal rocket-powered ship. They offloaded nineteen of the *Lances*, as well as the rear habitat module and oxygen tank #1. NASA engineers had designed the detachable rear compartment to land on Haumea with the strike team. They had not foreseen the need for the larger forward compartment to be easily detached. Because of time constraints, it would remain with the ship. Fifty-four bodies crammed into such a small space elicited cries of outrage and strings of colorful curses, but Colonel Sakiri ignored them as he oversaw the transfer.

Costas decried his dismay for anyone within hearing. "We're packed like sardines in here. I didn't sign up for this." Many voices rose in agreement. To Walker, he said, "Unless one of the female pilots wants to share my hammock, I'm officially pissed. I want to file a complaint."

"This ain't a union," Walker replied. "Suck that gut in and make room."

Costas looked down at his stomach. "What gut? This is all man meat."

Gate felt sorry for Costas. He reached out a hand and laid it on the sergeant's shoulder. "It's only for a few hours, Costas."

Costas did not look convinced. "Yeah, if our taxi shows up. If not, this is going to be one crowded coffin."

Walker did not meet Gate's gaze. He had refused until the last minute to give up on his plan to accompany Gate on the *Javelin*. Sakiri had finally made him see sense by threatening to pull rank, but he was no less disappointed. Gate understood Walker's dilemma. Ever since his inclusion on Fire Team Bravo when they had penetrated Kaiju Nusku to destroy it, Walker had assumed the responsibility of keeping him alive. Now, that was impossible. He would have to look out for himself.

"Aiden," he said, "it's the way it has to be. We all assumed the same risks when we left the Earth. If ... if anything happens, at least I'll have died trying to save lives. After what I've witnessed ..." He stopped, unable to continue. He had never spoken openly about Indiana, Chicago, or his adventure inside the Kaiju, not even to Walker. He had kept it bottled up inside, revealing only that knowledge which aided in the destruction of other Kaiju. Only recently had he learned to live with it. Even so, many nights he awoke in a cold sweat.

Walker looked at him with sympathy in his eyes. "We've been through a lot together, Gate. I wish this was on me instead of you."

"You're needed on Haumea. You have to stop the Nazir."

Walker nodded and held out his hand. "Good luck."

Gate gripped Walker's hand and shook it, trying to keep his own from trembling. "See you in a day or so."

"Jesus, you two!" Costas growled. "You're making me all teary-eyed."

He embraced Gate in a bear hug so tightly Gate thought the burly sergeant would dislocate his shoulders. When he released him, Gate backed up a couple of steps and looked Costas in the face, surprised at the emotion visible there. Gate glanced at the packed room one more time before sealing the hatch. All their lives depended on him doing his job.

The *Javelin* was as deserted as a sinking ship. The main living quarters, before so tightly packed, looked like a dance floor. The galley still smelled of the last warm meal the crew would have as they waited for the *Assegai*. Except for the quiet creaks and moans of the expanding and contracting hull and the hum of the life support equipment, the ship was eerily silent.

"Just you and me, Dr. Rutherford."

Gate looked up and smiled at Peters, who had Peters had volunteered to be his *Lance* pilot and fly the *Javelin*. It was good to see a familiar face. The thought of going out alone to meet the Kaiju pods had been disquieting. Better an experienced pilot at the controls of the ship than him. Of course, Peters had never sat in the control seat of the *Javelin*, but he had assured Gate it was simply a matter of inputting the correct coordinates and pressing the Go button. "A monkey could do it," he had said.

"Did you draw the short straw?" Gate asked.

Peters grinned. "I just wanted to take this baby for a spin. What say we buzz the others?"

Gate sat at Blivens' console to familiarize himself with the few controls he would need to destroy the ship. The process would be distressingly easy. Controlling the gravity drive was akin to harnessing an atomic bomb – one slip and oblivion. Blivens had downloaded a quick-reference users' manual for initiating the overload sequence of the gravity drive. Since it was a barely controlled spatial anomaly, the procedure was short and sweet, essentially a list of red-highlighted warnings that he was purposefully ignoring. If the generators could not produce enough power to strengthen the magnetic bottle, it would be a short journey.

Unsure if the *Javelin* would continue to function once the drive reached near-critical mass, he would wait until the last moment to overload it. The ship would continue toward its destination until seconds before the explosion. *Unless*, he thought, *it explodes in my face like a short-fused firecracker, or the gravity distortions rip apart both ship and crew.*

Twenty minutes later, Colonel Sakiri contacted him. "Tank #1 is connected to the module. We've moved the *Lances* and the module twenty clicks out as a safety margin. Everything is Go. Good luck, Dr. Rutherford."

Luck. Yeah, it will take some of that. "Thanks. See you later."

Peters fired the gravity drive. Again, the lack of pressure as the *Javelin* moved away disconcerted Gate. His mind told his body to expect a strong G-force, but none came. He relaxed when it became evident that Peters handled the ship as expertly as he flew his *Lance*. Leaving peters to his flying, Gate pored over the hastily written procedure provided by Blivens, trying to commit it to memory. He would not have the opportunity for a practice run and could afford no mistakes. It was a one-time only, do-or-die effort. If he did something wrong, he and Peters would not even know about it. They would be dead; atomic particles scattered over thousands of cubic kilometers of space.

To place distance between the *Javelin* and the abandoned crew, Peters pushed the ship to maximum. Each hour widened the safety margin but increased their return time to rendezvous with the *Assegai*. The *Javelin's* speed was tenfold that of a *Lance*. Peters' *Lance* would have to fly a wide intersecting arc to intercept the *Assegai's* flight path. If they missed it by a few degrees or if the *Assegai* veered from its course, they would drift in space until they depleted their oxygen.

Gate checked the approaching Kaiju often. At first, the data confused him. Given what they knew about the alien gravity drive, he did not doubt the gravimetric readings. They meshed with the data from previous Kaiju pods. However, they did not jibe with the mass spectrometer readings. He voiced his concern to Peters.

"We may have a problem. The mass spec readings indicate the Kaiju are larger and more massive than expected. Either the aliens have increased the power of their engines, or the pods are half again as large as previous pods."

Unlike Gate, who now had serious doubts about their mission, Peters maintained his composure. He looked as though he were out for a Sunday drive than speeding toward an enemy armada. "You're sure?"

Gate shook his head. "No. We're still too far away, but I recalibrated the equipment before running a second scan. The figures double-checked within five percent."

"Look, I'm just a space jockey, Dr. Rutherford. I know enough about gravity drives to fly my ship, and in a pinch, this one. I'm no engineer. If you say they're bigger or more powerful, I believe you. My only concern is that your plan will still work. Will it?"

"Maybe."

Peters arched his eyebrows and frowned. "Maybe? If this mission is a No Go, I need to know now, so I can turn this baby around."

"Their speed is constant, and the grouping hasn't changed. I am certain the explosion will destroy the Kaiju pods regardless of their size. In fact, the additional energy output of their gravity drives works in our favor. My concern is the aftereffects." He paused.

"Don't keep me in suspense, Doc."

"The explosion could be much larger than I calculated. We might not escape the danger zone."

Peters appeared to give the idea proper consideration, and then said, "We both knew this might be a one-way trip, so nothing has really changed has it? Mission is still a Go."

Part of him had hoped Peters would scrub the mission. Fear was creeping up from that place he had tried to imprison it deep inside him, sending fingers of doubt into his mind. He didn't want to die, but the likelihood was increasing with each passing hour. Despite his fear, he could not turn back now.

"Okay, we continue."

The decision made, a sense of liberation settled over Gate. Accepting imminent death freed him from the cloying fear and nagging doubt. He maintained a constant watch on the oncoming swarm in case of any changes. As the *Javelin* closed with the pods, the single pod that had changed course to intercept them veered sharply back toward the main body. The aliens did not suspect a trap. If they continued to hold their present course, the explosion would destroy all of them.

Wanting to place as much distance as possible between the explosion and the men of the *Javelin*, Gate had suggested a wide, looping intercept course. That had added hours to the already long journey but had seemed the best solution. That meant that Peters had to remain at the controls the entire trip. It was not as exhausting as flying a jet, but his mind had to remain focused on the various ships functions that normally three technicians controlled. He had placed himself into a personal state of autopilot, reacting only when the need arose.

To Gate, the intervening eleven hours crept by. He listened to music on his laptop to unwind. Finding himself tiring of jazz, he played Isao Tomita's *The Planets*. It was a bit astray from his usual jazz interests, but seemed appropriate. Unable to reach the state of serenity music usually took him, he gave up. Reclining in his seat, he closed his eyes and mentally went over the arming procedure until pangs of nervous hunger began to gnaw at his stomach. He realized he had not eaten in eighteen hours. The colonel had taken the bulk of the food and water for the habitat, but Gate located two meatloaf dinners with brown gravy and a bag of frozen rolls. It was not a banquet, but he hoped it would not be their last meal.

The clock on the forward screen counted down the last moments before contact. The numbers seemed to freeze in place, changing only when he blinked his eyes, as if playing mind games with him. The two lines on the plotting chart representing the *Javelin* and the Kaiju pods grew closer together.

Taking a deep breath and holding it before exhaling slowly to calm his nerves, he said, "It's time."

"Do it," Peters urged.

"Reduce our speed to twenty thousand miles per hour. I'll increase power to the magnetic bottle and initiate the overload sequence. If we stop the ship or slow too much, the aliens might become suspicious. We will have to release the *Lance* and drift away before you fire the drive. Maybe we can slip away unnoticed."

"It will be tricky," Peters replied. "Once we release the clamps on the *Lance*, the *Javelin* will be moving away at high speed. If we brush against her..."

He didn't have to elaborate. Gate understood the consequences of a mishap. Leaving the *Javelin* was not like launching from an aircraft carrier. Once they were free of the *Javelin's* gravity field, the relative velocities of the two craft would increase within seconds. From their perspective, the *Javelin* would disappear. If leaving a wake were possible in the vacuum of space, her wake would destroy the tiny craft.

"We have only one shot at this," Peters warned. "They won't give us a second chance."

Gate watched the line indicating the gravity drive output steadily climb toward the red danger zone. No one knew just how far into the red the drive would go before exploding. No one had been foolish enough to test it. The fluctuations of the magnetic bottle disturbed him, as gravity spikes pushed and tugged at the magnetic field surrounding the drive. Any slight deviation in power would release the gravity drive, now a barely controlled bomb, too early.

Peters looked at the countdown clock and grimaced. "We'll be cutting it close."

Peter's voice carried an edge of alarm. He had every right to be concerned. If the *Javelin* blew too soon, the gravity wash would envelop them. Gate didn't know what kind of spatial distortions they would encounter in such an instance. The ship could disintegrate or turn inside out. He tried not to dwell on it. It was like not thinking about an itch on the end of his nose.

Gate imagined he heard a Siren song inside his head as gravity distortions and changing lines of magnetic force played havoc with the fluids in his brain. He began reciting the names of stars to be certain he wasn't suffering random memory loss; then, stopped as he realized he would not know if he had forgotten a star. He decided it was a baseless fear, since he could do nothing to prevent it.

Fluctuations in the power grid affected ship's functions. Life support failed first; then, artificial gravity. As he floated free of his seat to don his spacesuit, the lights failed. During the few moments before the emergency lighting switched on, the absence of light sucked the breath from Gate's lungs. The utter darkness was a living entity drawing him into its mass. No darkness on Earth, except the bottom of the sea or the deepest caverns could match the total absence of light outside the ship. He welcomed the dim red emergency lights with utmost joy. He was reborn. For a terrifying moment, he forgot everything they had taught him about suiting up. He took a deep breath to relax, and tried again. This time, the process went more smoothly. The heavy gloves made typing on his keyboard difficult, but he entered the final overload sequence and hit the Enter key. Now, there was no turning back. An explosion was inevitable.

One hundred thousand miles from the estimated point the two alien craft would meet, they abandoned ship. This time, the short distance between the airlock and Peters' *Lance* was easier for Gate to negotiate.

There was no Earth below to disconcert him, only the vast blackness of space. He glanced around where Jupiter should have been. He discerned nothing at first; then, finally spotted a tiny dot a few million miles away. Once safely strapped into the seat in the *Lance*, Peters wasted no time disengaging the docking clamps. He fired the gravity drive in a short, low-power burst to move the craft away from the *Javelin*. Gate sensed a slight increase in gravity, and then an uncomfortable pressure in various parts of his body as the two conflicting gravity drives fought for dominance. The vague unease lasted only seconds before Peters cut the drive. The *Javelin* disappeared in a blur, as if swallowed by space.

After a brief moment of wondering how much cosmic radiation his body had absorbed outside the *Javelin's* magnetic field, Gate set an intercept course that would place them in the path of the *Assegai*, plus or minus four thousand miles. He hoped it was close enough for the *Assegai's* gravity detectors to locate them. They were engaged in a battle that would determine the lives of tens of thousands of people on Earth, but they sat alone in the emptiness of space thousands of miles from the scene of the battle. With the press of a button, the magnetic bottle containing the rampant gravity distortions of the *Javelin* would evaporate, releasing a fury.

Gate watched the final flight of the *Javelin* on the *Lance's* radar and gravity detector screens. The Kaiju pods had begun to spread farther apart, but he estimated they would still be within the blast radius. An aurora visible twenty thousand miles away surrounded the *Javelin*, as the lines of magnetic force of the shield encountered random electrons and cosmic particles. She looked like a fireball aimed at the heart of the alien armada.

"Do it," Peters urged.

"A couple of more seconds," Gate answered. Like Peters, his finger itched to press the button, but he had to be sure of maximum impact. He didn't want to miss a single pod. He glanced at his screen, and his heart skipped a beat. "Oh shit!" he said.

"What's happening?" Peters demanded.

"One pod is increasing speed and breaking away from the swarm toward the *Javelin*."

"Do it," Peters repeated with more vigor.

Gate pressed the button sending the signal to the *Javelin*. Seconds later, a small sun exploded into existence behind them as the *Javelin* disintegrated.

"Yes!" Peters yelled.

The incandescent orb expanded for twenty seconds before the outer edges tattered as the boiling gases cooled. The *Lance* lurched as gravity waves crashed against it and pushed through it. One moment, the ship drew his body down into the floor. The next, the front of the ship became a bottomless well into which he fell face first. His feet were heavy, but his head was light. His vision blurred as the fluid in his eyes swelled and swirled. His ears screamed from blood rushing through his inner ear; then, reversing directions. Time surged forward and snapped back to the present between the space of two heartbeats. The sensation passed quickly, but left him feeling exhausted and disoriented.

As soon as his vision cleared, he checked his screen. One blip emerged from the rapidly dissipating cloud of plasma. He did not have time to consider the implications.

"One pod escaped," he informed Peters.

"Pursuing us?"

Gate traced the pod's course. "No. It's still headed for Earth."

"Earth will have to deal with that one," Peters said. "We stopped the rest."

The triumph vanished from his voice, as the ship suddenly lurched again and lost power. Everything went dark inside the ship. For a moment, Gate feared he had gone blind. Panic rose in his chest. Then, he glanced outside the ship and saw stars. He wasn't blind, but the *Lance* was in trouble.

"What happened?" he asked, trying to keep the rising panic from his voice.

"All the needles are pegged out. The distortion caused a system overload. We have no power."

"Are we dead in space?" The thought of drifting aimlessly until they froze frightened him.

"The gravity drive is still functioning at full power. We're traveling 41.5 thousand miles per hour. I just can't see where we're going."

"How much oxygen do we have?"

"The tank is fully pressurized. We have about twenty-two hours left in it, plus an additional six in our suits."

Gate did a few calculations on his laptop. "We should rendezvous with the *Assegai* in twenty-six hours. That gives us a two-hour leeway. I calculated an intersecting course with the *Assegai* closing with us from behind. Of course," he added, "that depends on how long it takes to transfer personnel to the *Assegai* and dock the *Lances*."

"I'm flying blind," Peters reminded him.

Gate could help with that problem. "See the bright white star off to the left a few degrees?"

A few seconds later, Peters answered, "Got it."

"That's Vega, also known as Alpha Lyra, in the Lyr constellation. It's about 25 light years away and the fifth brightest star visible from Earth. Center the *Lance* on it. We'll reach the rendezvous point before the *Assegai*."

"How will we know haven't missed them?" Peters asked.

"If they don't find us before we run out of air, it won't matter."

Peters remained silent for almost a minute; then, said, "At least we accomplished our mission, even if we don't make the big one."

Gate wasn't ready to give up. Walker had taught him that. "As long as the drive is functioning, they can detect us from halfway to the Kuiper Belt. They'll find us."

"You're right, but will we still be alive?"

Gate had no answer for that one.

16

August 15, Dobbins Air Reserve Base, Marietta, GA –

LaBonner thought Paris had been sweltering. Stepping off the C-130 Hercules and onto the sunbaked tarmac at Dobbins was akin to walking into a sauna. The mid-morning heat bitch- slapped him in the face. A percent humidity of 96 percent leached the moisture from his flesh, and re-deposited it as a second clammy skin he could not wipe off. The only breeze to evaporate perspiration was the scorching air rising from the tarmac. The heat enveloped him like a cloud. Hot air crawled up his pants leg, singeing the hairs on his legs. He lifted one foot to make sure his boot wasn't miring in the soft asphalt.

"If this is morning, I can't wait for mid-afternoon," he said to no one in particular.

Although protected by burn ointment, bandages, and a long-sleeve shirt, his blistered skin grew a voice and begged him to put it out of its misery. He shaded his eyes with his hand to look at the approaching truck that would transport him and the nine men who had accompanied him from Lakenheath to their next ride.

He glanced at the new captain's bars gracing his collar glinting in the sun, his reward for a successful mission. They looked like twin shiny silver tombstones to remind him of the men and women he had helped kill. When offered the promotion, he had refused, but Colonel Eckhart had insisted. If he had pushed too hard, Eckhart might have demanded he take time off for medical treatment. Accepting the promotion was his only way back into the action.

Assigned to the 94th Airlift Wing stationed at Dobbins, they now waited for word on the inbound Kaiju pod. It was due to strike in less than five hours. The 94th's fleet of C-130s would quickly transport them to any Kaiju landing on American soil. As senior officer, Caulder was in command of the newly formed K-Team Zulu. LaBonner was glad to let the responsibility slide from his shoulders. In his eyes, his record was one of dismal failure. As the sole survivor of K-Team Charlie, he didn't want a second chance to kill more men. Caulder, Vance, Warski, and six others he had met only briefly had left Lakenheath twelve hours earlier for America. He had not slept on the journey across the Atlantic. His troubled mind would not allow it. A sense of betrayal that he alone of his team had survived consumed him. Remorse could kill a soldier as quickly as an enemy bullet. He had to find a way to live with his guilt or put all their lives at risk.

LaBonner recognized the same guilt in Caulder's haunted eyes. He had not slept on the flight either. He had paced the deck of the noisy plane with a grimace frozen on his lips, refusing to engage anyone in conversation. His silence spoke of his reluctance to broach the one subject that they all carefully avoided like a landmine – fear. Not a fear of the Kaiju, the Wasps, or Fleas – they had faced those fears – but the fear that they would make the same mistake again and more men would die. He could not read Vance or Warski but suspected they wrestled with their own inner demons.

He and the others were the lucky ones. Skill had little to do with their surviving their battles with the Kaiju. Bringing down one of the giant creatures was a team effort. Individual training, speed, and cunning meant nothing during the fight. One man could not do the job. Soldiers and comrades had died for that one golden moment that marked the difference between success and failure. Now, they had to learn to operate as a team instead of individuals, or none of them would survive. Afterwards did not concern LaBonner. Killing the Kaiju did. He owed it to the fallen.

LaBonner clung to one bit of good news. Somehow, the *Javelin* had destroyed nine of the incoming Kaiju, leaving only a single pod to deal with in the first wave. He didn't know how, or if anyone had sacrificed themselves to accomplish it, but he was grateful. Earth needed any break it could get. He needed the specter of an endless number of Kaiju lifted from his troubled mind. They slowly whittled down the number of Kaiju in Europe. Eliminating nine of the new creatures en route hinted at the possibility that someone had a plan for the other twenty on their way.

They had come to Dobbins because NASA had predicted a 90-percent probability that the Kaiju pod would strike the East Coast somewhere between Myrtle Beach, SC, and Jacksonville, FL. He could not shake the uncomfortable sensation that he stood in the center ring of a giant bulls-eye. He glanced upward at the sky hoping he didn't see a bright dot growing bigger.

Caulder caught him staring at the sky. "We still have a few hours."

"Maybe their watch is fast."

Caulder's face turned even grimmer. "If it strikes the ocean, the tsunami will wipe out half the cities on the coast, but it will give us more time to prepare. God help me, I'm praying it strikes the ocean."

LaBonner understood Caulder's coldness. Caulder was not callous or unfeeling. People were going to die no matter where it landed. The more prepared his team was, the better chance they had of destroying the Kaiju.

"They're evacuating the cities along the coast," LaBonner responded.

Evacuating the larger cities and coastal islands in twenty-four hours would be next to impossible. Many had only one or two exit routes that did not lead either north or south along the coast. The smaller cities stood a better chance, but without knowing where the Kaiju would strike, any place to which they evacuated could be in the target zone.

"Good luck with that," Caulder answered.

The truck pulled up with brakes screeching and stopped in front of them, followed by the stench of overheated brake fluid and scorched brake pads.

Caulder shouldered his pack. "Taxi's waiting."

LaBonner did the same, but winced as the heavy pack dug into tender flesh. The truck conveyed them to a cinder block building housing the Georgia National Guard Reserve, their new home for the duration. The governor had already dispatched the Guard to the coast. Next came the part LaBonner detested – the waiting. He was a man of action. Faced with danger, battle instinct and training took over. You made spur of the moment decisions. Sometimes they cost lives. During battle, you didn't have time to do a running analysis of your actions. That came later. Downtime, especially when waiting for the next battle, allowed time for retrospection. His men had died. He might never know if he could have saved them, but every decision, each move weighed heavily on his mind.

He could not dismiss the nagging doubt that rose above all others that everything they did was for naught. The aliens had proven resourceful and determined. They had already dispelled all the theories put forth by so-called experts as to their resources, which now seemed unlimited. They could stand off five billion miles and toss monster Kaiju at Earth until the planet crumbled under the onslaught. If nothing he did counted, was he foolish to throw away his life so cavalierly? His gut told him to head for the deepest desert or the highest mountain and bury himself in a deep hole.

Of course, he couldn't run away, abandon his comrades or his duty. He was a soldier. Everyone was afraid, but not everyone could fight. What separated him from the masses was that gift or curse that made first responders like cops or firefighters heroes. They ran into burning buildings or toward the sound of gunfire when everyone else ran away. It was a tough job, but somebody had to do it. Unfortunately, this time, it was him.

The team killed time by watching television, but found an unusual scarcity of news about the Kaiju rampaging in Europe, as if they didn't exist. Bad news was bad advertising. Only a fleeting banner scrolling beneath the commentator warned of the Kaiju targeting the southeastern coast, as if it were an approaching storm. Instead, reality shows, talk shows, and news programs about politics dominated the airwaves. The people most affected by the Kaiju didn't need to know, and those yet unaffected didn't want a reminder of what lay in store for them.

One local news story attracted his attention. The camera showed a knot of protestors marching down Peachtree Street carrying Judgment Day signs. They all wore black with a white cross emblazoned across their chests like some band of medieval Templars. He had heard of the group, people who believed the Kaiju were dark angels sent by God to cleanse the world of sinners, but he had never encountered any. He found it difficult to believe sane people could encourage the Kaiju, and even more difficult to believe they could actively work toward Armageddon by setting fires and destroying buildings.

"Insane fuckers," he mumbled at the screen.

LaBonner watched the news with his attention divided between the screen and the men who would soon be fighting by his side. He knew three of them by name – Caulder, Warski, and Vance – and had a nodding acquaintance with a couple more. Most of the others were young raw recruits. The Romans called them *tirones,* untested in battle. They had trickled into Lakenheath from all over Europe. The only thing that concerned him was that they were willing to die. He didn't want them to die. He wanted them to get the job done and go home to their families. Enough men had died already. Too many.

Caulder, Warski, Vance, and he had the same look in their eyes, the vacant battle weary stare from seeing too much, too many friends die, too many civilians die, and too many monsters. The others' faces displayed fear. That was to be expected. A man or woman would be a fool to face a Kaiju unafraid, but their young faces also showed a touch of excitement, as if beginning a great adventure against which they could test their worth.

The long sleep his beaten body had demanded at Lakenheath had helped heal his superficial wounds, but it needed more than a few hours' sleep and Band-Aids to heal properly. His blistered skin had tightened and threatened to split every time he moved. The shrapnel wound in his side throbbed constantly. He refused the pain pills offered by the base physician. His mind was cloudy enough without the additional fog of medication.

Confined to the base, they ate, dozed, played cards, and watched television. The one thing they did not do was speak of their experiences, not even when the new recruits asked. The only advice LaBonner offered one concerned soldier was, "You can't prepare for it. You just try to stay alive long enough for the perfect shot. Don't make any plans for the future." It was dismal advice and not the words of support the fresh young recruit had expected, but LaBonner had no encouragement left in him.

LaBonner watched television, losing himself in its mindless programming. The Kaiju arrived two hours early. He watched its approach on CNN, a blazing fireball low in the sky. Instead of striking the ocean off the Eastern Seaboard as predicted, it crashed less than sixty miles northeast of Atlanta in Commerce, Georgia, a small town near Interstate 85. The impact extinguished the entire population of 6,500 in a blinding flash of light, so quickly that no one knew what was happening. The impact created a dark cloud of smoke and dust that rose a mile high into the afternoon sky, blocking out the sun. Molten rocks the size of SUVs spewed from the crater and fell like brimstone on the surrounding countryside. Homes not demolished instantly by the impact burst into flame from the heat wave. Summer desiccated pastures and rain-starved forests quickly became blazing infernos. Superheated hurricane-force winds swept outward, incinerating anyone caught outside without shelter.

The 7.2 magnitude quake that followed the impact raced outward in a concentric circle, leveling buildings, bridges, and power lines. In Atlanta, shattered windows cascaded onto the streets from high-rise buildings downtown and in Buckhead. A Marta train jumped the buckled tracks and crashed into Brookhaven Station, creating a roadblock across Peachtree Road.

The barracks building shook for a full minute, knocking photos from the walls, cracking the ceiling, and upending tables and other furniture. The flat-screen television fell from the wall just as the power failed. LaBonner held onto the suddenly alive chair in which he sat, as it took him for a wild ride across the room. Then, as suddenly as it began, it was over. Sirens began wailing in the distance, as the city awoke to the crisis.

"Well, that was fucking different," Vance said, picking himself up off the floor. He rubbed the back of his head where it had banged the tile.

His hand came away wet from blood. He glanced at the blood, and said, "Shit."

Caulder pinned each man in the room with a hard stare. "Garb your gear. It's time to earn our pay."

LaBonner picked up his pack and weapon and strode for the door without looking at his fellow team members. His pulse pounded in his temple from a migraine, but he had given Thayer all his aspirin three days ago. He gritted his teeth and forged on.

K-Team Zulu loaded onto a UH-60 Blackhawk helicopter and was in the air within ten minutes. The runways were active with FA-18 Hornets loaded with AIM-7F Sparrow short-range and AIM-9 Sidewinder medium-range air-to-air missiles. A few carried BLU-26 cluster bombs outlawed by international treaty but revived as an efficient method of killing Fleas. The pilots nicknamed the bombs "Black Flags" after the flea spray. The 20mm M61 Vulcan cannons in the nose of each Hornet were effective against both Wasps and Fleas. The loud whine of the twin GE F404 turbofan engines as the Hornets took to the air drowned out the sound of the Blackhawk's engines, curtailing any possible conversation. It was just as well. No one felt much like talking.

Unlike the first Kaiju to arrive on Earth, which took hours to emerge, the Kaiju in the later European attacks became active within minutes. Within an hour, swarms of Wasps would control the skies above the craters, and hordes of Fleas would sweep outward in all directions. The Hornet pilots would have their hands full avoiding the often-suicidal Wasps. AH-1 Cobras, UH-1 Iroquois 'Hueys,' and UH-60 Blackhawks like their transport vehicle would strafe Fleas and Wasps with 7.62mm Gau-17A Gatling guns, 7.62mm M60 machine guns, 20mm XM-197 cannon, AIM-9 missiles, and 70mm *Hydra* rockets.

When the skies became too dangerous, the choppers would retreat to attack the leading edge of the advancing Fleas. The tactics had proven effective for the first few hours, but LaBonner had witnessed such attacks many times. Eventually, by the time the second wave of Wasps and Fleas hatched, they all failed. The Fleas and Wasps were fearless and relentless, and their greater numbers overwhelmed any attempt to stop them from the air. Each hour the Kaiju remained alive, it produced hundreds more Fleas and scores of Wasps. The only effective way to stop a Kaiju was a controlled nuclear explosion. If K-Team Zulu failed in their task, LaBonner was certain the military would resort to a larger nuclear bomb. In that case, the aliens would still win by default.

The size of the crater astounded LaBonner when he caught his first glimpse of the smoking pit reaching down to the bowels of hell. He had seen the massive craters blasted in Indiana and Nevada by the first Kaiju.

The craters from the European monsters were smaller. The crater below was bigger than Meteor Crater in Arizona. The impact had peeled back layers of gray Georgia clay in a three-hundred-yard-wide strip for half a mile, gouging deeper into the earth toward the crater end of the furrow. The splintered trunks of trees, demolished buildings, mangled vehicles, and strands of barbwire fencing lined the channel plowed through the Georgia countryside.

The crater was slightly oval, over a mile wide and more than five-hundred-feet deep. Black smoke poured from the crater and rolled along the ground, partially screening the ebony Kaiju pod deep within the crater. Patches of molten rock were visible through the smoke and haze. A ridge of shattered earth surrounded the pit, reaching a hundred feet in height at the terminus. Every building, farmhouse, and bridge within a six-mile radius lay flattened by the force of the impact and the aftershock.

As the Blackhawk approached the crater, the dense smoke roiling from the crater parted, allowing LaBonner a brief view of a dark shape moving just out of view. He leaned out the open door for a better look. The object was much smaller than any Kaiju he had seen. As its entire shape and size became distinguishable, his chest heaved with dread. The alien pod disgorged not a single giant Kaiju, or even two, but hundreds of smaller creatures, each ten feet in length. They scurried from the crater like baby spiders from a disturbed web and spread out in all directions so quickly LaBonner soon lost sight of them.

"Giant spiders! That is way fucked up," Vance said. His right hand rested on the glass of the door, as his gaze shifted to follow the Kaiju Spiders pour out across the countryside.

"I counted at least a hundred," Caulder said over the headphones, "maybe more." His voice expressed the disgust that LaBonner, too, experienced at the unsettling sight of giant alien spiders.

"This changes things," LaBonner replied. "Our nukes are useless."

"We've got Wasps," the pilot called out, as he banked the chopper sharply.

LaBonner focused his attention back on the pit. A large swarm of Wasps appeared through a break in the smoke. They had emerged fully developed from the pod. The aliens had once again changed tactics and caught them unaware. Instead of a giant Kaiju, they had sent smaller mobile units, Spiders and Wasps. K-Team Zulu had no time to prepare a proper defense. The aliens had sent an invasion force. The thought of twenty more similarly laden inbound pods sickened LaBonner.

He shook off the melancholy that gripped him. "Do we go after the Wasps or the Kaiju Spiders?" he asked Caulder.

Caulder stared out the window for a moment. Then, his face grew dark and grim. "Neither. Let the Air Force handle them. We're not equipped for a ground war against Spiders. We'll go back to base and regroup. We need some armored vehicles and heavier firepower. Take us home, pilot."

The Blackhawk dropped until it barely skimmed the tops of trees and power lines. The Wasps remained near the crater, forming a large swarm, and ignoring the chopper. Seconds later, the first group of F-18s began firing missiles into the swarm. It was like stirring a hornet's nest. The Wasps broke into small formations and went after each aircraft. LaBonner watched two F-18s go down with their engines clogged by Wasp bodies before he turned away. The pilots were valiant, but too few to make a difference.

"Those Spider things are herding back together," Vance announced. "They're headed southwest."

"Toward Atlanta," LaBonner said. "They'll reach the outskirts in a few hours."

"We'll be ready for them," Caulder said.

On the way back, as the chopper flew over Jefferson, Georgia, LaBonner noticed an elementary school at the edge of the small town busily loading children onto a line of buses. A quick count showed more children than buses. A line of buses waited on the road, blocked by fallen power lines. A Georgia Power crew worked feverishly to remove the debris, but it would take time, time the school did not have.

LaBonner patted Caulder's shoulder. "We have to help them." At first, he thought Caulder would refuse, but as he stared at the children and teachers milling about the parking lot in confusion, he nodded.

"Set us down in that field just east of the school," he ordered the pilot.

The pilot swung back around over the school and landed in a cornfield 200 yards away. The rotor wash flattened sun-dried stalks in a big swath, reminding LaBonner of a crop circle.

"Leave the nuke rocket launchers on the chopper," Caulder said. "Bring extra ammo."

They spilled from the chopper on both sides of the vehicle and fanned out. They had only minutes before the first of the Spiders would reach them. Two of the team carried modified Mk 46 machine guns. Gas-operated and belt-fed, the 7.62mm weapons had a maximum range of 3900 yards and fired 710 rounds per minute. Two men lugged EMG-148 *Javelin* anti-tank rocket launchers over their shoulders with SCAR 7.62mm rifles for backup. Four more formed two M224 60mm mortar squads. Caulder carried an M107SASR .50BMG sniper rifle, and

LaBonner had his SCAR 7.62mm. The small arsenal that would have been effective against any human foes, but LaBonner wasn't sure it would be of much use against Spiders. No one knew what the creatures were capable of or what it might take to bring one down.

They didn't worry about the Wasps. The Blackhawk lifted off immediately after they disembarked and remained in the area to protect them, as did the F-18s. The sky above them filled with the streaks of Sidewinder and Sparrow missiles and the chatter of M61 20mm Vulcan cannons. Occasionally, one of the F-18s would swoop over the field low enough to rustle the corn stalks, the shriek of their engines sounding like banshees from hell. Cobra and Huey helicopters arrived and worked the fringes of the Wasp swarm with their GAU-17A Gatling guns, M60 machine guns, and 70mm rockets.

LaBonner followed the battle with one eye, as he scanned the fields for sign of the Spiders. The cries of the children crying and the frenzied yells of the teachers fought for dominance over the sound of the battle in the sky. Listening to their pitiful cries, the cold pit of fear in his stomach gave way to the burning desire to kill. His finger ached from its position on the trigger of his rifle.

"I see them!" Vance yelled out.

The two mortars began firing, raising geysers of dust and smoke four hundred yards away. The first Spider came into view, climbing out of a ditch and striding over a fence. Others appeared behind it, a phalanx of black obsidian monsters standing six feet tall and ten feet in length. Unlike the Kaiju's segmented, angular body, the Spiders' body was smooth and rounded. A dozen multi-jointed legs sprouted from the cephalothorax, each tipped with three claws for grasping. The most forward pair of legs were shorter and raised in the air near the vertical mouth, which was surrounded by four tentacles, each three-feet long. Two large red eyes dominated the oval-shaped head. LaBonner wondered if the resemblance to spiders was intentional to strike fear into the beholder. If so, it worked.

The Spiders ignored the mortar explosions, striding through them at a pace much faster than a human could run. One lucky hit ripped off one Spider's leg, but the injury barely slowed it. Another creature, blown into the air by an explosion directly beneath it, landed upside down but quickly righted itself and continued. At three hundred yards, one of the rocket launchers fired. The *Javelin* missile, designed as anti-tank weapons, proved more effective than the mortars. The Kaiju armor-tipped missile destroyed its target. It at least proved the creatures were vulnerable. One man fired a second *Javelin*, but the Spider stepped aside from the missile's path. The *Javelin* struck an embankment and exploded behind it.

"Get ready!" Caulder sang out.

The Spiders – LaBonner counted over a dozen – had reached the edge of the cornfield. LaBonner followed their movement by watching the tops of dried stalks divide and fall as the creatures plowed through them. Vance cut loose with the Mk 46 machinegun, hacking a swath through the cornrows like a scythe. He concentrated on the lead Spider. LaBonner was relieved to see chips of ebony armor fly from the creature's head, as the Kaiju armor-piercing rounds struck. Finally, the creature tipped over and fell dead, its legs twitching in muscle spasms.

LaBonner picked up the Mk19 grenade launcher and fired six quick bursts into the midst of the Spiders, shattering legs and chipping away at their armor, but killing none. Caulder with his M109 SASR .50BMG sighted in on a Spider's eyes and fired. Spurts of yellow blood proved he had hit his mark, but even sightless, it still homed in on them using sound. LaBonner emptied the grenade launcher and picked up his SCAR. The SCARs, Caulder's SASR, and Mk46s were less effective against the Spiders than against Wasps, but they made a dent in the opposition. At close range, less than fifty yards, the armor-tipped rounds began penetrating the creatures' Kaiju exoskeletons. Six more quickly succumbed to their overlapping fields of concentrated fire. The remaining creatures halted their charge and attempted to bypass them, sensing easier prey ahead.

However, one Spider suddenly veered back in their direction and broke through their line before anyone could stop it. It leaped forward and landed on one of the men, a young recruit named Nixon. Its weight bore Nixon to the ground, and then savagely attacked him with its legs, chopping him apart. The creature's intense rage saved LaBonner, who stood only a few feet away from the dead man. He dove to the ground and rolled away, firing his weapon into its underbelly. Vance swung on it with the Mk46, standing face-to-face with the creature, and refusing to back down. Under the combined heavy assault, it retreated; then, swerved and charged a second soldier with his back toward it. He turned at the last moment. The Spider slashed at him with one of its clawed legs as he fell away. He went down with a deep wound in his chest.

The other Mk46 joined Vance. The two closed the distance with the Spider. Chunks of ebony armor flew from the creature's head. They continued chipping away until bullets began to strike exposed alien flesh. The Spider tried to back away, but it had waited too late. Another burst from the machineguns, and its legs folded under it. It collapsed dead on the ground.

The three remaining Spiders tried to flee, headed away from the school. One of the men fired the last *Javelin* missile. It struck a Spider's abdomen from the rear and killed it. The other two disappeared into an adjacent cornfield. The Blackhawk pilot, still circling overhead, noticed and went after them with its machineguns blazing. It returned a few minutes later. One of the gunners held out his thumb in a victory sign.

LaBonner strode over to the wounded man. The soldier clasped his hands to his chest, but blood seeped around the edges of his hands. "I'm hit," he said. LaBonner slapped his hands away to check the wound. The gash was six inches long but not deep. The young man's nametag read "McKay." LaBonner grabbed a bandage from his med kit to staunch the bleeding.

"You're lucky, McKay. You'll live and have a nice scar to show the girls in the bars."

"I'll live?" he asked. The look on his face showed disbelief.

"For thirty or forty more years." The answer seemed to satisfy McKay. He lay back on the ground and closed his eyes, as LaBonner sprinkled disinfectant powder into the wound and wrapped it with a bandage.

Caulder checked the dead man, Nixon. They could do nothing for him. The creature had slashed him so badly he was barely recognizable as human. Caulder reached down and took his dog tag, squeezing it in his fist.

"We got a dozen of them," Vance announced, pleased with himself.

"Another hundred or so are still out there somewhere," Warski reminded him. Warski had come through the fight uninjured, but splotches of Nixon's blood mixed with Spider blood smeared his uniform.

"They'll head to Atlanta," LaBonner said. "More people, more chance to do some damage."

Caulder nodded. "Yeah, you're right. We're going to need bigger weapons next time."

"And more men. This isn't a special ops detail. We're facing a horde of giant Spiders instead of a single Kaiju. We need some armored vehicles."

"I'll call the chopper."

LaBonner helped the wounded man to his feet. He moaned from the pain. Even with one dead and one injured, they had been lucky. Their first battle with the new Kaiju threat had not gone well, but they had saved the school. He watched as the last bus pulled away from the parking lot. He was certain that if the Spiders had been intent on killing them, they would have finished the job. They were just an obstacle between the Spiders and their destination – Atlanta. Next time, they would have to bring their A-game or the city would die. He had watched one city die. He did not want to witness a repeat on American soil.

17

August 16, *USS Assegai* –

Walker edged his way across the crowded room through the press of bodies, trying not to offend anyone. If not for the zero gravity allowing people to float horizontally above one another, traversing the space would have been nigh impossible. Each person wore their bulky space suit, further eroding any personal space, but with no room for both personnel and their suits, it was the only viable option. They did not wear their helmets. That might come later, as the air ran out and only suit oxygen remained. Walker did not care to think about that eventuality.

Fifteen hours had passed since disembarking the *Javelin*, just enough time for everyone to grow edgy and cranky. Neither he nor Sakiri could do much to alleviate the tension. It built slowly like ripples in a pond, but when it reached a crescendo, it would become a tidal wave. His own nerves were beginning to fray around the edges, but he could do nothing about that either. Presently, he was more concerned with Gate. They were nearing the time Gate had estimated it would take to intercept the pods. They would have no way of knowing if Gate and Peters had succeeded, or if the ten Kaiju pods had changed course on their way to destroy them or the *Assegai*. With no long-range detectors, any attack would be sudden and devastating. He tried to avoid that dark thought, as he searched for Costas. The sergeant could at least keep his team occupied to avoid any chances of conflict with the Air Force personnel.

He found Costas hanging onto a strap attached to the wall. "How are you doing?" he asked.

Costas' face turned bright red. "It's embarrassing floating around with a diaper load, but I couldn't hold it any longer."

"There are a lot of people here in the same situation. It's better than passing around a bucket."

Costas grimaced. "Whew! In Zero-G that would be nasty. It's just that I can't work up the balls to approach any of the women, not in my delicate condition."

Walker suppressed a grin and patted Costas on the shoulder. "You're a real hero, Costas, above and beyond the call of duty."

"I'll take my frustration out on the Nazir. When's our ride coming?"

They had not heard from the *Assegai* for eight hours. She had increased speed by fifteen percent, the most the engineers at NASA would allow. He had to assume everything was still on schedule. Even then, it was only a best guess. The *Assegai's* course was slightly different from the *Javelin's* due to the launch time difference. In addition, they had to locate the tiny habitat module in the vastness of space. He gave Costas the only answer he could. "Thirty-five hours or so."

"Tell them I'm pissed. Maybe that'll speed them up."

"Get our guys breaking down and reassembling their weapons. That might kill some time." Breaking down weapons in Zero-G was a challenge. Small parts tended to drift away unnoticed. The purpose of the exercise was to impress upon them the differences in the environment in which they might be fighting.

Costas guffawed.

Walker raised an eyebrow. "Is there a problem, Sergeant?"

"No problem, Major, but I've had these guys field stripping their weapons so often, they can do it in their sleep. It won't keep them amused for long."

Walker waved his arms in the air. "Have a weenie roast, sing some songs, anything; just keep their minds occupied, or we'll have a melee in here."

"Yes, sir."

Costas drifted off toward Alpha Team. Walker hugged the wall, searching the room until he found Sakiri discussing tactics with another pilot. He stared pointedly at the second pilot until he floated away to leave the two men as alone as they could be in the crowded space.

"Are you sticking to the same plan?" he asked.

"In thirty hours, we'll fire one of the *Lance's* gravity drives for two minutes at intervals of thirty minutes," Sakiri said. "It should help the *Assegai* home in on us but not attract unwanted attention from our neighbors. At the same time, we'll try to detect the Kaiju pods."

"Do you still consider them a viable threat?"

"I consider all threats viable." Sakiri's voice remained neutral, but Walker detected the edge of uncertainty in it. "If the *Javelin* fails, the

Nazir can figure out where we are quickly enough. If they arrive before the *Assegai* ... Well, the battle begins here."

Walker understood that placed them at a serious disadvantage. In space, speed was important. If the Kaiju pods sought them out while they were stationary, it would be a short battle, at least for the men in the module.

Walker shook his head and smiled. "You don't know Gate Rutherford. He won't fail."

"I wish I had your faith in him, I really do. I agreed to forward the plan to higher authority only because it offered a chance to alleviate some misery on Earth. If we fail in our mission, it will have become a moot point."

"If it succeeds, the real battle on Haumea starts two days late. Eisenhower had to reschedule D-Day several times before we landed in Europe."

"The Allies knew what to expect when they hit the beach. We don't. We have no reliable intel. We don't know if we're facing a small Kaiju-building outpost or the buildup of a massive invasion force."

Sakiri's statement struck home. Uncertainty had been the U.N.'s big worry, that beyond the orbit of Haumea, an alien invasion fleet waited for the monster Kaiju to decimate Earth's defenses before attacking Earth. Walker believed otherwise. He prayed he was right.

"Well, it sounds like a sage idea. I'm all for anything we can do to make it easier to find us."

"I won't make any new friends among this lot," Sakiri said, frowning. "To use the airlock to man the *Lances*, we'll have chase everyone out and cram them into the remaining available space. We can recycle the air, but tight quarters will heighten already taut tensions. We must stay on top of arguments and dissention lest it build to conflict."

Walker understood that Sakiri was referring to his team. Sakiri did not believe his pilots would resort to such crude behavior. He allowed the insult to slide. "There won't be room to do much but yell, but I get your point."

To Walker, the worst part of waiting was the uncertainty whether Gate's plan had worked or if he and Peters were still alive. He still regretted that he had let Gate go without him, but Gate had been right. His place was with his team. Even with the firepower of the *Lances*, he suspected it would take a boots-on-the-ground effort to stop the Nazir. Then, Allah willing, he and Costas could return to Earth to take on the Kaiju Gate could not stop.

* * * *

The *Assegai* arrived thirty hours later, nearly six hours ahead of schedule. After 45 hours of listless waiting, the crew of the *Javelin* welcomed its arrival with a spontaneous celebration. Sakiri and Walker allowed a few minutes of hugging, handshaking, and Zero-G dancing before herding them out the airlock to dock the *Lances* with the *Assegai* and transfer personnel. Sakiri insisted they attach the *Javelin's* aft module that had served as home to the rear of the *Assegai*. "We might find a use for it once we reach Haumea," he explained.

Walker didn't argue. The task took his mind off Gate for a short while, but he was eager to get underway and begin the search for Gate and Peters. The *Assegai* started her gravity drive and pressed forward toward Haumea. He was glad to have near normal gravity once again. One thing he had learned during the ordeal was that his body did not like zero gravity. His mind preferred a distinct up and down for reference, and his legs preferred walking rather than swimming through the air.

Searching for Costas, he found him in the galley. The sergeant noticed Walker's entrance and called him over.

"Man, even this crap beats that concentrated stuff. I was afraid to eat until I changed my diaper and took a real crap." He jerked his thumb toward the bathrooms. "You might not want to go in there without your helmet."

"Thanks for the warning." He eyed Costas' meal and decided it didn't look good enough to risk eating. A knot in the pit of his stomach gnawed away his stomach lining. He would get no relief until he learned Gate's fate. "You look like you're feeling better."

Costas lowered his spoon and looked up with a humiliated expression. "I was in a low spot. I felt like a senior citizen wearing my Depends diaper waiting for the nice nurse attendant to come around with my meds. I'm not cut out for this close-elbowed dumpster living. I need some space to move about and real air to breath, even that crappy, damp-assed Limey air at Lakenheath."

"We're on our way again."

"Yeah, seven more days of this. I can't wait."

"Plus ten days for the return trip, remember."

Costas ate a spoonful of his meal and looked at him sideways. "Yeah, well, I'll count those days when it looks like I might need to."

Costas' statement summed up the general air of the entire crew. Waiting had taken the edge off. No one believed he or she would survive the mission. Some thought it doomed from the beginning, an enterprise undertaken solely to appease the masses on Earth promised a quick victory by the politicians. The myth of the mysterious unseen Nazir had grown larger than the Kaijus destroying Earth's cities. Walker had seen such pessimism infect entire companies in Iraq where every person encountered on the streets could be a suicide bomber or an ISIS operative, every car, truck, or garbage can an IED. It raised doubts about the mission. Survival became more important than solution, shooting first more effective than waiting.

"That shit stops right now," he snapped at Costas, who jumped in surprise. "You're too good a soldier for that. If we die, we die, but we do the job first. Dying isn't hard. You just forget why you're fighting, and death will find you in a heartbeat." He looked around the suddenly quiet galley and raised his voice so that all could hear. "We came to do a job – stop the enemy. Stop the enemy. We can't win this war at home." He pointed toward the front of the ship. "The enemy is that direction – Haumea. That's where we're going. When we get there, we stop them any way we can.

"You all volunteered for this mission. I want all of you to make it home. Some won't. Maybe none of us will, but we'll complete the mission first if it's humanly possible. The mission is all. It's why we came. If you think your life more important than some civilian's on Earth whose city is under attack by the Kaiju, then you can remain on the ship with the technicians. It's no safer, but maybe you'll feel better. I only want men and women ready to do the job beside me when I put boots on the ground."

The silence that followed concerned him. He hadn't meant it to be a rousing speech; he was just venting, but he did expect some reaction, good or bad. Finally, one soldier in the corner called out, "Hoo ah!" Others quickly chimed in. Soon, the entire ship resonated with the call. He didn't know if he had stirred their hearts or won their minds, but he had gotten their attention. Sometimes that was enough.

Costas looked up with a sheepish grin on his face. "Sorry. I've always been by your side, Major. I just don't like this damned, insufferable waiting." He clenched his fists and waved them in front of him. "In Iraq, we choppered in, hiked in, drove in, or whatever, but we got there and the mission started. This being cooped up for days on end gives you too much time to think about things. I don't like it. It fucks with your head."

"This, coming from a man who lay in a puddle of his own urine for twelve hours to get a shot at an ISIS leader." He reached out and clasped Costas' shoulder. "I never doubted you'd do your job. I just want you to make that date with the Demarcos twins."

Costas grinned. "Yeah, they're both double-jointed. You wouldn't believe how they can –"

Walker released Costas' shoulder and chopped his hand in the air. "I don't want to hear it. Save it for your memoirs."

"Memoirs, schmemoirs, I'm gonna sell it to HBO for a movie of the week."

"You do that, but after you eat, have the team clean their suits. They probably need it."

After leaving Costas, he went forward to the bridge and found Sakiri already there. Both members of the *Assegai* crew were with NATO, Captain Stefan Renatto and Lieutenant Ki Ngabe. Blivens and Worthen had lost their bridge bunk space and now shared quarters with the Lance crew. Goodman, who operated the ship's environmental systems, had retained his berth, but he looked uncomfortable around so many military personnel.

"Thanks for picking us up," Walker said to Captain Renatto.

Renatto threw him a wave. "No problem. It was going to be a long trip with only Ki to talk to."

"You made good time."

Ngabe grinned. "We decided to push the engines a bit past the limits. They performed excellently."

"Can we reach Haumea in five days instead of seven?" Walker asked. Losing almost two days waiting had put them behind schedule.

Ngabe's frown spoke volumes. "That might be unwise. I can perhaps increase speed another two or three percent. It will shave a few hours off the trip." He glanced at Sakiri. "With the colonel's permission, of course, but any higher might compromise our magnetic shield."

Walker nodded. The magnetic shield produced by the gravity drive protected them from deadly cosmic rays and micrometeorites. "I see. I will appreciate anything you can do. My men are getting antsy." He did not want to admit that he, too, was growing restless.

"The *Javelin* succeeded. Only one pod escaped."

The news was a welcome relief. "Have you picked up Lieutenant Peter's *Lance*?"

"Nothing yet, but if he's out there, we will find him."

Walker nodded. He hoped they were right.

"A bit of bad news, I'm afraid. They're at the far edge of our scanners, but it appears the second group of Kaiju has increased speed."

"Any change of direction?" Sakiri asked.

"No, still on course for Earth. They may arrive a few hours earlier than expected. It might affect where they land."

"Have you notified command?"

"Yes, they are aware of the situation."

Whatever the situation on Earth, there was little that Walker could do about it. For the next seven days, he was just a passenger. All he could do was sit and hope they found Gate.

Costas burst onto the bridge a short while later. The sergeant's ruddy cheeks were even redder, his eyes flashing with anger, his voice almost a low growl, as he held out a soggy piece of paper.

"I found this in the toilet. Someone tried to flush it."

Walker was reluctant to take the wet paper, but something in Costas' voice told him it was important. He glanced at it and his stomach rolled. It was part of a Judgment Day recruitment pamphlet. Someone on the ship had brought it aboard. He looked at Costas. "This isn't good, Sergeant. We can't afford to allow a Judgment Day acolyte to sabotage the mission."

"How do we find him, or her?" Costas added.

That was the problem. They would need many pairs of eyes to watch the group, but whom could they trust? "Colonel?"

Sakiri's dour expression matched his own. "I'll review personnel files. I have one or two of my team I trust implicitly. I'll ask them to move about discretely and make observations. We should not make anyone else aware of this. If there is an acolyte aboard, he or she will become more difficult to ferret out."

Walker stared at Costas. "Sergeant, you don't have a discrete bone in your body. Talk to Cantrell. She's a little more subtle. She might have more luck."

"Yes, sir."

Costas' news disturbed him. They faced enough perils without the risk of sabotage by a religious fanatic. The means of destroying the ship or its killing its occupants were too numerous to list. The severity of the danger depended on who the fanatic was. *As if fighting an alien army wasn't enough.*

18

August 16, Aboard a *Lance* adrift in space–

Staring at the relative position of the unmoving stars, Gate was certain the *Lance* was stationary; however, Peters insisted the gravity drive was operating at near 100 percent. Unless the gravity distortion bubble that shut down their power had subverted all the laws of physics, they were speeding at close to 40,000 mph toward their rendezvous point with *Assegai*. He couldn't be certain of anything, except the fact that each breath reduced their chances of survival. In a movie, one of them would insist on dying so that the other might have all the oxygen and live long enough for a dramatic rescue. That was the movies. Even if either wanted to, they couldn't exchange their suit tanks while they were moving.

He had almost depleted the battery on his laptop trying unsuccessfully to pinpoint their exact location. He had used the last few minutes of power to record a message for Walker, unsure if he would ever hear it. Part of the message was technical data concerning the gravity drive overload. The rest was of a more personal nature, things he could not tell Walker in person. As he had spoken into the microphone, he had tried to put his disjointed thoughts into a coherent form. Now, as he listened to his own shaky voice, stared into his gaunt, worried face, he wasn't certain he had succeeded.

"Walker, the data I've included might help our war effort. I hope so. Earth deserves better than it has received, at least, most of it does. There are still a lot of selfish, foolish people who never seem to learn, even when the end of the world is likely. You're not one of them. You're one of the most decent human beings I've met. We're poles apart, but we share the same goals, and I'd like to think we've become good friends. I would venture inside a Kaiju with few people. In fact, you're it, you and Costas.

"I've watched a lot of people die, too many, and it made me angry enough to want to do something. Looking back, I was foolish to insist on tagging along when you went inside Nusku. I couldn't take care of myself and probably cost the lives of some of your men watching out for me. For that, I'm deeply sorry. I learned things about myself inside that, that monster. You probably went through the same kind of catharsis in your line of work – your first mission, your first kill, wondering if you were making a difference. You came out the other side a hero. No, don't be modest, Aiden. You are a hero in every sense of the word. You walk into a situation fully aware you might die, knowing only that you will do your best and save lives whenever possible. That's what a hero does.

"I came out cowed and afraid, a deep, cold fear that wrapped itself around my bones and wouldn't let go. The memories haunted my sleep and some of my waking moments. If the Nazir hadn't sent Kaiju Kiribati, I don't know what would have happened. I hate to think about it. There were times, late at night when I was alone … Well, I didn't. Maybe I was too afraid for that way out too. Kaiju Kiribati dropped me back into the fray, kept me from thinking. I buried myself in my work, but it didn't help. Did you know I went to a shrink, Aiden? I guess not. I didn't tell anyone. I surprised myself. She diagnosed it as depression and prescribed *Celexa*. The drugs screwed with my mind so badly I had to stop taking it. Acupuncture helped a little, but not enough to face the needles. I've always hated needles. In the end, I chose alcohol and jazz.

"I tell myself the director backed me into a corner when she convinced me to come on the *Javelin* mission, but in truth, I was already in one, a corner I walked willingly into. I guess I wanted revenge more than I was afraid of dying. Have you ever felt that way? Has that kept you going when others might falter? I'm glad I came. I think I did some good. Maybe a few more people on Earth will live because of what I did, what Peters and I did. I hope I haven't killed you and the others with this plan. I would like to have been in on the end, but I guess –"

The image flickered a few times and the screen went blank. He glanced at the flashing low battery light. The rest hadn't been important anyway. He checked his watch – twenty-one hours had passed since the explosion. That left another hour before they would have to rely on suit oxygen. He did not want to spend his last hours inside his suit breathing canned air. How should he spend his last day on Earth, or, at least near Earth?

"Did I hear you talking back there?" Peters asked.

"Just listening to a recording. I was hoping for some jazz, but my battery's dead."

"I prefer classic rock myself, you know, Aerosmith, Guns and Roses, Zeppelin. Something I can dance to."

"You won't do much dancing out here."

"You got that right. My seat is as tight as a Scot's purse. At least you can spin in circles in your seat."

Gate smiled. "Not anymore. No power."

"Oh, yeah. I forgot. What do the stars tell you?"

Gate sighed. "We're still on course."

"You think."

Gate caught the sarcasm in Peters' voice. "We're headed in the right direction. We should reach the rendezvous point in two hours. Then, we wait for our ride."

"Sounds easy when you say it real fast, but, really, what are our chances?"

Gate considered the question. "Sixty-forty."

"I think you're being generous. If the *Assegai* was delayed or anything happened … Well, at least we won't have to wait too long."

"And the view is spectacular," Gate added. "I'm sorry, Peters."

"Not your fault. I volunteered. You were right. We did some good. I always knew one mission would be my last. It looks like this is the one."

The finality in Peters' voice disturbed him. "Don't cash in your chips yet. We still have a chance."

"With no radio or sensors, we wouldn't know if they flew past us. We make a pretty small blip on a radar screen."

"As long as the jump drive is working, they can pick us up on a gravity wave detector."

"Maybe, if Jupiter doesn't mask our drive. I'll have to shut it down soon, or we'll continue well beyond our rendezvous spot. I can't even circle because without a visual it might become a spiral. That could doom us as surely as missing our rendezvous. Without the drive, we're just another speck floating in space."

"They'll come," Gate replied, but he wasn't sure if the queasy feeling in his stomach was from his nagging doubt or his last meal.

* * * *

"It's time to cut the drive," Peters announced.

Gate checked his watch and hoped his estimate of their location was accurate. Some of it he derived from visual clues – the position of the stars, the location of Jupiter – but much of it was just a guess based on estimated speed. The only thing accurate about the entire process was the time. His watch didn't lie and it said they had four hours of oxygen left.

They had been on suit oxygen for two hours. By his best estimate, the *Assegai* would not arrive for another two hours. It would be much closer than he was comfortable with.

"Looks like the spot," he remarked, trying to lighten the situation.

"Cutting the drive." There was no sensation of speed reduction. The view outside the canopy did not change. "I guess we wait."

"How long have you been flying, Peters?"

"Six years. I flew an F-18 in Afghanistan and made a few sorties into Syria before volunteering for the *Lance* project. I wouldn't fly anything else now. These babies are great. I feel like Neil Armstrong every time I strap in."

"Married?" As he asked, Gate kicked himself mentally for such a delicate question.

Peters answered without hesitation. "No. Times are too uncertain for a wife and kids. Maybe later."

"Sure. Later."

"How about you?" Peters asked.

"No wife, cat, dog, or girlfriend. No time for distractions."

"Got that. There's no certainty until we defeat the Nazir. I just want one more chance at them."

"We struck quite a blow with the *Javelin*."

Peters' voice dripped rage, as he said, "Yeah, but I didn't see them die. I want to see a real Nazir and watch him die under my guns. Then, I can die happy."

"We'll get there."

"You believe that?"

Gate understood Peters' skepticism. "With all my heart," he answered. His answer surprised him. In spite of the odds, he believed he would see Haumea. Going home – that was too far beyond his scope of vision.

"I wish I had your conviction. All I got is hope."

"Sometimes hope is enough."

"We'll see in about four hours."

* * * *

They sat in silence, each man embroiled in his personal conflict between hopes and regrets. Gate's gauge read 1.4 hours oxygen left – 84 minutes. At his normal 15 breaths per minute, he estimated he had 1,200-1,300 breaths left, less if he panicked. He had no desire to count them, tolling his death like counting rosary beads. He fought back the ghastly thought of choking, gasping for air that wasn't there. It was not a nice way to go. He wished his laptop were working. He badly wanted to hear some jazz to soothe his frayed nerves. At the lowest point in his life, he had toyed with the idea of suicide but could not go through with it. Now, it seemed the better option. He could shut down the air scrubber on his suit and choose to die of carbon dioxide poisoning instead of gasping for his last breath.

Maybe his last act should be to open the canopy of the *Lance* and float free of the ship to drift slowly toward the sun, and eventually to be spewed out again as new star stuff. He stared at Vega, 25-light years distant. Thousands of years ago, it had been Earth's northern pole star. In 12,000 years, it would once again be the Pole Star. Would he still be drifting in space as the Earth slowly wobbled back into alignment with Vega?

He resisted looking at his watch, but the urge overwhelmed him. He now had 62 minutes of oxygen remaining. What if his gauge was wrong? What if this breath was his last one? He considered one last word with Peters, the man who had risked his life and would ultimately pay with it to offer him a chance to escape certain death aboard the *Javelin,* but he suspected Peters was preparing himself for the end. What if he was already dead? The thought created a surge of panic in his chest he at first mistook for lack of oxygen. He had waited long enough. If he had the courage to crawl inside a Kaiju, surely he had the courage to choose his own end.

He accessed his suit computer. After fumbling through the menu a couple of times, he located the suit functions parameters. He reduced the scrubber by thirty percent, hoping it would allow him time to drift into unconsciousness before his air ran out. He gazed out the canopy at Vega, deciding it was not a bad star to die under. It was in the Lyra constellation, the Harp. It was serenading him in frequencies he could not hear. It was twice as large as Sol but only a tenth as old. Vega was the fifth brightest star in the night sky. Because it burned bright, Vega and the sun would die near the same time.

The star flickered. At first, he thought it was because of Vegas rapid rotation, which made it seem to dim and flare over time, but this seemed too sudden. Maybe his mind was playing tricks on him. He checked his oxygen. According to his gauge, he had another 10 minutes left – a lifetime. Then, slightly behind the *Lance*, movement caught his eye. The Angel of Death coming for him? No, nothing so dramatic. He swiveled his seat to look and gasped at the sight of the *Assegai.*

He tried to keep from yelling with joy, as he frantically brought his scrubber back online. "Peters! Our ride's here."

* * * *

August 16, *Assegai* –

Walker remained on the bridge as the *Assegai* searched for the tiny blip of a *Lance*. The process was slow and laborious. He mentally hurried them, but they worked as quickly and as diligently as possible.

"Got it!" Renatto shouted.

Walker strode quickly to Renatto's station. "Where?"

Renatto pointed to a peak in a wave graph. "There. About 1.2 million kilometers out."

"1.2 million kilometers, how could –?" He stopped as he realized Renatto had said kilometers. He made a rapid mental conversion to 750,000 miles. The *Assegai* could cover that distance in a few hours, but would they reach them soon enough? "Can you contact them?"

"They're running dark. No radio signal or telemetry."

"Why would Peters run dark?"

Renatto shook his head. "I don't know. Low power?"

"We need to go faster."

As Renatto glanced at Sakiri, Walker realized he had overstepped his authority. Sakiri nodded.

"Six hours is the best I can do without killing all of us."

Walker hoped it was fast enough.

He refused to eat or leave the bridge. Only the bridge's cramped quarters kept him from pacing. He should have been with his team, but he hoped Costas understood his concern. He and Gate had gone through a lot, and he shouldered a responsibility for him, like a big brother. Three hours later, when Renatto announced, "I've lost the gravity drive signal," he could only assume the worst.

Sakiri had more faith. "Peters would have shut down the drive when he reached the rendezvous point. He's a good pilot. He will fire it up again when he thinks we're nearby to give us a fix."

Walker appreciated Sakiri's attempt to lessen the blow, but he suspected as well as did Sakiri that Peters and Gate's oxygen supply was running low. They could already be dead. He drove that dark thought from his mind. Gate was a survivor. They would find them alive. He would cling to that thought.

A commotion in the galley attracted his attention. He tried to ignore it, but Sakiri was less inclined. He took two steps toward the hatch, but then backed up when one of the weapons specialists burst onto the bridge holding an MP5K in his hands, waving it back and forth.

"You must stop this ship," the man said. "It's against God's word to continue."

Walker kicked himself mentally for failing to secure the weapons after Costas had found proof of a Judgment Dayer aboard the *Assegai*. The 30-round magazine could kill everyone on the bridge and damage the delicate equipment before someone stopped him.

"Put the weapon down, Blaylock," Sakiri ordered.

Blaylock whirled on him, aiming the weapon at his belly. "No! I didn't act earlier because I thought the Kaiju would stop us. Then I realized God waited for me to act. A human must shed his blood in sacrifice."

"I'll shed your blood for you, Blaylock," a gruff voice yelled from the galley. Walker recognized it as Costas.

"Shut up!" Sakiri ordered. "Look, Blaylock. Sometimes it difficult to understand God's will, but do you really think that he would want you to kill everyone aboard the *Assegai* and doom Earth?"

"Earth is doomed."

"Then why would God want to stop us? Do you think God is afraid of us?"

Blaylock shook his head, but his gaze never wavered. "God fears nothing. He is omnipotent and all seeing."

Walker understood what Sakiri was trying to do, calm Blaylock down with reason, but he doubted Blaylock was swayable. He had come with the intent of destroying the *Javelin*. Now, he would destroy the *Assegai*. He would try to carry out his plan, and people would die. It was even possible stray weapons fire could damage the ship enough to compromise its structural integrity.

"Blaylock, you can't believe –"

"Don't tell me what to believe, Colonel," Blaylock snapped. "You are a heathen. God is not interested in what you think. I'm not interested in what you think." He pointed the MP5K at Renatto. "Push the gravity drive to maximum."

"I won't. The drive will overload." Renatto crossed his arms over his chest. Walker hoped Renatto didn't push the deranged Blaylock too far.

"That's the idea. Now, do it."

Renatto shook his head. "I refuse."

Walker looked into Blaylock's eyes and saw madness and anger. His right cheek twitched. He would shoot Renatto. It was time to act.

"Costas, are you seeing this?"

"I have eyes on him, Major," Costas replied from the galley.

Blaylock swung on him. Walker stared into the barrel of the MP5K and saw how steady it was in Blaylock's hand. He was no longer frightened. He was determined. He realized he could not destroy the

140

ship, but he could kill the upper echelon. Walker hoped he didn't pull the trigger before he could act. His belly itched from the thought of a bullet slicing into his gut from five feet away.

"You won't accomplish anything, Blaylock. You missed any chance you might have had. You blew it because you didn't want to die. At most, you might kill one or two of us before the others bring you down. They'll toss you out the airlock without a suit." He took another step forward, slowing moving to Blaylock's side. Blaylock's gaze locked on him. Beads of perspiration dotted his upper lip. As Walker hoped, he moved as well to keep Walker at a distance. Walker continued, "Your eyes will freeze first. You'll feel them freezing, burning like fire as the last breath of air leaves your lungs. You'll be blind by the time your flesh begins to freeze, but you'll still feel it. Oh, yeah, you'll feel it. You will die alone, in the dark, a billion miles from home, and accomplish nothing."

At first, Walker thought he might make it to Blaylock to disarm him, but something snapped in the man. His face paled, as he raised the MP5K. "No! I'll take you with me. I'll kill all of you."

Blaylock was in position in front of the hatch. "Costas," Walker called. Blaylock tried to turn, but groaned and slumped forward, Costas' knife embedded in the center of his back. Walker lunged and grabbed Blaylock's arm, but not before the dying man's finger pulled the trigger. The MP5K exploded beside Walker's head, followed by the loud hissing of escaping air. He wrenched the weapon from Blaylock's dead hands.

"Someone please place a patch on that leak," Sakiri shouted. Men rushed to comply. A minute later, the hissing stopped. Sakiri stood over Blaylock's body. "You didn't have to do that, Major. I could have –"

Walker cut him off. His ears still rang from the noise of the shot, and his eyes watered from the flash. He had been lucky. A couple of inches more and he would be dead. "With all due respect, Colonel, I don't think you could have. He was a dangerous, unhinged man with a loaded weapon. We got off lucky."

"Perhaps, but he was under my command."

"Yet a member of Judgment Day managed to hide it from you and join the *Javelin's* crew. How did that happen?"

"We might have learned more from him. If Sergeant Costas hadn't –"

"Costas acted under my direct order. If not for him, more people might have died. Frankly, I don't care about Blaylock's motivation. He posed a serious threat."

Sakiri noticed the stares leveled at the two of them. "We'll speak more about this later in private."

Walker took a deep breath to calm down. His heart still raced from the adrenalin rush of fear and excitement. He could not let his emotions taint the discussion. Too much was at stake.

"If you wish, Colonel, but I suggest we lock up the weapons until needed."

Sakiri paused a moment before nodding curtly. Sakiri had taken the fact that the culprit was one of his men too personally. Walker thought he might have as well if their roles were reversed. He regretted creating a possible wedge between them, but it was up to Sakiri to move on. He hoped that time would make him see reason. In the meantime, he would grill his fire team to find out if Blaylock had an accomplice.

* * * *

When they reached the location of the last fix on Peters' *Lance*, they found nothing. Sakiri ordered all *Lances* to execute a search grid of the area. Placing all his ships in jeopardy was unlike the Air Force colonel, but Gate understood they could not waste too much time. The enemy waited at Haumea.

Sakiri had not broached the subject of the Blaylock incident. They had spaced the body out the airlock after a short ceremony. Walker noticed few hard stares leveled at him and Costas, but no one had said anything. Whatever feelings they may have had for the dead weapons specialist, they realized Costas had saved their lives.

For an hour, none of the *Lances* reported anything; then, "*Lance* 7, here. I see them. I'll go alongside to give you a beacon."

The news made Walker lightheaded. They had found a silver needle in a pitch-black haystack, but were they too late.

"I see movement. Yes, they're both alive."

Walker released his pent-up breath.

Sakiri took the com. "*Lances* 7 and 9, help Peters and Rutherford into your craft and hook them to ship's oxygen. They must be nearly dry. *Lance* 2, tow *Lance* 11 back to the *Assegai*. We'll close on your position, *Lance* 7."

Sakiri grinned at Walker. "Don't worry, we'll get them back."

Walker wanted to hug Sakiri but thought it might send him into apoplexy. Instead, he shook his hand, and then saluted. "Thank you, Colonel."

19

August 15, Atlanta, GA –

LaBonner surveyed the men standing around the hastily assembled convoy. They were a motley crew of National Guard stragglers, Air Force military police with a few flight crew thrown in, and an Army infantry platoon originally bound for training at Fort Benning. Until the main force of the 29th Infantry and the M1 Abrams tanks and Bradley fighting vehicles of the 69th Armored Division arrived from Ft. Benning, they would be the ones holding the line – 106 men and women, who, to LaBonner, looked too young to be out of school much less defending the jewel of the South. As with most battles, men and women too young to understand what they would be facing would fight this one. For some, it would be their first and last fight.

The convoy consisted of six deuce-and-a-half trucks for transport, each towing an M102 105mm howitzer. Four men, including Warski, claimed some knowledge of the howitzers' operation. Caulder placed him in charge of the battery. The others would receive on the job training. Eight Humvees mounting two 7.62mm M60 machineguns and two M136AT4 anti-tank weapons, and two eight-wheeled Strykers with a 105mm M68A2 gun and a .50 caliber M2 Browning machinegun rounded out the convoy. LaBonner took his place in the lead truck with Caulder, who had command of the mission. His expression revealed his thoughts on his troops. As a member of Kaiju Killer Team Foxtrot, Caulder had worked with pros – men and women specially trained for the job. Now, he would face a deadly enemy with untrained personnel. LaBonner watched Caulder's gaze flick from man to man, as he tried to size them up, determine who was up to the task.

LaBonner didn't feel like fighting a battle, but he was adamant in arguing against Caulder's suggestion he remain behind to heal properly. The fight with the Spiders had ripped open a few of the stitches in his side, but he didn't have time to have them seen to. When they had dropped off the injured man, McKay, at the base hospital, he had pilfered a bottle of acetaminophen to help numb the dull ache. Ready or not, the Spiders were coming. A little pain helped him focus. Besides, a few aches and pains meant little to a man dying from radiation poison.

Where the giant Kaiju had been slow and plodding but impossible to stop with conventional weapons, the Spiders were small and swift, scattering out over the countryside to make them more difficult to track. Their goal was simple – kill as many humans as possible. The Air Force unloaded on the crater but not before a second batch of Spiders emerged. Now, several hundred of the creatures, as well as scores of Wasps, were bound for Atlanta. They appeared in no hurry. Small scavenging groups broke away from the main body to attack towns and farms. The Air Force could not bomb them while in populated areas. Until they again massed for the attack on Atlanta, the jets and helicopters merely harassed them.

Near Norcross a few miles outside the I-285 Perimeter, the Spiders finally regrouped along I-85, which pierced the heart of the city like a dagger. Smoke rose from Jimmy Carter Boulevard, one of the main East-West thoroughfares crossing I-85, less than 20 miles away. The smoke came from businesses and homes reduced to rubble by the swarm of creatures and by bombs and missiles from F-16s and F-18s. To the people living in the homes, it mattered little that they were collateral damage. Their lives were irrevocably shattered, their futures left in doubt.

Before the convoy moved out, two men rolled up on Harleys. They parked their bikes and walked over to the LaBonner's truck. Both sported long beards and colorful tattoos peeked from beneath the sleeves of their jackets. LaBonner recognized an army vet when he saw one; mostly by the way they walked. One had an oxygen cannula and tube running to his nose from an oxygen bottle clipped to his waist.

The one with the oxygen bottle stared at him for a moment before saying, "Name's Jackson, Captain. He's Hodges. We were in Nangarhar with the 75th. We want to help."

The 75th Army Rangers had fought ISIS and the Taliban in one of Afghanistan's most dangerous provinces. The pair had seen serious action. LaBonner did not doubt their experience. Since the arrival of the Kaiju, LaBonner didn't know if any troops remained in Afghanistan. More dangerous things than ISIS now faced humanity.

"Talk to him." He pointed to Caulder. "He's in charge."

"You're on oxygen," Caulder pointed out.

"That's 'cause I'm dying, sir. Picked up some damn bug in the desert. I figure I can sit at home and wait for the Grim Reaper, or go out and find the dark bastard like a man oughta. I can operate a Ma Deuce like a fucking pro. Hodges here can feed the bitch." He scanned the frightened faces of the young troops on the trucks. "Seems to me you could use some talent."

A lump formed in LaBonner's throat when Caulder nodded and said, "Climb on."

LaBonner handed Jackson a 7.62mm SCAR from a stack at his feet as he climbed into the truck. Jackson picked up two grenades from an open crate and stuffed them in his pockets as well.

"Thanks," he said. "I'll put these to good use."

In spite of the news reports and the arrival of the alien pod, the city had not quite awakened to the threat of the Spiders. LaBonner expected southbound traffic to be heavy as the city evacuated, but a nightmare snarl of traffic filled all the lanes, like a rainy Friday afternoon before a holiday weekend. People didn't know where they were going; they just wanted to leave. Thousands of turn signals blinked as frustrated drivers tired switching from one slow-moving lane to another. A constant susurration of honking horns and belligerent voices provide the background music for the nightmarish evacuation. The convoy bulldozed its way through the snail-paced line of vehicles, the big deuce-and-a-half truck shoving vehicles out of the way when necessary, leaving in its wake a throng of angry drivers and dented vehicles.

Near the exit for Roswell Road, they passed a group of protestors beside the road haranguing the motorists. A solid black banner bearing a white cross and the words Judgment Day flew over them.

"I'd like to frag the lot of them," Warski said, sneering at the small crowd.

The group saw the military vehicles and their yells and chants became more frantic. The gunner in the leading Humvee pointed his machinegun at them, and the chanting subsided.

Warski spat over the side of the truck. "We should use them for target practice."

"Save the fight for the Spiders," LaBonner advised.

Squadrons of F-18s and F-16s had followed and harassed the swarms of Wasps from the crater, eliminating half of them, but the deadly creatures had taken their toll on aircraft as well. Low on fuel, the jets had returned to base to refuel and rearm. Slower, but well-armed A-10 Thunderbolt IIs poured steady fire into the advancing Spiders, as HH-60 Pave Hawk helicopters kept the Wasps off their backs. Fires sprouted in a score of locations. A pall of dark smoke slowly spread over the area obscuring visibility beyond a few miles.

LaBonner glanced at the men in the truck with him, a nine-man infantry squad. A sense of deja vu threatened to overwhelm him, punching him in the gut like a hard-knuckled fist, as the bloodied faces of his dead K-team replaced the faces swimming before him. He fought back the survivor's guilt plaguing him. Swallowing hard, he allowed the anxiety bleed away like the last breath of a dying man. Dying wasn't hard when it was inevitable. Only the slim hope of surviving made facing death difficult. They were the first responders, the men and women called on to hold the line until the main force arrived. They were throwaways, disposable. They would keep the enemy engaged for as long as possible.

The Spiders, whether by plan or simply from seeking the easiest path, congregated along I-85 as they neared Atlanta, sweeping through businesses and homes on both sides of the corridor, leaving a mile-wide swath of destruction as they scampered toward the heart of the city. Caulder decided to make their stand at the intersection of I-285 and I-85, the Tom Moreland Interchange, known more colloquially as Spaghetti Junction for its multi-layered, twisted ribbons of concrete and asphalt that brought heart palpitations to most residents and intimidated all visitors. Missing one's exit could add miles to a trip in search of a place to exit and turn around for a second attempt.

The convoy would not have this problem. They were going nowhere. First, they had to clear the interchange of vehicles by blocking all east and westbound Perimeter traffic and diverting it south onto I-85. The process was slow and arduous, made more difficult by irate drivers. LaBonner, tired of the harassment and verbal abuse, leveled his weapon at one particularly garrulous driver and threatened to shoot him. The tactic worked. The driver shut up and cooperated. Finally, the way cleared, Caulder directed their convoy vehicles to various on-ramps and off-ramps. By taking positions along the westbound lanes of the perimeter, he set up a multi-layered and multi-leveled defensive ring, allowing them to fire down onto the Spiders from different locations and to bring to bear firepower from different groups on one target. LaBonner approved of Caulder's tactics, but doubted they could hold for the three or more hours until ground reinforcements arrived.

They placed the howitzers in a vacant lot beside the northbound lanes of I-85 inside the perimeter, with a spotter on the overpass to direct fire. The objective was to decrease substantially the enemy's numbers before engaging them with small arms fire. They could do nothing about the continued southbound traffic on I-85, but as the Spiders drew closer, people would abandon their vehicles and flee on foot. If not, dying by friendly fire was no worse than the fate that waited them from the alien creatures. With a certainty, civilians would die. They were already dying. Their deaths added precious minutes of preparation time to the main battle force assembling to defeat the Spiders.

LaBonner urged the Spiders forward. The day was dying, and he would rather fight them in the daylight than at night. A night battle would be confusing and cost more lives. When the stream of southbound vehicles slowed, and then became a trickle, he knew the Spiders were getting near. A pickup truck loaded with boxes and furniture was the last vehicle through. Small groups of pedestrians followed. The lull afterward announced the arrival of the Spiders.

Breaking through the low-hanging shroud of smoke like birds of prey, an A-10 dropped to ground level to unload on the Spiders. Nose-mounted GAU-8 rotary cannons fired 3900 depleted-uranium, armor-piercing rounds per minute. The whir of the seven spinning barrels pierced the low growl of the twin jet engines. A second Warthog followed close on its heels and released two laser-guided bombs from only a hundred feet above the ground. The twin explosions hurled burning vehicles, chunks of asphalt, and pieces of Spiders in all directions. The concussion rocked the Warthog. The brave pilot risked death by shrapnel to deliver his ordinance on target. He waggled his wings as he passed overhead to indicate he was the last aircraft in the immediate area.

Moments later, the 105mm howitzers began firing. At first, the firing was sporadic as the inexperienced crews learned their jobs. The noise was a raging thunderstorm a few yards from his ears. He cupped his hands over his ears to muffle the noise. The shells fell well short of the main body of Spiders over six miles away, inflicting more damage to the highway and surrounding buildings than to the Spiders. However, the Spiders were nearing the range as quickly as their twelve legs could carry them. Even an untrained crew could drop shells in the same area twice in a row.

LaBonner was more concerned about the Wasps. He was certain the helicopters had not eliminated them all. Acting as aerial support, wherever there were Spiders, they would also find Wasps. Searching the skies, he noticed several ominous dark shapes embedded in the churning smoke. He nudged Jackson, who had set up the .50 caliber Ma Deuce beside him, and pointed upwards.

"We're expecting visitors."

Jackson tilted the barrel of the .50 caliber. His face remained calm, but his eyes revealed the hatred and turmoil within. LaBonner imagined the same look was visible in his eyes. Hodges, sitting beside him, gripped the ammunition belt tightly and scooted a second ammo box closer. His expression was serene, almost blissful. Like LaBonner, both men had come expecting to die, but they intended to do some damage first. Their example encouraged him. LaBonner picked up a loaded RPG launcher, rested it on his right shoulder, and sighted toward the spot he had glimpsed the Wasps.

The Wasps were clever; using the smoke screen as cover, they came within a hundred yards of the interchange before attacking. Machineguns on two of the Humvees began firing just as Jackson cocked and fired his Ma Deuce. The .50 caliber chattered away, as he swung the barrel back and forth searching out targets. Slowly, as they noticed the Wasps, others began firing at them as well. The Wasps dove at the men on the overpasses, buzzing them like mosquitoes at a backyard barbeque.

LaBonner picked one cluster of Wasps, followed them with his sight, and fired the RPG. The rocket soared skyward, struck one of the Wasps in the abdomen, and exploded, killing two of them and injuring two others with shrapnel. Silently cheering, he watched their bodies fall to the ground. The two injured ones crawled around trying to escape, but bursts of machinegun fire killed them. He didn't get cocky. There were plenty more Wasps waiting for a chance to kill them.

Their combined firepower held the creatures at bay for a while, but eventually, enough of them slipped through their defenses to cause havoc. A Wasp snatched a man from the overpass, thrust its stinger into his chest, and dropped him over the side. He fell screaming thirty feet to his death. Another descended on the gunner of one of the Humvees, using its forelimbs to hack the man to pieces. The driver inside the Humvee poked his SCAR through the opening and fired point-blank into its head. Small pockets of battle raged everywhere. Several of the creatures landed together on the overpass and attacked a Stryker vehicle. Their sharp claws dug deep gouges in the armored steel and ripped the rubber tires to shreds. The gunner inside the Stryker attempted to lower the .50 caliber remote-controlled machinegun to sweep the Wasps from the vehicle, but the barrel would not deflect sufficiently. One soldier foolishly left the safety of the vehicle through the rear door to fire at them with his weapon. The Wasps swarmed him and killed him; then, rushed inside the vehicle, killing the entire crew and knocking it out of commission.

LaBonner dropped his PRG, saving it for Spiders, and grabbed his SCAR-H, using it to ward off Wasps intent on attacking Jackson and Hodges on the .50 caliber. The untried collection of soldiers and airmen fought well, but the aliens had designed the Wasps as fearless, tireless fighting machines. As the battle dragged on, men tired and weapons jammed or needed reloading. A single distracted moment was enough for the Wasps. LaBonner watched as men and women died all around him. He could do nothing to help them, instead channeling his rage into killing Wasps.

As twilight fell, the muzzle flashes of the howitzers drew Wasps like moths to a porch light. By full dark, the howitzers were silent, their crews dead. So too had the gunfire lessened from the pockets of resistance. One Stryker, three Humvees, and less than two dozen men remained. The firing became sporadic. He had lost track of Captain Caulder and Sergeant Vance, but they were veterans of such battles. He was certain that, like him, they had managed to survive.

LaBonner was not sure why the Spiders had halted their advance. Perhaps it had been to allow stragglers to catch up or to allow the Wasps to wipe out the defenders. They could have easily gone around the howitzer fire, or attacked in coordination with the Wasps and overwhelmed the defenders. Instead, they waited just out of range until the howitzers presented no more threat before advancing. As if aware their black coloring would act as camouflage in the dark, the Spiders attacked just as the sun slipped beneath the horizon. A flare soared skyward from off to his right. Its brilliant glare revealed a sea of Spiders shoving aside abandoned vehicles and surging forward, crawling over vehicles and concrete construction barricades. He stared down at the mass of creatures and saw in their numbers the end for the small band of remaining defenders.

He picked up the RPG and began firing rockets as quickly as he could reload. He didn't need to pick individual targets. Anywhere a rocket landed struck a Spider. He delivered death and destruction in epic proportions; yet, the number of Spiders seemed not to diminish. Jackson's .50 caliber Ma Deuce joined the remaining armored vehicles and the lighter weapons fire. A blaze of tracers crisscrossed the battlefield like a grid map. The only sound from the Spiders was the steady tapping of their legs as they scurried along the highway, punctuated by explosions and weapons fire.

A large band surged up one ramp and attacked the remaining Stryker vehicle. Its weapons operator continued firing even as the creatures rolled it over and shoved it through the concrete guardrail onto the pavement below. It burst into flames and exploded a few moments later. No one escaped. The Stryker gone, the Spiders rushed up the ramp toward him. LaBonner turned his RPG on them, but there were too many. He fired his last rocket and picked up his SCAR-H.

More Spiders climbed the concrete supports and scampered over the sides of the ramps surrounding them. Men's screams pierced the night, as the creatures ripped into them. LaBonner fired his weapon into the face of a Spider rising directly in front of him. It raked his chest with one of its short feeding legs, ripping open his shirt and slicing a gouge in his chest armor. If not for the armor, the blow would have sliced him open. He fell back, as Jackson's .50 caliber raked it. The Spider toppled backward off the ramp into the darkness below. Then, the machinegun went silent. Hodges sat back on his heels staring at the empty ammo belt as if it was his fault.

"That's it," Jackson said, picking up the SCAR rifle. "No more ammo."

The screams of the dying faded as their numbers dwindled. Small pockets of gunfire dotted the ramps and the roadway below. It was too late to try to regroup. They would die as they fought – alone and in the dark. LaBonner reloaded his weapon with his last magazine, and faced the horde of Spiders pushing up the ramp toward him.

Suddenly, a spotlight burst into life above him, flooding the ramp with light. The beam swept across the river of Spiders, revealing their malevolent hungry eyes. Machinegun fire tore into the first rank of Spiders, ripping them to shreds. He glanced to his side and saw a Pave Hawk helicopter rising above the level of the ramp. The gunner standing in the open doorway fired his GAU-17/A Vulcan minigun with deadly accuracy. From twenty yards, the 7.62mm armor-piercing rounds tore through the Spiders like BBs through cream cheese. The Gau-17/A was the big brother to the M134 Gatling gun Chalmers had used so effectively against Wasps in Paris, firing 6,000 rounds per minute. The gunner swept it across the line of Spiders, concentrating his fire until one creature was dead before moving to the next.

The pilot risked crashing the helicopter by hovering beside the raised roadway. A man stepped to the door with an Areas *Shrike* 5.56mm machinegun. LaBonner saw that it was Vance. Vance fired until the 200-round soft pouch magazine was empty, tossed it aside, and waved for them to climb aboard. He ignited a handful of flares and tossed them in front of the line of advancing Spiders.

"It's not time to die yet, Jackson," LaBonner said. "Let's go."

The three men raced for the chopper. LaBonner emptied his SCAR as he ran. Vance reached down and pulled him aboard. The sudden yank started a fire blazing in his injured side. He bit back on the pain and turned to help the others inside the chopper. As he watched on in horror, a Spider crawled up the side of the ramp, balanced on the concrete railing, and leaped at Hodges, pinning him to the ground. The creature's legs became a savage blur, stabbing repeatedly into Hodges' back until they came away dripping with blood.

Seeing his friend in trouble, Jackson stopped running. He glanced at LaBonner, wheezing from lack of breath, and apologized with his eyes for what he was about to do. He ripped the oxygen cannula from his nose and produced two grenades from his pockets. Guessing Jackson's intent, LaBonner searched the helicopter for a weapon, but the Vance's *Shrike* was empty, and the GAU-17/A gunner was busy holding back the Spiders. He watched on helplessly, as Jackson pulled the pins from the grenades with his teeth and ran at the Spider screaming like a banshee.

The Spider thrust a foreleg into Jackson's chest, skewering him. Jackson stood erect, his body trembling from muscle spasms. Using his last remaining strength, he pitched the grenades underhanded. They rolled beneath the Spider and exploded. The blast ripped Jackson from the impaling leg and hurled his crumpled body backward against the concrete guardrail only inches from his friend Hodges' body. The Spider disintegrated, as hot shrapnel sliced through its torso. The concussion rolled the helicopter, throwing LaBonner hard to the deck. He slid across the deck and slammed into the edge of the opposite door, bringing on a second bout of pain. The pilot banked sharply to avoid a collision, gunned the engine to lift it above the roadway, and turned toward the city.

A thud drew LaBonner's attention to the open doorway where the gunner had stood. He was no longer there. A Spider was. It had made a tremendous leap from the elevated roadway to the moving chopper, throwing it off balance with its added mass. The pilot fought the stick to keep the chopper level. Unarmed, LaBonner watched helplessly as the Spider slowly surveyed its surroundings as if deciding which human to kill first. Vance, unarmed, stood, and faced the creature. LaBonner did not have time to consider options. He shoved Vance to the deck and charged the Spider with his combat knife. Before he could reach it, the Spider lashed out, catching him in the side with one of its legs. The blow didn't slice deeply, but the pain brought tears to his eyes.

The co-pilot did not have a safe shot with his AR-15. Instead, he slid it across the deck toward LaBonner. He went to his knees as he moved, snatched up the rifle, and slid beneath the Spider. The edge of one gnashing mandible caught him in the chest. He fought down the sudden burning pain, jammed the barrel of the AR-15 just below its head, and squeezed the trigger. He emptied the magazine into the creature. Hot Spider blood splattered his face and hands. The pilot tilted the chopper even farther to the left to send the injured Spider over the side. Both LaBonner and Spider slid toward the open door. LaBonner grabbed the mount for the GAU-17 and hung on. The Spider slid past him and tumbled into the darkness below.

As he lay there catching his breath, the first of the F-18s arrived. Using the flares as guides, they unloaded their bombs on the Spiders. Massive explosions rocked the area. Sections of ramp collapsed in clouds of concrete dust and smoke. Twenty F-18s made a pass over Spaghetti Junction, reducing it to rubble. A few minutes later, a second squadron arrived, dropping napalm. The jellied gasoline exploded, covering the entire area in a sea of flame visible for miles. Spiders burst like ticks put to the match.

The Pave Hawk hugged the ground as it left the area to avoid the jets, but LaBonner watched the fire until only the glow remained visible.

"How many?" he asked Vance, groaning as the sergeant helped him to a sitting position.

Vance's face was bloodied and bruised, his uniform reduced to rags. When he looked at LaBonner, his eyes told the story. "Nineteen."

"Captain Caulder?"

Vance shook his head. "No. Captain Caulder was not one of them, or Warski." He glanced back at the intersection, now a blazing funeral pyre. "We lost a lot of good people tonight."

As they flew south along I-85, a line of trucks, M1 Abram tanks, and Bradley fighting vehicles rolled northward, the reinforcements. To them would fall the task of mopping up the remaining Wasps and Spiders. They had won, but as always, the price had been high. He had lived, while others had died. It seemed to be his fate to survive when he shouldn't. He grinned.

The co-pilot saw and asked, "What's so funny?"

"Twenty more pods are headed our way. I get to reload and start over."

The co-pilot stared at him a moment. "Man, you need some rest." He pointed to LaBonner's side and chest. "You're bleeding too."

LaBonner reached down and felt his side. His hand came away bloody. He chuckled. "It's okay. It won't kill me."

He didn't think he was slipping over the edge into insanity, but would he really know if he did? He was tired, hurt, and dismayed by the death around him. Death surrounded him like a black cloud, touching everyone but him. Everyone he knew but Vance was either dead or on their way to Haumea to fight the aliens, an almost certain doom. He lay back against the bulkhead and closed his eyes. He wouldn't die until the radiation poisoning drained the life from his body. He would let the docs fix him up and send him back out to do what he did best – kill Kaiju.

20

August 18, Yacht *Doria* –

Pope Clement stood on the crowded foredeck of the yacht *Doria* watching as a young mother breast-fed her infant son. She looked barely out of her teens, skin smooth and unblemished. The child appeared cherubic. The beatific smile on her face relaxed him, reminding him of the Virgin Mary and Jesus. If he accomplished nothing more in his life, at least he had helped save a mother and her child from the perils of the Kaiju in Italy. It pained him that he had forced the separation of families with his decision. He prayed the fathers would soon join them in Malta, though by what means he was uncertain.

To the ire of the crew of the *Doria*, the dozen refugees they had picked up at Marina de San Nicola had just been the start. Once at sea, they had rescued another thirteen people – three men, four women, and six children – from three makeshift rafts in danger of capsizing. The captain warned him that the *Doria* was herself in danger of sinking from the additional passengers, but Johan would not relent. He would allow no one to drown as long as a square meter of space remained. He had given over his cabin to the more urgent needs of a large family, much to the consternation of O'Bannon.

He was anxious to reach Malta. The eighteen-hour voyage had already lasted four days. A host of delays filled his mind with turmoil and his heart with doubt. He wondered if God was guiding him away from the island instead of toward it, throwing obstacles and tests in his path.

Ten hours into the voyage, one of *Doria's* three engines had decided to become uncooperative. Instead of her usual 30 knots, they had limped along on the remaining two engines while the mechanic worked on it, reaching the Sicilian port city of Selinunte midday of the second day out. After anchoring offshore, they had waited a day and a half while the engineer and chief mechanic went ashore for spare parts. Just as they had given up all hope of their safe return, the two had shown up with the marina's owner and his family, their safe passage the price of the needed parts. It took the crew until after midnight to repair the engine.

They found no fuel at Selinunte. The fishing fleet had emptied the marina's tanks as they fled the island. Wishing to avoid large ports such as Marsala and Palermo, they had followed the southern coast to Licata, where they had purchased five-hundred gallons of diesel at four times the normal price. The captain had at first refused to pay such an exorbitant price, but O'Bannon produced a large wad of cash from his jacket pocket and gave it to the captain. Seeing Johan's astonished expression, he had explained, "The Vatican bursar always keeps large sums of money in the safe for such emergencies. I took five thousand U.S. dollars for our journey. This is the last of it."

From Licata, they continued to Gela, where they had finally topped off the 30,000-gallon fuel tanks. These tasks took another full day and a half. Though Malta lay only 300 kilometers away, the captain would not continue without full tanks. Once he had delivered his human cargo to Malta, he and the *Doria's* crew would remain at sea, where they hoped to avoid contact with Kaiju or their attendant host of alien creatures. At Gela, two families left them, hoping to find relatives in Sicily. Johan wished them luck and prayed for them.

On the morning of their fifth day at sea, while drinking coffee with Peter O'Bannon on the flying bridge, Johan finally spotted the coast of Gozo, Malta's northern island. A sense of relief washed over him, tempered by a deep sadness that he had abandoned the Vatican, his home for four years. Its loss would haunt him all his life. So much was lost, not just in irreplaceable treasures or the vaunted Vatican archives, but as a symbol of the Catholic Church; two millennia of tradition destroyed by an alien creature. Upon his shoulders rested the responsibility of rebuilding. He hoped to make it a better church.

He studied the craggy coast of Gozo. "Upon this rock, I will build my church." He found new meaning in the pronouncement of Jesus to Peter.

O'Bannon overheard him, amused. "Better it than me. The original inhabitants built a megalithic structure on Gozo a few thousand years ago, Ggantija Temple. You will have to visit it someday."

O'Bannon knew of Johan's love of ancient buildings. It was why the loss of Rome struck him so hard. "Have you been there?"

"Yes. I spent an entire day exploring the countryside around the temple. Very beautiful."

Johan spotted a gunmetal gray ship approaching from the strait between Gozo and Commotto Island. Machineguns bristled from her foredeck and amidships. "Who is that?"

"That is an Armed Forces of Malta *Protector*-Class patrol boat. The AFM patrol the territorial waters. They have intercepted many refugee boats and rafts from Africa, mostly bound for Italy. I assume they are very active nowadays."

By O'Bannon's dark tone, Johan assumed the AFM had repatriated anyone they intercepted, or worse. The patrol boat veered in their direction and increased speed, throwing up a plume of water behind it. "Will they stop us?" Johan wanted no more delays. During the passage, he had learned he did not like ships. The weather had been mild and the seas calm, but the constant rolling motion took its toll on him. He was eager to plant his feet on firm ground.

"No, we fly the Papal flag. They are merely curious." Even as he spoke, the patrol boat made a lazy turn and headed out to sea. "However, assuredly they will search the ship at Valletta. Our passengers might have a difficult time seeking asylum, as would any refugees these days. Malta is a small island."

"We will give them sanctuary in the church if necessary."

"It may become so. The people of Malta have long memories. German and Italian aircraft bombed the island daily during WWII. Many people died. Italian refugees will not be welcomed with open arms." He looked at Johan. "Some might resent even a Pope."

"It was a dark time in our country's history. I will address the problem as quickly as possible. Besides," he added with a smile, "I will remind them I am Dutch."

"Malta barely supports herself. They import much of their food and water. Perhaps you could direct some of the Church's resources here. It might smooth the way."

Johan smiled at O'Bannon's candor. The Church had lost much, but its resources spanned the globe. "You still love this island, don't you, Peter? Very well, your task will be to divert what funds you deem appropriate to the Church in Malta and to whatever Maltese organizations you think best serve the people." He wagged a finger at O'Bannon. "Keep in mind there are millions of people suffering throughout the world."

As practical as ever, O'Bannon replied, "We must start somewhere."

"Agreed." Johan set his coffee cup on a table. "I must go comfort the children. I can offer them so little else but comfort."

O'Bannon reached into his pocket and withdrew a small brown paper bag. The bag was crinkled and worn through much handling. He clutched it by the twisted top. "These sweet treats might help."

Johan arched an eyebrow. "Is that your much-hoarded stash of peppermints, Peter?"

"Alas, I must give them up sometime. Now, seems appropriate." He offered the bag to Johan.

"God will bless you for this gesture."

"Perhaps he already has. He has sent me back to an island I love."

"Malta. May it persevere as it has through all other invasions."

A scowl creased O'Bannon's face. "This is not Napoleon, the Spanish, or Hitler's Nazis. They were merely evil tyrants bent on conquest. The Nazir are godless alien monsters who wish to wipe us from the face of the Earth."

Hearing the vehemence and hatred in O'Bannon's voice, Johan searched his own soul. He did not know if the Nazir were godless, as O'Bannon asserted. Men proclaiming God's name had spread much death and destruction in the past. God took no sides, but one could take God's side. God had a plan, he was certain. He only wished he were wise enough to understand it.

21

August 23, Atlanta, GA –

LaBonner languished in a hospital bed for eight days, this time the medical center at Dobbins. It was not by choice. The battle with the Spiders had torn open his stitches, and the gash from the Spider mandible had become infected. Colonel Eckhart had insisted he tend to his wounds before joining any fire teams and brooked no argument otherwise. LaBonner didn't mind the confinement as much as he thought he would. His anger at the aliens and his guilt over surviving when his team didn't had driven him to push himself beyond his limits in the fight with the Spiders, and his body had rebelled. Now, every ache, each sharp spasm of pain reminded him that he was only human. If he continued pressing, his body would fail, and more people depending on him would die. He could not always avoid making bad decisions or becoming mired in untenable situations, but he could eliminate his physical weakness as a liability to others.

Therefore, he rested and healed, reluctantly but quiescently. He ate the food the attendant brought to him without complaint, he swallowed the pills the nurse handed him without argument, and he willingly submitted to the battery of tests the doctor requested. He became the model patient. The infection abated, and his wounds slowly healed. He felt he was fit. He was eager for the doctor to discharge him.

On his eighth day in the hospital, his physician dropped by. When he pulled up a chair and sat beside the bed, LaBonner knew this time something was different. He hoped he was getting his walking papers.

"You received an unhealthy dose of radiation in Paris, but not a fatal one," the doctor said.

The doctor delivered the test results without emotion, but LaBonner listened as a fog slowly enveloped his mind. He watched the man's mouth as he spoke, noting the thin, almost bloodless lips and the equally thin mustache not quite touching the upper lip. He stared at the lips, trying to read them to determine if the spoken words matched the lip movements. The words made no sense to him. He wondered if his mind was conjuring what he wanted to hear.

"I ... I don't understand," he stammered.

"Monitoring of the blast area in Paris indicated radiation levels at half a mile radius from the blast zone ranged between 400 and 600 millisieverts. Tests suggest you received a higher initial dosage, perhaps 1,000 m/Sv. Without a blood sample from your initial hospital stay, I'm guessing. At your age, and with the proper anti-radiation regime, such as DBIBB, a lysophosphatidic acid, your chance of dying from a radiation-induced cancer is less than 5%."

LaBonner stared at the doctor in disbelief. "But the burns, my aching muscles, the migraines, my ... my mind." He could feel the radiation worming its way through his body, like a parasite leeching away his life. The doctor was wrong. He knew it.

"The burns are from the heat flash and consist mostly of minor first-degree and some second-degree partial-thickness burns. Your skin will heal with some minor scarring. The wounds in your side and your chest are healing nicely, as is your infection. As to your aching muscles – my God, man, they found you in a collapsed church. Of course you would be sore." He hesitated before continuing. LaBonner read more in the man's shifting eyes than in his words. "As to your mind, what human could endure what you have and not come away confused? Perhaps some counseling might help, but I found no organic causes for your anxiety."

Could the doctor be right? If he were ... "I thought ... I knew ..."

"You were lucky, Captain. The ancient brick of the church might have shielded you from the blast." He shrugged bony shoulders. "Maybe it just wasn't your day to die. I'll get you started on the anti-radiance drugs today." He rose and loomed over LaBonner. "I'll release you later today if you promise to remain in your barracks and continue to mend. We need the rooms for the severely injured."

After the doctor left, LaBonner tried to piece his world back together, but the pieces did not quite mesh. He wasn't dying. It took a while to digest that information. He had been so certain. He had given up on life, had tried to throw it away in the battle with the Spiders. Now, his world was in disarray. It meant he could get back into the fight. He had to get back in the fight. While he lay on his back in bed, the men and women of the 69th Armor and 29th Infantry from Ft. Benning had hunted down and eliminated the remaining Spiders and Wasps. Atlanta was safe for the moment, but the rest of the world was not. Twenty more pods had arrived, four in the U.S. The battle must continue. Quitting was not an option.

The doctor was true to his word and released LaBonner later that afternoon. However, LaBonner did not complete his part of the bargain. He had no time to rest. Given his new lease on life by his doctor, he no longer desired a quick death. As long as he had any fight left in him, he would expend his remaining energy against the Nazir.

When he met with Colonel Eckhart, the colonel looked haggard and older. LaBonner suspected things weren't going as well as the official news reports indicated. He eyed LaBonner standing across from him trying to look the picture of perfect health.

"I suppose you want to get back in the fight, Captain."

"Yes, sir. It's been a week. The doc says I can."

Eckhart didn't argue. Instead, he let out a deep sigh and sagged back into his chair. To LaBonner, it looked as if he deflated, leaving skin and a uniform. "Well, we can use you. I guess you know about the recent incursion."

"Yes, sir, at least what the news channels report, which is pretty skimpy, but it looks bad."

Eckhart nodded. "The aliens caught us flatfooted. Because of the pod that landed here, we assumed the next twenty would be similar, just larger. We deployed our forces around the world accordingly. Three pods landed in Canada, two in Australia, one in India, three in northern Africa, and two in the Middle East. Russia nuked two of the three pods in its territory – one in the city of Perm, just west of the Ural Mountains, and another in Khabarovsk at the edge of China's northeastern border. The third landed near Petersburg. Instead of only Spiders and Wasps, the pods contained two giant Kaiju, as well as hundreds of Spiders and Wasps. They swept through the city within hours, killing tens of thousands.

"China fired several land-based *Dong Feng-11* short-range ballistic missiles at the pod in Xi'an, simultaneously vaporizing it and the tomb of China's first emperor, Qin Shi Huang, and his terracotta army. A second pod landed just outside Beijing. One of the missiles destined to destroy it went astray, landing in the heart of the city, killing an estimated 11 million people. Alarmed by Russia and China's indiscriminate launches, the nuclear member nations of the United Nations have readied their nuclear arsenals. Son, the world's going bat-shit crazy."

The news was dire, but LaBonner's concern was the U.S. "What about the four that landed here? The news is kind of sketchy."

Eckhart grimaced. "That's because almost everybody in the vicinity of a pod landing is dead, and any forces we send in to stop the Kaiju are quickly destroyed. The four pods landed along a roughly north-south line in the center of the country, from the Texas Gulf to Iowa. One pod crashed eight blocks from the center of Sioux City, Iowa, instantly vaporizing the city and killing 85,000 people. Hundreds of Spiders and Wasps spilled from the pod almost immediately after impact, spreading across the countryside. Thank the Almighty the President decided against using nuclear weapons. Nukes would have been ineffective anyway and would have irradiated thousands of acres of valuable cropland for decades. Troops moved in to surround them to prevent the Spiders from dispersing further. The cornfields of Iowa are now a hot battle zone.

"Something is different about this attack. The two Kaiju from each remained on station beside the pod. They haven't moved. We don't know why, but you can bet your ass it isn't good."

LaBonner now understood Eckhart's haggard appearance. If the Nazir had changed their tactics, the military would be playing catch up, as they had in Atlanta.

"A fleet of B1 bombers saturated the entire area around Sioux City with 1,000-pound CBU-89/B bombs, dispersing thousands of antitank and antipersonnel mines using the GATOR mine deployment system. The mines will remain active for forty days before their batteries deplete. If we haven't stopped the Spiders by then, it won't matter. They will spread across the country like a plague of locusts.

"A second pod crashed halfway between Topeka and Kansas City, Kansas. We fought a bitter battle to bottle up the alien creatures while authorities evacuated the cities, but hundreds broke through the lines and destroyed large sections of Kansas City. We're in the process of pulling back and regrouping. A third pod struck just outside Norman, Oklahoma, and overwhelmed the National Guard defenders in less than an hour. We haven't heard from the area commander in four hours."

The colonel let that bit of bad news hang there a moment before continuing, "The fourth pod landed in Texas City, Texas, just outside Houston. Because of Houston's prominence as a port city and the vital refineries, the President ordered a significant portion of available forces deployed to the area. The lines are still holding, allowing Houston time to evacuate, but Spiders are ravaging towns and communities along the coast from Port Lavaca to Port Arthur. Troops deployed on the I-45 bridge across Galveston Bay into Galveston prevent Spiders from overrunning the city, but bays and lakes don't stop Wasps. The death toll in the city of 50,000 has risen to 12,000, almost as many as were killed during the devastating 1900 hurricane."

The colonel's report stunned LaBonner. 24-hour news channels, unable to enter the affected areas, relied on official reports and detailed a valiant effort to stem the alien tide. Uploaded cell phone videos hinted at a darker outcome, but even they fell short of the full scope of the disaster.

"Are we going to win?" The words slipped out unbidden. He had not wanted to voice his personal doubts.

Eckhart shook his head. "I don't know. If we can't beat them by conventional means, the President will consider a nuclear option."

"I want to be there, sir, with a Kaiju Killer team."

Eckhart nodded. "Assuredly, Captain. We have no experienced personnel available. You'll have to train them on the job."

"Is Corporal Vance still here?"

Colonel Eckhart nodded. "He is. I promoted Vance to sergeant. Take him. Take what supplies you need. Get the job done, Captain."

LaBonner saluted. "Yes, sir."

As he left, LaBonner knew he had no time to spare. He found Vance in the barracks, along with half a dozen other men he did not know. Vance smiled when he saw LaBonner enter.

"I thought you had decided to stay."

"The chow sucked. We've got a mission."

Vance clapped his hands. "About damned time! I've been sitting here on my ass waiting for someone to do something."

"Get everyone armed, equipped, and loaded on the transport in thirty minutes. We're going to Louisiana."

Twenty-eight minutes later, Vance herded the squad onto a C-135 bound for Lafayette, Louisiana, where the army had established a Forward Operating Base to deal with the Texas City threat. 6,000 troops, 200 tanks and armored vehicles, 300 pieces or artillery, and 125 helicopters poised for an all-out offensive against the Kaiju.

When the C-135 landed at its destination and opened its rear hatch, the familiar bayou air hit him in the face like a wet homecoming kiss. LaBonner hadn't been home in four years, but it was as if he had never left. All the memories of his childhood came flooding back. A drizzle of rain fell as he marched down the ramp, and layers of gray clouds laden with moisture heralded the approach of Tropical Storm Deidre working its way up the Gulf of Mexico. If they did not move fast, weather would ground the aircraft and helicopters, leaving the troops in the field without air support.

General Stuart S. Montgomery, in charge of the task force, called for a meeting with all officers. LaBonner gathered with other officers along the edge of the field. Montgomery, a stocky, broad-shouldered man wearing desert fatigues and baseball cap, paced up and down the line with his hands clasped behind his back.

"We will divide our forces," he announced, his voice deep and gravely. "The artillery batteries, the armor, and 5,000 personnel will form a blockade along I-10 east of Port Arthur near the Texas-Louisiana border. Once the area is secure, they will advance westward until they meet the troops north of Texas City. The remaining troops will fly in to relieve Galveston. So far, the aliens have concentrated along the coast, using the bayous and undergrowth as cover, making them difficult to locate and destroy, but eventually they will break out toward Houston. Our job is to stop them."

As someone who had lived his life among bayous and swamps, LaBonner understood the dangers they faced. Rattlesnakes, coral snakes, cottonmouths, and alligators could be just as dangerous as alien Spiders and Wasps. Fields of reeds, ponds covered with water lilies, and cypress swamps could hide entire armies. Except for the occasional dry hummock, anytime they left the road, they would be waist deep in black water. With a storm surge and heavy rains, the water would rise over their heads.

"You officers instruct your men that the line must be held at any cost. We cannot retreat. Okay, dismissed."

LaBonner remained standing where he was.

"What's your problem, Captain?" Montgomery asked.

"My name is Captain Francis LaBonner, sir. I brought a Kaiju Killer team with me. We need a ride to the nearest Kaiju."

Montgomery stared at him for a moment; then, nodded. "I see. I'll have Major Dickerson assign you and your team a chopper. So far, both creatures are just standing there near the pit. We can't get a drone close enough to see what they're doing. God knows what they're up to, but I'll take every minute we get. Once they start moving ..."

LaBonner saluted. "Good enough, sir."

"Once you're on the ground, we can't provide much support. You'll be on your own."

"We always are, sir."

"If the President decides on a nuclear option, we can't give you much warning. It might be impossible to evacuate."

"Understood, sir."

"Gather what munitions you need. Good hunting, son."

"Thank you, sir."

Within the hour, he, Vance, and seven other men were aboard a Blackhawk helicopter cruising south twenty feet above the swamps at 175 mph. They flew in formation with twelve other Blackhawks transporting the first troops to Galveston. Approaching from the south over the Gulf was less risky than a direct eastern approach. They encountered two small swarms of Wasps along the coast, but the creatures paid their armada little heed, as if intent on a destination farther east. He spotted several dark shapes in the murky water below that could have been Spiders or large gators. Wide crushed paths through the reeds indicated Spiders had passed through the area. The pilot radioed in his report. Troops behind them would deal with the Spiders and Wasps. His target was much larger.

The leading edge of the storm buffeted the aircraft mercilessly. A slanting rain blew in through the open cabin door, stinging his face, but he relished the cool dampness that smelled of his childhood. Tropical Storm Deidre was building up to be a major storm front. When it hit land, it would be difficult to see their hands in front of their faces much less locate and track a Kaiju. So far, the two ebony behemoths had not strayed from the pod in which they had arrived. When they did move, stopping them would not be easy.

Vance crawled over next to him and yelled in his ear. "I don't like this. Why aren't they moving?"

It worried him too. He didn't like surprises. "I don't know. They're waiting for something."

"No one's ever killed two Kaiju except Walker. We could make history."

"If we're not careful, Sergeant, we'll be history."

Vance smiled at LaBonner's use of his new rank. Unlike him, Vance was proud of his promotion.

Their helicopter broke away from the others. "The other choppers are going in first," the pilot announced. "They will take some of the heat from us. I'll shoot straight north to the crater. We won't encounter any Wasps until the last few miles. Hold on. It's going to be rough."

The pilot was right. The chopper danced like a marionette on a string in the strong cross gusts. He flew so low to the water that the tops of whitecaps sheered away by the wind deluged them. At times, LaBonner couldn't tell if they were flying or floating. The rain was too heavy to make out much of Galveston Island spread out below them, but what he saw disturbed him. Scholes International Airport was a sea of wrecked aircraft. Small Beechcraft and Cessnas, their wings and fuselages shredded by Wasps, lay strewn over the tarmac. Larger Gulfstream and Lear jets had fared no better. Several displayed large holes in their fuselages where Wasps had pried away doors, windows, and stripped pieces of metal from their roofs.

Scholes was home to several companies operating helicopters serving the Gulf of Mexico oil platforms. The shattered and burned remains of Eurocopter EC-135s, Bell Jet Rangers, and Sikorsky S-61s attested to the ferocity of the alien attack. Smoke poured from the terminal building and several hangars. An aviation fuel truck had exploded while refueling an S-61. Charred parts of the chopper lay scattered around the fire-gutted vehicle.

Beyond the airport, the hulls of shattered and half-submerged boats littered the waters of Offatts Bayou on the south terminus of the I-45 Bridge. The residents of Galveston had no means of escape. The Wasps had trapped them to make hunting them easier. Explosions on the eastern end of the island marked a pitched battle between the military and swarms of Wasps, but distance and the intervening storm denied him any view of who was winning.

Crossing West Bay between Galveston Island and the mainland, they approached Bayou Vista where the pod had crashed in the middle of the fourteen artificial canals connecting with Bayou Highland. Once, rows of stately one and two-story homes with private docks had lined each side of the canals, a bedroom community for Texas City and Houston. The neighborhood was now another lake. Most of the homes were gone, pulverized by the massive impact of the Kaiju pod. Others were piles of splintered wood jutting from mounds of mud and earth pushed up by the impact and forming the crater walls. Smashed cars and boats dotted the ruins like raisins in a pudding.

The pod had struck at a shallow angle, skidding for 4,000 feet before embedding itself in the mud and the soft limestone and shale, forming a teardrop-lake. One end of the ebony pod protruded 20 feet above the surface of the muddy water. Both 1200-foot-long-Kaiju stood like enormous sentries flanking the pod, water up to their ebony bellies.

Though they were stationary, they were not idle. The long tentacles surrounding their maws whipped beneath the surface of the water, withdrew small black objects from the pod, and deposited them into the blister openings along their flanks. Glowing purple lines zigzagged along the pod's surface. Unlike previous pods, this one had not broken open upon impact and was an integral part of the reason the Kaiju had come. He did not wish to guess what that purpose might be; however, he knew it did not bode well for humanity.

"Call in what you're observing to HQ," he told the pilot. "They need to be aware of this."

They circled the water-filled crater while the pilot reported his observations. The lack of Wasps in the area disturbed him. He had never seen a Kaiju without Wasp air cover. The aliens were employing yet another new tactic. The significance eluded him. With no Wasps or Fleas delivering food to the Kaiju and with dense clouds blocking most of the solar energy, the Kaiju depleted their storehouses of energy.

"I'll set us down as close as possible," the pilot said. "I spotted an unbroken stretch of asphalt road about half a click away."

LaBonner nodded. That placed them just over two clicks from the crater. The less time they spent slogging through the muck and mire, the better he would feel. He fought down the hard knot of anticipation growing in his stomach as the chopper settled onto the road. It was not exactly fear, although fear was a reasonable sensation facing a Kaiju; it was more a sense of finality, as if one way or another, this would be his last battle. The prospect of death did not bother him. He had counted himself among the dead long ago. Each day alive was just an aberration. He wanted his epitaph to read better than 'He Tried.'

No matter how many times he faced a Kaiju, the image of an ant attacking an elephant popped into his mind. These new Kaiju acted differently, and he hated the unexpected. The unexpected could kill you. He checked the sky for jets but saw only rain-laden gray clouds. The Air Force was busy over Houston. Command was allowing his team first shot at the twin Kaiju. If they failed, or took too long, or if the Kaiju began moving toward Houston, they would be on ground zero of a devastating nuclear attack. It was an uncomfortable position.

"Okay, lock and load," he called out to his team.

He exchanged glances with Vance. Only the sergeant's tightly clenched jaw betrayed his concern. A few of the others, on their first mission, appeared uneasy at their first close-up sight of a Kaiju. They looked miserable in their rain-drenched uniforms, water running down their faces, but they stood like soldiers, backs straight, faces grim with determination. Their bearing made him proud. He offered them a few words of encouragement. *For what they're worth.*

"We just need to get close enough to deliver our nuclear rockets. The targets are stationary. That makes the job easier. No sweat. The sergeant and I have done this before."

Vance raised a questioning eyebrow but said nothing.

They followed mud-splattered, cracked streets through rows of homes damaged by the impact until the houses disappeared beneath the water and the streets became small islets of asphalt surrounded by a sea of mud. Spalled outcroppings of shattered rock disgorged by the impact, some as large as dump trucks, lay scattered across the shallow end of the basin formed by the impact. A rim of shale, chalk, and mud surrounded the northern and westward slope of the crater. Occasionally, small avalanches of mud created by the heavy downpour cascaded down the slope into the water.

"We'll make our way to the southern dike formed by the impact. It should make movement easier."

When he waded in, the cold water caught him by surprise. He had expected it to be warm from the impact. It stank of salt and oil released through cracks in the salt domes deep beneath the surface fractured by the Kaiju-induced quake. He urged his team to move quickly. Whatever the Kaiju were doing, their blisters remained open, offering a prime target. He didn't know how long the opportunity would present itself.

The mud beneath the water sucked at his boots. Each laborious step required reclaiming his leg from the thick mud that fought to bind him in place. They moved in slow motion, sitting targets for any Wasps that might attack from the low-hanging gray clouds. Vance and one other soldier, each carrying M60 machineguns, trudged more slowly through the muck, lagging behind. The 23-pound weapons, plus the 100-round belts of 7.62mm ammo, weighted them down. He waited on Vance and relieved him of his ammo can.

LaBonner's weeklong stay in the hospital without exercise had weakened him more than he had anticipated. Though sufficiently healed of his wounds, his muscles had not had time to readjust. The effort of trudging through the thick mire carrying the heavy ammo can exhausted him before he reached dry land.

The steep slope of loose rock and mud offered poor footing, especially crossing the rivulets of muddy water pouring down the slope, but at least it didn't actively fight his progress as the mud had. As they neared the two Kaiju, he got a closer look at the objects the Kaiju were removing from the pod and depositing in their blisters. A short, stubby protrusion at one end of the oddly shaped black lumps looked uncomfortably like the barrel of a weapon. He wondered what purpose they served, and if a weapon, for what creature they were intended.

He waved the two men carrying the nuclear-tipped rockets forward. They were dangerously close to their target, but any Kaiju Killer team was expendable, even his, as long as they completed their mission. Too many lives depended upon them. The city of Houston depended on them. Nine men versus tens of thousands – the coldness of the simple equation no longer troubled him. Numbers mattered. He had not seen the truth of this earlier. As a leader, his efforts had been to complete the mission and get his men safely home. He had failed in that part. He now realized the lives of his team were beyond his control. He could do all the right things, but it might not matter. His job was to keep them alive until they got close enough to take their shot. After that, it was in God's hands.

"The blisters remain open for about two minutes," he told them after observing the Kaiju's actions. He tried to read the men's names from their nametags. The mud obscured some of the letters. "Time your shots accordingly. Brewster, you take the creature on the left; Agnew, the one on the right. You both need to fire at the same time. We might not get a second chance."

"It's Brewsley, sir, not Brewster."

"Okay, Brewsley. You ready?"

Brewsley swallowed hard and nodded. He balanced the heavy launcher on his shoulder, and waited. Beside him, Agnew did the same. Both men were tense but ready. The lack of Wasps improved the odds of hitting their targets. Seconds later, everything changed. Both Kaiju stopped what they were doing and lowered until they lay half submerged in the water. LaBonner placed his hand on Brewsley's shoulder to stop him from firing. The blisters had closed. They had missed their best opportunity.

They waited ten minutes, while the Kaiju remained immobile, and the blisters closed. Then, all the blisters on both creatures opened simultaneously. It looked as if the Kaiju were bleeding Spiders, dropping into the water with hardly a splash. They maneuvered through the mud on their thin legs as nimbly as their Earth namesakes did. LaBonner noticed the strange objects the Kaiju had been removing from the pod attached to the Spiders' backs and knew he had been right. The Spiders, deadly enough in their own right, were now weaponized.

But what kind of weapon?

It did not take long to find out. Most of the Spiders quickly scurried from the watery crater moving northeast toward Texas City. The Kaiju blisters closed once again, and the giant creatures rose to their full height and followed. Confused by the emergence of the Spiders, his team had missed its best chance to kill the Kaiju. Waves created by the monsters' passing crashed against the hummock on which LaBonner stood, eroding it beneath his boots. He backed up the slope while keeping his attention fixed on the new threat. Twenty Spiders remained behind. He was certain the creatures were aware of his team.

As if on a silent order, all the Spiders attacked simultaneously. The first weapon discharged, blasting a small crater in the dirt a few feet from LaBonner, splattering him with hot mud and gravel. The high-temperature beam's passage through the rain left eddies of steam.

"Lasers!" Vance yelled in warning. "They've got goddamned lasers."

The balance of power had shifted once again. Now, their enemy was armed as well as deadly.

"Scatter!" LaBonner called out. "Aim for the spot beneath their heads."

This time, they had no mortars, only SCARS, two M60 machineguns, and grenades. They returned fire. One soldier went down when a laser beam sliced him in half. The upper portion of torso toppled and slid down the slope into the water, while his lower trunk remained planted firmly in the mud. Vance tossed a hand grenade, but the water acted as a cushion, shielding the creature from most of the concussion and shrapnel, causing little damage. LaBonner fired at the closest Spider with his SCAR, finally bringing it down after emptying a magazine, but the creatures behind it continued to advance. Vance stood in mud up to his calves, firing his M60 in short bursts to save ammunition. The armor-piercing rounds chipped their ebony carapace and tore into the Spiders' soft spots, but each time Vance replaced a belt, the creatures moved closer.

Two more men died as the Spiders' lasers zeroed in on their positions. The creatures were learning quickly and adapting their tactics.

"Take cover!" LaBonner yelled. The only cover was behind the ridge of debris on which they fought. As they clambered up the steep, muddy slope, another man died when a laser tore through his chest. As Vance struggled up the slope backward firing his M60, lasers striking all around him, LaBonner grabbed his belt and dragged him over the ridge to safety. He plopped onto his belly and continued firing. The battle had lasted less than a minute, and the creatures had reduced their numbers by almost half. The ridge offered some shelter. Laser blasts passed close over their heads or struck the opposite slope, showering them with scalding water and hot mud. They killed two more Spiders by carefully selecting targets and combining their firepower, but the remainder had almost reached the slope.

LaBonner knew they could not survive a concentrated attack. They had nowhere to run. Vance was down to his last two belts of ammo for the M60. Once the Spiders crested the slope, they would all die. Brewsley still carried his rocket launcher with the nuclear-tipped rocket. Vance followed LaBonner's gaze and nodded that he understood what he was thinking. If they had missed their chance with the Kaiju, they could at least take out the Spiders. Dying for something was better than dying for nothing.

Before he could tell Brewsley to fire, a loud roar overhead drowned out his words. With a blast of air, the Blackhawk that had brought them swept over their heads and opened fire on the Spiders. The .50 caliber GAU-19 and twin 7.62mm M240 machineguns raked the creatures with a withering field of fire, killing three and confusing the rest. The pilot almost stood the chopper on its side, making a steep banking turn to bring the aircraft back around quickly for a second run. Laser beams danced across the sky. One struck the underbelly. The chopper shuddered in midair. Smoke billowed from the undercarriage.

The pilot emptied both pods of M229 70mm *Hydra* rockets, each weighing 13 pounds and measuring 42 inches in length. The fourteen rockets barely had time to arm themselves before they lanced into the creatures. Kaiju armor-tipped and packed with 17 pounds of explosives, the rockets ripped the Spiders to shreds.

The pilot fought to keep the Blackhawk level, but the laser blast had severed his controls. The chopper began spinning. The skids struck the water and dragged the chopper down. It struck hard nose first, bounced, and hit the slope opposite LaBonner and the others. The loose earth shuddered from the impact. The spinning chopper blades dug into the mud, burying them beneath a shower of mud and dirt. It cart-wheeled over the ridge and landed upside down in the water. The blades broke away and skipped like stones flung across a pond. One 6-foot-long section of blade embedded in the ridge beside LaBonner. Smoke and flame erupted from the fuselage. Seconds later, before any survivors could escape, it exploded. The Blackhawk crew had saved their lives, but at the cost of their own.

LaBonner stood. He was tired of other people dying for him. "Come on. We still have our rocket launchers. Let's chase these bastards down and put a stop to them."

It was a bold boast, one which he had little hope of fulfilling, but he was not about to give up. The creatures were just a stone's throw from Louisiana, his home state. He wouldn't let them in without a fight.

22

August 22 Haumea –

The *Assegai* slowed as it approached the dazzling speck dead ahead. Five billion miles from the sun, now just a tiny bright speck in the sky, the oblong dwarf planet glowed with an ethereal light. To Walker, it did not seem possible. *136 108 Haumea*, one of the larger of the Trans-Neptunian Objects in the Kuiper Belt, ellipsoidal because of its rapid four-hour rotation, looked like a bright, shiny Easter egg spinning in space.

Although they had entered the area at minimum speed, Walker was certain the Nazir had picked up emanations from their gravity drive. It surprised him that there were no preparations, no spaceships, no Kaiju waiting to pounce. Either the aliens were waiting to spring a trap, which worried him, or they assumed the *Assegai* posed no serious threat in spite of the destruction of nine of the thirty Kaiju they had dispatched to Earth. The latter worried him more than the former.

Sakiri sat at the controls on the bridge, guiding the *Assegai* to Haumea using Hi'iaka, the dwarf planet's largest of two moons as cover. Namaka, one-tenth as large as its sister moon, was hidden behind the dwarf planet. Four *Lances* flew Combat Air Patrol for the ship. The CAP provided an early warning of an attack, as well as a defense. Handling the large craft as deftly as he controlled his smaller *Lance*, Sakiri brought the ship to a stationary position behind the moon. He sat back in his seat; then opened and closed his cramped hands to re-start the circulation from gripping the controls too tightly.

He turned to Blivens. "Shut down the drive and artificial gravity." To Walker, who stood behind him sharing his nervousness, he said, "Once we've reconnoitered the situation, we'll drop your two teams on the surface, while we do as much damage as possible and provide cover for you."

Walker grasped Sakiri's shoulder, felt the tension in the bunched muscles beneath his hand. A week had passed since Blaylock's death, but the colonel still had not brought up the subject. Walker was certain he had not forgotten it. The incident loomed between them like an unspoken curse.

"From what we've seen, the factories must be underground. We've spotted two possible entrances. It was a wise decision bringing the *Javelin's* aft module with us. Now, I can safely split my team."

Gate stood in front of the forward view screen. "We learned in 2017 the Haumea had rings, but I never expected this."

600 miles out from the surface, a thin disc of rubble over 50 miles wide circled the dwarf planet. Comprised mostly of dust and ice, some chunks were as large as the *Assegai*.

"Chariklo and Charon, both asteroids, have rings, but it is an unusual occurrence for small objects. Haumea must have received quite a wallop eons ago, that heated it and threw off a debris field. While molten, its rapid spin elongated the main mass and the rings formed from leftover material from the twin moon formation. Its mass is lower than we thought. That will affect the gravity. We can't really classify Haumea as a dwarf planet. It's just a large asteroid."

"I'll think of it as a planet, if you don't mind," Walker said. "It will make me feel better about crawling around on the surface."

Walker pressed the screen with his finger to indicate a double line of nearly invisible objects circling the planet and knotted his brow. The sheer number of objects alarmed him. They had seriously underestimated the aliens' capability. "Those dark masses must be Kaiju pods."

"Or spaceships," Gate offered. "We have no idea what their ships look like."

"True, but they haven't moved, and I'm certain they are aware of our presence. I'm putting my money on the bet that they are Kaiju awaiting final assembly and pose no threat to us. The gaps in the line indicate missing Kaiju, the ones they've already sent to Earth."

"They are much larger than any previous Kaiju pods. Earth must be sheer hell right now."

"You lowered the odds with your bold plan to destroy the first swarm," Sakiri said.

Gate blushed at Sakiri's unexpected accolade. "Twenty-one got through."

"It was a good call. Nevertheless," Sakiri insisted, "if we fail here, there are almost fifty more Kaiju waiting out there to attack Earth."

"No matter what happens," Walker said, "we can't allow them to launch those Kaiju."

Sakiri glanced up at him over his shoulder and blinked once to indicate his agreement. If the mission seemed about to fail, they would destroy the *Assegai* just as Gate had the *Javelin*. Fifty-eight lives didn't matter. *Fifty-seven*, he reminded himself.

One thing puzzled him. "Why is the surface of Haumea visible? Out here in eternal darkness, I assumed we would be fighting with night vision gear. Hell, I can see shadows down there."

Gate shook his head. "I'm not sure."

Worthen cleared his throat. "Er, I might have a theory." When no one interrupted him, he continued. "It is possible that the gravity drive energy can be used for more than artificial gravity or as a means of propulsion. What if the Nazir can fine-tune gravity waves much as we do radio waves?"

Worthen was taking over his head, but Walker noted from Gate's expression that Worthen's comment interested him. "And do what with them?" he asked.

"We know the ebony material is energy absorbent and channels kinetic and EM energy to the Kaiju power source for storage, a kind of organic battery."

Walker nodded. He had seen the massive battery inside Kaiju Nusku.

"What if it has other capabilities?" he paused. "I believe the orbiting pods are radiating light waves, invisible to us because of the vacuum surrounding the planet, but its effects are evidenced by the shadows."

Gate burst out laughing and slapped Worthen on the back, shoving him halfway across the room. "By God, you're right! It's simple really, once you think about it. It's not magic. It's elementary science." Gate's face became animated. "Think about it! With more study, the principals of the gravity drive might be used to power and illuminate entire cities. We could view distant planets and stars in real time. The same drive that powered a colony ship to the stars could tame the planet, we could …" His voice trailed off and a look of stricken horror crossed his suddenly ashen face. "I'm blathering madly."

"We need to power down the ship to avoid detection," Sakiri announced.

"Powering down life support to minimum," Worthen said. The lights dimmed, and the ventilator fans shut down.

"Shutting down artificial gravity," Blivens announced.

Walker's body lifted from the deck. He held onto the wall to prevent drifting away.

"You will have to get used to this," Gate told him. "Haumea's mass is less than 6 percent of Earth's moon, or 1/1400th of Earth. With an escape velocity of .9 km/s, you could literally take a flying leap and leave the surface. The surface temperature is 50 degrees Kelvin, four degrees below which oxygen becomes a solid. The high albedo indicates amorphous ice covering much of the rocky surface. Fighting under such adverse conditions will be rough for someone on the ground."

"Yeah," Walker replied with a grin, "but at least we won't be in the dark."

Gate pointed out dark spots mottling the white surface of Haumea. "The darker areas are olivine and pyroxene with a few organics added. Spectral analysis indicates fewer volatiles than previously believed. The impact that deformed Haumea into an oblate shape happened a billion years ago, and the dwarf planet and its attendant moons and rings migrated here over the eons from a less dense part of the Belt."

"It worries me that they haven't attacked yet," Blivens said.

Walker stared at him. "Are you in a hurry to die?"

"They must have ships. They arrived in our system somehow. They can't mine all the material they need on Haumea; therefore, it stands to reason they mine the Belt."

"Let's hope their ships are a long way off."

"My men will provide air cover," Sakiri promised. "We'll keep any ships or Kaiju off your backs while you plant your nukes."

"It's not what's orbiting the planet that bothers me. I'm betting the underground facility is teeming with an interesting assortment of creatures, not to mention the Nazir. It won't be a cakewalk."

"You'll get the job done," Gate assured him. "You always do."

"I appreciate the vote of confidence, but this is a little different from slipping inside a Kaiju, as difficult as that was. If it looks as if we've failed, we'll set off the nukes. I'll try to provide ample warning for you to move your *Lances* and the *Assegai* to a safe distance, but I don't know what conditions we'll encounter. It may not be possible."

"Understood," Sakiri replied. "Do what you have to do." He rose from his seat and floated across the cabin. He grabbed a handhold and stretched to ease his aching muscles after the grueling task of piloting the *Assegai* into position.

"I'm going with you," Gate said.

Gate's announcement caught Walker by surprise. He stared at Gate, wondering if he had misunderstood. "With me? Why?"

Gate shrugged. "What you just mentioned – intel. We know quite a lot about the Kaiju but nothing about the aliens. Worthen's analysis of the gravity drive's capability makes it imperative. Any knowledge we glean, no matter how trivial, could prove useful in case," he cleared his throat, "in case we fail."

"If we fail, intel won't be much use. You're more useful guiding the ship. You risked your life once already. Don't push your luck."

"We have two people capable of plotting a course back to Earth." He glanced at Worthen and Blivens. Worthen beamed at the accolade. Blivens, his face now ashen from Zero-G nausea, did not look up. "I have the opportunity to see an alien, the source of all our ills. I can't pass that up. I can transmit anything we learn to the *Assegai*. They can forward it to Earth."

Walker gazed at Gate a moment, proud to be his friend. He recognized how much courage it took for Gate to volunteer, especially after his near-death experience in the *Lance*. He nodded. "Your priority is intel and transmitting it to the *Assegai*. Mine is destroying the Kaiju factory."

Gate's smile was slightly forced and fleeting. "Thanks."

Colonel Sakiri encompassed both Walker and Gate with his gaze. "We've been twelve days getting here. I suggest we deploy our forces quickly. If we have caught the Nazir by surprise, I don't want to waste an opportunity. One *Lance* should handle each of the drop modules easily enough. The other eighteen will fly cover and do as much damage as possible."

"My teams are ready," Walker replied. He looked at Gate. "Gate, you come with me and my team. Once we breach the surface, we move fast and stop for nothing."

Gate nodded. "Understood."

Walker hoped the astrophysicist fathomed what he was getting into. This mission would be balls-to-the-wall fast and furious while wearing life support equipment in which the tiniest slash could be as deadly as a Wasp's stinger. He was certain the aliens would have a few surprises in store for them. In spite of the initial lack of concern, they would not let invaders waltz in unopposed. He had witnessed Gate's ability with a weapon and had no doubts he could handle himself under fire, but he feared the scientist's curiosity might place his in danger.

He applauded Gate's desire to transmit intel to Earth, but doubted the information would be of any use. If their mission failed, Earth would not have the time or the resources for a second attempt. For that reason, every member of the team was expendable, even Gate.

"I'll meet you at the aft airlock in five minutes," he told Gate. "I have something to attend to."

Finding a space to be alone for prayers was almost impossible in the small ship. Walker had solved the problem by utilizing the only spot that offered privacy, the Zero-G toilets. He had been lax in his prayers on the journey. Things got in the way. He was certain Allah would understand.

Time had a way of becoming moot in a spaceship. He checked his watch to be sure of the hour of day – 6:05 p.m. GMT. To prepare for his *salat*, he must perform *Taharah* or purification. That included *wudu*, ablutions before prayer. Water for cleansing was limited on the ship. A second option was *Tayam mam*, or dry purification, except he had no dirt. A happy medium was washing with a moist paper towel as best he could.

One important ritual was *Najas*, or the casting away of anything filthy. A toilet used by fifty-eight men and women was the most unclean space he could imagine, but he needed privacy for his own peace of mind. He wiped down everything with his moist paper towel, and then used a second to wash his hands. Flushing the complicated Zero-G toilet took his mind from his prayers. He closed his eyes and meditated a moment before beginning. His prayer rug was a simple folded thin cloth he had brought aboard ship inside his uniform, but it would suffice. He had prayed in worse situations.

The sunset prayer, *Maghrib*, seemed out of place in a sunless void, but in his mind, the ritual of five daily prayers was more a means of attaining inner peace than for asking Allah for guidance. With barely room to stand in the tiny toilet, made especially difficult in zero gravity, he laid his makeshift prayer rug on the floor with its niche representing the *mihrab*, a prayer niche featured in all mosques, facing toward Earth and Mecca. Using one of the handholds, he pulled his body down until his feet pinned the rug to the floor. He could not prostrate himself, so he bent as far as the tiny space would allow.

He did not have the time to complete the entire ritual, nor an Imam to announce the *rak'at* verses for him to answer. He spoke directly to Allah. At first, he thought Allah had abandoned him in the vastness of space, but then a feeling of grace, a sense of bliss enveloped him. He clung to the feeling as one would a beloved friend, savoring the aura of peace. He took it into himself and let if suffuse his body, flushing away the days of tension and mantle of responsibility. He knelt for what seemed like hours, basking in Allah's light, but it could have been only minutes. Then, a heavy pounding struck the door.

"Hurry it up in there!" someone yelled.

Walker smiled, picked up his prayer rug, and tucked it into his shirt. As he floated out of the toilet, he said, "All yours."

When he reached the aft compartment, Gate, and Fire Team Alpha were waiting. As Walker led his team into the airlock, he stopped to speak with Costas.

"Sergeant, I'm expecting you back here in six hours with your hide intact. You got that?"

Costas floated in front of him, twirling his long mustache with his finger. He offered Walker a big grin. "Sure thing. I got a date with one of the weapons specialists. I've already got a private corner of a broom closet picked out for our tryst."

"If you find a vital target, set your nuke for thirty minutes and get the hell out of there. Both nukes are synced. Activating one will activate the other. I'll know when you've done it. Transmit a signal to Sakiri to pull back his *Lances*. Don't wait on me. Just do it."

The grin faded from Costas' face. "Got it," he replied.

Walker slapped Costas on the shoulder, sending him floating backward. Costas grabbed onto a handhold. He and the sergeant had survived many missions together by defying the odds. He was afraid their luck was running out.

His five members of Fire Team Alpha would perform a spacewalk to reach the *Javelin's* module attached to the *Assegai's* stern. They would go in first and draw any alien defenses away from the second team. Costas and the five remaining team members would remain in *Assegai's* aft module and follow them twenty minutes later. Dividing his troops was a dangerous risk, but doubling the area they could cover might make the difference between success and failure. Faced with two possible entrances, either of which might be heavily guarded, it was unwise to simply guess. Both could yield valuable intelligence or offer the solution to destroying the Kaiju factory. The added advantage of his team going in first was that it might pull alien opposition away from Costas' team, giving him a slight advantage.

Inside the airlock, he helped Gate attached the armor plates to his suit. Donning the suits in Zero-G required teamwork. After he suited up, he issued Gate a weapon from the weapons locker in the floor. Gate took the strange looking device and frowned.

"What is this?"

"That is an H&K L200, basically a mini-RPG. Firing a regular rifle in low gravity could send you sailing backward from the recoil. To reduce inertia, the HK fires low-yield armor-piercing rockets. You hold it under one arm. The flame emerges from the rear of the launcher, so be sure no one's standing behind you before you fire. A cable from the HK connects with your suit computer. You aim with your suit video camera and fire by pressing the firing stud. It automatically reloads. Each magazine holds six rockets. Just yank the empty one out and slap a fresh one in."

Gate shook his head. "I don't think –"

Walker grinned at Gate's nervousness. "You'll do fine. Just don't shoot anyone we know. It's for emergencies. We'll keep an eye on you."

Gate pointed to bags other members of the team carried in addition to the HKs. "What about those?"

"Two are Maxwell-Atchisson 12-gauge automatic shotguns with 32-round drum magazines. The others are 9mm H&K MP5Ks. The heated and insulated bags keep the moving parts from freezing solid. We're carrying them in case we find an atmosphere. Otherwise, we use the HKL200s."

Two of the weapons lockers required the use of two keys. Costas produced his and inserted it into the lock. Walker did the same. The loud click when they turned both keys simultaneously made several of the team jump. Inside, two silver cylinders lay cradled in shock webbing.

"These, gentlemen, are the nuclear payloads from two B61 bombs. Each one is set for a 340-kiloton yield. Together, they should be sufficient to get the job done. Each weighs about eighty pounds, but in the low gravity, that should not present a problem. When activated, we have thirty minutes to get clear. They are electronically synced, so arming one arms both."

When all seven of them were suited up and equipped, Walker cycled the airlock and opened the outer hatch. The *Javelin's* recovered aft module sat at the rear of the *Assegai* attached by quick-release brackets. Walker had ordered cables strung between the two modules. Walker made sure everyone properly secured their tethers to the cables, and then pushed off. He pulled himself along with his hands, feeling like a pro until he forgot to reduce his speed before he reached the other end. He grabbed the cable with both hands, but his inertia wrenched the cable from his hands. He slammed into the module much harder than intended. His face pressed against his visor, bruising his nose. Unable to reach his nose through his helmet, he twitched it to make certain he hadn't broken it. He recovered and warned the others.

"Watch your inertia, or you'll bloody your nose."

Once the others arrived, he opened the outer hatch.

"Leave your suits on and grab something to hold to. We'll be leaving shortly."

Four minutes later, Sakiri's voice blared over this suit radio. "I'm attaching cables now."

Metallic clangs signaled the brackets releasing. The module jerked. Walker gripped the floor tighter. In zero gravity, he felt no sensation of movement.

"I'm deploying my *Lances* above each opening," Sakiri said. "We'll cover your landing, and then pull back."

The journey to Haumea took fifteen minutes. He tensed his body waiting for a Nazir response to their encroachment, but none came. The lack of a response only intensified his trepidation. Were the aliens waiting until the last minute for deadly accuracy? His weight increased slightly as they neared the surface. The module slammed onto the hard rock like a free-fall elevator from the second floor. The impact threatened to wrench Walker's shoulder from the socket as he held on. One soldier lost his grip, tumbled across the floor, and slammed into the wall. He sat up groaning, but was otherwise uninjured. Walker ran a quick diagnostics of the man's suit to be certain it had not suffered damage, and then slapped him on the back.

"Be careful." He turned to the only woman on his team. "Cantrell, you carry the nuke. The rest of you keep a tight formation on the ground."

On low gravity Haumea, the eighty-pound nuke weighed only a few pounds, making Cantrell's job easier. He had no doubt she could have handled the nuke in full gravity. At 5'10" and heavily muscled from constant workouts, she was as strong or stronger than any man on the team except Costas, and Walker wouldn't have wanted to witness a knock-down drag-out fight between them, though Costas might have enjoyed the prospect. She grabbed the case by the handle, set it on her shoulder, and wriggled her ass. She grinned and asked, "Does this make my ass look big?" Her comment elicited a few laughs, relieving the tension.

Walker opened the outer door, revealing the dismal, stark landscape of Haumea. Rocks, their edges razor sharp for lack of erosion, protruded through drifts of a dirty snow of frozen gases. No surface buildings were visible, but a plume of vapor rose from a deep pit a hundred yards from their position. He craned his head to search the dark sky above them, but could not see the Kaiju pods circling overhead.

By whatever method and for whatever reason the aliens conjured the light flooding Haumea's surface, Walker was grateful. He didn't like fighting in the dark. The ambient light was the equivalent of a full moon, making it easy find their way to their target. On the negative side, they became highly visible targets for any alien gunners.

Despite the heaters, the deep cold penetrated Walker's body armor, chilling his flesh wherever the suit fit snuggest. The sensation reminded him of a package of outdated chicken with freezer burn. Even the air he inhaled seemed unnaturally cold and damp. He fought a panicky moment of claustrophobia by focusing on his destination.

"Don't bunch up," he told his men. "Spread out fifteen yards apart. Not you, Gate," he told Gate as he began edging away. "You stick close to me."

They didn't run as much as bounded. It was an efficient means of covering ground quickly, but the sharp rocks posed a problem with each landing. They could easily rip a suit and expose flesh to vacuum. He twisted slightly in midair to adjust his landing spot to avoid one stony knife thrusting up from the sandy surface.

The pit was wider than it first appeared, almost eighty feet across. Condensate from the vapor lined the sides and settled around the rim like salt on a giant margarita glass. The sides were smooth, sheer, and vertical with no means of access. His suit radar indicated a bottom sixty feet below, too far to jump even in low gravity. They would have to rappel. He rued they had no drone to survey the pit, but with no atmosphere, one would not fly.

Instead, he tossed a slow flash grenade down into the pit. When activated, the grenade produced a bright light by mixing two low-temperature reaction chemicals. The transparent casing magnified the light. The grenade flared seconds after leaving his hand. He leaned over the side and watched it descend. The sides of the pit were as smooth and featureless as the rim, except for a ledge thirty feet below the surface. The bottom was flat with an opening along one edge, but even with the light, he could not see into the tunnel because of the angle.

Two men drove metal rods into the edge of the pit with percussion hammers, silently due to the lack of atmosphere. After belaying three thin, flexible steel hawsers – ropes would have crumbled to dust from the extreme cold – Walker clipped onto the cable and stepped off the side of the hole. He checked his descent with his gloved hands, using the cable as a safety line. After landing on the ten-foot-wide ledge, he peered over the edge. The light from the slow flash grenade faded as the extreme cold froze the chemicals inside, but it revealed a wide, uninviting dark tunnel that extended deep into the surface. Walker saw no aliens or alien machinery, but he smelled a trap. A smaller opening in the wall by the ledge looked more promising. It was from there the vapor originated.

Cantrell lowered the nuke first; then, slide down and took a guarding position while Walker helped Gate land and unhooked him. The others descended and grouped around him. He looked into their faces. They all showed concern but no fear. They had all faced Kaiju and survived. He was confident they were capable of meeting any challenge the Nazir threw at them.

His suit light revealed a cylindrical tunnel eight feet in diameter at one end of the ledge. A slight wind pushed a cloud of vapor along the tunnel. White crystals formed on the ceiling. Gate reached up and stuck his finger in the condensation. It crystallized on his glove.

"I think this is liquid oxygen condensate. Oxygen changes from a gas to a liquid at minus 218.4 degrees Celsius or 54.8 Kelvin, the mean temperature of Haumea."

"Why would they vent pure oxygen?" Walker asked.

"I have no idea. It might be a waste by-product of some process. That would indicate the Nazir are not oxygen breathers. Blivens was right."

"I'm sure he'll be delighted." Walker turned to the others. "Through here," he said.

Walker noted the ripples in the stone floor of the tunnel and did not think they were a natural occurrence, but rather the results of high heat, as if a laser had bored the tunnel. That the Nazir had lasers concerned him. Any tool could become a weapon. A large laser would have been required to bore the tunnel, making it formidable weapon. As they continued down the sloping tunnel, Walker detected a vibration through his boots that grew steadily stronger the farther they went. The tunnel continued for two hundred yards before ending in a large chamber. Walker activated another flash grenade and rolled it across the floor, revealing a hemispherical cavern two hundred feet across. The chamber walls were smooth and perfectly formed, not a natural geological feature.

Two large machines sat in the middle of the space, or he assumed they were machines, though they were unlike any machinery he had seen. Parts of them billowed and contracted as if breathing, but metal pipes and ducts entered the bulk of the machines from holes in the walls of the cavern. A chute exited one end and entered an opening in the floor. Walker could not see what was in the chute because of the sides, but steam rose from it, as if whatever product the machines manufactured was warm.

He approached the closest structure and examined it. It towered over his head and was as big around as a California sequoia tree. He laid his hand on its uneven, pebble-textured surface and detected movement, a grinding inside.

"It's warm. It doesn't feel like metal. I think it's some kind of alien cyborg."

He and Gate approached the front of the machine to get a glimpse of the product it produced. Ten-foot-wide sheets of ebony armor slid down the chute and disappeared into the floor.

"Kaiju armor," he exclaimed. "This is an armory."

Gate reached out and caressed a piece of armor as it slid by. "The Nazir take whatever raw material required and feed it to this ... half-machine/half-animal, which forms it into armor material. They must have a means to adhere the smaller sections together to form solid Kaiju shells. Amazing."

"Destroying these should slow them down," Walker suggested. He began removing explosives from his pack.

"They must have more," Gate cautioned him. "Judging by the output, it would take these two machines a year to produce sufficient material for the Kaiju armada circling the planet, much less the ones on Earth."

He decided Gate was probably right. Destroying the machines would serve little purpose other than alerting the enemy to their presence. "Okay. Then we go deeper into the heart of their operation."

Gate continued to examine the machine. "I'd like to study this more. Maybe we can learn how to produce our own Kaiju armor instead of salvaging it from downed Kaiju."

"We don't have time."

"But –"

"We don't have time," Walker repeated. He understood Gate's desire to learn all he could about the Kaiju, but destroying their manufacturing capacity was vital and took precedence over intel. Seeing the bitter look of disappointment on Gate's face, he relented. "Okay, two minutes while I contact Costas. Take photographs."

He set his suit radio for Costas' frequency. "Alpha Team One to Alpha Team Two. Come in Costas."

Costas replied a few seconds later, huffing and puffing, his normally deep voice high-pitched over the radio. "Team Two here. We've breached the surface, and we're following a tunnel. Nothing to report yet except that these suits weren't made for climbing."

"We located a small manufacturing area. We're going deeper underground to continue our search."

"We haven't encountered anything, but we've seen lots of tracks on the ground, so we're not alone down here. I can't wait to see what this bitch throws at us."

"Watch your ass, Costas. Report anything you find. Remember, don't wait on us. If you run into real trouble, set your nuke and leave. Team One out."

Walker turned to Gate. "You ready?"

Gate took one last photograph. When he looked at Walker, his face was pale, as if he had guessed what Walker's off-line conversation with Costas was about. "I think I'm going to be sick."

Walker fought to keep from chuckling. "I wouldn't advise it in a space suit."

"It all just kind of hit me all at once. Did you ever feel this way before a mission?"

Walker smiled at his friend. "Every damn time."

Gate shook his head. "That should make me feel better, but it doesn't." He took a deep breath. "As to whether I'm ready or not, how do you prepare yourself for first contact with an alien species, a hostile one at that?"

Walker understood what Gate meant. Although Gate had endured things most humans had not, he had been on Earth facing the aliens' invading creatures. Now, he was the invader.

"If you see a Nazir, don't stop to shake hands or take photos. Kill the bastard and move on. Don't forget, twenty Kaiju pods are hitting Earth today. We have to win this war quickly."

Gate swallowed and nodded. "For Earth."

23

August 22, Malta –

For four days, the authorities at Malta refused to allow the passengers of the *Doria* to disembark. Though given permission, Johan had refused leave his fellow passengers for fear they would be refused entry onto the island. He hoped his weight and authority as Pope would sway them to do their Christian duty to those in need. It was easy to dismiss others' fears and trials when concerned with one's own misfortune. The mark of a true Christian was compassion during adversity.

Neat rows of stark white tents erected by the U.N. Higher Commission for Refugees adjacent to the docks housed hundreds of refugees. In stark contrast to the controlled UNHCR endeavor, beyond the docks clusters of ramshackle tents sprouting up haphazardly in any open area attested to the overcrowding of the island. Malta faced a crisis, and he hoped he had the determination to guide them through it on the moral high road.

He stood on the deck with O'Bannon drinking coffee, wondering if it might be his last cup. With its overpopulation, Malta needed every cubic meter of cargo space for essentials. Coffee and other so-called luxury items would be difficult to find and undoubtedly would become more so after the new wave of Kaiju landed. He savored the Italian *Lavazza* brand coffee. He preferred it without cream or sugar. Unlike most of his fellow Italians, he had never developed a taste for latte or cappuccino. He drank coffee for the caffeine.

"At some point, Your Holiness," O'Bannon said, "you must leave the boat. Your duty calls you to your new diocese."

He balked at the delay, but remained firm in his conviction. "And what of these people, Peter? If they cannot enter Malta and must leave with the *Doria*, the captain might drop them off on some foreign shore with no resources and without hope. It would be a death sentence. I must show the Prime Minister and the legislature that their fate concerns me."

O'Bannon shrugged. "As you will. I share your concern, but also understand the government's position. At what point will Malta's generosity break the country's back?"

"God will provide."

A bright light high in the sky moving east to west caught his attention. "What is that, an aircraft?" The object's speed was considerable. It covered several degrees of sky in seconds. Its size was difficult to estimate, but it looked too large for an aircraft and moved too fast. As he watched, it seemed to aim directly at the small boat, upon which he stood. He experienced a moment of panic.

O'Bannon shaded his eyes with his hand and gazed at the object with a frown on his lips. "I believe it is a Kaiju. The radio reported twenty more pods were due to strike Earth today."

In his discomfort aboard the ship and administering comfort to his fellow refugees, Johan had forgotten. He flinched as the pod passed directly overhead at less than five miles altitude. The roar of its passing shook the ship. Many of the children, and a few of the women, began to cry. He did not blame them. His bowels had turned to jelly as the Kaiju pod had blotted out the sun.

"We are safe," O'Bannon said. "It looks as if it will land in the deserts of Libya."

Johan made the sign of the cross. "We must pray for them. We must pray for everyone. Then, we must pray for the crews of the *Javelin* and the *Assegai*. Our future may depend on them."

"If they succeed in destroying the aliens, we might pray that they have a home to return to."

Two officials approached the dock. They stopped to stare at the Kaiju pod as he had, and then continued on their way across the dock. Their bearing and gait lent an air of importance to their mission. Johan knew their destination was the *Doria*. He hoped it was good news.

"Perhaps God has moved the government to allow us all to leave this boat," he said.

"That would be lovely indeed," Peter replied.

Johan and the captain met the two men dockside. The oldest, a tall, slim man with weathered hands and wrinkled face glanced at the ubiquitous clipboard he held in one hand.

"Your Holiness, the Prime Minister bids me to inform you that the legislature has agreed to allow all the passengers of the *Doria* onto Maltese soil with the stipulation that the Church agrees to help with their resettlement and welfare."

It was the news for which he had prayed. Now he could get on with his real task – serving the Church from its new home. "The Church will make funds available for as many refugees and residents as it can. Our coffers are not limitless, but what we have is yours."

Both men bowed. "Thank you, Your Holiness," the younger one said. "If you will follow me, we will deliver you to St. Peters."

Johan's first steps on dry land were a bit shaky. He did not know if it was from his sea legs or nervousness. Now, the entire weight of the Catholic world lay on his shoulders. He prayed he was man enough for the daunting task.

Around him, the refugees and the Swiss Guard poured off the boat, eager to set foot on the soil of their new home. Lines of officials waiting with clipboards questioned each one as they disembarked in a too-often unsuccessful effort to place them where it would do the most good. Health officials moved among them, offering inoculations to stop the spread of communicable diseases. The scene repeated itself in every country under siege by Kaiju, people forced to flee and ask their neighbors for help. Some obliged; some did not. If the world were to survive, all its people would have to learn to think differently. The aliens did not acknowledge artificial divides and borders. Neither could mankind. It would be a hard lesson. He took a deep breath of Maltese air, so different from that of Rome; and yet, so similar. Many things would change for him, but many would remain the same. He was now Pope Clement XVI, but he was also still Johan ten Boom.

"Peter," he said, "do you know what day this is?"

"I believe it is Sunday, Your Holiness."

Pope Clement smiled. "Yes, it is. Let us begin our new journey with a special mass."

As Johan strode through the crowd, touching people's extended hands, concern for the fate of the world, the Catholic Church, his tenure as Pope, and his new life on Malta troubled his mind, but his greatest fear was the inoculation he now faced. The new Pope had a deathly fear of needles.

24

August 22, Haumea –

Gate knew he was going to die; knew it with the certainty of one of his mathematical computations: aliens + deadly alien environment = death. He tried not to display his fear to his companions, but was sure they could see it in his eyes. He had come fully expecting to die, not because he was a hero or because he enjoyed challenging death, but because Earth needed whatever information that he could glean, even at the cost of his life. Walker could provide intel on armament and military threats, but he was no scientist. Of all the humans now prowling the dark bowels of Haumea, only he knew what might be important from a scientific standpoint. Blivens or Worthen might have been better suited for the task, but they were essential to the *Assegai*. He had examined the exotic organic crystalline cyborg controlling apparatus and communications systems of Kaiju Nusku and possessed a rudimentary grasp of the basics of the alien technology. Fit or not, he would have to do.

The modified rocket launcher he gripped so tightly in his hands reminded him of the peril of his situation. He had used shotguns and assault rifles against Wasps and other creatures inside Kaiju Nusku, but he had been familiar with them if not proficient in their use. The rocket launcher felt unnatural. He feared that with it, he posed a bigger threat to his companions than he did to the aliens, but he was afraid to lay it aside. Without some type of weapon in his hands to stoke his confidence, he thought he might run screaming from the dark tunnel.

The tunnel eerily reminded him of the passageways inside Kaiju Nusku, dark, alien, and foreboding. Composed of stone rather than ebony Kaiju material, it was nonetheless intimidating – a cross between wandering helplessly inside a Kaiju's body and lost in a deep abandoned mineshaft. In spite of the low gravity, he imagined he could feel the rock pressing down on him. He rushed to suppress the sense of deja vu and its frightening connotation before it found a place in his mind to root and feed his growing terror. He faced enough problems to keep him occupied without reliving old ones.

As they progressed deeper into the heart of the planetoid Haumea, following the conveyor bearing Kaiju armor plates, the ground throbbed with the beat of some heavy alien machinery. Walker insisted on inspecting each of several openings they stumble upon, a series of side caverns excavated by the same process the aliens had used in constructing the tunnel. Two such chambers proved storerooms piled high with stacks of Kaiju armor plates, enough for a dozen more Kaiju. A bulky multi-armed machine removed armor plates from the conveyor and stacked them onto an open tram. The vehicle rode a single metal rail. When loaded, it trundled the plates to an empty spot, tilted, and dumped them onto the ground. When adding to a higher stack, the entire tram lifted on hydraulic legs to the desired level.

A third cavern contained four, enormous, sealed vats, each twenty feet tall and fifty feet in diameter. A clear inspection window running from the floor to the top of the vat revealed a bioluminescent organic substance inside, slowly rotating. The material quivered and pulsed as if alive. Three vats contained a thick ocher-colored material. The fourth's contents were the color of congealed blood. Numerous tubes pierced the sides of the vat supplying the organic material with nutrients, while others drained away waste material. Gate recognized the substance inside the vats.

"This is like the organic substrate we saw in the Kaiju. They initiate growth in these tanks, transfer it into a completed Kaiju shell, and allow it to develop into the desired organic components. Considering the complexity of organic material that we saw in Nusku, there will be more vats like this, and more where they develop fully functioning organs from the genetic material."

Walker frowned. "We severely underestimated their production capacity. They could keep sending Kaiju until they wear us down."

Gate agreed. "After they wipe out mankind, they probably plan to utilize specialized Kaiju to harvest whatever raw materials they want from Earth. They have planet harvesting down to a science."

Two caverns were empty. The sixth turned Gate's stomach when they entered it. Memories from inside the Kaiju flooded back so fast it made him dizzy. A chill crept up his spine. "It's a crèche."

The chamber was a duplicate of one of the nursery crèches they had discovered inside Nusku. Rows of crystalline pods lined the walls of the eighty-foot-diameter space. Each translucent coffer along the bottom row contained an immature creature unlike any they had seen. Measuring slightly taller than a human being, the arthropodal creatures possessed three distinct body segments. The larger lower half, the abdomen, bore rows of raised, sharp-edged parallel ridges along the back. Four thin, multi-jointed legs, folded together in the youngest specimens, connected to a bundle of muscle tissue near the center of the abdomen. Two pairs of legs, each ending in three claws, extended from the cephalothorax – one pair for manipulating objects and a second, shorter pair resembling arachnid mandible parts. A vertical slit-like mouth in the center of an ovoid head bore rows of wiry cilia instead of lips, reminding Gate of the long feeding tentacles of Kaiju. Frills of crimson flesh surrounded twin nostril pits above the mouth. The most disturbing features of the creatures were their eyes.

Unlike the other alien creatures they had encountered, the four, large round eyes set in a diamond pattern contained pupils consisting of a series of concentric rings of muscle acting as irises. As Gate stared into the row of opened eyes, he imagined he saw intelligence behind them. As he shifted position, the eyes followed him.

Corporal Cantrell glanced into one of the containers and grimaced. "Ugly bastards, aren't they?"

Walker pointed to the empty cocoons on the top two rows. "Some have hatched already. I wonder what function they serve?"

A growing realization brought a shiver to Gate. "I think these are the Nazir."

Walker stared at him. "Are you sure? They look like more caretaker creatures to me."

"There's something about the eyes." Unable to better define what he meant, he shook his head. "I don't know. Maybe I'm just imagining things."

Walker stared into one of the caskets; then, jumped back in alarm. "They're awake!"

"They can see, but I don't think they're fully cognizant of us. It's as if they're not complete. Maybe they gain intelligence as they move up the tiers and mature."

Walker's voice had a hard edge when he said, "I won't leave these things here. Cantrell. Reynolds. Wire this place for demolition. Use one-kilo blocks of PVV-5A."

The PVV-5A plastic explosives had been a gift of the Russians used in their MON-50 Claymore-type mines. Walker ordered the team to place the explosives along the base of the incubators and the nutrient tubes feeding them. Gate stared into the closed coffers at the creatures that would become the Nazir, and did not try to stop him. He felt an odd sense of regret at destroying what were essentially alien children, but murder was the reason they had come. Any sympathy he might have had for the Nazir had long ago vanished in smoke like that rising over the destroyed cities of Earth.

When they had finished, Cantrell grinned and said, "That should fuck them up real nice." Her eyes bore the bloodthirsty look of a hardened killer. She had been on a Kaiju Killer team and had witnessed what the aliens were capable of. She shared none of Gate's regrets. For her, it was a blow for Earth, savagery with a purpose.

"They won't have left their young unattended for long," Walker warned. "We'll blow the room, and then move deeper into the facility." He looked hard at Gate, as if sizing him up. "It's going to get tough from now on. They'll know we're here. You up to it?"

As frightened as he was, returning alone to the surface was not a viable option. He needed to see the job through. Some things he could not avoid. Chickening out would haunt him for the rest of his life. He nodded. "Let's do it."

Walker set the timers for ten minutes – sufficient time to penetrate deeper into the complex, but not too long to risk an alien guard stumbling over the explosives and removing them. A hundred yards farther down the tunnel, they encountered a shimmering, transparent wall across the width of the corridor. Hundreds of thin tendrils dangled from the ceiling, reminding Gate of the beaded curtain in his college dorm room. Taking a deep breath, he placed his hand into the curtain. The tendrils were as rigid as icicles; as well, they should have been at 54.8 degrees Kelvin. The farther his hand penetrated, the more pliable and warmer the tendrils became. He extended a probe through the curtain wall. It registered an atmosphere beyond.

"It's some kind of atmosphere barrier," he told Walker. The Nazir technology surprised him, a mixture of advanced science and bio-tech. "Very ingenious."

Gate pushed through the barrier and emerged into an area several hundred degrees warmer than the section of tunnel he had just left. The high heat triggered a red light in his suit panel. He dialed down his suit heater to compensate.

"It's 60 degrees Fahrenheit in here," he said. "We must be getting closer to the heart of the facility." He checked his instruments. "There is too much carbon dioxide in the atmosphere for humans, as well as very little oxygen."

Walker checked his watch. "Twenty seconds to go." Walker began unzipping the insulated bag he carried slung over his shoulder. "It's warm enough for these." He extracted one of the A-12 shotguns and inserted the ammo drum. The others began unlimbering their weapons as well. "Remember," he warned, "with no gravity to hold you down, these things will have a hell of a kick. If you have to fire them, brace yourself against something."

With no atmosphere beyond the shimmering wall, they did not hear the explosion in the crèche chamber, but the quaking floor attested to its force.

"That should raise a few alien eyebrows," Gate said. He felt less guilt for destroying a Nazir hatchery than he thought he should. The aliens wanted to wipe out humanity. He hadn't murdered doctors, painters, or philosophers. He had killed a potential army.

Just as he spoke, the tendril wall turned opaque. Alarmed, he tried to force his hand into the wall. It would not penetrate beyond a few inches. The barrier had become solid. In the distance, a shrill one-note whistle repeated. Gate's gut tightened. The aliens were now aware of the intruders in their midst.

Walker hammered at the wall with the butt of his shotgun to no effect. "Damn it! We're sealed in. I'll warn Costas." He tried his suit radio and frowned. "No signal." He looked around. "We'll have to abandon the main tunnel." Gate followed Walker's gaze to an adit diverging from the tunnel. "Come on. We had better find what we're looking for and fast."

Sealed in the alien burrow, Gate's expectations of leaving again dimmed. He had waited too late. Now, he could not inform the *Assegai* of their findings. All he had learned would be lost. That bothered him more than the probability of his own demise.

"Oh, God!" he heard someone utter.

He turned to look and saw a horde of Ticks scuttling down the corridor. Gate understood the man's shock. He remembered his horrible first glimpse inside Kaiju Nusku of the mottled gray, bloated creatures they had named Ticks. They moved on ten multi-jointed needle-like legs. Each rounded, bulldog-sized body ended in a wicked pair of mandibles capable of severing human limbs or ripping open a man's stomach. He wasn't sure the battle armor would protect them.

"Use your weapons to drive them to one side of the tunnel," Walker called out. "We have to get past them to reach the side tunnel."

Walker fired his RPG until empty. Each explosion ripped into the horde of Ticks, sending chunks of flesh and yellow ichor flying in all directions. Gate was glad for the suit air. He remembered the nauseating stench of the dead Ticks from Nusku. The rockets and the gunfire from MP5Ks and AA-12s produced the desired effect, diverting the Ticks, but their numbers increased from a constant flow of reinforcements. As the creatures began climbing the walls, Walker herded his team toward the adit.

A scream through the com band rattled Gate's ears. He glanced back to see one of the soldiers writhing on the floor of the tunnel beneath a Tick. Its two-foot-long mandibles closed around the man's neck, severing his head. Head and helmet rolled across the floor, as the man's legs kicked wildly in his death throes. Another creature dropped from the ceiling, seeming to float down in the low gravity. More were scampering across the ceiling toward them.

Reaching the safety of the side tunnel, Gate stopped and fired his HK200L until it was empty. His hands shook too badly to extract the empty magazine and insert a fresh one. Walker noticed his problem and did it for him; then, braced himself and fired his AA-12 into the front ranks of Ticks. The shotgun blasts ripped into the creatures' unarmored bodies, gouging out handfuls of flesh and splashing blood across the floor and ceiling. The viscous blood dripped from the ceiling in long, slimy strings.

"Aim for the roof," he said to Gate. "Try to collapse the entrance."

With unsteady hands, Gate aligned the launcher with the ceiling at the entrance to the adit using his suit's view screen. He pushed the firing stud three times in rapid succession, firing three rockets. The armor-piercing rockets penetrated the rock before exploding. Though packed with low-yield explosives, they possessed enough punch to shatter solid rock. Shards of rock pelted his suit but none pierced the heavy fabric of the armor. A slab of ceiling broke away and collapsed onto the leading line of Ticks, crushing them beneath tons of rock. An avalanche of boulders piled up until they blocked the entrance.

As Gate stood admiring his handiwork, Walker shoved him in the back. "Move it!"

Once again, Gate wished for real gravity. The low gravity forced him to consider carefully each step as he bounded down the tunnel lest he slam his head into the low ceiling. He soon reached his stride in a stooped, loping gate. He focused on a light at the end of the tunnel. Abruptly, the tunnel ended on a balcony at the edge of a gigantic cavern. He tried to skid to a stop, but with his running inertia in the low gravity, he slid across the balcony. There was no railing, but he grabbed one of three metal posts marking the edge of the balcony and clung to it.

He stared down past his feet into a cavern that plunged to a depth of over a quarter of a mile. On the floor of the cavern, rising almost to their balcony level, a dozen Kaiju pods stood on end undergoing final assembly. Rows of low-power red lights ringed the cavern from ceiling to floor, spaced twenty yards apart. A flurry of activity at their bases drew Gate's attention.

"Nazir," he said, spotting mature versions of the strange arthropod creatures from the crèche.

Some of the hundreds of Nazir carried objects into the pods, while others operated machinery ringing the pods. A handful carried short cylinders, using them like torches to seal the pods. A second entrance to one side of the cavern was large enough to admit a full-sized Kaiju.

"They look like workers," Walker said. "Hmm. I wonder where the soldiers are. They can't rely only on the usual assortment of creatures for defense."

Despite Walker's claim, he thought the Wasps, Fleas, and Ticks he had encountered posed sufficient threat to guard the facility. "This must be the final assembly," he said, as he watched the activity below. "Just what we were searching for." He pointed to the underside of the ceiling sixty feet above them. "The ceiling is retractable. They launch the pods from here."

Walker studied the cavern. "We need to find a way down there to set the nuke."

"We can't go back the way we came," Gate pointed out, "and I don't see any stairs."

Walker smiled. "We still have our cables. We can rappel down."

Gate glanced down into the depths of the cavern and hoped Walker was kidding. "Down there?" Although he had rappelled several times inside Kaiju Nusku, and again to enter the cavern, it still frightened him to dangle from a slender thread.

"Sure. There are more balconies below this one. We can rappel from level to level. The deeper we go, the more damage the nuke will do."

Gate wasn't sure a few hundred feet would make a difference to a nuclear blast, but he understood Walker's need to be certain of success. If the Kaiju pods in the cavern were active, it was possible their ebony material could absorb a significant portion of the blast. The closer they were the better. They would have only one chance to end the Nazir threat. They could not afford less than a maximum effort.

After securing a cable to one of the metal posts, Walker went first down the line. Gate followed. In his mind, he knew descending the cable was no more dangerous than while entering the pit, but the 1,200-foot-plus drop pulled at him. More appalling, at such low gravity, the fall would not be a quick one. He would fall for an interminably long time before hitting the bottom with sufficient force to crush his spine.

They descended three levels, almost half the distance before encountering more creatures, this time Wasps. It was not an entire swarm, just a few individuals, but their instinct to attack anything different made then dangerous. Five of the team had reached the balcony, but their sixth member was still on the cable when the Wasps attacked. Unable to release the cable to fire his weapon and prevented from further descending by a Wasp directly below him, he looked down at them begging for help. Gate's RPG was useless in such a situation, but the others fired their MP5Ks and AA-12s in an attempt to protect him. After killing one Wasp and injuring a second, the creatures changed tactics, remaining out of range above the descending man, using him for cover. Walker saw it as a delaying tactic.

"They're playing for time, waiting for reinforcements. Move it, Reynolds," he yelled at the man on the cable. "Loosen your grip and slide."

Reynolds free fell. He made it to within twenty feet of the balcony before a Wasp plunged downwards and blocked him, chewing on the cable to sever it. Reynolds wrapped his legs tightly around the cable, released both hands, and fired a burst from his MP5K. The recoil sent him swinging away from the Wasp. He almost lost his grip and fell. He dropped his weapon and grabbed the cable with both hands. As he swung back like a pendulum, he realized his danger. He kicked at the creature with his feet, but the Wasp ignored his futile blows and plucked him from the cable with two of its legs. The claws ripped into his battle armor, venting his atmosphere. Reynolds groaned over the radio. Then, the Wasp released him.

Gate watched him fall past the balcony in dream-like slow motion, reaching out his hand in a futile gesture to for help. Reynolds' screams echoed in his head.

Cantrell yelled, "Reynolds!" and then fired a burst from her MP5K, killing him. She looked at Gate, her eyes tearing inside her helmet. "I couldn't let him fall."

Gate nodded. Her guilt was misplaced. "You did him a favor."

Now, the remaining Wasps came at them full force. In a flurry of gunfire, they killed all but one. Gate raised his HK200L, aimed carefully, and fired at the sole remaining creature. He willed the rocket to the target, not trusting his aim. The Wasp failed to see the rocket's approach until the last moment. The rocket punched through the Wasp's armor before exploding. It was as if the Wasp disintegrated. A puff of smoke, a cloud of ocher blood, and the Wasp was gone. Pieces of the dead creature cascaded to the ground below, falling slowly like confetti. Cantrell patted him on the back.

"Nice job, Doc."

They now had to hurry. Their display of firepower had not gone unnoticed. Activity on the ground below increased.

"We can't use the ropes," Walker said. "We're too vulnerable."

Gate could see in Walker's eyes that he felt responsible for Reynolds' death. He wanted to offer a word of solace, but knew Walker would not appreciate it. Instead, he suggested, "The aliens must have another way of traversing up and down the complex, an elevator or stairs."

"We have to find it, and we don't have much time."

The grim tone of Walker's voice worried him. If faced with another delay, Walker would order the bomb armed and the timer set. Although delivering the nuke was the reason they had come, Gate wasn't ready to give up yet. Before failure of the mission, he thought he could accept dying, but a small kernel of hope inside yelled at him to keep moving and keep trying.

The balcony led to a tunnel lined with small alcoves. Each alcove contained stone troughs at different heights, feeding stations. A thick slurry dripped into the troughs from holes in the walls. Gate remembered the creatures drinking from the digestive pool in the Kaiju mouth, nutrients derived from pulped humans. He was glad his suit masked the nauseating smell, or he was certain he would have thrown up.

They met with some minor good luck. The only creatures feeding were smaller ones. He recognized Mice from Kaiju Nusku, small cleaners than scrubbed and polished the floors. Others were unknown, coming in a variety of shapes and sizes, from tiny insect-like fliers to hand-sized triangular beetles with rows of centipede legs. If he had brought a cage, he would have tried to collect samples for study, because if all went as planned, they would soon cease to exist, immolated in a nuclear fire.

One of the flying insects landed on Cantrell's armor. "Little shit." She smashed it into pulp with her glove. Moments later, the other denizens of the feeding station became agitated, milling about the ground. She jerked back her boot when one of the triangular beetles walked across it. "What the fuck did I do?"

"The dead insect released pheromones," Gate told her. "They may go into defense mode."

"We can kill them," she replied. "There aren't many."

Walker intervened. "No. We don't have time to waste on small change. We search for a way down."

As they left the feeding station, a few insects followed them, but stopped after a few yards when the pheromones dissipated. Minutes later, they stumbled upon another chamber. This room contained several small pedestals with curved thick opaque crystal screens jutting from the upper surface. One of the screens, illuminated from within, displayed a linear script flowing across its surface. The symbols resembled drunken chicken scratches, but Gate recognized a few of the symbols as similar to ones Walker's team had discovered inside Kaiju Kiribati. He touched the screen, and the script disappeared, replaced by several cryptic icons. Pressing one, a 3D holographic image appeared inside the screen, rotating slowly. The image consisted of a vertical spiral line intersected in several places by curved horizontal lines. Each point of intersection was a node displaying information. The nodes lower on the spiral were all illuminated. The few nodes remaining above the upper horizontal line were blank.

"It looks like a graph, a progress report of some kind," he told Walker. "According to this, they've almost achieved their goal."

"Maybe they'll get a big year-end bonus," Walker said. "Come on, we don't have time for this."

Gate protested. "It could be invaluable."

"We can't take it with us, and we don't have time to destroy it."

Gate took a photo of the graph and the room, sighed at the missed opportunity to learn more about the Nazir, and followed Walker out.

Twenty paces farther down the corridor, they found a narrow shaft in the wall that dropped to the floor of the cavern.

"It might be a transport tube for smaller flying creatures," Gate said, "or maybe just an air vent. It's too small for Wasps."

"Too small for us, too," Walker said. He stared down into the shaft, using his suit light to illuminate its depth. "The nuke will fit though."

Gate's throat tightened with dread. Walker was proposing arming the bomb and lowering it into the shaft by cable. No matter how convenient or expedient the shaft might be, activating the nuke left them with no way out of the alien facility, not in the thirty-minute timeframe. He alerted Walker about his concerns.

"That doesn't give us much time."

"We've lost contact with Costas' group. For all we know, they failed. We can't pass up this opportunity. Once the nuke's armed, we concentrate on escaping. We might get lucky."

Gate thought they were already pushing their luck too far. "We might not."

"I'll give you and the others fifteen minutes before I arm the nuke and lower it. If you're not out in forty-five minutes …"

His voice trailed off. Gate understood the implications. He also understood that Walker intended to sacrifice himself to give them a few extra minutes. "I can't let you do it, Aiden."

Walker smiled. "You can't stop me. I outrank you. Carry your intel back to the *Assegai*. Tell Sakiri … Tell him to carry on. Blow this place to hell. Win this damn war."

Gate was dumbfounded. It had finally come down to his worst-case scenario. Walker did not intend to leave Haumea. He had no words to express how he felt. Walker had seemed like a stone wall, unperturbed by any crisis and unbeatable. He knew he could not dissuade Walker from his chosen course. Instead, he offered Walker his hand. "It has been a pleasure working with you, Aiden."

"Same here, Gate. When you see Costas, tell him no flowers."

"I'll do that. You'll find a way out of this," he blurted, knowing it was unlikely.

"I don't think so this time. It's time to pay the piper. Cantrell."

"Yes, sir," she answered.

"You're in charge. Get Wilson, Doctor Rutherford, and Ramirez out of here. When you reach the surface, put as much distance between you and this place as you can."

"Yes, sir," she replied.

"Now, go. Don't waste time with long goodbyes."

Cantrell and the other two team members walked away. Gate lingered a moment longer; then, turned and followed. He could think of nothing more to say. He fought the urge to turn for one last look at Walker, thinking it would somehow jinx him. Walker would find a way out. He always did.

25

August 22, Haumea –

The tunnel that Costas and his team investigated sloped downward into Haumea's depths. After trudging three clicks, passing only empty chambers along the way, he wondered if the tunnel pierced to the heart of the planetoid and exited on the far side. He faced his explorations with a mixture of equal parts gratitude and disappointment – grateful the aliens had not yet discovered them; disappointed he had not had the chance to shoot something.

"This looks interesting," he said, as he stood before a translucent curtain suspended from the ceiling like beads of frozen water droplets on strings. He tapped one with his gloved hand. "Solid." He shoved his hand through the curtain. "They're soft on the other side. Feels warmer, too. Here goes nothing." He pushed his way through the curtain and emerged in a space filled with atmosphere. "Well, this is different."

The temperature beyond the barrier was that of a spring day in New York, sweltering compared to the ambient temperature of the planet. To his disappointment, the air was not breathable. He would have to remain inside his bulky, uncomfortable, and claustrophobic suit. He immediately removed his MP5K from its protective bag.

"At least we can use these," he said. He felt safer with a real weapon. The H&K L200 was club compared to the MP5K, a finely crafted tool.

A short distance past the barrier, they chanced upon a large chamber through an open doorway carved into the solid rock of the tunnel. Inside, he swept his suit light over a stack of parts composed of the alien ebony material – trusses, rods, blister covers, and most gruesome of all, thousands of replacement Kaiju teeth. His rage rose when he saw the teeth. He had witnessed countless people sliced and ground up by similar teeth before going into the Kaiju gullet. He immediately wanted to blow them up but knew their explosives were

197

useless against the super dense material. He could at least make them more difficult to use by burying it.

"Nicholson, you and Mullins rig the entrance with that Russian explosive we brought. We'll see if it's any good. Wegman, Tate. You two keep watch."

It worried him that so far they had encountered no alien threat. The Nazir had to know they were there, but were ignoring them. Did they discount the human threat so easily? He watched Nicholson and Mullins place the kilo blocks of plastic explosive above and on each side of the entrance, noting the expert manner in which the two men handled the explosives. They worked as if it were a training exercise and not a dangerous situation on an alien-inhabited planet. In spite of their suits and gloves, the two made quick work of the task. Costas noted the rock was a loose aggregate fused by the laser used to excavate the room. The explosion would bring down the entire ceiling on the supply cache.

"Set the timer for five minutes. The noise will probably bring every mother lovin' alien bitch to investigate. We want to be long gone."

They made it only 1,000 yards down the tunnel when an alarm sounded. "Well, they know we're here," he said. "Watch your asses." He assumed the alarm was for Walker's team. He hoped Walker's team was still viable.

They did not have long to wait for the first visitors. Fifteen spindly, bi-pedal, avian monstrosities with vicious beaks and bladelike appendages for wings rushed down the tunnel toward them. Instead of feathers, their eight-foot tall bodies sprouted sharp spikes. Their backward jointed legs ended in three enormous raptor claws, like those of a giant condor. They reminded Costas of the giant birds from *Sinbad the Sailor*.

"Kaiju Rocs," he said while loading his rocket launcher. "Is it just me, or do these Nazir assholes just try to freak us out with things from our legends or giant fucking bugs? Let's fricassee these bastards."

The rockets made short work of the Rocs, leaving pieces of smoking flesh and pools of yellow blood spreading across the floor of the tunnel. Costas discarded his empty launcher and sprayed a couple of the twitching carcasses with his MP5K just in case. It felt good to shoot something. It was the reason he had come.

"Let's hump it before more of these Rocs show up."

He stopped, uncertain which way to proceed when the tunnel divided. Flipping a mental coin, he chose the right-hand path. They passed more storerooms, some empty, some filled with things he didn't recognize. The only creatures they encountered were tiny Kaiju Mice gliding along the floor cleaning it with their abrasive undersides. The tunnel emptied into a massive chamber six hundred feet wide. Dim red lights in the three-hundred-foot ceiling barely illuminated the cavernous space. The true dimensions of the open space were difficult to determine in the dim light. Although the cavern appeared empty, the nape of Costas' neck began tingling.

"This don't look Kosher. Keep your eyes peeled for hostiles. Anything moves, shoot it."

As they marched down the cavern, he began to discern shapes in the distance, still unclear in the muted light. When he finally recognized one object, a chill enveloped him.

"Kaiju," he whispered over the comm.

Three giant Kaiju, each one larger than the original three monsters that had attacked Earth, loomed in the darkness. They stood on partially folded legs near a series of openings in the wall of the cavern. A balcony eighty feet above the floor of the cavern ran along the wall parallel to the blister openings on the Kaiju. They had stumbled upon a Kaiju assembly room. He motioned the team against the nearest wall, the only available cover. After watching for several minutes, he determined the Kaiju were not active.

"These are some damn big buggers. I'd better contact the major about this. Sheesh, as if he doesn't have troubles enough."

He tried the comm link but got only static. Cursing, he said, "No dice. At least we've got team coms so we won't have to butt heads to talk."

He spotted a wide zigzagging ramp leading up to the balcony level. It looked like a good place to go. It at least offered a better view of the cavern. Expecting an alien attack at any moment, they bounded up the ramp. At the top, an unwanted surprise awaited them. Dark objects that Costas at first mistook as alien machinery or stacks of supplies suddenly reared on multiple jointed legs and regarded them with their two large red eyes. Tentacles ringed their vertical mouths. He immediately recognized them from the report from Atlanta.

"Spiders," he yelled. "More fucking nightmares. Watch yourselves."

The Spider watchdogs, all six of them, attacked together. The width of the balcony allowed only two of the ten-foot-long creatures at a time to confront them, but others crawled along the edge of the balcony to encircle them. Mullins fired his H&K L200. The rocket struck the first creature in the cephalothorax with a glancing blow. The warhead exploded, but only scored the dense carapace and the flesh beneath it. The Spider leapt backward, leaving a trail of dark blood, but remained on its feet.

Costas fired his MP5K at the creature's eyes, attempting to blind it. He grinned with satisfaction, as he dug a small crater in one red orb with the 7.62mm armor-coated rounds. The Spider regarded him warily with its one good eye, thick blood oozing from its other the shattered orb. The alien Spiders proved difficult to kill, but rage swept aside Costas' revulsion and fear of spiders. He emptied his weapon into the open wound, striking a vital organ. The Spider convulsed and tipped over dead. He quickly discarded the empty magazine and shoved in a fresh one.

Tate took out one of the Spiders crawling along the edge of the balcony with his RPG, but a chunk of flying stone caught Wegman in the side and knocked him down. Costas stepped between the downed man and the Spiders, giving Wegman time to regain his feet, shaken but not seriously injured.

"You good?" Costas asked him.

Wegman shook his head to clear it. "Yeah, just sore."

"Well, get back in the fight."

Wegman nodded and fired his AA-12 at a nosy Spider, bracing himself against the wall and pumping shells into the chamber as quickly as he could. Costas probed for weak spots on the Spiders, finally finding one where the legs joined the body. He concentrated his fire there and amputated two legs on one creature, leaving a gaping wound. He emptied a second magazine enlarging the hole; then, changed magazines a third time, knelt, and continued firing into the creature's underbelly. It roared in pain and died, falling off the balcony in its death throes.

Nicholson stepped too close to one Spider and went down when the creature swept him from his feet with its front legs. In an instant, it hovered over him, slashing at his body with its sharp, clawed feet. Costas fired into the creature's open mouth until it retreated, but he was too late. Nicholson was dead, his armor ripped open and a large gash in his chest exposing his lungs, muscle, and bone. Enraged to lose a man, Costas advanced on the Spider. His charge took it by surprise. Instead of attacking, it circled him warily. Out of the corner of his eye, he saw Tate shoulder his RPG and fire again. The rocket struck the Spider's rear and exploded. Costas ducked, as bits of the creature and gouts of blood splashed his suit. He stood and wiped his faceplate clean with the back of his gloved hand.

"Yuck! Spider guts."

Two Spiders remained. Tate had no more rockets, and they were all running low on ammunition. "Concentrate your fire on the nearest creature. Kill it, and then go for the second one."

Both Spiders continued to press the attack, but now the fire team could work as a unit. Their target danced around the platform, refusing to allow the second creature around it to attack. By focusing on one creature and firing at its vulnerable areas, they managed to kill it. The second Spider, sensing the danger, attempted to flee, but they chased after it, dismembering its legs with well-placed bursts. Even disabled and dying, it continued to pull itself across the ground using only its two short front legs. Costas closed with it from behind to avoid the thrashing tentacles and placed three rounds into the back of its head from two feet away.

The battle left Costas breathing heavily. He needed a break, but he didn't have time. Tarrying too long gave the aliens time to regroup and attack.

"Come on, you alien-slaughtering mother humpers. We've got a job to do."

"We've got problems, Sarge," Tate called out. He stared at the nuke in his pack. "This thing's active."

"Son of a ..." Costas checked the device and saw two minutes and forty seconds of the thirty-minute countdown had elapsed. It had activated while they were fighting. "I never did like the fact the two nukes were synced. We've got to find a place to leave this baby and get the hell out of town." He looked around. "Here is as good as any other place. Maybe we can take out some Kaiju."

Tate shoved the nuke underneath the corpse of the Spider they had just killed. "This will do."

"Okay, people. Move your asses like your life depended on it, 'cause it damn well it does."

He chose a tunnel at random. It sloped downward, not the direction he wanted to go, but the solid curtain wall cut off their direction of retreat. They had less than twenty-seven minutes to find a way to the surface, or sweet Mama Costas was going to be missing her finest son.

26

August 23, Haumea –

Gate knew they had stumbled upon an important part of the facility when he saw the vast array of electronic equipment in the room. Two aliens stood in front of one panel, looking almost as surprised to see him, as he was to see the aliens. Though they were larger duplicates of the creatures in the crèche pods, he did not have time to study them. Cantrell opened fire as soon as they entered the chamber. The aliens had no weapons and died quickly under her withering fire. Though he longed to examine the alien corpses, Gate turned his attention to the exotic equipment.

Like most Nazir machinery, it consisted of a disorienting fusion of manufactured and organic components. Tubes containing liquid connected the machines, as well as cables clearly electrical in nature. One particular piece of equipment aroused his curiosity, an oscillating globe floating above an ebony crystal pedestal. The globe material was opaque but glowed from within with lights that morphed through the visible spectrum from violet to red. A deep resonant rumble in his chest reminded him of the loud bass guitar he had heard once at a Houston nightclub. The heavy metal band was as different from his usual jazz trios as wine from water, but he had gone at a friend's insistence. It had been a miserable experience. He wondered if the low frequency emanating from an Extreme Low-Frequency generator could be a means of short-range communication inside the underground facility or with the Kaiju in orbit. One panel screen displayed a number of objects represented by glowing icons. Dim icons remained stationary in a semicircle at the edge of the screen, but several were brightly lit and in movement. The number corresponded with the pods in orbit around Haumea, furthering his theory. He pushed and twisted projections and protuberances until hitting upon the one he sought. The moving icons dimmed and stopped moving. He hoped that meant they were offline.

A thick ebony crystal cable ran from a second console to a small version of a Kaiju pod, less than three feet in diameter. A web of azure lines illuminated the crystal portion of the metallic filigree teardrop, which he recognized as a gravity wave generator, the heart of the communication device.

"Cantrell, we've got to destroy this."

She looked up from nudging one of the dead aliens with her boot. "Why?"

"It's how the aliens control the Kaiju."

"I thought the Kaiju acted independently now."

"To a certain degree, but they have small brains that need constant updating. They feed data back to their masters, and the Nazir use that data to determine a series of courses of actions. If we destroy that link, we might confuse them."

"Gotcha, Doc. Ramirez, help me wire this shit."

Gate studied the apparatus while Cantrell and the others planted the last of their plastic explosives. A small metal box attached to one machine contained round depressions in its surface. Four of the depressions held crystal cylinders. A dozen similar cylinders lay nestled in a box beside it. It reminded him of a flash drive for a computer. If it contained alien data, it could prove invaluable. Lacking the proper tools to remove it, he used the butt of his MP5K as a hammer and broke the box free of the machine. He hoped he hadn't rendered it useless.

Much of the equipment consisted of small semi-organic modules attached to larger metal machinery. He ripped away as many as he could carry and placed them in the empty explosives bag. He didn't know their function, but by studying them, the scientists on Earth might gain some knowledge of Nazir technology.

"Ready," Cantrell announced. She held a remote detonator in her hand.

"Give me a minute." He knelt beside one of the aliens. Its fragile anatomy denoted their home world as a low-gravity planet, explaining why they had chosen Haumea as a base and used Kaiju on Earth to do their dirty work. The heavier gravity would have killed them.

"We don't have much time, Doc. We have to blow and go."

Her reminder that they were racing twin nuclear blasts urged him to move faster. The odds of escaping were dismal, but he refused to quit. Walker was giving his life to give them every minute he could. He could do no less to provide Earth with valuable information.

They took shelter against the wall of the corridor outside the chamber. He nodded and Cantrell pressed the detonator's remote trigger. Gate expected a large explosion. Instead, it sounded muffled, like firecrackers going off. The size of the blast worried him. He looked inside the chamber and saw that Cantrell had placed the explosives in an expert manner. No piece of equipment remained undamaged. Fluids ran across the floor. Sparks flew from severed power cables. Chunks of metal and crystal littered the floor.

"That should slow them down," he said.

"If the nukes work, it will be a moot point," she replied. "We have about twelve minutes."

Gate checked his watch. The second had seemed to spin like a top around the dial, ticking off the time remaining. He noted that it was 1:30 a.m. ship's time, based on Houston's Central Daylight Time. The threat of imminent death pushed back his exhaustion. He hurried his steps, as they retraced their path until they reached the beaded atmosphere curtain across the corridor. It now dangled limp and allowed them to pass through. They had damaged its controlling mechanism with the explosion.

They reached the pit through which they had entered the network of caverns. Low gravity made climbing the cable easier than descending. Despite his fatigue, Gate grabbed the steel cable and pulled himself up. His eagerness to escape added an additional impetus to his efforts. On the surface, Gate noted the absolute darkness. By shutting down the Kaiju pods, he had also eliminated the source of the light. They would be running in the dark. Determined to place as much distance as possible between him and the blast, Gate's long-legged, low-gravity bounds left him off the ground for so long his mind tried to convince him he was falling. He fought down the panic by concentrating on his footing on the treacherous ground. His suit light was sorely inadequate for the task, illuminating only a small patch of black ground, and then only when he was so low to the ground he could not alter his trajectory to pick a safe spot to land.

He didn't know where they were going. The module that had delivered them was nowhere in sight. Their only hope was getting safely away and signaling their location to the *Assegai*, if it was still there. He had no idea how the battle around the planet had been going. Had they lost? Was it only a matter of time until the Nazir found them? He lost track of time, but the explosion caught him while he was on the ground. The force of the blast heaved him high into the air, tumbling like his first spacewalk. He tried to right himself, but only made things worse by his frantic efforts. The shockwave roared across the flat, rocky plain silently in the vacuum, a cloud of dust, smoke, and rock. It swept across the surface of the small planet, gripping him in its warm embrace.

He felt as if a thousand fists were pummeling him, rocks slamming into his limbs and sides. If not for the armor, the rocky onslaught would have pierced his suit in a hundred places. The bag across his back holding the alien apparatus took the brunt of the attack and protected his air supply. He hoped the explosion had not damaged it. He curled into a tight ball to protect his damaged faceplate. He watched the surface dwindle below him as he rode on the turbulent current of air.

He waited for the inevitable fall when he would crash back to the surface to his death, but it did not come. The force of the shockwave had propelled him into orbit. Clouds of smaller rocks and dust surrounded him, making seeing the others impossible. He did not know if they had survived the blast. He was not traveling fast, but he was moving farther away from Haumea toward the thin band of rings. He tried his radio, but the blast had damaged it.

Once again, he could do nothing but wait for death.

27

August 23, Haumea –

After ten minutes had elapsed, scratching noises loud enough to hear through his helmet reverberated down the corridor. Walker knew it was not good news. He was afraid he might not be able to give Gate and the others their fifteen-minute head start. He hadn't heard from Costas, but feared the worst. If Costas' team had triggered their device, he would know about it. If anything happened to him, the entire venture inside Haumea could be for nothing. Taking no chances, he initiated the thirty-minute timer on the nuke. There was no backing out now.

As he lowered it down the shaft, the first creatures appeared from around a turn of the corridor. He had expected more Ticks, or even Fleas. He did not expect the alien Nazir in person. Four of them stood twenty yards away staring at him with their twin sets of eyes. He could not read their alien faces, but he assumed they examined him with curiosity, much as he did them. They wore no clothing to distinguish them from the lower creatures with which he was familiar, but as Gate had correctly pointed out, their eyes held a glimmer of intelligence. Though unclothed, they were not unadorned. The longer pair of four grasping arms cradled short cylinders similar to the ones he had seen carried by the aliens in the lower cavern. He had no doubt they were deadly.

He released the rope and let the bomb drop the last fifteen feet. In the low gravity, its descent took longer than he expected. He wondered why the aliens did not immediately attack. When the sharp thud of impact echoed up the shaft, one alien jumped slightly on two of its four legs, but still they did not attack. Walker slowly thumbed off the safety of his AA-12 shotgun, smiling at the aliens like an imbecile. He was too far away for the shotgun to be effective, but he expected to be a lot closer very soon. He reached into his pocket and brought out a fragmentary grenade.

"Hey, glad to meet you," he yelled to them. "Here's something I brought from the good ole U.S.A. for you."

He yanked the pin and tossed the grenade, simultaneously hitting the ground. The aliens correctly interpreted his actions as an attack. One of them fired his cylinder. A loud hiss accompanied the beam of light that struck the wall behind where he had been standing. The rock sizzled and glowed red for several seconds. Hot shards of rock splattered his armor but caused no serious damage, although it would have easily fried his naked flesh. *So, they have smaller versions of the tunneling lasers. This should be interesting.*

Seconds later, the grenade exploded. The concussion slammed his chest against the solid rock of the floor. A piece of shrapnel ricocheted from his helmet with a sharp ping. He quickly rose and raced toward the aliens through the cloud of smoke with his shotgun leveled ready for action. They were dead, incinerated by the blast. Pieces of leg and torso lay scattered across the tunnel floor. Ocher goo dripped from the walls.

"They may be great bioengineers, but they're lousy soldiers."

He had struck the first blow directly against the aliens. They were more fragile than the creatures they created to do their bidding. He looked down at their shattered remains and felt no remorse. They had come to Earth as hostiles and deserved no sympathy from him. He was more concerned with their weapons. The blast had damaged three of the lasers the aliens carried. He picked one up, its metal casing split, and a handful of powdered ebony crystals spilled out. Walker slung his shotgun over his shoulder and retrieved the undamaged laser. It was awkward in his grip but simple enough to operate. A single stud activated the weapon.

"This might come in handy."

The bomb was active, and the aliens now knew where he was. He had no reason to linger. He didn't expect to make it out alive, but it was not in his nature to stand around waiting for death to come to him. At the very least, he would meet it halfway. He hoped he would encounter more aliens. His bloodlust was up, and killing aliens seemed like a good way to go. A nuke was too impersonal. His grim visage as he marched down the corridor would have frightened any human he encountered. He didn't know if aliens could interpret human miens, but he would give be glad to give them a quick lesson in facial recognition.

He chose corridors at random, killing a few Ticks and smaller creatures along the way with the laser, taking delight in its power. The aliens' defenses seemed frenzied and haphazard, as if they had bigger worries than him to attend to. He hoped it was Costas' doing. The big sergeant had a way of strewing destruction wherever he went. Walker emerged in a large room where giant machines along the walls hummed and throbbed. He had no idea of their purpose, but decided to put them out of commission. The laser was perfect for the job. He fired until the leaser began heating up in his hands, punching holes in machinery, and severing ducts and cables. Streams of viscous fluids ran across the floor of the room. The machines still functioning after his frenzied attack developed a decidedly sickly sound.

His assault drew attention. More Ticks poured into the room, followed by a dozen aliens herding them like sheep. He thought it strange that only four of the aliens carried weapons. He took shelter behind one of the machines and fired the laser until he could no longer hold it in his gloved hands. He had killed two Nazir and a dozen Ticks, but many more remained, and they had him pinned down. He took careful aim with his shotgun and began firing, picking off the nearest Ticks, wishing the aliens were within range. He hoped the laser cooled down quickly. The aliens' laser blasts splattered molten globs of metal and chips of stone from the walls and machinery around him, spreading the carnage. The aliens were finishing his job for him.

Without warning, the rear rank of aliens exploded. As the smoke cleared, he saw Costas and three of his fire team. Their sudden and unexpected appearance caught the aliens by surprise. RPGs, shotguns, and MP5Ks blasted into their exposed flanks. Ticks milled about in confusion uncertain whom to attack. Walker left his refuge and waded among them, firing his shotgun from inches away, ignoring the goo splashing his suit and faceplate. When he and Costas met in the middle of the room, no aliens or Ticks remained.

"You made it," Walker said to a grinning Costas.

"When I heard the commotion, I knew you would be in the middle of it." He glanced around. "Where are the others?"

"I sent Gate and the remaining three of my team to find a way out. I set our nuke," he checked his watch. "We have sixteen minutes."

"Yeah, ours activated when yours did. We placed it in a cavern with some truly enormous Kaiju a level below this one. We killed a shitload of these Nazir buggers along the way, so the day hasn't been a total loss. Funny, they don't act like soldiers. They have no tactics. They just looked at us. Most of them weren't even armed."

Any other time, Costas' observations would have struck a nerve with him, but he was too tired to give it any serious consideration. He had matters more pressing on his mind. "Nothing to do now but wait for the fireworks."

Costas took a seat on a low stone bench. "I wish I had a cigar. And some Scotch," he added. "A nice cigar and a glass of Scotch with fireworks afterward."

Walker ignored him and began walking back the way he had come.

"Hey, where are you going?" Costas asked.

"To find a balcony. I want a good seat for this." Sitting in the corridor waiting on a nuclear blast seemed too enclosed and depressing. The cavern was open space. It wouldn't be as good as looking at the sky, but it would have to do.

Costas shrugged and rose from his seat. "What the hell. I'll join you."

They encountered no more alien creatures along the way. Walker guessed they were in a frantic struggle to finish the remaining pods. When he walked out onto a balcony, the pit below was in frenzied activity with aliens directing giant Kaiju into the pods like cowboys herding cattle. *At least this bunch isn't going anywhere.*

Costas leaned over the rail. "I wish I could take my helmet off and spit on the bastards."

Walker grinned. "Or unzip your pants."

"Yeah, that too. I'd like to take a massive dump on them and shout, 'Manna from heaven.'"

Walker felt the balcony quiver. A second tremor brought a shower of rock from the cavern ceiling. As he looked up, the entire ceiling slid aside, grinding as it retreated into recesses in the pit walls. Seconds later, the air in the cavern began rushing outward through the opening. Two missiles shot through the opening and exploded on the cavern floor, causing even more chaos among the aliens. The cyclone of air swept down the corridor, trying to push Walker and the others off the balcony. He clung to a metal post.

Struggling to be heard over the radio in the din of noise, Walker warned, "Hang on to something!"

One soldier rolled by Walker and hung halfway off the balcony, gripping the ground with his gloves. Walker reached down and grasped the back of his suit, pulling him back. After two minutes, the blast of escaping air diminished, as the aliens activated more of the atmosphere barriers. Glancing over the side, he saw dozens of aliens lying dead on the ground. Others had escaped.

His suit com buzzed. "This is Colonel Sakiri. I boosted my signal to cut through the dampening field. Do you read me?"

Walker hurriedly hit the send switch. "Walker here. Glad to see you, Colonel. Now, clear the area. You've got eight minutes before our nukes explode."

"Plenty of time. I'm here to give you a lift."

At first, Sakiri's comment confused Walker. The *Lances* had room for two people, no more. They couldn't possibly ferry everyone to safety in eight minutes. Then, he saw the aft airlock module that had delivered them dangling from cables suspended beneath the *Lance*. The airlock door was open. The colonel was trying to save their ass by risking his own.

"If you insist." Walker guided him down. "We're on the third balcony below you to your right."

Free of the dampening field, Walker's radio picked up chatter from the other pilots fighting the Kaiju pods. Normal nuclear missiles were ineffective against the dense, energy absorbing alien armor. Instead, Driller missiles coated with Kaiju armor latched onto pods exteriors and drilled through the armor before their nuclear warheads exploded. The pilots played cat and mouse with the pods as the pods tried to ram them. Some of *Lances* lost the game. One in three missiles failed to destroy the pods. The numbers were on the aliens' side. Then, the game suddenly changed.

"They've stopped," one pilot said.

Walker heard Sakiri ask, "What do you mean?"

"They've stopped moving. They're just dead in space, doing nothing."

"Disengage," Sakiri ordered. "I repeat, disengage. Reform around the *Assegai* in case it's a trap."

Walker didn't know if it was an alien ruse, as Sakiri suspected, but he was glad for the respite.

Whatever had stopped the pods, it did not affect the Nazir. Below, more aliens appeared wearing opaque bubbles over their heads against the vacuum, firing lasers at the *Lance*. Several blasts struck the module, but none struck the aircraft. Sakiri dropped into the cavern until the module swung near the balcony. It would take too long to steady it. They would have to take their chances.

"Jump for it," he told the others.

Waiting until the module's pendulum swing brought it closer to the balcony, he leaped. Two others leapt with him. A laser bolt caught one of the men in the middle of his leap. He exploded in a bright flash as his oxygen tank combusted. Walker hit the deck and rolled inside. Sakiri edged the module closer until it banged against the balcony, bending one of the metal posts. Costas and the remaining men raced aboard. Before they could find something to hang on to, Sakiri lifted. They braced each other as the module rose swiftly up the cavern. Laser blasts struck the bottom and sides. One blast punched a hole in the floor. Another holed the open air-lock door. If they didn't hurry, the module would look like Swiss cheese.

Finally, they were out. As they flew across the landscape, rising higher in the Haumean sky, Walker checked his watch – *two minutes*. The *Lance* was twenty clicks above the surface when the two bombs exploded. The nukes were too small to shatter Haumea, but the detonation of two, 340-kiloton bombs in a confined space was still a spectacular sight. The surface rippled from the epicenter of the blast. Frozen patches of frost heated instantly to gas from the heat. Loose rock bounced on the surface. A plume of flame and smoke shot from the mouth of the launch cavern. Seconds later, twin columns erupted from the two pits through which they had entered the underground facility. Walker was confident the two bombs had scoured the entire facility clean of any life forms and destroyed any alien machinery. Any Kaiju that survived now lay buried beneath thousands of tons of rubble.

"Did you pick up Doctor Rutherford or any others?" he asked Sakiri.

Sakiri paused before replying, "No. No contact with Doctor Rutherford or anyone else."

Walker offered up a silent prayer for Gate. He had tried to give them a head start. Instead, he had escaped. They had stopped the aliens and destroyed their base, but the price had been a steep one.

* * * *

When Walker and the other survivors arrived at the *Assegai*, they transferred to the *Assegai's* main habitat module. Seeing it almost empty was a shock. The pilots and weapons specialists were in their *Lances*, leaving only the five technicians aboard. Walker unsuited and went directly to the bridge.

"How bad is it?" he asked Worthen.

Worthen's face betrayed his concern. "Eleven *Lances* are gone, but they destroyed sixteen pods."

The math wasn't in their favor. There were many more pods than *Lances*. "Is there any further activity from the pods or on the surface?"

"No. They're just sitting there. We've picked up no signals from the surface."

"Scan Haumea's surface. Doctor Rutherford and the rest of my team might have escaped." Worthen hesitated. "Do it!" Walker yelled.

"Major," Blivens said, his voice surprisingly calm. "The surface is covered in dust and smoke, and a cloud of material ejected by the explosions is shielding the surface. Until it settles, our scanners won't be able to pick up anything."

Walker tried to control his anger. Taking his frustration out on the hapless technicians was not going to help find Gate. He took a deep breath and nodded. "Inform me as soon as it becomes possible. I won't give up on them."

Back in the ready room, Costas was stowing his spacesuit. He glanced at Walker when he entered the room. "He's hard to kill."

Walker sat on a bench. It felt good to be at near Earth normal gravity after hours on Haumea. His muscles ached from the jostling during their escape. He rubbed his right leg calf muscle to ease a cramp. "If he didn't make it out …"

"If anyone could do it, Gate could. He's got the luck. Besides, he had Cantrell with him. She's as hard-assed as they come."

Walker wished he had the sergeant's confidence. Luck only went so far, and Gate had used up all his.

The intercom buzzed. "I've got Colonel Sakiri here."

"Put him through to me. Walker here, Colonel."

"I'm having my men manually attach Driller missiles to the pods. They remain inactive, but for how long, I don't know."

"While you're at it, lob a couple more nukes down into the alien facility. We can't take any chances."

"Good call. I'll see to it."

"Have you heard anything?"

"From your missing team members? No. We can't do a visual search of the surface yet, but I promise you I will before we launch missiles."

"No. Begin the attack as soon as you're ready. Waiting is too risky."

Costas looked at Walker with pleading eyes, but Walker shook his head. His heart tightened in his chest. If Gate and the others were alive, he had just doomed them. The mission came first if Earth were to survive. The odds of Gate having survived were small, but experience had taught Walker that odds sometimes lied. Even so, he believed Gate would understand what he was doing. At least, he hoped he would.

Something about the whole Haumea set up troubled him. They had come expecting an alien military base with a Kaiju factory. They had found the factory, but nothing they encountered had seemed military. Even the lasers the aliens carried looked too bulky for weapons, as if they were tools hastily utilized as a weapon. They had met no organized resistance even when the aliens knew they were there. They acted more like technicians, workers, and supervisors thrust into a dangerous situation defending themselves. Had the Nazir depended on their distance from Earth to protect them? Even so, they should have been better prepared.

He let the thought slip from his mind, as he leaned forward the crack his spine. He was exhausted and too concerned for Gate's safety to think any more about the aliens.

"I'll be in the galley," he said to Costas.

* * * *

"I've located them," Worthen shouted down the corridor fifteen minutes later.

Walker sat drinking coffee waiting for Sakiri to blast Haumea. He pushed the cup aside and bounced down the corridor to the bridge so quickly he banged his head on the ceiling.

"Where?"

Worthen pointed to a screen. "There, about ten kilometers above the surface. It's a light flashing SOS."

Walker slapped Worthen on the back. "Good job! Can we get to them?"

"No. There's too much debris in the way. Besides, the colonel ordered us to maintain position."

"Contact him. Let him know we have survivors." Walker did not know if the signal originated from Gate or one of the others, but the fact that someone was still alive gave him hope. "They don't have much oxygen left."

As Worthen contacted Sakiri, Walker listened in.

"I can't spare any *Lances*. We don't know how many are required. Our priority is preparing the pods for destruction. We don't know if they might reactivate at any moment."

Walker cursed under his breath at the delay, but Sakiri was right. Completing the mission came first. However, Sakiri was not finished.

"I can send one *Lance* to breakaway and pick up the second air-lock compartment. If anyone is still alive, we'll find them."

Walker sighed in relief. "Thank you, Colonel."

"According to you, Doctor Rutherford carries vital intel about the Nazir. We need every scrap of knowledge we can get. Once they are aboard the *Assegai*, move her away from the planet. When we detonate our nukes, we will follow and rendezvous outside the Kuiper Belt."

Walker didn't know if Sakiri was attempting the rescue solely for the possible intel, or if he was simply using it as an excuse. He didn't care as long as Gate and the others were safe.

The next thirty minutes were nerve-racking, as Walker waited on word from Sakiri. Finally, "I located someone," the *Lance* pilot announced. "They're not moving." Walker held his breath. "Their faceplate is broken. I'm afraid they're dead, Major Walker. My weapons specialist is going outside to bring the body on board the compartment."

Not knowing the identity of the dead person was the worst part. It could have been any one of his four missing team members. Ten minutes later, the pilot reported, "Two more. One of them is flashing suit lights." He held his breath until the pilot announced, "They're both alive. Delbertson is helping them aboard." A few minutes later, he said, "The survivors are Corporal Cantrell and Private Ramirez. The dead man is Private Wilson."

Walker fought back the bitter disappointment that none of the survivors was Gate. "Good job. Bring them home."

"Will do, Major."

"Are we just leaving Doctor Rutherford out there?" Worthen asked.

"We don't know that he's there, or if he survived the blast."

"The others did," Worthen pointed out.

"Two did, but we're running out of time. We have to move the *Assegai*."

Worthen looked as if he wanted to argue, but he held his tongue. Walker knew how he felt. Gate was his friend, but the safety of the ship and crew was too important to risk.

"I've got something, Major, farther out than the others."

Gate reached for the microphone and took it from Worthen's hand. "What?"

"Another body. I'll move closer. Three minutes. There's a lot of debris here." Three minutes later, the pilot announced, "No movement." Gate sagged as disappointment washed over him; then, "No. Wait. He's alive."

Walker wanted to shout into the microphone. "Pick him up and get back here ASAP." He smiled at Worthen. "They got him. Gate's coming home."

28

August 23, Haumea –

When Gate saw the aft module from the *Assegai* moving slowly toward him through the dust and rubble, he almost cried out in joy. He had thirty minutes of air remaining and did not want a repeat of his earlier adventure after destroying the Kaiju pods with the *Javelin*. Cantrell and two others stood in the open airlock pointing at him. He was glad to see them. The pilot of the *Lance* transporting the module maneuvered it deftly and scooped him up like dipping goldfish from a pond with a net. Cantrell and one of the others grabbed him and reeled him in until he grabbed a handhold on the wall. Like his, her radio antenna had sheared away from the blast. She leaned forward and placed her helmet to his to speak.

"I was beginning to worry about you, Doc."

"I'm glad you decided to come after me." He pointed to the body floating at the rear of the module. "Who's that?"

"Wilson. He didn't make it. Just me and Ramirez."

"Did anyone …?"

Cantrell grinned. "Major Walker and Sergeant Costas are on board the *Assegai*. As soon as we dock, the *Assegai* is moving off to let Colonel Sakiri blow the rest of these Nazir bastards to hell."

Gate panicked. "I couldn't send my data to the ship. They need it."

"Relax, Doc. Whatever you did, you stopped the pods. They're just sitting there now like lumps of coal. We'll reach the ship in ten minutes."

Gate stared out at Haumea, now merely a dark shape in the distance. He could not see the pods or the other *Lances*. Destroying the communications equipment had neutralized the pods in orbit, but he worried they had a failsafe system that overrode the signal from Haumea. They could reactivate at any moment.

"We don't have much time."

"I'll tell the weapons specialist to inform the pilot. Maybe she can speed things up."

As she pressed her helmet against the *Lance's* weapons specialist, Gate remembered his low air supply. He detached the hose from his nearly depleted tank, removed the tank, and replaced it with a full one from one of the lockers. His first breath of fresh air tasted sweet. No matter how efficient the suit's air scrubbers, after six hours, the air became stale.

When he caught his first sight of the *Assegai*, his heart nearly burst through his chest protector. As small and confining as the ship was, it was a piece of home, the nearest piece of Earth for 5 billion miles. The pilot deposited the module off the *Assegai's* port side. The second module held a position on the starboard side.

"We'll just attach a safety cable to the ship to hold the module in place," Cantrell told him, "and then transfer across. We can properly secure them later. The major wants us out of here double time." She glanced over at Wilson's body. "We'll leave Wilson's body inside and give it a proper spacing later," she added.

After floating in space around Haumea, the prospect of a spacewalk from the module to the ship seemed less daunting. He surprised himself by making the leap across to the airlock without hesitation and expertly grabbing the handhold. He entered the *Assegai* through the smaller forward airlock.

Walker was waiting for him. "Welcome aboard!" he yelled, grinning as he slapped Gate on the back.

"Thanks. I need to transmit this data to Earth," Gate replied.

Walker nodded. "Do it. We're leaving as soon as the module is secured."

Walker followed Gate to the bridge. Gate's warm reception surprised him. Even Blivens seemed genuinely pleased to see him.

"Colonel Sakiri said we have to leave now," Worthen said. "He's moving his ships away from the planet. He'll stay behind to launch missiles at Haumea."

"Get us underway as soon as possible," Walker said.

Gate began stripping his suit. When he saw its condition, he was thankful to be alive. The crack in his faceplate ran almost its full width. Rips in several places in the outer layer of insulation material exposed the fine network of fluid tubing operating the heat exchange system. Dents in the air tank and scrubber revealed the extent of the damage by flying debris. The bag carrying the alien artifacts contained numerous holes. He hoped the contents were still in good enough condition to study. He handed the bag to Walker.

"Here. This might shed a little light on the Nazir."

Walker looked at the contents. "Looks like a good haul. You've been busy."

Gate shrugged. "Just a few things I picked up along the way."

His muscles ached from the pummeling his body had taken from the blast, and he longed for sleep. He looked longingly at his hammock, but he had no time for rest. The next few hours were going to be crucial. If the Nazir had any offensive capabilities remaining, they would attack. If not, the crew of the *Assegai* had the opportunity to end the war.

Walker picked up Gate's helmet and examined it. "I hope you won't need this. It's scrap."

"Don't knock it. It kept me alive. Any word from Earth?" Gate was eager to learn if destroying the communications equipment had affected the Kaiju on Earth.

"Last report was a few hours ago. Twenty pods landed. Four hit the U.S."

"Where?"

"Kansas, Iowa, Oklahoma, and Texas."

Gate's heart jumped. "Texas?"

"Yeah, Texas City. They're threatening Houston."

Too close to home. Galveston, too, where former Director Caruthers now lived. The war with the Nazir became more personal each day that passed.

Cantrell, Ramirez, the pilot, and the weapons specialist cycled through the airlock. "The module is secured, sir," Cantrell reported to Walker.

"Thank you, Corporal. Take us out of here, Blivens."

The only indication of movement was the rapidly shrinking Haumea in the view screen. Within minutes, the Assegai was 100,000 kilometers distant from the planetoid and her two moonlets.

"Hold position," Walker said.

"The other *Lances* are on their way here," Worthen reported. "Colonel Sakiri is making a run at the planet to launch his missiles."

Gate's chest tightened with apprehension. So many things could go wrong.

"The colonel reports missiles fired. Detonation of all devices in thirty seconds."

The *Lances* appeared around the ship. Gate noted their dwindled numbers. He knew now that the hours he had spent study the Kaiju had been worth it. His familiarity with the Nazir technology, as limited as it was, had allowed him to neutralize the pods around Haumea, thereby saving lives. He wished he could do the same for the Kaiju on Earth.

"Fifteen seconds."

Gate willed extra speed to Colonel Sakiri's ship. He was cutting it close. Gate barely listened to the countdown; then, scores of bright flashes burst into existence around Haumea, too many to count, the Kaiju pods exploding. A cheer went up on the bridge, but he still held his breath. Moments later, a larger explosion blossomed on Haumea.

"That probably shattered the planet," Worthen said.

"No," Blivens countered, "but it –"

A second, much brighter flash blinded them. The lights in the cabin flickered. Gate felt as if the deck had turned to Jell-O. He tried to move, but his feet mired in the deck with his first step, and then bounced with the next. His ears screamed from the blood rushing through them, and his stomach crawled up his throat with tiny dagger fingernails. The sensation passed as quickly as it came, leaving him disoriented and queasy.

Blivens, overcome by nausea, leaned over by his console and vomited.

"The explosion detonated a gravity drive," Renatto said, as he checked ships systems for damage. "I think we were far enough away. Systems returning to normal."

"What about Colonel Sakiri?" Walker asked.

Worthen checked his screen. His voice cracked, as he announced, "Haumea is gone. So are her two moons."

"Gone? What happened?" He confronted Blivens. "I thought you assured the colonel that the nukes wouldn't affect the gravity drives."

Blivens looked up at Walker, wiping spittle from his mouth. His face was ashen. He looked almost in shock. "It, it shouldn't," he stammered, taken aback by Walker's ire.

Worthen intervened. "An inactive gravity drive is safe. There must have been an active gravity drive on the planet. We didn't think to check for one after the pods became inactive."

Gate thought he knew the answer, and he didn't like it. "They use a gravity drive for communications. I thought I shut down all communications. I must have only killed the link to the Kaiju pods. It's my fault." Walker and Blivens stared at him, Walker with disbelief and Blivens with relief that the blame had passed from him. Gate wished he had a corner he could hide in. "If I had checked to see if the Kaiju on Earth had been affected, I would have known." He shook his head. "I didn't."

"No," Walker said, shaking his head. "This all happened too quickly. No one has contacted Earth since we lost you and the others after the blast. It's not your fault. It's an unforeseen consequence of events, which I set in motion. I told the colonel to blast the planet. If anyone is at fault, it's me."

Walker looked around at the people on the bridge. Gate saw such remorse in his gaze; he wished he could have offered him some comfort, but no one could relieve his guilt, deserved or not.

"You were willing to let me off the hook," he said. "You can't hang yourself out to dry in my place. It happened. We have to move on."

"Inform the *Lance* crews what happened, if they haven't already guessed by now. Make sure they're all okay; then, bring them in and let's go home. We're done here."

On the view screen, the fireball had died away, but the consequences of the massive explosion were still expanding. Haumea and her two moons were shattered. The rings were gone, vaporized by the blast. A gravity ripple moved outward from the blast's epicenter, nudging rocks and chunks of ice slightly out of their eons-old orbits. The full effect of the explosion's aftermath would be impossible to determine for years. All the maps of the Kuiper Belt were now useless. An entire new field of astronomy would open up, but Gate wanted no part of it.

Any trace of alien technology in or around Haumea was gone. All he had left was a few photographs and a handful of technology scraps in a polyester bag. *Of course, there is more than enough Nazir technology on Earth.* He hoped he had discovered something useful in the battle against the Kaiju ravishing his world.

29

August 23, Texas City, TX –

LaBonner's fixed his gaze on the two giant Kaiju lumbering northwards toward Houston. He paid scant attention to his surroundings. The ripped-up asphalt of the roadway, the smashed houses, and the crushed automobiles were simply markers to guide his path, as if he needed such things. The two Kaiju were clearly visible just a few miles ahead, but his team could not close the gap between them, and their chopper had gone down with its entire crew saving their lives. The laser-armed Spiders had moved north ahead of the Kaiju, and the Wasps were south around Galveston. His greatest fear was that the military would decide to use a nuclear option, a much larger response than the small nuclear-tipped rockets they carried. His team was the scalpel, and the military was leaning toward a hammer.

"There's a truck," Brewsley said, pointing to a used Chevy F-250.

"Check for keys. See if it will crank. Vance, check our ammo." LaBonner checked his weapon. "I've got half a mag and two extra."

LaBonner next decision could doom them all, but he saw no other option. Stopping one Kaiju wasn't enough. They had to stop both of them.

"Vance, look for a second working vehicle. I want you to take Agnew, Hawthorne, and Thompson. Your target is Kaiju Number Two, on the right. The rest of us will attack Kaiju One. We'll coordinate our attacks by radio."

Vance stared at him. He knew what the sergeant was thinking. As close as the two Kaiju were, even a small nuclear blast would probably take out both teams. Two blasts made it a near certainty. If they did not get a firing solution that included both creatures simultaneously, they would have to settle for one, thereby ending the opportunity at the second Kaiju. If they got lucky and the two Kaiju separated as they approached Houston, their odds improved, but so did the chance that the brass would become proactive and beat them to the punch. Either way, the odds were not in their favor.

"Good Kaiju hunting," Vance replied, as he walked away to check their ammo.

He's a good man. I wish I had a better plan to offer. LaBonner had known when he volunteered for the Kaiju Killer Teams that it was a suicide squad, but that each victory hastened the end of the war with the Nazir. He thought it was worth it. He and Vance had survived their Kaiju kills and three battles with Spiders. They were both pushing their luck, and Vance knew it.

"Chevy's running," Brewsley reported a few minutes later. "Sergeant Vance found a Miata." He smiled. "He said it was the perfect Kaiju hunting vehicle."

LaBonner glanced at the car, saw the barrel of the M60 protruding from the rear seat, and smiled. "He would. Load your launcher and whatever ammo Sergeant Vance can spare into the truck. You and I are going Kaiju hunting."

Brewsley's face grew grim. "It's why we came after all, isn't it?"

So many good men have to die. So many have died. "Let's see if we can raise some hell."

The Kaiju Vance's team pursued strode toward Texas City. LaBonner assumed it would follow Galveston Bay north into Houston's eastern neighborhoods. LaBonner's creature took a northwestern course that would take it through Santa Fe, Alvin, and Sugarland on Houston's southwestern side. He drove up I-45 until he reached Main Street in La Marque, cutting across to Hwy 6 in hope of closing the gap with the Kaiju. The pod landing to the south had shaken and damaged the town's buildings, creating large cracks in the streets. The authorities had hastily evacuated the residents before the Kaiju emerged from the pod. The Kaiju had bypassed the heart of the city, but the Spiders had not. Buildings and cars still smoldered from laser blasts. He saw no bodies, but after witnessing a Kaiju feeding, he doubted he would.

Reaching Highway 6, he was dismayed to find what had once been a state highway had become a broken ribbon of asphalt. The impact quake had cracked and shattered the asphalt, creating wide gaps in some places and ridges of buckled asphalt in others. He swerved around giant potholes and bounced over others, mouthing a silent prayer he didn't kill them in a rollover before they could catch it. He dodged burning wrecks and downed power poles. He took to the front lawns of one row of houses where the road became impassable, tearing through white picket fences and hedgerows. A narrow bridge across a bayou had partially collapsed, but it held the truck's weight, although it creaked ominously as they crossed.

If the Spiders followed in the Kaiju's wake, he and Brewsley had no chance of surviving. They could not fight off dozens of Spiders armed with lasers. However, if the Spiders were traveling ahead of the creature, they might get a clear shot at it. He tried to shake the images of pursuing Kaiju Paris for three days, losing most of his team along the way and the remainder at the end of the chase. This time, he had lost half his team in less than an hour. He hoped it was not a continuing trend.

They passed dozens of smashed cars, demolished buildings, and flattened homes. A Suzuki motorcycle laid crushed beneath a fallen billboard, the bloodstained asphalt bearing witness to the driver's fate. Flames and billowing black smoke shot into the air from a gas station destroyed by the creature's passage. In the parking lot, an overturned tow truck lay half atop a smashed station wagon.

The cities of Santa Fe and Alvin had fared no better than La Marque. Both areas looked as if pounded by saturation bombing. Entire city blocks were mounds of smoking debris. Fires raged through neighborhoods. The Kaiju was intent on doing the most damage possible in its trek north to Houston. They passed small groups of people, survivors of both Kaiju and Spiders, milling about the wreckage in various states of shock. He felt sorry for their plight but wondered why they had refused to evacuate. Were they the same people who remained during a hurricane? Did they see the Kaiju as just another natural storm to endure? One man wearing only his underwear, oblivious to his state of dress or his surroundings, sprayed water from a garden hose onto the remains of his home totally engulfed in flames. It was a futile effort, but he persisted as though he made a difference.

Am I like that man? Am I making a difference, or am I simply fooling myself? LaBonner gritted his teeth and pressed the accelerator harder. *No, I have made a difference, and I will again. I will stop this monster.* He refused to believe otherwise, for in the face of such an enemy, doubt would eat away at his confidence.

Just south of Sugarland, the Kaiju turned northeast toward the heart of Houston. The heavy rain half-obscured it, as it stomped its way across neighborhoods, leaving carnage in its wake. Just south of Sam Houston Parkway near Fondren Gardens, the Air Force finally made an appearance. Squadrons of F-18s streaked through the dark sky. Their target was not the Kaiju, immune to the tiny stings and pinpricks of conventional weapons, but rather the Spiders presaging its arrival by seeking out stubborn survivors and destroying everything in their path.

He swerved the truck to avoid a wrecked car and bounced over a fallen streetlamp post. Beside him, Brewsley slammed his head into the roof.

"Slow down," he cautioned. "You're going to wreck us."

LaBonner nodded but he did not reduce speed. However, he did focus his attention on his driving. They were gaining on the Kaiju, now only a few blocks ahead of them. To each side of them, he noticed Spiders burning houses and buildings, the lasers on their backs bright flares briefly illuminating the storm-dimmed light. The rain had become a torrent, running through the streets. The truck splashed through deep puddles, throwing sheets of water onto the windshield faster than the wipers could remove it. At the last moment, he saw a mangled bicycle in the street. With no time to avoid it, he barreled over it. A sickening crunch resounded through the truck, as metal pierced metal. The transmission rattled like dice in a cup before the truck shuddered and finally stopped.

"I guess we walk," he said to Brewsley, who tried his best not to say what he was probably thinking. "Grab the launcher. Let's do this before it's too late."

Even as he said it, he knew it was too late. The Spiders had moved closer. It would not be long before they spotted them. The Kaiju had stopped moving. It stood like a black cloud over the suburbs. Only the heavy downpour prevented the city around it from becoming an inferno.

"Why isn't it moving?" Brewsley asked.

"Who cares? Maybe it used all its energy. This rain and cloudy sky isn't allowing it to collect solar energy. That's good for us. Makes the job easier."

He had not convinced Brewsley any more than he had convinced himself. Although the Kaiju was stationary, the Spiders were not. They would remain in the area. They would be lucky to get within two blocks of the creature.

Almost as if his thinking of them had conjured it into existence, a Spider stumbled from the ruins of a building and crossed the street only yards from them. It paused, fixed them in its cold-eyed gaze, but strangely, did not attack. Instead, it turned and raced up the street away from them.

"Well, that's different," Brewsley said.

"Yeah. I wonder why it didn't attack."

Farther away around the Kaiju, the battle for Houston had not relented. F/A-18E *Super Hornets* swooped dangerously low over buildings and aerials to drop their payloads of CBU-87 Combined Effects Munitions on Spiders. Each cluster bomb delivered over 200 bomblets. At low altitude, the bombs spun slowly on their way down, covering less than 10,000 square feet in an effort to reduce destruction to private property and save lives. Puffs of smoke marked the explosions before the sound reached LaBonner. He hoped no one living had been beneath the canopy of destruction.

Twin laser beams raked one *Hornet* as it pulled out of its dive. Smoke billowed from its starboard engine. The pilot banked the craft sharply in a losing battle to keep it level and in the air. Then, all control lost, it turned upside down and crashed into a strip mall. A fireball rose from its grave.

A second wave of *Hornets* emptied their M61 20mm nose canons into the Spiders. He cheered them on. The more Spiders the *Hornets* took out, the easier their job to destroy the Kaiju.

"We have to move fast."

Brewsley knew what he meant. When the jets cleared the area, the next explosion might be nuclear. They had to stop the Kaiju first. He contacted Vance.

"Team One Zulu to Team Two. Come in, Vance."

Over the crackling of static, he heard Vance's voice muffled by nearby explosions. "We can't get close to the target. It's too far out in the bay. Repeat. No go on Target Two. Surrounded by Spiders. Blackhawks are keeping them back for now, but we can't break out."

That was unwelcomed bad news to LaBonner. They could not coordinate their attacks, but he could not wait. They would have to settle for one Kaiju. "Dig in. We're going for Target One."

"Roger that," Vance replied. "Maybe our target will come in closer. It's just standing there in the bay out of range."

"Roger, we'll ... Repeat that last." He knew he had missed something important.

"Target Two immobile in the bay. No shot."

"Roger. Thanks. Over."

He looked at Brewsley, an idea forming in his mind. "Why aren't they moving?"

"Yeah, that was my question, remember."

"Sorry I dismissed you. This could be significant. Why haven't the Spiders attacked us? That one Spider clearly saw us but ran off. Why haven't more Spiders shown up?"

"Got me there. They did just shoot down a *Hornet*."

"Yes, but it had attacked. Maybe they're still capable of self-defense."

LaBonner was unsure of his next move. He was afraid he was grasping at straws, reading more into events than was there. All logic told him to take the shot before the Kaiju started moving or the Spiders regrouped, but his instinct told him to wait. This was not like earlier when the Kaiju standing by the pod were arming the Spiders. They had stopped midstride, as if waiting for orders. The Spiders were not acting in any coordinated way. He thought he knew the answer.

"The team on Haumea must have accomplished their mission. Do you remember how the Kaiju stopped moving when Colonel Langston destroyed the communications pod on the moon? This is like that. I think they're without guidance and are waiting for orders."

"Seems like the best time to kill it before it starts moving again."

Brewsley was right, but he didn't want to lose any more men. Enough people had died following him. "If I'm right, maybe the war's over."

Brewsley stared at him. "Over?" He glanced around at the destruction surrounding them. "Over," he repeated, mouthing the syllables slowly, as if tasting them.

"Over." Saying the word gave LaBonner a strange sense of relief. Even if the Kaiju had stopped, the battle wasn't over. The Spiders, Fleas, and Wasps remained. Even without direct control, they were still dangerous, but without the Kaiju as base support, they were a minor problem. He watched a *Hornet* fire four AGM-65 *Maverick* missiles into a mob of Spiders a block away. They accepted their fate without returning fire with their lasers. It was a good sign.

"Let the Air Force handle this one. They can launch a nuclear missile from a safe distance." He shrugged. "If that doesn't work, we go inside and blow it like Colonel Walker did."

LaBonner raised his head and let the rain wash over him and run down his face. It was cold and struck with enough force to sting his flesh, but it felt good. The war was over. For the first time in weeks, he felt clean.

30

August 25, *Assegai* –

The war was over. Walker had a difficult time accepting that. He felt as if he had been fighting Kaiju his entire life, although it had been just over a year. The alien base on Haumea and the entire planetoid were gone, blasted into dust by a combined nuclear and gravity bomb explosion. So were Colonel Sakiri and twenty-six good men and women. A message from Earth reported that the Kaiju had stopped moving.

When he read aloud the message to everyone on the ship, the shouts were tumultuous. An air of jubilation swept through the *Assegai*. People wept, shouted, and prayed. They were going home after a successful mission, the most important successful mission of their lives. The deaths, though still fresh on their minds, were offset by the lives they had saved on Earth. The Kaiju spread across the globe had stopped moving with the destruction of Haumea. The military was finishing off the remaining Spiders, Wasps, and Fleas, still a daunting task in spite of the lack of coordination among them, but not an impossible one.

When Walker found him, Costas sat on the floor in a corner of the aft module, now firmly reattached to the *Assegai*. The frown on his face looked out of place among the other rejoicing soldiers. Walker strode over to confront him.

"Why the long face, Sergeant?"

"No broads or booze," he quickly replied.

"We're all suffering."

"Naw. I been thinking," he admitted.

"That could pull a muscle or two."

"Ha. Ha. No, I been thinking about the Nazir."

Curious, Walker asked, "What about them?"

"They didn't act like any military unit I've ever seen. They should have kicked our collective asses."

Walker had considered the same thing but wanted to see where Costas was going. "But they didn't."

"No, and that worries me. Even the lasers they used seemed more like tools than weapons."

"They weren't expecting us to attack."

"They acted more like a bunch of nerds caught with their pants down." He looked at Walker. "Don't tell me you haven't been thinking the same thing."

"Okay, you're right. It bothered me too. I think we stopped a commercial venture rather than a military invasion."

"Huh?"

"What if the aliens were simply a corporation searching for minerals on other worlds? They move in, nullify the local threat, and take what they want."

"You mean like a hostile takeover, Nazir style?"

"Exactly. It wasn't as much as an attack as a business venture. Oh, they would have wiped us out, but just as a side bar, not because they wanted us dead. We posed a threat to their venture. We posed no risk to their home world."

Costas scratched his head. "I'll be damned. Corporate stuffed shirts."

"We stopped them. Somewhere, an alien accountant is looking over the books and deciding if Earth is worth the investment. I'm betting it isn't. I'll think they'll cut their losses and try somewhere else."

"Some fucked up universe. We finally meet aliens, and they're from Wall Street running a pyramid scheme with us on the bottom. We should teach them a real lesson."

That had been Walker's thought. "Somewhere in the data Gate brought back, we might find the location of their home world. If we do, we might pay them a visit to warn them off."

Costas grinned. "I want in on that."

"It might be a while. First, we have to rebuild and unite."

A frown crossed Costas' face. "That might take some doing. China and Russia might have other plans."

"Resources for rebuilding are going to be limited. A little nudge in the right place and their citizens might reconsider their restrictive forms of government. There's no place left for stifling regimes. We all work together, freely, or we won't survive."

"You sound like a diplomat. I say drop a few gravity bombs on them and call it a day."

Trust Costas to be direct. "There's been enough death. We need to heal first, hearts and minds. Something good may come of all this."

"If you say so. I ain't got as much faith in my fellow man. Now, Russian women, that's different. They've got cold faces but are on fire inside. Must be the vodka. You make nice to the Ruskies. I'll go with you, but I'm looking out for Mama Costas' number one son."

"As long as you've got my back."

"Always, Major. Always."

Walker felt an itch to do something, and he had an idea. They were still eight days from Earth. He went to the bridge to find Gate. He was poring over his notes on the aliens and scanning photographs. He looked up as Walker entered.

"This is a gold mine," he said. "We can learn so much from this."

"You've got time to study all that later. I have a question."

"Shoot."

"Do you feel like an adventure?"

Gate frowned. "An adventure? After what we've been through?"

"I thought, as long as we're in the area, we might drop by Mars. What say we pose in front of Mars Rover's camera for the folks back home? We could pick up a few samples for NASA. Who knows when we'll get back out here? There's a lot of work to do back home."

Gate looked at Worthen. "What do you say, guys? Want to say hi to your friends at Johnson from Mars?"

"Won't the brass back home have something to say about it?" Worthen asked.

"I'm in command," Walker said. "Let them hang me."

Worthen smiled. "I'll set a course for Mars."

"What's next for you, Major?" Gate asked.

"Fishing for trout in Idaho."

"Really? I never took you for a trout fisherman."

"Never fished in my life, but a few days of lying on the bank in the sun sounds like heaven."

"Need some company?"

Walker shook his head. "Not this time. By the time we reach Earth, we'll all be tired of each other's company."

"Earth," Gate said. "It's good it'll still be there waiting for us."

"You'll probably be a hero."

Gate shook his head. "Not me. No heroes here. We left the real heroes on Haumea."

"Yes, Sakiri and the others. I hope the world doesn't forget them too soon."

"Not this time. Someone once told me the world needs heroes."

"Heroes and heroines," Walker added. "When the world requires them, someone always steps up to bat."

"That's humankind for you, Major. Maybe we're worth the price others paid. We'll see."

"Yes, we'll see. The aliens caused some damage, but maybe it's time for the world to change. We as a species have some growing up to do."

"If the Nazir are out there, other races must be too. Maybe we can seek them out as allies. It might prove mutually beneficial."

Walker smiled. "Now, there's a job for you, Wingate Rutherford, ambassador to aliens."

Gate shook his head. "Not me. I'm too hot-blooded. Ambassadors require a cooler head. I'll stick with the stars. They're quieter."

"I think a lot of people will be searching for some peace and quiet after all this. Find your spot early."

"Yeah, a three-day jazz festival. That's what I want."

"Take Costas with you. He needs some culture."

Gate chuckled. "Culture and Costas don't belong in the same sentence."

"Yeah, but if things ever get rough …"

"I wouldn't want anyone else by my side," Gate finished.

"Three and a half days to Mars, Major Walker," Worthen announced.

"Let's hope there are no Martians," Walker said. "I'm through with fighting for a while."

THE END

SEVERED**PRESS**

 facebook.com/severedpress
 twitter.com/severedpress

CHECK OUT OTHER GREAT KAIJU NOVELS

ATOMIC REX: WRATH OF THE POLAR YETI
by Matthew Dennion

It has been fifteen years since Captain Chris Myers used his giant mech to draw the kaiju of North America into each other's territory to have them destroy each other. Once all of the kaiju had battled to the death only Atomic Rex was left standing. In Antarctica, the kaiju known as Armorsaur has entered the frozen valley of the yetis and attacked them. Devouring all but one alpha male yeti who was exposed to the kaiju's blood and left dying in the snow. The yeti awoke to find himself transformed into a kaiju with an obsession to destroy Armorsaur. Chris and Kate are forced to protect the people of their settlement by drawing Atomic Rex into South America where he will battle the kaiju there to usurp their territory and claim their hunting grounds as his own. As Atomic Rex enters South America from the north the enraged Polar Yeti enters the continent from the south. The two most powerful kaiju in the world will battle their way through a multitude of giant monsters as they are set on a collision course with each other!

KAIJU CORPS
by Matthew Dennion

They are four soldiers who were genetically created to be mankind's last line of defense against potential world ending threats. They are soldiers who can transform themselves into gigantic monsters. They are the Kaiju Corps and they are facing a threat that is beyond the scope of even their fantastic abilities.

SEVERED**PRESS**

f facebook.com/severedpress
𝕏 twitter.com/severedpress

CHECK OUT OTHER GREAT
KAIJU NOVELS

POLAR YETI AND THE BEASTS OF PREHISTORY
by Matthew Dennion

A team from Princeton University searching for a lost tribe in Antartica discover a hidden valley filled with wooly mammoths, saber toothed tigers and other Ice Age beasts. Seizing the opportunity of a lifetime, the team set up camp to study the amazing creatures. But there is something else that lives in the Valley. Something terrifying. Something beyond imagination. POLAR YETI!

TITAN WARS
by M.C. Norris

Millions of microscopic alien life forms escape a sample canister of water from the frigid depths of outer space. Invisible to the naked eye, a menacing menagerie of more than seventy deadly species react to Earth's warm and fertile seas by launching into metabolic overdrive. Waves of gargantuan abominations begin to rise from the sea, transforming our world into a zoo without cages, where humans plunge to the bottom of the food chain.

In dire need of a zookeeper, the Allied Navy turns to "Psyjack," a bickering geek squad with an outrageous plan to hack into the minds of the megafauna with some reengineered neurosurgical technology. The young gamers hope to level the uneven playing field by fighting monsters with monsters, but they couldn't have anticipated how deadly their technology could be, if it ever fell into the wrong hands ...

**SEVERED**PRESS

facebook.com/severedpress
twitter.com/severedpress

CHECK OUT OTHER GREAT KAIJU NOVELS

MURDER WORLD | KAIJU DAWN
by Jason Cordova
& Eric S Brown

Captain Vincente Huerta and the crew of the Fancy have been hired to retrieve a valuable item from a downed research vessel at the edge of the enemy's space.
It was going to be an easy payday.
But what Captain Huerta and the men, women and alien under his command didn't know was that they were being sent to the most dangerous planet in the galaxy.
Something large, ancient and most assuredly evil resides on the planet of Gorgon IV. Something so terrifying that man could barely fathom it with his puny mind. Captain Huerta must use every trick in the book, and possibly write an entirely new one, if he wants to escape Murder World.

KAIJU ARMAGEDDON
by Eric S. Brown

The attacks began without warning. Civilian and Military vessels alike simply vanished upon the waves. Crypto-zoologist Jerry Bryson found himself swept up into the chaos as the world discovered that the legendary beasts known as Kaiju are very real. Armies of the great beasts arose from the oceans and burrowed their way free of the Earth to declare war upon mankind. Now Dr. Bryson may be the human race's last hope in stopping the Kaiju from bringing civilization to its knees.
This is not some far distant future. This is not some alien world. This is the Earth, here and now, as we know it today, faced with the greatest threat its ever known. The Kaiju Armageddon has begun.

www.ingramcontent.com/pod-product-compliance
Lightning Source LLC
Chambersburg PA
CBHW020106180626
46812CB00006B/2492